What bookworms are saying about

Book 1: Haiku of the Vampire

"… held me spellbound from beginning to end…"

"… a creative and mesmerizing story…"

"Fascinating, edge of your seat action… this book has everything you didn't know you wanted."

"One of the very best!"

"I've been searching for a worthy epic and this is it."

"… action-packed bloodshed that leaves you wanting more!"

"I loved this book!"

"The jumps from the present to the past were infuriating and perfect."

"I couldn't put it down!"

"The best vampire story I have ever read."

Here Comes the Jampyre

Here Comes the Jampyre

Book 2

of

The Vampire Haiku Chronicles

Arakaki Soto

Here Comes the Jampyre
Copyright ©️ 2020by Arakaki Soto

Published by ArDayne Press

Editor: Caroline Barnhill
Book Cover Design: SelfPubBookCovers.com/ArtStyleAlice
Book Cover Back Image: Engin Akyurt from Pixabay
ISBN 9781675824641

Dedicated to my wife,
who allows me to stretch
my imagination.

Table of Contents

Part One

The soul of your soul,
has more layers to behold.
Magic sparks the flame.

chapter 1

Cyprian Dugas looked over the line of Wolves currently crouched before him. Sweat beads poured off their faces onto a battlefield that had been demolished from a hard-fought war. Some had blood running down their limbs from vicious encounters. But the Wolves all still had eyes of hunger, sensing their eminent victory. After all, there was only twelve seconds left on the clock, and Cyprian's football team had only one play left. And eighty-three yards to the end zone.

The score was 49-45.

The Frederick A. Douglass High School Bobcats' undefeated season was about to come to a heartbreaking end at the hands of their crosstown rivals, The New Orleans High School Wolves, in the Louisiana State Championship. Cyprian had broken school records in yards rushing, yards per carry, became second all-time in career touchdowns, and was on the verge of signing a contract to play for LSU, but none of that seemed as important as the moment he faced right then under the Friday night lights.

Twelve seconds left.

And eighty-three yards.

Quarterback Derek McDowell had a decent arm, but a Hail Mary pass/play was out of the question. So all of the receivers were told to run a "fly route," straight up the field, as fast as they could, as deep as possible. Cyprian's assignment was to run a hitch, partly as a decoy and partly as a last alternative. And when the football was finally snapped, everything seemed to move in slow motion.

Cyprian ran about eight yards and then curled back towards Derek, who was looking down field at his receivers. But they all had defensive backs and safeties flanking them like a dog on a bone. The quarterback faked a pass to Cyprian, but when he realized his prized running back was actually the best possible option, he gunned the pigskin to him.

As soon as he caught the football and secured it into his torso, Cyprian heard a squeal from the stands—

"Go Sippy!"

It was his younger eight-year-old sister Lucie, waving a ginormous cardboard cutout of Cyprian's face on a stick. Her smile was a beacon of hope in a moment that had none.

And that's all it took for Cyprian to transform into beast mode.

This is for you, Lucie.

The Wolves' linebacker was the first to approach the Bobcat running back. But Cyprian sidestepped him, sending the big oaf sliding across his own sideline and demolishing a helpless water boy. Cyprian then waited for his own offensive linemen – who immediately chased after the ball once it was passed – to throw a couple of well-timed blocks before he kicked it into high gear and ran thirty more yards. It was the moment the halls of Frederick A. Douglass High School would be talking about for the rest of the year.

This is for you, Lucie.

Every defensive back and safety left their man to meet Cyprian at mid-field. The running back stiff-armed his first foe backwards, knocking him into a teammate behind him. Cyprian then twirled a perfect pirouette, like a heavyweight ballerina, to elude the next defender. When he righted himself toward the end zone, Cyprian only had one defender standing in his way: the Wolves' free safety, who himself had signed a Letter of Intent to play for powerhouse Alabama.

This is for you, Lucie.

Cyprian ran a slant, but the free safety was up to the task, sliding across to block his path. With the opposite sideline drawing close, Cyprian turned straight up field and faced the defender now directly in front of him. The free safety motored ahead as well; it was like two locomotives heading for a collision at full speed. And now Cyprian knew there was probably only one thing he could do: leap.

This is for you, Lucie.

But the free safety knew that would be Cyprian's next move. Both football players jumped at the same moment, colliding in midair. The entire stadium hushed as both polycarbonate helmets violently smacked against each other with thunderous force. Their shoulder pads made a resounding crunch. And when their interconnected bodies finally fell to the ground, the football palmed in Cyprian's hand landed into the end zone.

Touchdown!

The game ended as the clock buzzed. Final score: Bobcats 51, Wolves 49.

That was for you, Lucie.

Cyprian was hoisted up into the air by his teammates. And even though he would learn later that he suffered a cracked rib because of that collision, he didn't feel any pain at that moment. The world was his. He had reached high school legend status with one glorious play that would be retold for years to come. But Cyprian wasn't completely satisfied. There was one other thing he wished he could do at that moment:

He wanted to hug Lucie.

"Good job, Sippy." Her little voice drifted through the air.

Cyprian scanned the bleachers for his little sister, but she was no longer there. In fact, Lucie never was.

She had died seven months earlier.

chapter 2

If Cyprian had a coffee mug that read "World's Best Brother," it wouldn't have been a lie. To little Lucie, he was the literal definition. From the day she was born, ten-year-old Cyprian took a personal vow to always protect her. To always nurture her. To never let his own life come between their relationship.

At night, Cyprian often read stories to her. And not that their parents were ever neglectful of their children, but Cyprian and Lucie had an unmistakable bond recognized by most and allowed to prosper. They were like kindred spirits, sharing their common love of Baskin Robbin's Daiquiri Ice, Disney movies, and football.

Lucie was Cyprian's biggest supporter and critic. She had an inkling early on that her big brother could achieve amazing things if he just put his mind to it. Starting with each game as a high school Sophomore, Lucie graded each of Cyprian's rush attempts as an A, B, C, or F. An A meant a touchdown occurred as a result of the play. When she gave him an F, it was usually because the other team's defense anticipated the play, or one or more of Cyprian's offensive linemen blew their assignments, resulting in a loss of yards. If her big brother received a B or C grade, then she was sure to give him reasons.

"I gave you a solid C on that one, Sippy," said Lucie on one such occasion.

"Why?" disagreed Cyprian. "I got a first down."

"Are you satisfied with just a first down? Cuz if you would've gone straight at the thirty-eight-yard line instead of cut to the left, then you could've picked up at least five more yards."

"I was efficient," said her big brother.

"You can be efficient and be great at the same time, Cyprian," remarked Lucie.

If Lucie ended her argument with Cyprian's full name and not "Sippy," then Cyprian knew the conversation was over. And quite honestly, Cyprian always knew Lucie was right. She had become a budding connoisseur of the game and quite the tactician.

The duo never missed a New Orleans Saints' game on TV, and even had the opportunity to see the Saints live at the Mercedes-Benz Superdome on several occasions, including the now infamous and ill-fated NFC Championship playoff game against the Los Angeles Rams and the botched pass interference call. That day marked the first time Cyprian ever heard Lucie utter a curse word:

"Are you kidding me right now?!" screamed Lucie at the referee, as she jumped up onto her folding chair to get a better view. "That was pass interference! Throw your fucking flag!"

Cyprian raised a brow at his kid sister, as the fans all around them cheered Lucie on. Of course, they all wholeheartedly agreed with her, too. When the game was over, Lucie shed a tear for her fallen hometown heroes. She thought for a flitting second that the NFL powers-that-be might have had a hand in determining the outcome of that game, but brushed it off knowing that it was over and nothing was going to change the end result. She went on to root for Tom Brady and the Patriots in the Super Bowl, despite her best moral judgements.

It was almost two weeks after the Super Bowl when Lucie was admitted into Children's Hospital New Orleans with fever chills and subsequently diagnosed with acute myeloid leukemia. The cancer spread rapidly, prompting aggressive chemotherapy.

Cyprian missed Spring football camp to be with his sister every day after school. He continued to read her stories, even though she slept most of the time. Lucie stayed fairly optimistic through the whole ordeal, citing that God recognized her talents and needed her by his side as soon as possible. That was the only time in their lives that Cyprian completely disagreed with his little sister, arguing that she wasn't going anywhere since it was he who needed her by *his* side.

"Why do you need me, Sippy?"

"Because you are my light and my fire. You keep me grounded, yet you keep me reaching for the stars," answered Cyprian.

"You can do that when I'm gone."

"How?"

"By just remembering me."

Cyprian shook his head. "I don't want to *just remember* you. I don't want anything to remind me of you. I just want you to be here."

"God needs me, Sippy."

"I could care less about what God needs right now. He has others to choose from. I only have you."

"But he sees me as special."

"You are special. And you'll always be special. But he can wait ninety-years."

Lucie pondered. "There must be an urgent need in Heaven right now. But if I go, I'll always be by your side. I'll always be a part of you, no matter what."

"How can you be sure?"

"I just know."

"What if it doesn't happen?"

"I'll find a way to make it happen."

"Promise me."

Lucie held out her little pinky. "I promise, Cyprian."

And with his full name stated, Cyprian knew that was the end of their conversation. He obliged by locking his own pinky with hers and accepted her promise as gospel.

That was the last conversation Cyprian would ever have with his little sister.

Lucie died early the next morning.

chapter 3

The following few days were the toughest on Cyprian. He was a shallow mess of his former self. It was as if his soul was abruptly taken from him and he now walked the Earth as someone without purpose. Someone incapable of being. Someone incapable of living.

Lucie's funeral came and went like a blur. Cyprian paid no attention to how many people attended, let alone who was actually there. It wasn't until the reception at his house afterwards, when he hid in Lucie's bedroom, that someone familiar finally broke through his remorseful shield.

It was seventeen-year-old Shanice Roberson.

"Hey, Cyprian. Your mom told me you were up here."

Cyprian looked up from Lucie's leather-clad Build-A-Bear that he was cradling and seemed to let out a sigh that he'd been holding in for days. "What's up, girl?"

She sat next to him on the bed. "How are you holding up?"

"I haven't even begun to hold up anything."

"I know. I mean... I wouldn't know since I've never had to deal with something like this. But you're the strongest guy I've ever known. And I'm not just talking about your muscles," said Shanice, seemingly trying to coerce a smile from Cyprian.

But Cyprian didn't smile. Instead, he sighed again. "My strength came from her. Where's it going to come from now?"

"Nothing's changed," answered Shanice. "Even though Lucie's physical body is gone, she'll always have a permanent place in your heart. And that's where you'll now channel your strength from."

Cyprian nodded, even though he still wasn't in the mood for a pep talk.

"And you know what?" said Shanice. "She'll be watching every single football game you play from now on, from the greatest seat in the world." She pointed to the heavens.

And for the first time, Cyprian grinned.

Shanice smirked proudly. "Why don't you come downstairs? Everyone wants to see you. It'll be good for you."

"I don't know if I'm ready."

"You can meet my new girlfriend, Zenia. She's probably dying down there in awkwardness without me right now."

"Girlfriend?"

"Yeah."

"You're gay?"

"Yeah. Duh."

"Since when?"

"All my life."

Cyprian had that dumbfounded look as his shallow and naïve masculinity filtered through his hardened exterior.

"But I only realized it in the seventh grade," added Shanice.

"Seventh grade?" Cyprian pondered for a moment. "But you and I made out in the seventh grade."

"And then I threw up in your mouth," responded Shanice bluntly.

"Oh, shit – you did. I remember. But I thought it was cuz of me, not cuz you were gay."

"Well," said Shanice. "It *was* because of you. You're a boy. That was gross."

It took another moment for Cyprian to comprehend, but then he couldn't help but chuckle. And it was the first time he saw some semblance of his former self. He started to nod. "Okay. I'll be down in a minute. Go save your girlfriend from the awkwardness."

Shanice gave Cyprian a shoulder hug and left Lucie's bedroom.

Cyprian let out a third sigh, this time deep enough to seemingly snap him out of his sullen funk. He knew that it would take time to completely get over Lucie's death, but he also knew that being selfish and moping in solitary confinement wasn't helping anyone. Others needed him to help them cope, especially his own parents. And when the reception was over, and days turned to weeks since Lucie's death, Cyprian had a renewed sense of purpose. He continued forward with his own life and dedicated every ounce of breath to Lucie's memory. His actions were her own actions. His dreams, her own.

When Cyprian would later hold a football again, he convinced himself he was carrying Lucie's soul. His goal was always to take her soul to its ultimate destination – the End Zone – which was his metaphorical Heaven. And that was where Lucie deserved to be and would watch over and protect her big brother, as he had done during her brief stay on Earth.

Little did Cyprian know, however, that it would take another year for Lucie's soul to finally arrive at her final destination.

But it wasn't Heaven.

And Cyprian would be the cause of that detour.

chapter 4

The Bobcats won the 5A Louisiana State Championship, and Cyprian was the hero. He was convinced that Lucie's spiritual presence in the stands guided him and his team to victory. Most nights after her death, he would hear her voice in his dreams as if she was narrating them. He never remembered one spoken word the morning after, but he knew she was with him. And when the one-year anniversary of Lucie's death arrived, Cyprian made sure he paid his respects tenfold.

Cyprian visited Lucie's grave almost every week, but on that monumental day, he didn't hold back with the tributes to her. Instead of his customary pint of Daiquiri Ice, he brought a gallon. He played not one, but three Disney movies back-to-back-to-back on his cell phone – usually the latest releases. And he brought a football signed by Saints' Quarterback Drew Brees that he bought on Ebay. To ease some of his predicted mental pain, Cyprian brought himself a bottle of smuggled Obsello Absinthe. By the time the live-action version of "The Lion King" was over, Cyprian had passed out behind Lucie's tombstone.

It was three o'clock in the morning when a green mist began to blanket the cemetery. The cool air became stagnant and humid. Crickets abruptly silenced as if someone pushed a mute button on life.

Cyprian slowly woke up to the sudden silence and the smell of something burning. And then wafting through the air in whispers was some kind of playground chant in a different language. He slowly peered around the tombstone and saw near the gated entrance two old African women with tribal paint on their faces, wearing dirty, gypsy-type shrouds.

They started to dance like young sprites around a grave.

Their odd song was indecipherable, but it stopped when they ceased dancing. One of the old women sprinkled green powder all over the grave, but when it hit the ground, a solid red vapor returned to the air instead.

Once it dissipated, the African women repeated the process on the next grave. Each turn took about twenty seconds and ended with the same red smoke pluming upwards. They continued down the row, until they reached the next one, and then finally – about thirty minutes later – reached Lucie's row.

And five graves later, they arrived at hers.

Cyprian curled himself into a ball and stayed hidden behind the tombstone. The women started to chant with what now sounded slightly African, slightly Cajun, and one hundred percent eerie. It was high pitched and had an evil cadence to the flow. And even though the old women looked to be in their eighties, they danced with more energy than your average teen.

Once the green dust was sprinkled – and the red vapor took its place – Cyprian expected them to move along. But that didn't happen. When the dust hit the grass, a vibrant, neon green smoke emanated instead!

The African women squealed in delight. They whispered to each other for a moment – in another language – and then waved to someone in the distance. From the shadows, an African-American man in his late thirties approached. He wasn't dressed in the same ragged attire, but in something completely different – a modern day Urban Outfitters-esque wardrobe.

He was also holding a shovel.

"This one?" he said, pointing at Lucie's grave. He read the tombstone slowly and whispered, "Lucie Dugas. Whoa, she was young!"

The women cackled and nodded.

The mysterious man sighed in reluctance, looking all around. "Are you sure this is necessary?"

That time, the women turned grim. It was as if they suddenly lost all of their patience and were ready to kick his ass with witchcraft.

"Okay, okay!" said the man, holding his hands up. "This better be worth it." He shoved his shovel hard into the top soil over Lucie's grave.

Behind the tombstone, Cyprian continued to listen. And when he heard the ominous sound of the shovel breaking the ground over Lucie's grave, his eyes widened in terror. He was conflicted with what to do. But there was no way he was going to let anyone desecrate his little sister's resting place. He gritted this teeth, squeezed his fists, got ready to spring up when—

"What is that?" said the man. "It looks like a cell phone. Is that ice cream and a football?"

Cyprian closed his eyes, cautious. Even though he was about to make his appearance and throw down like a Gotham vigilante, he was curious to see what the trio's next move was.

But there was complete silence.

Even the shoveling had stopped.

When Cyprian opened his eyes back up, he was met with something terrifying.

Both of the African women stared down at him with pupil-less eyes. They had no expressions, yet the current ambiance of the cemetery made them horrifically macabre. And at that proximity, Cyprian was convinced they must've been centuries-old.

Cyprian remained crouched, unable to move. He began to speak, even though he now realized his mouth was completely dry. "This grave. It belongs to my little—"

But before he could finish, one of the women opened her mouth – flashing her incredibly sharp incisors – and instantly blew the green dust into his face, wreaking havoc on his constitution. Cyprian's eyes watered, his throat shriveled, and all of his muscles simultaneously stiffened.

His body slumped to the ground to wavering consciousness.

From that point on, Cyprian only saw hazy images. One of them was the mystery man standing inside of Lucie's grave, clanking his shovel against her coffin. Another was the old women huddled together, sharing an odd pipe with a large bowl that had two stems extending to each mouth (and green smoke curiously filtering out). The next image was the coffin being pulled out of the grave and landing with a precarious thud. And then the shovel wedging the coffin wide open.

The final image – right before Cyprian passed out for good – was Lucie's slightly decomposed corpse draped over the man's shoulder.

chapter 5

"I'll always be a part of you, no matter what. I promise, Cyprian."

Cyprian woke up to Lucie's voice and found himself sitting upright against a wall in the cargo hold of a large wooden boat that rocked from the ocean waves outside, splashing against the exterior.

He instantly vomited his Absinthe, Daiquiri Ice, and stomach acid mixture all over himself. But before he could wipe it clean, he realized his hands were shackled from behind.

"That was gnarly, Bro," said L'Trell – the mysterious black man wearing Urban Outfitters from the cemetery. He sat on a bench, trying to keep his balance from the oceanic calamity outside.

"Where am I?" asked Cyprian.

"Somewhere in the Atlantic."

"Where are we headed?"

"Somewhere in Africa."

A woman's voice spoke softly from an opposite corner. "A region called the Xhosa."

Cyprian looked over to find Atalia, an African-American woman in her late twenties, sitting casually on her own bench. She was quite undeterred by the motion of the high seas. "What exactly did you just throw up? It looks like toxic waste. Smells like it too."

"Why are we going to Africa?" asked Cyprian, ignoring Atalia's question. "And why am I the only one chained up?"

Atalia and L'Trell exchanged bemused glances.

"You want to tell him?" asked Atalia.

"No, you tell him," responded L'Trell. "You know more about it than I do."

Atalia stood and walked calmly over to Cyprian. She crouched next to him and pulled out a switchblade. She then cut off his soiled shirt and wrapped the vomit inside, throwing it to the opposite corner of the room.

"Thank you," said Cyprian.

Atalia seemed to admire his stocky physique for a moment, and then sat across from him on the opposite wall. "How old are you?"

"Eighteen."

"Eighteen? What a shame," said Atalia.

"Why?"

Atalia sighed, now seemingly regretful for being nominated to tell Cyprian the truth. "You are about to be food."

"Food?"

"Yep. Fed to the wolves, so to speak."

Cyprian looked over at L'Trell, who turned away shamefully.

"What about the two of you?" asked Cyprian.

Atalia smiled. "Mr. L'Trell and I are to be mated and bonded," she said with a sarcastic undertone. "I don't know how exactly, though."

"With sex, I hope," chimed in L'Trell.

"Yeah, I'm sure you do."

"And I hope it's in front of everyone, for the whole tribe to watch."

"I highly doubt that will happen." Atalia rolled her eyes and feigned a smile at Cyprian, who now looked completely befuddled. "Consider yourself an ingredient to our ritual transformation in becoming vampires."

At that moment, the boat hit a massive wave and shot almost vertically, until it rested back down.

Atalia and L'Trell both watched for Cyprian's reaction. But he had none. "Where is my sister's body?" he said instead.

"That was your sister? The eight-year-old?" asked a surprised L'Trell. "Oh, shit."

But Atalia looked a bit shameful. "Your sister? How did she die?"

"Leukemia," said Cyprian. "Where is she?"

Again, Atalia and L'Trell exchanged glances. That time L'Trell explained.

"A virgin sacrifice is also needed in the ritual," he said.

"But she's already dead," said Cyprian.

"Her body is," clarified Atalia. "But not her soul. The *Impundulu* believe they can retrieve someone's soul from its resting place, as long as they have the physical body. It acts kind of like a conduit."

Cyprian furled a brow. "*Impundulu?*"

"That's the vampire breed," said Atalia.

"Wow. You're not letting go of this *vampire* thing."

Both Atalia and L'Trell silenced, expecting the skepticism. Atalia returned to her original bench, closing her eyes to rest.

Cyprian waited for either of them to tell him more, and especially the truth. But when the silence continued through the smashing waves outside, he reluctantly nodded. "Okay. So let's say I believe both of you are becoming vampires. Your choice? Why?"

"Who wouldn't want to be a vampire, Bro?" said L'Trell. "I'll get to live forever. Have lots of sex. I heard they have orgies all the time."

"Yay. Orgies," said Atalia facetiously.

"What about you?" Cyprian asked the lone female.

"Why do I want to become a vampire?" repeated Atalia, as she seemed to choose her answer carefully. "I served two stints in the Army in Afghanistan as a linguistics expert. I saw a lot of shit go down that I didn't agree with. On both sides. I'm just tired of this fucked up world, and I'm ready to blow up shit in a different way."

Cyprian nodded, seemed logical. "So… did you two just answer an ad in the newspaper or something? 'Vampires wanted?'"

"The military and the U.S. government know about vampires. But they keep it undercover so people don't panic," said Atalia.

"So like they do with aliens?" asked Cyprian.

"No. Aliens aren't for real. That's dumb."

Cyprian looked over at L'Trell for his explanation. "When your family's wealthy like mine, then you get connected and have access to everything and anything you're not supposed to. The best drugs, the most exclusive clubs, friends who have friends who have friends who have vampire friends. They met a Mexican vampire in San Antonio that talked about the *Impundulu* and how they can only recruit black people."

There was a long silence as Cyprian almost seemed tired of the preposterous story.

Atalia summed it up. "So apparently, when the *Impundulu* recruit new members, they only do two at a time – one male, one female. Both of us are supposed to be infused with a virgin's soul, which will be the spiritual caretaker of not only our own souls, but our magic and powers as well. We then have to unite—"

"—hopefully with sex," interrupted L'Trell.

"Hopefully with *no* sex and then drink your blood as our first meal." Atalia pointed at Cyprian, who was hung up on another detail.

"Do you only have one virgin body?" he asked.

"No," said Atalia. "I had to find my own and dig him up. Had to be the opposite sex. Turned out to be an overweight forty-year-old, who had just died a week earlier. I think his name was 'Moe.' Both bodies are in a cooler on the top level of this boat."

Regardless of how true the vampire angle might or might not have been, Cyprian was still pissed that Lucie's body was even dug up at all. Whether she was to be a part of some kind of stupid and hokey vampire ritual, or was just disrespectfully removed for something else entirely, Cyprian knew there was only one thing he needed to do:

Get Lucie's body back to the cemetery, where it belonged.

And he didn't care if he died trying.

chapter 6

The two African women from the cemetery periodically visited the cargo hold and left fish and water for their mortal guests. The fish were on sticks, apparently caught right from the Atlantic Ocean and broiled over an open flame. Each of the women took turns feeding Cyprian, since he remained shackled. They also escorted him to the restroom in an adjacent compartment when needed, wiping him clean afterwards. The eating and bathroom process repeated for the next nineteen days, since that was how long it took to finally arrive in Africa.

The conversations between Cyprian, Atalia, and L'Trell were limited, mostly because Cyprian thought they were full of shit, and Atalia and L'Trell didn't seem to care for each other. At one point, L'Trell did ask Atalia if she wanted to rehearse having sex, but she opted to masturbate in the corner. Cyprian had a feeling she was used to the practice, having undoubtedly been propositioned by fellow troops on her tours in Afghanistan.

There was only one other time during the trip when Atalia tried to bring Cyprian around to the notion that vampires truly existed.

"You're from New Orleans. Surely you've heard rumors about them?" she asked on day eleven of the cross ocean trek, when L'Trell was asleep.

"Of course."

"So then why is it so hard to believe what we're telling you?"

Cyprian said, "I chalked up the rumors about vampires to the same stories about haunted hotels and Big Foot and aliens – which you've already discounted."

"Big Foot is a myth. And before you ask, so are werewolves and mermaids. Ghosts and spirits? There's been definite proof of their existence. But the nightly news in New Orleans is filled with reports about missing persons and victims mutilated by animals. You've never questioned that?"

"No," said Cyprian. "I've always just figured that every big city was like that."

Atalia sighed in defeat. "Well… you'll see soon enough."

Cyprian shrugged. "So the military was how you got all of this vampire intel?"

"That's right. Including the language."

"Oh, yeah – *Linguistic expert*. How many do you know?" asked Cyprian.

"I'm fluent in seven," answered Atalia. "But I have a passing knowledge of four others."

"What's your favorite?"

Atalia's eyebrows raised. "Ooooh, good question. I'd have to say Japanese."

"Japanese? Huh. Have you found much use in it?"

She laughed. "Unfortunately, no. But I'd definitely like to practice. Perhaps I can make it out to Japan someday."

They both nodded, as if visiting Japan was on both of their bucket lists. But then Atalia seemed to remember that she was talking to a soon-to-be-dead man. She quickly changed the subject.

When the boat finally docked, it was in the middle of the night. Cyprian was led out of the boat by the two African women and joined Atalia, L'Trell, and several African men, who apparently crewed the boat. Bringing up the rear of their caravan, a seven-foot-tall African man with twice the amount of muscles of any normal man, carried Lucie and Moe's corpses on each shoulder. Cyprian took note to ensure his sister's body travelled with them.

The full moon and the twinkling stars seemed incredibly low wherever they were in Africa and were the only lights illuminating a rocky dirt path splitting a coastal zone of mostly sea oats and wax myrtle. But after a couple of miles, the darkness turned to blackness. The moon and the stars were suddenly covered by what looked like a thick cloud.

Except it wasn't a thick cloud. It was a solid mass of birds.

Lightning birds, to be exact.

They were completely silent, staying in formation and seemingly tracking the entourage below. There must've been several hundred.

"What's that?" whispered Cyprian to Atalia.

"Lightning birds. It's their spirit animal," she said. "They also feed on human blood."

"Oh. Great," said Cyprian wryly.

Cyprian continued to look back every so often to ensure Lucie was still back there and wasn't being bothered by the strange birds up above. If he wasn't still shackled, he would've offered to carry Lucie's body in his own arms, to protect her journey.

In the distance, Cyprian finally noticed specks of light peppering the landscape and even up into the air. When they got even closer, he realized the higher lights were instead stationed on a mountainous escarpment littered with thatched huts. They overlooked a large clearing with a stack of wood in the middle.

Up above, the lightning birds all flocked down and landed on various huts and posts. The moon and the stars reappeared, illuminating even more of the small village. And when the stack of wood was lit – creating a massive bonfire – nothing was hidden in darkness anymore.

But Cyprian wished it was.

The two African women he had come to be familiar with for the past three weeks left their group and joined another on the other side of the bonfire. It was a group that looked exactly like they did: old African women in shrouds with stringy gray hair and no pupils. There must've been hundreds. In fact, if Cyprian didn't know any better, their numbers matched the exact amount of lightning birds, currently perched and watching. *Waiting.*

"I was not expecting this," said L'Trell.

"What were you expecting?" asked Atalia.

"Honestly? Something like Wakanda."

The seven-foot man placed the two corpses in front of the bonfire and then joined all of the other African men behind the women. Atalia and L'Trell remained on the other side, with Cyprian in the middle.

"What happens now?" Cyprian asked no one in particular.

"I'm not entirely sure about this part," said Atalia.

"No military dossiers on this?"

"No military dossiers on this. I just know that they've all been standing there without food or water since we left, and what's supposed to happen at the end."

"They've been standing there for three weeks?!" Cyprian almost shouted his dismay. He looked across the bonfire at all of the women. There was one in the middle that did seem a little more distinct than the others. Her garb had black and yellow accents. And she was silently motioning to something in the bonfire.

"That must be Kwan'de'melu'da," said Atalia. "She's the High Priestess of the *Impundulu*. Some say she's a goddess disguised in human form and over five-hundred-years-old."

Vampires? And now goddesses? Cyprian rolled his eyes.

Kwan'de'melu'da approached the bonfire and began sprinkling various colors of powder into the flames. After each, she chanted a mumbled verse, "*Wen-sa. Zun-lee. Fin-oh.*" Once she was finished, the flames continued to burn with a green hue. She then began dancing around the bonfire, much like the two women had done in Lucie's cemetery.

"Three weeks standing and now she's dancing," said L'Trell. "I'm getting Plantar Fasciitis just watching her."

The High Priestess must've been dancing for thirty minutes when something curious happened. A nondescript Westland Lynx helicopter flew into the area and landed in the plains behind them. But oddly, no one in the *Impundulu* tribe paid it any attention. It was as if they expected it. And Kwan'de'melu'da didn't even miss a beat.

Cyprian turned to see several French men in suits climb out of the helicopter. They were all government officials from the Castille of Charlemagne in New Orleans.

One of them was Balzac St. Laurent.

Another was Chancellor Viktor Valiquette.

chapter 7

"Oh my God," exclaimed Atalia.

"Who are they?" asked Cyprian.

"The leaders of the vampire world. That's Chancellor Valiquette in the middle."

The French vampires shielded themselves from the gusts of wind the helicopter propeller produced. When they arrived to the clearing of the village, they all readjusted their suits and remolded their perfectly coiffed hair.

"Ah, good. We didn't miss it," said the Chancellor. They watched Kwan'de'melu'da for a moment, until Viktor approached Atalia and shook her hand with a wide smile. "Hi. I'm Chancellor Viktor Valiquette from the Castille of Charlemagne. You must be Atalia Venable. I thank you for your service to our country. And we are very excited to have you join our ranks."

"The pleasure will be mine," said Atalia, with a half-curtsy.

Viktor skipped right over Cyprian – without any eye contact – to L'Trell. "L'Trell Ward. Thank you for your family's contribution to our causes. I hope we have their continued support, as you join our family." They shook hands.

L'Trell only nodded, obviously intimidated by the supreme leader of the vampire world.

The Chancellor then turned back to the show, as Kwan'de'melu'da continued to dance.

"Hey, Mr. President," said Cyprian to Viktor. "You ain't going to shake my hand?"

Viktor turned to Cyprian and smirked smugly. "And how would we shake hands? Are they not bound behind you?"

"So, just a thank you then," said Cyprian. "I understand I'm going to be a meal."

The Chancellor approached Cyprian and seemed to scrutinize his body, admiring his muscle tone. "Indeed you are. And plenty to go around for everyone, I'd say."

The other French vampires chuckled. Balzac puckered his lips with a desirable gaze.

"I can be a vampire too," said Cyprian, grasping for straws.

"Unfortunately," said Viktor. "We don't have another dead, female virgin for you. Unless Mr. Ward would like to give up his and take your place?"

"Hell no," said L'Trell. "I paid thirty-six thousand dollars for this."

Viktor shrugged apologetically at Cyprian, who quickly said, "Then let's find another virgin."

"The *Impundulu* are only allowed this ritual once a year," said the Chancellor. "And only one male, and one female at a time. So, you, my friend, are out of luck – oh look, the High Priestess has stopped dancing."

Kwan'de'melu'da had indeed stopped, now approaching the trio of mortals. The French vampires backed away, remaining a safe distance away from the action.

"*Len pon-su zee me intok oxlo fin din kee*," said the High Priestess.

Atalia nodded.

"What did she say?" asked Cyprian.

"It's time for the transference of souls to the nesting fire," said Atalia, through her teeth.

Kwan'de'melu'da walked back to the dead bodies of Lucie and Moe. She knelt in between them and placed a hand on both of their bare chests.

Cyprian made a move toward Lucie's body, with eyes welling up. But Atalia held him back and shook her head. "If you still don't believe in any of this, then this is the best time to continue that."

The High Priestess closed her eyes and began to chant. Her hands started to glow green. The chests of each corpse rose into the air, until a bright light shot from their bodies and into Kwan'de'melu'da's hands, which she promptly shot back into the bonfire directly in front of her.

The flames billowed upwards in an explosion of sparkling embers. The smoke seemed to waft towards all of the lightning birds, still perched silently in their various positions.

Cyprian watched as Lucie's body collapsed back to the ground. Even though she was already dead, he couldn't stand to watch her small body go through such trauma. Tears rolled down his face.

Kwan'de'melu'da returned to the trio. "*Zenkwe po la va no mandu kwanulu.*"

Without a prompt, Atalia translated. "Now it's time for L'Trell and myself to become vampires."

The High Priestess motioned L'Trell and Atalia both to get down on their knees. Once they did, L'Trell was approached first.

"Oh shit, oh shit, oh shit," he cried, as Kwan'de'melu'da sunk her fangs into his carotid artery. L'Trell's eyes bulged out. "Fuck this hurts!"

When the High Priestess finished, L'Trell collapsed to the ground and began convulsing. His mouth opened and gasped for air, like a fish out of water.

It was Atalia's turn. But she was calm, only letting out a slight wince when Kwan'de'melu'da bit into her neck. Atalia slowly descended, so her body didn't have that far to fall once the process was over. And when it did, her body reacted much the same way as L'Trell's did.

Cyprian continued to stand awkwardly between Atalia and L'Trell, still squirming on the ground and kicking up dirt. He watched in horror as the High Priestess backed away, her mouth and chin covered and dripping with blood. He looked over at the French vampires, but most of them seemed uninterested in this portion, looking at their cell phones instead.

It took about twenty minutes for Atalia and L'Trell to collect themselves and rise to their feet. Their skin now looked like effervescent cocoa, and their eyes were a shade lighter. Their faces glowed with a renewed vigor, as if they were on a perpetual Red Bull drip.

Kwan'de'melu'da spoke again. "*Len pon-su zee me intok oxlo fin kwen kwanili.*"

Cyprian did not expect Atalia to translate this time, but she did. "And now we disrobe and connect with the souls that will guide our spirits."

"Connect?" asked Cyprian.

Atalia pointed into the bonfire. There were two distinct green shapes within the flames. One of them was shaped like Lucie.

"No, no, no! That's my sister! You can't put her soul into a stranger!" cried Cyprian to the High Priestess.

And oddly, she perked a curious brow. Apparently the High Priestess understood English, but didn't speak it. "*Pin a loxli nu?*"

Atalia answered for Cyprian. "Yes. That is his sister."

Cyprian nodded appreciatively to Atalia, and then back to Kwan'de'melu'da. "Please. She was the light and purpose of my life and wherever I end up after this – whether it be Heaven or Hell, or some other weird place we don't know about – I won't be able to live with myself if her soul is stuck in this ass-hat." He motioned to L'Trell.

L'Trell was taken aback. "*Ass-hat?!* Hey! I didn't pick your sister! It wasn't my fault she was the only fucking virgin in that cemetery!"

Cyprian ignored him, trying to burn his pleading eyes into the High Priestess's conscience.

She laughed and said, "*Min tow fa zenkili?*"

"She asked what do you propose?" translated Atalia.

Cyprian was surprised, never for a million years thinking a High Priestess slash goddess slash vampire would even give him the time of day at that point. "Um. I don't know. Maybe… let us fight for her soul?"

"What?!" yelled L'Trell. "That's bullshit! I paid thirty-six thousand dollars for the right to become a vampire! Chancellor Valiquette! Tell them!"

Off to the side, Viktor seemed immensely amused and entertained by the sudden interruption of events. "I'm here to support the High Priestess, so it's ultimately her decision of who she wants in her clan."

"What the fuck?!" L'Trell gave Cyprian the stink eye.

"But may I propose an idea… just to be fair," said the Chancellor. "I suggest the man in shackles remain bound during the fight."

L'Trell barked, "There will be no fight! I paid for this fair—"

"—I accept the terms!" yelled Cyprian.

"No, no, you can't do that," countered L'Trell.

"Aren't you a vampire now?" Cyprian asked him. "Don't you have some kind of super strength and the ability to bite into my jugular and rip out my vocal chords like I was cotton candy?"

L'Trell looked over at the French vampires, who shrugged and nodded in confirmation.

"You can probably even turn into a bat and claw out my brain or something," added Cyprian.

This time, all of the French vampires adamantly shook their heads.

"And I've got my hands bound behind my back."

L'Trell looked at Cyprian's hands, still bound tight in metal shackles. He then looked back at all of the other vampire faces. They all looked eager for a good-ole-fashioned-fight-for-a-soul throw down.

"You'll win easy peasy, *dahling*," said Balzac.

It took another moment of contemplation before L'Trell finally said, "Fine."

There was a low rumble of excitement as everyone turned to Kwan'de'melu'da, who already seemed to be pondering. She started to nod, outlining the new plan. After each sentence, Atalia translated:

"Lok fu tan mir xolik."

"A circle will be drawn in the dirt."

"Krit pon bak, zenli quina."

"Both men will face each other with only their birth skin."

Off to the side, Balzac silently clapped in glee.

"Spee liv mir bak tik kroon intok."

"They mustn't leave the circle until one is dead."

"Oxlo plan bi luk zenkwe tik la xypi liv kwanilo pak quil bak liv oot rag orez rola vok lam ho nib zenktu ray ere thin emo kwis tar nadil nas luf zalap sav ficee weiv reg nif nalp bi liv oot rola ere la tik zenkxo ba ficol wassir sin mal zenkwo zenkwo pak..."

As the High Priestess continued to talk, L'Trell leaned over to Cyprian and whispered, "When this is over – and you are dead – I'm going to fuck your sister's soul."

Cyprian gritted his teeth and simmered. He closed his eyes, waiting for Kwan'de'melu'da to finish her rules. But she didn't seem like she was going to be silencing any time soon.

So Cyprian turned and head-butted L'Trell's nose.

It promptly shattered and spurted blood and dropped the new vampire to the floor. He clutched his nose and writhed in the dirt.

And then Cyprian went ballistic.

Using his feet, he clamped L'Trell's head in between his Air Jordans and over a half-buried stone. He then violently stomped on L'Trell's head and crushed the skull with one ferocious step. And then he continued the onslaught, until the brain was sufficiently squashed and the spinal cord detached from the body.

L'Trell's headless body continued to twitch for a moment, until it didn't.

There was a long moment of silence. When Cyprian caught his breath, he looked up at everyone to expressions of dismay. When he looked at the High Priestess, she was fucking pissed.

And about to unleash Hell.

chapter 8

It was like she was charging up.

Kwan'de'melu'da had closed her eyes and clenched her fists. Her veins bulged and her skin began to glow green. When she finally opened her eyes, she looked right at Cyprian and spat an evil curse, "*Vad a zuul mi por!*"

But before she could unfurl her voodoo magic on Cyprian—

"Wait!" barked Chancellor Valiquette. He rushed over and stood between the *Impundulu* High Priestess and Cyprian.

Kwan'de'melu'da backed down, but continued to fume.

"Killing this man will do you no justice," said Viktor. "Do you still not need someone to complete this ritual? Here you have a perfectly abled body. Otherwise, you will waste the talents of this woman and must wait another year for your clan to grow." He approached Atalia, who seemed clueless that the death of L'Trell could jeopardize her transformation.

The High Priestess was none too pleased with her quandary and didn't want to give in. She spoke, "*Tak lo venzu paratok fi lis dun dun kin pa no kwin ti fo lis tak kwahili nee din fi oxlo zenbi praka.*"

Viktor turned to Atalia, who was hesitant in translating. But she did anyway. "She is upset that he disrespected her process, but now more worried at how much power he will have, considering his spirit will be guided by a direct blood relative."

"Oh my," exclaimed the Chancellor with school boy enthusiasm. "Oh my, oh my! I had no idea that could make a difference. Then we absolutely must see what happens!"

"*Ki lepu ton fa zili fo*," added the High Priestess.

Atalia said, "And she said the first meal is no longer, since L'Trell died with vampire blood."

Viktor looked down at L'Trell's body and then shrugged with no concern. "We have two more fresh bodies in the copter. How do you think *we* were going to eat?"

Kwan'de'melu'da sighed, out of excuses.

Suddenly – from the crowd of male *Impundulu* vampires – the seven-footer who had carried Lucie's corpse quickly approached his High Priestess. He whispered something into her ear. And whatever he said made her eyes perk.

Cyprian and Atalia exchanged curious glances.

The tall vampire then retreated back to his group, leaving the High Priestess in quiet contemplation. She studied Cyprian and seemed to have a quiet inner conversation with herself. She then nodded and oddly seemed appeased.

"You need not worry, High Priestess," said Viktor. "I will take full responsibility for what happens to this man. If he becomes too powerful, then we will simply kill him."

Kwan'de'melu'da remained silent, almost indifferent now.

The Chancellor took it as an affirmative. He turned to Cyprian and whispered, "What is your name?"

"Cyprian Dugas," he said.

Viktor nodded. "Well… Cyprian Dugas… if this process works, then you owe me your life. Understand?"

"I understand."

"You will work for me as a dutiful soldier in my VES."

Cyprian had no idea what the Chancellor was referring to, but nodded anyway. "Sure."

Viktor added, "I've already recruited the lovely Miss Atalia here, so you will instantly be among friends."

Atalia raised a brow at Cyprian and shrugged coyly.

"I do have one request," said Cyprian to the Viktor.

"I believe you've already made enough requests, Mr. Dugas. And a request to die to live forever surely trumps them all."

"Then call it a favor," said Cyprian. "When this is finished, I would just like to return my sister's body back to her grave."

Chancellor Valiquette softened, as if he was realizing what a big heart Cyprian had. "Mr. Dugas – you have my word your sister will be returned. And in fact, I will ensure that she rests in the finest coffin money can buy."

Cyprian nodded appreciatively.

Viktor twirled back around to the High Priestess with a flourish, "Then let's finish this!"

Kwan'de'melu'da approached Cyprian and motioned him to kneel down. She stared into his eyes sternly for a moment, and then plunged her teeth into his neck.

Cyprian's eyes rolled back in pain as he tried to man up. The heat from the bite radiated and sent shock waves through his cerebral cortex. He heard the flutter and cawing of what seemed like a thousand lightning birds within his subconscious. His blood boiled and popped through his veins and when the chaos in his body finally subsided, he slowly opened his eyes and climbed to his feet.

But everyone was gone.

No vampires. No High Priestess. No Chancellor. No Atalia.

The helicopter was missing as well. In fact, Cyprian couldn't even see remnants that a helicopter had ever landed in the nearby clearing. And even more curious, the bonfire had been extinguished. It was eerily silent all around, until a lightning bird chirped from up above. Cyprian looked up to find every bird still on its perch.

"Hello?" he said. It remained quiet, except for the howling wind twisting around the homemade shacks and huts ascending the mountain. Cyprian swiveled around to the Atlantic Ocean side. Miles away, he could hear the breaking waves.

And something giggling?

It was macabre, like a banshee playing pranks.

Cyprian moved around the pile of wood in the bonfire, which was curiously cold to the touch. In fact, there was no evidence that it had burned at all. The wood was perfectly unblemished and newly stacked.

"Where is everyone?" he asked, now standing directly in the center of the clearing and only then realizing his hands were no longer bound.

Suddenly, the swirling wind stopped. The ocean waves in the distance disappeared, like they were swallowed up into a vacuum.

And then the banshee's laughter again. But even that was cut-off.

Cyprian then heard the rustling of feathers. He looked up to see every lighting bird with their legs cocked in attack formation. They were also staring back at him with murderous intentions.

It seemed like an eternity before they finally attacked.

Straight towards Cyprian.

Hundreds of lightning birds shot down and swarmed around him, taking turns pecking at his skin. Blood started to spill as Cyprian was stabbed over and over again, until his flesh gave way to bone. The birds were relentless, taking larger chunks of meat.

Cyprian tried to swat them away like overgrown flies. It wasn't until one of the lightning birds pried out his left eyeball that he finally took off running.

Towards the ocean.

Towards the banshee.

The birds pursued him, diving all around, tripping Cyprian up every few steps. He kept his face and remaining eye shielded with his hands, until he finally reached the coastline and dove into the ocean.

Cyprian swam as deep as he could, as some of the birds braved the salt water and plunged in after him. But they soon gave up and retreated, leaving Cyprian in the darkness of the Atlantic Ocean. And when he finally bobbed up to the surface for air, all of the birds were gone.

The calm of the sea in the dead of night was a welcome solace.

For a moment.

The chilling laughter of the banshee returned. Except now it wasn't a lone banshee. But several. And it was loud, as if the source was only a few feet away.

Cyprian turned to the coastline, but no one was there. On either side of him, the waves continued to break. He turned back around to the vastness of the ocean, shimmering from the moonlight. The reflection of the moon sprayed in front of Cyprian.

And that's when he saw the heads slowly pop out of the water.

It was the clan of old, female *Impundulu* vampires. Their stringy gray hair even more so from the wetness of the ocean. Their eyes glowed green as they approached Cyprian like poisonous sea serpents. And, of course, they were still laughing.

Cyprian began to swim back towards the coast.

Mimicking a shark's dorsal fin, the heads of the vampires remained just above the water, as they kept getting closer.

And closer.

Cyprian began to tire as he finally reached the shallow end and trudged through the water the rest of the way. He collapsed into the sand and turned around.

The vampires had also reached the shallow part. They began walking, revealing their nude, weathered and wrinkled old bodies. They were all infested with lesions, glistening with puss and mossy residue.

Cyprian looked down at his own skin, looking grotesquely similar from the vicious injuries he sustained from the lightning birds.

The laughter of the *Impundulu* vampires now echoed across the ocean.

Cyprian made an effort to move, but two female arms burst out of the sand – *with a tiger's roar?* – and wrapped around his chest, holding him down. But they weren't arms belonging to an *Impundulu* vampire, or even a black woman for that matter. They were young and silky white, with an Oriental-themed tattoo sleeve adorning one of the arms.

The vampires were now upon him; their laughter now shattering decibel levels. Their open wounds oozing neon green acidic goo. They reached out for Cyprian and started clawing at him with razor sharp nails, giving him gashes anywhere he wasn't already hurt.

As Cyprian relented and accepted his fate – and just before he lost his remaining eye – he managed to see past the vampire witches to find the High Priestess.

She suddenly rose from the ocean, standing on a wave that extended fifty feet into the air! Lightning and thunder cracked all around her as Kwan'de'melu'da began to cackle devilishly.

For one brief moment, Cyprian regretted the actions that led him there. Especially when he visited Lucie's grave on the anniversary of her death.

And then he died.

chapter 9

It had only been thirty minutes since Cyprian was bitten before he finally woke up from the dead. He instantly freed himself from his shackles like they were made of paper, and then felt his eyes. They were still there. And his body was completely free from any of the injuries he sustained from the birds and the vampires. He looked up to find Atalia smiling back at him.

She said, "Trippy, huh?"

Cyprian nodded.

"Did all of the birds attack you?"

Another nod.

"Did you see a bunch of old, naked titties?"

"Yeah."

"Lose both of your eyes and get strangled to death by a snake?"

"Yeah – wait, no. I lost both of my eyes… but there was no snake. Maybe a tiger?" Cyprian recalled the two arms that held him down, but he kept it to himself.

Atalia crinkled her forehead in curiosity. "Huh."

Cyprian finally stood and focused on all of the other faces looking back at him. As a new *Impundulu* vampire, the details were amazing. He could see every wrinkle and mole on the other tribe members standing fifty feet away. Every feather on the lightning birds had vivid lines in their design.

And then he realized he could smell something that was absolutely intoxicating.

Behind him, Balzac and another official had pulled out one of the aforementioned corpses from the helicopter.

"Smells like… candy?" said Atalia, who also latched onto the scent.

"*Len pon-su zee me intok oxlo fin kwen Kwanili*," said Kwan'de'melu'da.

Atalia started to translate, "And now we disrobe —"

"—and connect with the souls that will guide our spirits," finished Cyprian, who had remembered that translation and was already naked. He stared at the shape of his little sister, eager to reconnect with her, regardless of the nature.

Of course, Balzac stepped closer, giddy for the free show.

For the first time, Atalia was now the one who seemed less confident. Even as a new vampire, she was a bit embarrassed to disrobe completely.

"C'mon, girl," said Cyprian. "You got this."

Atalia nodded and stripped off her clothes. She then stood next to Cyprian in front of the bonfire; the flames highlighted their impressive physiques, each with distinct, contoured muscle tones and zero percent body fat.

"Now what?" asked Cyprian.

On cue, the High Priestess said, "*Pok ni zin.*"

Atalia furled her brows. "She just said to walk into the flames."

Both of them paused in trepidation. Cyprian looked at Lucie's shape in the flames, and it almost looked like she was beckoning him to join her. She then held out her pinky finger. And then Cyprian heard her voice in his subconscious.

"*I'll always be a part of you, no matter what. I promise, Cyprian.*"

Cyprian looked down at his own curled pinky finger, remembering her promise. He nodded and smiled.

And then walked into the flames.

His skin sizzled briefly, but he appeared mostly unfazed. He climbed the bonfire until he reached the top and joined Lucie's shape, which was instantly absorbed into his own body with a resounding spark. It was only then that Cyprian finally made a sound; a primal grunt that seemed to indicate accepting Lucie's soul into his body was not a completely smooth transition.

Meanwhile, Atalia followed suit and took the same steps Cyprian had, joining her own virgin soul waiting for her. She screamed in anguish as the connection took place and a fireworks display continued. Once the two shapes were completely gone, Cyprian and Atalia both climbed down the other side of the bonfire and patted down any remaining smoldering flames.

That's when they noticed a neon green lightning bird symbol glowing from their left shoulders. When the symbols hit the open air, they sizzled to reveal a black – and embossed – permanent tattoo.

Kwan'de'melu'da stood before them. "*Si li kwanti pon may fi zen ti xylo len suso.*"

"The lightning bird symbols act as the portal to our borrowed souls, who will take ownership of our inherited powers," said Atalia.

Cyprian looked at his tattoo proudly, almost as if he could see Lucie's face.

"*Lo ba tu zinzin,*" said the *Impundulu* High Priestess, as she pointed to the ground.

Atalia laughed and shook her head.

"*Lo ba tu zinzin?*" repeated Cyprian, since she hadn't translated yet. "What does that mean?"

"It means it's time for us to mate – *right here* – in front of everyone," said Atalia, still giggling and red with embarrassment.

"Right here? No pillows or champagne or nuthin'?" said Cyprian to the High Priestess, who didn't look very amused.

"L'Trell would be so pissed if he could see this right now," mused Atalia. "If you hadn't squashed his eyeballs."

Cyprian nodded. "Yeah. I almost feel bad now."

Atalia turned her body towards Cyprian and slid her already erect nipples just under his torso. She now had her game face on, sweat glistening seductively down her neck.

Cyprian glanced down at his new tattoo one last time.

If you can see this, Lucie, you better close your eyes.

He then cupped Atalia's cheeks in his hands and kissed her passionately.

chapter 10

If there was a Top Ten list of the hottest sex scenes ever to happen on our Earth, then the one between Cyprian and Atalia would crack it. Not just because of the literal bonfire sparking and illuminating their perfect bodies behind them. Not just because their body temperatures were a simmering one hundred and ten degrees from having just bathed in the open flames. But because as two newly minted *Impundulu* vampires, their hunger was insatiable, and the enhanced vigor their bodies had never experienced before found a suitable practice field.

It didn't take long for Cyprian and Atalia to zone out their hundreds of spectators. Once they kissed and swallowed each other's fresh vampire juices, they melted as one body and knew of nothing else. Even when the French vampires came around the bonfire to get a better view, the couple was already on another hedonistic level of their own.

Each *Impundulu* vampire took turns taking control, testing out their new strength. At one point, Cyprian stood and hoisted Atalia into the air as her legs stretch over his shoulders. He continued to thrust without missing a beat; his muscular legs bulging as he backed her into the bonfire. Atalia screamed in ecstasy as she showed off her new fangs and the flames sizzled all around her.

The female vampire was equal to the task as she flipped Cyprian around and smashed his buttocks into the burning wood, riding him with such force that the bonfire collapsed and splintered all around them. But nothing would deter their commitment and their passion. When they finally rolled out of the bonfire and away from the burning embers, Cyprian rested his body on top of hers and filled it with one last gratifying thrust, sending both of them over the top with an orgasmic crescendo.

They both stayed connected for another hour, each not wanting to break the union and staring into each other's eyes.

"So, Cyprian," whispered Atalia. "Do you believe in vampires now?"

"I keep waiting for myself to wake up from a dream."

"I know. This is so unreal. Even when I knew I wanted to do this, I never imagined *all* of this."

"What did you imagine?"

"Honestly? Just getting bit in an alley and waking up with sharp teeth."

"This is no alley."

"No, it isn't." Atalia caressed Cyprian's cheek. "Thank you for taking his place. I can't imagine having to do this with that – what did you call him?"

"Ass-hat."

"Right. Ass-hat."

"I wish I could say I did it for you."

"I know. I know you did it for your sister. But I hope this wasn't entirely… *unsatisfactory*… for you."

Cyprian's eyes widened. "Unsatisfactory? Are you kidding? You're one of the most beautiful women I've ever met."

"That's sweet. Thank you."

"And I'm only eighteen… so I really haven't been with any *women*."

"Oh yeah, I forgot you were so young. Not really sure what to think about that."

"Don't think about it," said Cyprian. "Just feel."

Atalia's eyes rolled back as she felt Cyprian's manhood expand inside of her once again.

"I think I might get used to these vampire powers," said Cyprian.

"So will I," said Atalia. "So will I."

And then they had sex again. In fact, they would engage another time before they finally separated and realized they were still being watched. The French vampires never once looked at their cell phones during the whole show; a couple of them even satisfied themselves. And even though their union was sealed the first time, the *Impundulu* High Priestess and the rest of her clan allowed the couple to take their time, since it was the last step in the long process. And also, because Kwan'de'melu'da was engaged in her own ritual.

The High Priestess crouched down and split her legs wide open. After several guttural screams, a speckled *Impundulu* bird egg peeked out from her birth canal. It then plopped out to the ground. It was followed by another.

That's right, Kwan'de'melu'da had laid two eggs.

Since Cyprian and Atalia were still so intertwined in a ball of sex juice, they didn't notice the odd birth. And when they finally finished, they were allowed to drink the blood of their first human corpse.

The two new vampires ravished it like there was no tomorrow. It was like that first drink of water after running a marathon. That late night greasy taco after a bout of binge drinking. The first orgasm after forty days and forty nights of Lent-induced abstinence.

The *Impundulu* vampire population increased by two on that night, and would possibly go down as the most important in their rich and vast history.

Part Two

The path cannot cease.
The prongs will still lead a way.
Each point is finite.

chapter 11

Cyprian and Atalia spent the next morning in the village of the *Impundulu*, where they drained the rest of their corpse for breakfast. It was then they learned that they weren't actually mated for life, but rather only for the particular ritual of becoming an *Impundulu* vampire. It wasn't any type of marriage ceremony. Both of the new vampires were slightly disappointed, but thought it might be for the best as they ventured through that new and unpredictable phase of life.

Before departing, Cyprian and Atalia paid their respects to Kwan'de'melu'da and then boarded the helicopter with the French vampires. A short journey took them to a landing strip, where Chancellor Valiquette's private jet awaited them for the trip back to New Orleans.

During the long flight, the new vampires sat across from Balzac, who was head of initiation for the Castille of Charlemagne. He spent most of the trip educating Cyprian and Atalia about the rules.

"And don't go turning every African-American into Vees, *dahlings*," he said. "We must keep the population controlled so we always have an abundant food source without raising suspicion. Do you understand?"

"But wouldn't we have to go through the whole process of taking them to Africa and sacrificing virgin souls and stuff?" asked Cyprian.

"Not for a regular *Impundulu* Vee," said Balzac. "But if you want more with what we like to call the 'B.M. Class' then yes."

"B.M.? Does that stand for 'Bad Motherfucker?'" asked Cyprian, as he turned to Atalia with a wink.

"Mother fucker is two words," she said dryly.

Balzac wasn't amused and said bluntly, "B.M. stands for Black Magic, *dahling*. Pun most definitely intended."

"Oh," responded Cyprian simply.

"Only those who go through the ritual with the High Priestess will be bestowed with your voodoo and witchcraft powers," said Balzac wryly, with a smidge of jealousy. "And that's why the Chancellor limited the recruitment process to only once a year."

There was a moment of silence as Cyprian looked out the window to the clouds. But Atalia had more questions.

"How many vam – I mean – *Vees* are there?" she asked.

"One thousand, two hundred and thirty-three," said Balzac quickly. "Which reminds me, once we arrive back to the Castille, I must get the both of you registered. I will only need a snapshot and a pint of blood."

"Was everyone back in Africa registered?"

"They are. In fact, the *Impundulu* comprise of almost half of our Vee population. Boy, that was a day and a half of fun," chuckled Balzac. "But there will now only be seventeen of you stateside – all but one residing in New Orleans. Ajax the Façade actually lives in Los Angeles and does work as a stuntman."

"Ajax the Façade?"

"Surely you remember the delicious, seven-foot chocolate man from last night?"

Cyprian chimed in, without looking from the window. "The one who carried my sister and the other guy from the boat."

"The one who may have saved your life with a whisper," added Balzac to Cyprian. "I wonder what he said to her?"

Cyprian looked back at Balzac, recalling that moment. He shrugged and also wondered what Ajax had said to make the High Priestess have a change of heart.

Balzac narrowed his eyes in suspicion at Cyprian. It seemed that the whisper gave the French vampires cause for concern.

"Right – that guy," said Atalia, also remembering. But she continued her own line of thought instead. "Are the rest B.M. Class?"

"Nine of them are," answered Balzac.

"Is Ajax the Façade?"

"Most certainly he is. His own father as well."

Atalia continued to grill Balzac as Cyprian turned back to the window with his first moment of reflection. He was still quite curious about the profound whisper. He also wasn't entirely sure that he had Lucie's "soul" inside of him, controlling his Black Magic. But he was certainly glad that her body was being returned to the cemetery, with a new coffin to boot. And thinking about Black Magic, how were he and Atalia supposed to learn how to use it?

Balzac continued to educate them on the rules, paying special attention to the Crossbreeding Ban of 1972, the Social Media Ban of 2015, and the frowned upon practice of biting a human who was already tainted with another vampire's blood (through the *Revendique*). Neither Cyprian nor Atalia could imagine any scenario where they would break those rules, let alone any other rule. And, of course, they learned about the Vampire Extraction Squad (VES), who enforced the rules and both of whom were recruited to become new members.

When they finally touched down in New Orleans, Cyprian and Atalia were ushered over to the Castille of Charlemagne and registered. Balzac then gave them a personal tour of the underground fortress and its many components, including the Great Hall of Bastien, chapels and oratories, cabinets and boudoirs, solars, dovecotes, kitchens, larders and butteries, among others.

"Would we live here?" asked Atalia, who seemed mesmerized by the beauty and grandeur of the Great Hall of Bastien. They passed by the painting of Chancellor Valiquette.

"No, *dahling*," said Balzac. "Only the Chancellor does. You will have to live among the mortals, like I do. But you will have unlimited access to the Castille and most definitely find yourselves taking advantage of its many amenities..."

Balzac took them past the parlor of the Great Hall of Bastien and through double doors. Down another hall, he slowly cracked open a door to reveal a large, velvety room.

And a vampire orgy in progress.

It must've just started, since any mortal humans involved were still alive. There was no blood to be seen. And everyone wore their customary green, gold, and purple Mardi Gras masks.

Atalia pushed the door further, fascinated with the erotic scene. It was a room full of beautiful vampires blended together in a canvas of continuous, perfect skin. Her nose flared to the intoxicating scent. "Do I smell human blood?"

"You most certainly do, *dahling*," said Balzac. "If you'd like to partake, *the pleasure is all yours*."

Atalia took a step and then caught herself. She looked back at Cyprian, who actually didn't look very interested. "No," she said. "Some other time."

Balzac smirked as if he knew they would refrain for the moment.

When he finished giving them the tour, Balzac gave them each a business card. "That's my number and address. If you have any questions, feel free to call, or better yet, stop by. I'm always having some kind of shindig."

"And these numbers?" asked Cyprian, who had flipped the card over to find two phone numbers scribbled in ink.

"One belongs to a Vee named Tebeau," said Balzac. "He will get you acclimated to the VES and train you properly. The other is Imamu. He can show you how to use your Black Magic."

"When do we call them?"

Balzac answered, "Whenever you are ready. Although the Chancellor does expect both of you to report to Tebeau sooner than later."

"I have to finish high school," Cyprian said bluntly.

Atalia snorted out a laughter louder than she wanted to.

Balzac smiled wryly, "You will no longer need high school, *dahling*. And you might want to start thinking about what you're going to tell your parents. Being a member of the VES will likely require you to travel for great amounts of time."

"And what do I say about having been missing for a month?"

"You were held captive by ISIS and managed to escape," offered up Atalia. "Now you've already joined the Army so you can help bring the bastards down. Boom. Two birds. One stone."

Cyprian and Balzac each perked a brow, impressed.

After the trio went their separate ways, the Chancellor sent a couple of vampires to assist Cyprian with burying Lucie again. She was given an ornate bronze coffin with a white satin interior. Afterwards, Cyprian went home to his distraught parents. Since he had rarely given them any problems as a child, they were quick to accept Atalia's fabrication (with the help of Castille-influenced *validation* from local police and the FBI) and were just glad that their only child was still alive.

Of course, Cyprian wasn't alive. He was just undead.

chapter 12

"We use swords," said Tebeau bluntly. He was the French, turtleneck-wearing vampire assigned in training Cyprian and Atalia, and he already seemed too bothered to care. His often short answers made it seem like he was giving a Cliffnotes version on how to perform as a member of the Vampire Extraction Squad.

The trio stood in the armory of the Castille of Charlemagne.

"Swords?" said Cyprian, scoffing.

"Just pick one from that rack."

Tebeau pointed to a rack that held a bunch of swords, most of them resembling Scottish claymores.

"Yeah, but... *swords*?" said Cyprian again.

The long-haired blonde vampire sighed in annoyance. "If you want to kill a vampire, it's the easiest way. You *can* introduce tainted blood into their system, but that takes preparation, precision, and patience. That vampire will likely get some blows in before it takes effect. Now, pick a sword."

Atalia wasted no time in choosing a sword.

Cyprian tried a couple of different hilts, and then settled on one that had gold accents in the pommel and cross-guard.

"How many vampires do you normally have to kill?" asked Atalia.

"I don't know. Four, five, six, or seven a year, I'd say," said Tebeau with another yawn. "The both of you won't have to kill so many, since I'm around. But if it so happens I'm preoccupied on another assignment, then you may get the call. If The Cowboy doesn't first. Otherwise, your duties will mostly encompass guard and escort detail for the government officials."

"Did you say 'Cowboy?'"

"The only non-vampire employed by the Castille. Consider him a sort of 'double-agent.' He's quite the bounty hunter for a mortal."

Cyprian was a bit relieved to hear that he wouldn't have to go around killing vampires all the time. He knew that becoming a professional football player was no longer in the works for him (although a few vampires had been), but becoming a vampire hitman was certainly not on his short list. Or long list. Or any list for that matter.

Tebeau went on to explain some more intricacies of the job, but it was pretty much cut and dry: if you got called upon to kill a vampire, you would find said vampire and kill him/her. No trial. No jury. There should be no questions asked, since by that point, the Castille would have done its dutiful and thorough investigation in such matters. Only on the rarest occasions did Chancellor Valiquette request a vampire returned alive for questioning, but even more rare was allowing that same vampire to survive afterwards.

For the next several days, Cyprian and Atalia were assigned sparring sessions, which mostly consisted of slicing watermelons off the shoulders of varied sizes of headless dummies. They also practiced the art of disposing vampire corpses, by mixing rat's blood, venom from a Golden Lancehead viper, and fire.

After the mediocre training with Tebeau, Cyprian and Atalia rarely saw each other. Atalia fully immersed herself into the vampire world and absorbed all she could. It was, after all, something she had wanted for herself for a while. And since Cyprian was "technically" still a teenager, Atalia sought company from vampires more her "human" age.

Cyprian, on the other hand, was a reluctant vampire and hoped he would never get the call from the Castille. For the next two months, he holed up in his parents' house and only went to the Castille when he was hungry (he didn't want to kill his own humans yet). Otherwise, there was nothing vampire about his lifestyle. Cyprian continued to visit Lucie's grave on a regular basis, but his disappointment kept growing as he felt nowhere near closer to his sister than before her body was kidnapped. If her soul was supposed to be a major component in his *Black Magic,* then where was it? Would it take the *Impundulu* vampire Imamu to show Cyprian how to connect with his sister?

Deciding that he couldn't procrastinate any longer, Cyprian finally made that call.

chapter 13

Imamu ran a curio shop in the French Quarter of New Orleans. He was an African man who looked to be about eighty years old with a perfectly white beard and one glass eye. He sat in the corner of his shop and smoked from a hookah most of his days.

The tiny store was filled with dusty shelves with such eclectic items as bottled bones, leather quivers, pewter drinkware, tapestry maps, and stuffed lizards.

The door chimed as Cyprian walked in. He didn't see Imamu, since the old *Impundulu* vampire almost blended in with his merchandise.

"Why did you take so long to come?" he asked, without confirming who Cyprian was. "Your sire-mate came almost two months ago."

"I know. I'm sorry. I just needed to… *collect myself*," said Cyprian. "Atalia was eager to learn everything."

Imamu smirked. "You two put on quite the show during the ceremony."

"You were… *there*?" asked Cyprian, suddenly embarrassed.

"Not physically."

Cyprian waited for more of an explanation, but Imamu took another drag off his hookah instead. "So… you're supposed to teach me about Black Magic or something?"

"Mm hm. Something."

"Is that going to make me some sort of witch?"

"A witch?" Imamu busted out in laughter. In fact, he couldn't stop himself, crying and choking on his hookah. "A witch! A witch, you say!"

Cyprian joined him with a chuckle. "I know, right? A witch?! *Pfft.*"

"Yes! That is so dumb!" cried Imamu. "Only a woman can be a witch! You are a man! You are a warlock!" He continued to shake his head, as if it was the most ridiculous thing he'd ever heard.

Of course, Cyprian's face dropped. "A warlock?"

"Mm hm."

"So I'm a vampire slash warlock?"

"Vampire slash warlock slash running back! Ha, ha! I saw you in the State Championship last year!"

"You were there?"

"Not physically," answered Imamu again. "But yes, if you are a man who needs titles, then you are an *Impundulu* vampire warlock."

"Seems kind of unfair, doesn't it?" asked Cyprian. "That we can use magic and other vampires can't?"

"*Los Vampiros Oscuros* have the essence of their creator – Queen Mictecacihuatl, the Goddess of the Underworld – flowing through them. She has used her divine powers through their actions. And the French vampires have ruled over everyone with an iron fist for centuries. Their influence has always tamed and tempered the others. So we all have certain, advantageous traits."

Cyprian nodded, taking a closer look at some of the merchandise. He picked up an oriental vase decorated with a sprawling tiger and recalled the roar he heard during his transformation into a vampire. "So... how long have you been an *Impundulu* Yoda?"

Imamu furled a brow. "Yoda?"

"Trainer. You know... teaching the ways of Black Magic."

"Ahh. No, I am not a trainer. Just a guide for the soul you are using."

Cyprian choked up more than he wanted to. If the process was true, then Lucie's promise to always be a part of him would come to fruition more than he ever imagined. "So then... what do I need to do?"

"Come with me."

Imamu led Cyprian through a beaded curtain into a back room. It was mostly dark, except for several votive candles and burning incense. The flickering lights, however, moved shadows across macabre figurines and masks depicting several Louisiana voodoo spirits called *loa,* including *Damballa* and *Mami Wata,* and *Bondye,* the Supreme Creator.

"Take off your shirt and lay down," said Imamu, as he motioned to a straw cot in the corner.

Cyprian obliged. He took off his shirt and laid down, the cot creaking and barely holding his weight.

Imamu then opened up an antiquated jar and smeared a translucent green paste on Cyprian's lightning bird tattoo, spending an unusual amount of time trying not to cross over to his bare skin.

"Let that sit for a few minutes."

"It's warm."

"Mm hm. In two minutes, it will burn."

Cyprian's eyes widened as Imamu walked over to a small cabinet and started to take out various items, including what looked like string, loose cotton material, and a naked voodoo doll. He began humming a tune which sounded oddly like "Witchcraft" by Frank Sinatra, as he used a thread and needle to fashion miniature hair and clothes.

As Imamu kept working, the paste on Cyprian's tattoo started to sizzle.

"Um. Is this supposed to happen?" he asked.

Without looking over, Imamu responded, "All that occurs right now is supposed to happen. Don't worry, you will not perish."

Cyprian didn't look very reassured as he grimaced from the burning sensation.

Imamu kept fiddling with the doll until he finally held it up and nodded. Satisfied, he turned it towards Cyprian.

It looked exactly like Lucie.

"What the fuck?" exclaimed Cyprian. "That looks like my sister!"

"Is she not the soul you are using?"

"Well, yeah, but... how did you know what she looked like? And what her favorite outfit was? Have you seen her before?"

"Not physically." Imamu placed the voodoo doll of Lucie on Cyprian's chest and then adjusted his hands to cradle it. "Keep her right there."

"Wait. Is this going to hurt her? I mean... *hurt her soul?*"

Imamu paused and looked perplexed. "I don't know. No one's ever asked me that question before." He then opened a *gris-gris* (voodoo amulet) and pulled out a thick incense stick. After lighting it on a nearby candle, Imamu began wafting it with a straw fan towards Cyprian's face. It smelled like a mixture of cloves, vinegar, and shit.

Cyprian coughed and felt another sting. He looked down at his tattoo.

It was hollow.

Cyprian leaned over and peered inside.

He could see the universe with planets and stars and flying comets, as if it was all swimming inside of his own body.

Cyprian leaned back, incredulous. And then he passed out.

What happened next was an existential acid trip for the ages.

Lucie moved Cyprian's fingers away from her body so she could stand up on his chest and then tiptoed over to his shoulder *where the lightning bird tattoo* was now a portal to another universe, and she dipped her foot inside like she was testing the temperature of a **swimming pool** and then clumsily fell in where she began *f l o a t i n g i n t o   s p a c e* and the opening into her big brother's shoulder got farther and farther away and she could see Imamu peering inside and waving hello *(or was it good-bye?)* and her back hit a cloud with a backdrop of pink skies *(was this Heaven?)* and she wondered if she could just lay there for the

REST OF ETERNITY

since it was very much like the place she'd been staying for the past year but the cloud descended until it reached the Earth's atmosphere and continued to the

Xhosa region of South Africa

and finally noticed that the cloud was not a cloud at all but the backs of thirty **LIGHTNING BIRDS** side by side supporting her body and there was the

High Priestess Kwan'de'melu'da

waiting for her with all of her *Impundulu* vampire minions behind her and their glowing green eyes but the birds didn't stop and carried Lucie into the raging bonfire where she disappeared through the burning wood

and then into the ground and could see the distinctive   details of
earthworms and other various insects   burrowing through
the soil and   there was even a mole
and down she kept going until she found Cyprian *(wasn't he supposed to
be asleep?)* sitting on a throne made of more

LIGHTNING BIRDS

and there were green flames all around *(was this Hell?)* and she felt
compelled to genuflect and was instantly taken back up to the Earth's
surface and this time the High Priestess threw dust on Lucie and now she
was in a tunnel with all of the other

Impundulu vampires

and they were putting a hand on her body with glowing green eyes
that had no pupils and then suddenly felt an immense amount of POWER
and REJUVENATION and now all she could think was her promise to her
big brother was fulfilled as she would now always be a part of him so she
closed her eyes to

BLACKNESS
BLACKNESS
BLACKNESS
BLACKNESS

BLACKNESS
BLACKNESS
BLACKNESS

BLACKNESS

BLACKNESS

                                                            BLACKNESS
                                    BLACKNESS

and then reopened them and was now seeing out of Cyprian's eyes
who was still clutching the voodoo doll   and Imamu
was drinking tea and   wearing   a different outfit
and not even paying attention   at
all to Cyprian who
            was trying
                    to speak
                        and
                            finally
                                said

chapter 15

"What just happened? I feel achy."

Imamu put his cup of tea down and approached Cyprian. "Your sister's soul has settled into your spiritual realm. And you've been lying in that dormant position for two days."

"Two days?!"

"Mm hm. Moving souls is not like moving furniture."

Cyprian looked over at his tattoo, which appeared normal again. He then glanced down at the voodoo doll, which he had been squeezing the whole time and was damp from his own palm sweat.

"Besides your stiff muscles, how do you feel?" asked Imamu.

"Um," Cyprian tried to focus on his mind. "Actually, I do feel more at peace. And... a little closer to my sister." He curled a smile.

"As you should."

"I don't understand."

Imamu placed a hand on Cyprian's forehead. "This is yours." And then on his heart. "This is also yours. But when you seek the guidance of your inner *Impundulu* powers, call on your sister." He then placed three fingers under Cyprian's ribcage. "Her soul is the keeper of that magical realm and will never lead you astray. You are very lucky."

"Lucky?"

"One who enters my home never has such a loyal and loving soul. Together, your outer and inner strengths will be unmatched."

Cyprian looked concerned. "Did… all of this prevent Lucie from going to Heaven?"

"That all depends on your translation of Heaven."

The new vampire continued to ponder. After a moment, he nodded in satisfaction. "So, now how do I learn to use this magic?"

"You don't need to. Your borrowed soul knows."

That time, Cyprian looked confused. Imamu noticed. "But if it makes you feel any better, I have a book of spells I can give you." He pointed to a book on a shelf that looked hundreds of years old and ready to fall apart.

"You're giving me that?" asked Cyprian.

"Of course not. I have Xeroxed copies," said Imamu. "Oh. And I need the doll back."

Cyprian looked at Lucie's voodoo doll and didn't look like he wanted to part with it. "What are you going to do with it?"

"I will store it with all of the other souls." Imamu opened an antiquated chest to reveal a pile of voodoo dolls. The chunky one on top was probably Moe – Atalia's virgin soul. Lucie was placed right on top.

"Can't she have her own shoebox or something?" Cyprian asked with concern.

"Bring me a shoebox," said Imamu with a shrug. "I'll put her in a shoebox."

Cyprian nodded. Regardless if Imamu was joking or not, Cyprian was going to find a nice shoebox and perhaps even put some of her belongs inside.

They both walked into the shop. Imamu opened a drawer and handed him a stack of paper, bound by a simple binder clip. "Your spells."

"Thanks."

"So, do you feel like a Jedi Master now?" asked Imamu with a grin.

Cyprian smirked, now realizing Imamu actually did understand the "Yoda" reference.

When he left the curio shop, the *Impundulu* vampire warlock heard a faint squawk. Cyprian looked up to see a lone lightning bird, staring curiously back at him.

Cyprian had never seen any in New Orleans until then. And it would take several more encounters for him to realize that the bird would always be somewhere in his vicinity.

It was his own, personal spirit animal.

Naturally, he named it "Lucie."

Since Cyprian told his parents he had joined the Army, he was going to have to play up the charade. So he moved out and found himself an apartment on the East side of New Orleans. Since the Castille was paying him a salary of a thousand dollars per week as a member of the VES, he had enough money to support himself and then some. Especially since he didn't have to spend any of it on food.

It was late October when Cyprian finally killed his first human. He met a tourist named Monique at a Halloween party and invited her back to his apartment. As they were engaged in sex and he was thrusting Monique from behind against the wall, the nape of her neck grazed his lips. And that's all it took for Cyprian to *accidentally* bite her as he had an orgasm.

Cyprian fed on Monique's body for a couple of days and then stealthily took it to the Castille of Charlemagne for disposal late one night. For a small monthly fee, they accepted corpses by utilizing an incinerator. (And three months later, started its first "corpse pick-up curbside" service called "BodyCaddy." It was a very successful set-up and one that kept money flowing into the French vampire government).

When December arrived, Cyprian spent some time at home and *pretended* to be on military leave for Christmas. He attended a football playoff game for his former high school, but sat on the visitor's side so that he wouldn't be recognized and asked a zillion unwanted questions. It was also his first real test to be around so much fresh blood without falling to his temptations.

His anonymity was going well until he ran into Shanice.

"Cyprian?! Oh my God!" She gave him a hug. "How are you?! I heard you were kidnapped by terrorists, and you joined the Army so you can get revenge!"

The *Impundulu* vampire thought the story now sounded utterly preposterous. "Yeah. Something like that."

Shanice rattled on, "What was that like? Did they torture you for information? Did you have to sleep on a concrete floor with mice? Were you molested? How did you escape? What's the Army like? Do you have to do push-ups all the time?"

"Well, I, uh..." Cyprian stammered, until Shanice realized—

"What are you doing on this side? You should be on the home side so everyone can bask in the glory of last year's hero!" she said.

"Well... I didn't wanna have to answer a zillion questions about the whole terrorist and Army thing," Cyprian answered wryly.

Shanice gave him a stink eye. "Whatever. I'm *not* just anybody. Anyways, do you remember Zenia? From Lucie's funeral?"

Zenia peered over Shanice's shoulder, as if she was hiding. "Hi."

"Hey. Yeah, I remember."

"And that's why I'm on the visitor's side too," said Shanice. "Zenia isn't ready for the world to know about her yet." She gave a disapproving side-eye to her. "Anyways, are you wearing contacts? Your eyes look lighter."

"No."

"Are you high right now?"

"No."

"Cuz your eyes look *reeeaaally* light. Right, Zenia?"

Zenia shrugged, still on a perpetual lookout for any witnesses.

"Probably just the stadium lights or something," offered Cyprian, who was also tired of all his relatives asking the same thing and assuming he was on drugs. "So what are you up to these days?" he asked, trying to change the subject.

"I got a volleyball scholarship to the University of Texas in San Antonio."

"That's dope!"

"Yeah," said Shanice. "Just in town for the holidays. I called Zenia cuz I missed how she tastes."

Zenia smacked Shanice in the shoulder. "You suck!"

"I will later," said Shanice playfully, shimmying her shoulders. "Anyway, Cyprian – we should hang some time. When do you come back into town?"

"I don't know," said Cyprian, not wanting to commit.

"Maybe Mardi Gras," offered Shanice. "I think it's during Spring Break next year. I'm gonna try and bring my roommate."

"Is she hot?" asked Zenia, who was suddenly concerned.

"Oh my God, she's sooo hot. No joke. She's Japanese. Are you jealous?" said Shanice.

Zenia only rolled her eyes and slid back behind her.

"So, maybe Mardi Gras then?" Cyprian started to back away, desperately wanting to leave the situation.

"Yeah, for sure," said Shanice. "I'll call you. Do you still have the same number? If not, I'll get it from your mom."

Cyprian slid away, without finishing the game. And when he returned home, he received a call from the Castille.

It was time for his first VES assignment.

chapter 16

Emmanuelle Emond was a French vampire who lived in New York City as a museum curator. She took pride in the works of art she chose to display, since they always invoked some kind of personal emotion. One collection from an English artist reminded Emmanuelle of her childhood with paintings that depicted the European countryside where she had spent many summers. Another from a Filipino artist showcased abstract images in various hues of pink and blue, which were her mother's favorite colors, before she passed away when Emmanuelle was a teen.

And the latest collection was no different. An Argentinian by the name of Hugo Acosta crafted watercolor paintings of couples in love amidst chaos all around. For example, a loving, African-American couple held a newborn baby and kissed, with several Caucasian police officers killing young, black teens behind them. The image in the foreground was a stark contrast to the violence in the back. Another depicted a young couple making love with fantasy-inspired vampires bathing in human blood all around. The entire collection was called "Dichotomy Mil" and quickly became one of Emmanuelle Emond's favorite works; it was beautifully nuanced and thought-provoking.

As customary, Emmanuelle first had coffee with her potential client. When Hugo walked into the café, she was instantly captivated. He had an air about him that she didn't see in most artists. Or other mortals for that matter. Hugo was confident, and every word he spoke had meaning and passion.

"The coffee in Bariloche opens every sense in your body to allow each experience of life to be unforgettable," Hugo said with a strong accent, comparing his tepid coffee to that served in his hometown.

"Is that so?" said Emmanuelle with her own sexy French accent, hanging on his every word.

Hugo reached over and twirled her golden locks and gazed into her blue eyes. "You should have a cup with me some time as the sun rises over the water, it will shine and reflect in your eyes as one."

After the successful art exhibit, Emmanuelle indeed travelled to Bariloche, Argentina with Hugo and shared a cup of coffee in his villa, overlooking Nahuel Huapi Lake. It was the beginning of a whirlwind romance, and each spent equal amounts of time at the other's residence. The "vampire reveal" would come several months later – with no concern from Hugo – and he would later permanently relocate to New York City.

But Hugo didn't move entirely because of Emmanuelle.

Back home, Hugo had amassed a large amount of debt with a local drug cartel warlord named El Mangosta that he could not satisfy. He hoped that by escaping to New York City, El Mangosta would forget his debts.

But he was wrong.

The warlord tracked Hugo down several months later. It was during one of Emmanuelle's new art exhibits with an abstract painter much like Jackson Pollock. On that occasion, the collection invoked feelings of nostalgia when Emmanuelle first became a vampire and her transformation was a mental blur of psychedelic shapes and images.

Emmanuelle and Hugo stood in the main exhibit hall when El Mangosta's men pulled up in front of the museum and began shooting into the building with high-powered Uzis. The bullets riddled the entire room, instantly killing all of those in the area. The paintings were ripped to shreds, and those that remained up were layered with a new coat of crimson splatter.

When the rain of bullets subsided – and El Mangosta's men drove away – only Emmanuelle and Hugo were left standing. Emmanuelle had turned her back towards the gunfire and shielded her mortal lover. When she finally looked up at the carnage, she realized in a strange twist that life had suddenly imitated art. Much like one of Hugo's paintings, the couple stood in an embrace in the center of a sea of bloody chaos.

But alas, the image was too good to be true.

Hugo had taken a bullet in the neck and was quickly fading. He looked up into Emmanuelle's eyes and tried to utter his final words, but his vocal cords had been severed.

Emmanuelle never took her "vampire rules" into consideration. Pure love and the desire to hear her lover's voice once again drove her to instantly turn Hugo into a vampire. She did it right then and there, before anyone could witness. And then she fled the scene with Hugo – and in a complete reversal – landed in Argentina.

Not only did she vow to retaliate against El Mangosta, but she also knew she needed to escape from the Castille of Charlemagne.

When Cyprian boarded the private jet for his journey to Argentina, he found himself sitting next to Atalia.

chapter 17

"So, how's life as a vampire?"

Atalia glowed. "I love it, Cyprian. I just feel so full of life."

The ironic statement didn't escape either of them, as they shared a smile.

"What about you? Have you learned to use your magic yet?" asked Atalia.

"Not really," said Cyprian. "I haven't found any need."

"It's pretty bad ass. I'd at least practice if I were you."

"If I don't use it, I lose it?"

Atalia shrugged. "Maybe."

They both looked out the window as the jet soared over the Gulf of Mexico. Lucie (the lightning bird) was flying with another similar bird, just above the wing.

Cyprian then noticed Atalia's sword. It had a curious set of gold dice dangling from the cross-guard. And it also had blood dried on the blade.

"Have you already been on an assignment?" he asked.

"Yup. In Vegas. There was an underground Texas Hold'em Tournament between vampires where they were betting live humans. The winner couldn't wait to feast on his winnings, but that human was still claimed."

"But he won it in a bet."

"Doesn't matter. He still should've waited."

Cyprian shook his head, in disbelief how serious the Castille was about its rules. "This is my first assignment."

"I know. They asked me to come as a back-up, since you haven't been very vampire-y thus far."

"What do you mean? I've killed."

"Cuz you were hungry and needed to eat. Have you hung out at the Castille?"

"To have an orgy?"

"No, just to mingle. Immerse yourself into the culture. Learn about their history. Meet other vampires. Listen to them about their experiences," said Atalia matter-of-factly. "The French vampires are a little snooty at first, but they're cool. The Mexican ones are hot as Hell."

Cyprian remembered Imamu's fact about *Los Vampiros Oscuros*. "Did you know they were created by some Goddess?"

"I did," said Atalia with a hint of petulance. "Learned it in the library of the Castille."

The *Impundulu* vampire warlock smirked.

"Did you know that Balzac is transgendered?" Atalia asked Cyprian, her turn in quizzing him. "I mean... *like*... he's *almost* transgendered. Like he didn't get to finish or something."

"No. You learned that in the library too?"

"Don't be dumb. I went to one of his soirees and found out."

"He just... *told you*?"

"No, I saw it. I mean... *I didn't see it*," said Atalia, suddenly confused at the proper vernacular. "We were all pretty drunk and having sex. Oh! And guess who I had sex with?!"

"I don't know. Imamu?"

"Seriously? You think I fucked *Impundulu* Yoda?"

Cyprian only shrugged, not thinking it was so farfetched.

Atalia hit Cyprian in the shoulder. "No! Eww."

"Ajax the Façade?"

"Oh my God – I wish I could climb that man. Isn't he in California, or something? He's definitely on my sexual bucket list." Atalia seemed to get lost in thought about Ajax the Façade, a horny little grin plastered on her face. She then snapped out of it and said, "No, I had sex with the Chancellor."

Cyprian stared into Atalia's overly excited face. "Isn't he like hundreds of years old?"

"He sure doesn't fuck like it."

"And he just hangs out at Balzac's with everyone else?"

"Oh, no. Of course not. He invited me to his chambers one night at the Castille."

"Let me guess," said Cyprian facetiously. "You had been in the library, studying about vampires?"

Atalia scoffed, annoyed. She settled back into her seat, seemingly content to stay silent the rest of the trip.

Cyprian grinned, finally noticing the folder sitting in Atalia's lap. "Is that what I think it is?"

Atalia opened it to reveal a picture of Emmanuelle Emond. There was also a piece of paper soaked with blood, sealed in a plastic sandwich bag. "Her and the guy she illegally sired. His name is Hugo Acosta."

Cyprian stared at the photo of Emmanuelle. She was too gorgeous to die. And even though it was only a picture, Cyprian could instantly tell she had a dignified intellect behind those bright, blue eyes. "So we just kill them?"

"Yep."

"Doesn't even matter why she broke the rules?"

"Nope."

Under his breath, Cyprian muttered to Emmanuelle's photo. "Must be a good reason."

When they finally arrived in Bariloche, Atalia unsealed the bloody paper swab and took a whiff. She then handed it to Cyprian for his turn. They both turned their noses up to the air.

"I can smell her. You?" asked Atalia.

"Yeah. I think I can. But—"

Cyprian stopped short, confused. So did Atalia.

"Yeah. I smell it too. It's surrounded by other blood."

Both of their noses flared to something decadent, intoxicating.

"Human blood," said Cyprian. "Lots of it."

chapter 18

By the time Cyprian and Atalia had arrived at El Mangosta's sprawling compound outside the city of Bariloche, all thirty-seven men, women, and children present were dead. That included El Mangosta's wife, seven children, his mother, his mother-in-law, and eight housekeepers. Most were savagely killed by their insides being clawed and ripped out, or their jugulars bitten. And the blood was still oozing.

For a vampire, the situation equated to a child being let loose in Willy Wonka's chocolate factory. It was a free buffet of sorts, with blood types ranging from A to B to AB to O to A positive to O negative. Each had a distinct smell. Each had a distinct taste. Some vampires would say that A positive was the sweetest. O negative was more on the bitter end of the spectrum. Regardless, every vampire had their preferences and would never pass up a taste test, especially since there was no question on how many humans were too many within the vampire quota; they were already dead.

So Cyprian and Atalia did just that.

They went around the entire compound and took sips of various corpses. When they found one they especially liked, they would call each other over for a sample. It was actually quite comical, expecting one of the *Impundulu* vampires to raise their heads at one point and exclaim, "This one tastes like Snozzberry!"

When their bellies were full and they were on a "sugar high," Cyprian and Atalia sat on a wicker couch on the patio of El Mangosta's gorgeous house, decorated with Christmas flair of red and white garlands. Their mouths and chins were caked in fresh blood.

"That right there... might've been better than an orgasm," said Atalia, basking in a euphoric glow.

"That *was* an orgasm," said Cyprian, with both of his hands resting on his stomach like it was about to explode.

"Did you taste the children?" asked Atalia, which sounded way more sadistic than it should have.

"I did. They tasted like—"

"—Fruity Pebbles," said both of them simultaneously, and then laughed like two stoned teenagers.

The two vampires continued to vegetate on the couch, until Atalia's eyes suddenly shot open. "She's still here."

Cyprian was half-asleep and instantly smelled the same thing. He turned his game face on as they both looked towards the interior of the house and scanned upwards.

"She's upstairs."

They drew their swords and crept into the house. In the foyer, a *pesebre* (Nativity scene) was toppled over and speckled with blood. The large Christmas tree was in disarray, many of the baubles, lights, *papai noel* figurines, and cotton balls scattered on the floor. A couple of the housekeepers were dead on the colorful Talavera-tiled floors of the dining room, already prepared for the feast of the Annunciation. There were also two more children with broken necks. Cyprian and Atalia rounded another corner to find a brass staircase lined with green, gold, red, and white flowers, ascending to the second floor.

Atalia immediately put her military experience to use and silently motioned Cyprian to stay quiet and follow her on the other side of the stairs. He obliged, welcoming her take-charge attitude.

When they reached the landing, their noses took them to a room on the opposite end. The door was currently closed. They crept towards it, swords poised and ready. When they reached it, Cyprian and Atalia heard the unmistakable sounds of a man and woman having intercourse.

Atalia slowly pushed the door open.

What they saw next was ghastly.

Hugo was on top of Emmanuelle in what must have been El Mangosta's bed. The vampires were soaked in blood, as well as the satin sheets underneath. And El Mangosta was lying next to them.

He was skinless.

And he was still alive.

The drug lord was catatonic. His eyes moved around in traumatic shock; the whites of them a stark contrast to the blood bubbling from the rest of his exposed, pulsating muscles. The cartilage of his nose was barely attached, hanging from one loose epidermis strand.

And it was only now the two *Impundulu* vampires realized that Emmanuelle and Hugo were having sex with El Mangosta's bloody, outer shell – *still in one whole piece* – sandwiched in between them. The mask of his hollow face danced in between Emmanuelle's breasts.

Cyprian instantly gagged.

And that's all it took for the two fugitive vampires to be alerted to their presence.

Emmanuelle reached behind her pillow with lightning speed and threw a razor sharp wooden stake at Atalia, hitting her in the abdomen. The *Impundulu* witch instantly buckled and collapsed to the ground, rendering her paralyzed and completely helpless. Another stake was thrown at Cyprian, but he managed to tumble away just in time, losing his sword in the process.

Hugo leapt off the bed in all his nude glory and landed in front of Cyprian.

But Cyprian kicked his groin, landing a hard foot against his equally hard – and amazingly still erect – shaft and sent him flying out of the window.

"Run, Hugo!" screamed Emmanuelle, as she tossed El Mangosta's hide to the floor and slid off the bed, exposing her sculptured physique. She wasted no time in kicking Atalia's head through the wall for good measure and then immediately pounced on Cyprian.

The *Impundulu* vampire was no match for the French one.

Emmanuelle hoisted him up into the air with one hand around his throat and then threw him out of the bedroom, smashing through the rails of the landing and crashing to the first floor in a heap.

Cyprian managed to turn on his back, but had no time to react as Emmanuelle jumped from the second floor and landed over him, straddling his body.

"You are who the Castille sends these days?!" barked the female vampire in her normally-cute-but-not-today French accent. "*Patheteek!*"

Emmanuelle picked Cyprian up again and raised him over her head, flinging the vampire through a wall into the kitchen, where he slid across the counter of an island and then smashed against the oven. Pots and pans and utensils of all sorts scattered to the floor.

"Viktor is going to have to do better than this!" said Emmanuelle, as she walked through the new hole in the wall and stepped to Cyprian, who was bleeding profusely. His hand was shaking and holding a sleek, all-metal butcher's knife.

Though it would've been futile, he still had no strength to use it.

Emmanuelle laughed. "Here, let me help you." She bent down and allowed the knife to pierce her stomach. She then settled her nude body seductively onto Cyprian's, rested her chin across clasped hands, and stared into his battered and beleaguered eyes. "How old are you? Not vampire years."

"Eighteen," grunted Cyprian.

The French vampire shook her head. "Now *that* should be a law. No one under twenty-five should be turned."

"I didn't give them a choice."

"Oooh, that's interesting." Emmanuelle shimmied up Cyprian's body; the butcher's knife continued to slice through her belly, but she wasn't deterred. Her stiff, blood-dried nipples were now close to Cyprian's chin. "Tell me more."

"It's a long story."

"Tell me the short version."

Cyprian sighed and chose his words. "I killed a vampire who was to partake in an *Impundulu* ritual, thereby forcing them to use me as a replacement."

"How did you kill him? With your bare hands?" asked Emmanuelle, eyes perked.

"My hands were bound, actually. I used my forehead and feet."

Emmanuelle nodded, impressed. "No wonder the Castille gave you this job." She slid off of Cyprian and extracted the blade from her stomach.

Blood gushed out and sprayed his face. "Well, I need to get back to my lover. He didn't finish fucking me. Any last words before I rip your head off and send it back to the Chancellor in a box?"

"Yeah. What hole is Hugo going to fuck?"

The French vampire grinned. "Any hole he chooses."

"Then I'm going to fuck this one!" And with that, Cyprian picked up a wooden ladle and plunged the handle into her still-open knife wound.

Emmanuelle shrieked and stiffened, collapsing backwards to the kitchen floor. She tried desperately to move, but she was now paralyzed, much like Atalia. "*Trou de cul!*" she screamed in French.

Cyprian calmly stood and wiped glass and debris off his body. He tore off several squares from a roll of paper towels and wiped his face. He then walked back up to the second floor, retrieved his sword, and returned to Emmanuelle. He raised his sword up over her neck.

"*S'il vous plait!*" shouted the French vampire, pleading with misty eyes.

"I just want to know one thing," said Cyprian. "Why? Why did you do it?"

The tears flowed down Emmanuelle's cheek, and she offered up only one word. "*Amour.*"

Cyprian didn't know French, but knew enough to understand what that meant. He stared into the vampire's soft eyes, witnessing the pure humanity and raw emotion for the first time. For being a vicious bloodsucker, she almost looked angelic.

And then he sliced off her head.

chapter 19

Atalia was wheezing when Cyprian finally extracted her head from the wall. He carefully slid the wooden stake out of her belly and then held her head in his lap, brushing her hair back in comfort. He remembered Balzac's lesson about wood, the paralysis effect it had on vampires, and how long it took to recuperate (depending on what areas of the body were affected).

But Cyprian and the *Impundulu* had an advantage other vampires didn't.

The vampire warlock hybrid began rubbing his palms together. His eyes started to radiate with a green hue. And then under his breath, Cyprian chanted, "*Oxlo mandu, Kwanili fino, Zenkwe in-tak.*"

But nothing happened.

"*Oxlo mandu, Kwanili fino, Zenkwe in-tak.*"

Suddenly, nothing happened again.

Cyprian squinted and pondered. He rehearsed the *Impundulu* spell in his mind. And then he heard a little girl's faint voice.

"*In-tok, Sippy,*" she said.

One word was wrong. Cyprian grinned at the sound of Lucie's voice and for the first time, realized her soul would truly be guiding his magic. "Thanks, Lucie. *Oxlo mandu, Kwanili fino, Zenkwe in-tok,*" he said, emphasizing that last syllable.

From his clasped hands, green smoke began funneling out. Cyprian quickly placed it on Atalia's wound and repeated the chant, much quicker this time. *"Oxlo mandu, Kwanili fino, Zenkwe intok. Oxlo mandu, Kwanili fino, Zenkwe intok."*

Satisfied, Cyprian lifted his hands off of Atalia and returned to stroking her hair.

It took forty minutes for Atalia to recover (instead of taking a normal three hours for that type of wound, without the aid of *Impundulu* Black Magic).

"You lied to me," said Atalia when she spoke for the first time. "You *have* been practicing your magic."

"Maybe a little," responded Cyprian, who had memorized only the ones that seemed pretty useful and practical.

"Well, thanks for that. Did you get those fuckers?"

"I got her. But he ran off."

"Where is she?"

Cyprian led Atalia back into the kitchen, where Emmanuelle's body laid still. Her head had rolled over to the refrigerator. The ladle remained protruding from her stomach.

"You stabbed her with a wooden spoon?"

Cyprian lifted his hands and shrugged.

"Nice job," said Atalia. "I had my doubts about you – being so young and all and knowing only how to score touchdowns – but yeah, I think you'll make it."

"Gee, thanks."

Atalia reached down to Emmanuelle's hand and pulled off a silver ring with a garnet shaped like a heart. She slipped it on one of her fingers.

"What are you doing?" asked Cyprian.

"That's going to be my thing," said Atalia. "I'm going to take something as a souvenir for every job I do." She pointed to the pair of gold dice hanging from her sword, apparently from her kill in Las Vegas. "You should, too."

"No, thanks. I'll just etch some prison notches into my bed post."

Atalia shrugged. "So I guess we need to go after Hugo?"

"I guess so."

It did not take long to find Hugo. The rookie vampire got hungry and took the life of a homeless Argentinian. That scent helped Atalia and Cyprian track him down near a retail center called Shopping Patagonia, where he had stolen new clothes. Atalia swiftly moved behind him and held his arms, while Cyprian quickly beheaded him.

Newly turned vampires were usually easier to kill.

Cyprian picked up Hugo's brand new, beige cabana hat – still with the price tag attached. He placed it on his head and modeled it for Atalia. "Maybe I'll take their hats as a souvenir."

"Because most vampires wear hats," said Atalia, rolling her eyes with a smirk.

They disposed of Hugo's body and walked around the shopping center for a moment, collecting themselves. It was night, and the bright, twinkling Christmas lights adorning all of the storefronts seemed to be a nice break from the day's violence. Both of their lightning birds rested on a lamp post with a big, red ribbon. It seemed like they were chatting.

Cyprian and Atalia were back on a return flight to New Orleans by midnight. With the starry night sky outside the window and the cabin lights on low, Atalia took the opportunity to thank Cyprian for using his magic on her by performing oral sex. Cyprian obliged by returning the favor, and when it was over, neither of them said another word the rest of the trip.

For the next couple of years, Cyprian and Atalia rarely saw each other. She went on to become a favorite VES agent and traveled around the world on various assignments. She eventually did have sex with Ajax the Façade and couldn't walk straight for days. Cyprian took on more local work, but still tried to remain out of the vampire spotlight. It would take almost two years for the two *Impundulu* vampires to finally cross paths again.

It was during one fateful day in Tokyo, Japan.

Part Three

A love not returned,
is still love that may be turned.
Time can be a friend.

chapter 20

Chancellor Viktor Valiquette was impressed with Cyprian's disposal of Emmanuelle Emond and Hugo Acosta. Atalia had given him a detailed account of this accomplishment and how Cyprian also helped her recover with his use of black magic. That prompted a private conversation, since the High Priestess of the *Impundulu* vampires was concerned with how much power Cyprian was capable of achieving.

"How long did it take for Atalia to heal?" asked the Chancellor, as Cyprian sat across from him in his large office at the Castille.

"Forty minutes or so?"

"Forty minutes?! My, oh my!" Viktor was giddy.

"That's fast?"

The Chancellor leaned in. "Without any *Impundulu* magic, it would've taken about three hours to heal. With the magic – in my experience and the stories I've heard – ninety minutes tops. You've cut that time in half, my boy."

"Maybe the injury wasn't so bad. Missed organs or something," said Cyprian.

Viktor grinned and leaned back. "Powerful *and modest.*"

Cyprian looked around the office as the Chancellor seemed to contemplate. There was one wall of shelves lined with first editions of such classics as "Moby Dick," "Wuthering Heights," and "The Catcher in the Rye." The Chancellor was – after all – old enough to have been able to personally amass the collection. Cyprian zeroed in on another title. "Is that what I think it is?"

He stood and pulled out a first edition of "The Narrative of the Life of Frederick Douglass, an American Slave." It was in great condition for its age.

"I read that one when it was first published in 1845."

"You remember that?"

"I remember it well. I was in France, and it was the first book to create such buzz and excitement since the works of the Marquis de Sade. It was later renamed to 'My Bondage and —"

" —My Freedom," said Cyprian.

Viktor smiled. "You can have it if you'd like."

"No, no, I couldn't."

"Its words will resonate with you far more than with me."

Cyprian nodded appreciatively. "Thank you. Is there anything else you need from me?"

"Yes. Back on the day you were transformed, Ajax the Façade whispered something to your High Priestess. Any idea what that was?"

The *Impundulu* vampire had forgotten about that moment, but realized it was still an unanswered mystery. "No. I… I don't. Sorry."

"No need to apologize."

"Maybe you can ask Ajax?"

The Chancellor curled a grin. "Perhaps I will." He then abruptly stood and offered Cyprian a handshake. "I will have a report card sent back to your High Priestess."

"You'd think the High Priestess would know it all already."

"Oh, she does," said the Chancellor. "But I want her to know that I know."

Cyprian shook his hand and left.

Over the next couple of months, the *Impundulu* vampire was only assigned local work that mainly consisted of surveillance and escort duties. Not many vampires broke the laws – but if they did – Tebeau or The Cowboy or Atalia or other VES agents were assigned. The Castille was still a bit apprehensive about allowing Cyprian to get into situations where he might "discover" his true abilities.

So Cyprian began settling into the life of a vampire and even visited the Castille more frequently, taking Atalia's advice and learning the history and customs of his new *family*. He figured the extra knowledge would serve him well if and when he had to kill again. He met other vampires as well, including some from clan *Los Vampiros Oscuros*.

Cyprian did not participate in any vampire orgies, even though they occurred quite frequently and seemed like a natural part of the culture. He felt timid, but also thought his little sister Lucie would not approve, since she was – *after all* – a part of him now. In fact, many of his decisions were based on that odd dilemma. At times he thought he heard an internal and very stern *"Cyprian, no"* in her voice, when his motives were in question. And for the most part, Cyprian always listened to Lucie.

Except for one day during Mardi Gras.

That morning began with a strange dream. In fact, it would be the same dream that would end many nights to come.

Cyprian walked through a flooded rice paddy field and grazed his hands over stalk that was calmly swaying from a light wind. He happened upon a baby tiger, swaddled in a blanket that was stitched with the symbols of the Japanese goddess of the Sun and Universe. The vampire picked up the cub and held it against his chest, looking out over the rice paddy for its mother. But there were no other tigers in the area.

Suddenly, there was a voice.

"Cyprian, no."

The *Impundulu* vampire whirled around to find his sister Lucie standing at the edge of the rice field. She was shaking her head, holding Cyprian's lightning bird on her arm. She leaned over and whispered something to the bird. It then took off and landed on the belly of the tiger cub, still cradled in Cyprian's arms. It began to chirp excitedly – but also angrily – at the vampire, who had no idea what it was saying.

"I don't understand. Speak English!"

But then the bird pecked at one of the tiger cub's eyes and pulled it out.

Cyprian screamed. "What are you doing?!"

The bird couldn't respond, since it had an eyeball skewered on its beak which prevented it from opening. Cyprian plucked the eyeball from its beak and placed it back into the cub's eye socket, where it oddly resumed its functionality.

"Now speak," said Cyprian.

The bird chirped in indecipherable sounds again. And again. And again.

Cyprian looked over at his sister, but it was no longer Lucie. She was replaced by Amaterasu-O-Mi-Kami – the Japanese goddess depicted in the cub's blanket. She wore a floral, pink kimono with flowing fringes.

But the goddess said nothing, only letting the bird continue to chirp incessantly. It continued at annoying decibel levels and became almost unbearable and—

Cyprian was awakened by his chirping cell phone. He looked over – confused at first – and then answered it.

"Cyprian?" said a woman's voice.

"Yeah. Who is this?"

"Shanice! Got your number from your mom. You in town?"

Cyprian had forgotten that others thought he might or might not be stationed overseas in Afghanistan. "Yeah, of course."

"Me too! Doing Mardi Gras with my roommate, and I was seeing if you wanted to hang tonight? Marco and Flora and Jam Jam said they were game – you remember them, right?"

"Uhhh... yeah." Cyprian was finally waking up, weary of the conversation.

"Cool. We're staying right on Bourbon Street, so we'll be around. You have my number now, so text me, and I'll tell you where we're at."

"Um. Yeah. I'll check my... *schedule*... and see."

"You better! I want to see you!" And with that, Shanice clicked off.

Cyprian had no intention of texting Shanice. In fact, he went back to sleep and never gave it another thought. When he finally crawled out of bed and went about his day, getting drunk with old high school friends was the furthest thing from his mind. But when midnight rolled around and Shanice texted a selfie of herself and her college roommate completely hammered and flashing their breasts with a caption that read "WHERE U AT?" Cyprian was intrigued.

But not just because of the unsolicited photo of bare breasts.

It was because of Shanice's roommate. She looked exotically Japanese, and the picture captured a mysterious aura about her. She was sweet and innocent, yet mischievous. She was enjoying life and new things to the fullest, yet had an unmistakable confidence and determined persona. It was only a selfie, but it seemed to reveal so much more to Cyprian.

She was also wearing a watch with an animated tiger on the face.

Cyprian remembered the interesting vase from Imamu's curio shop with the artsy tiger. He also recalled the "tiger's roar" he heard when he was transformed into a vampire, and then the slender, tattooed arm with the Oriental markings that seemed to hold him down on the beach in South Africa. And of course, that strange dream from the morning with a baby tiger and a Japanese goddess.

Surely it couldn't be a coincidence?

Shanice's roommate did not seem to have a tattoo arm sleeve, so that didn't match. But still, something was drawing him towards her.

And Lucie didn't seem to like it.

"*Cyprian, no,*" said her voice faintly, drifting through Cyprian's subconscious.

But that only seemed to fascinate her big brother more. How could this woman – a random college roommate of an old high school friend – be a danger to Cyprian? What made Lucie even care that he was thinking about joining them for a drink or two? And why was he so drawn to her enigmatic beauty and – *lately* – Japanese culture in general?

Those three questions were all Cyprian needed to go out that night.

It did also help that the Japanese woman's breasts were shaped like perfect tear drops.

chapter 21

"*Cyprian, no.*"

Cyprian found himself standing outside of the Spotted Cat Music Club. The jazz music and drunken revelry spilled through the open doors as people came and went. He had a sense of dread and couldn't bring himself to enter. Especially since he'd be surrounded by a smorgasbord of human blood laced with alcohol. *The best kind.*

"*Cyprian, no.*"

"Fuck this," said Cyprian softly. He promptly turned to leave when he ran into Jam Jam, a former high school football teammate who was an offensive lineman, which meant he was a big boy.

"Yo, Nigga! You lost? We're in there!" Jam Jam fist bumped Cyprian and then pointed inside of the club. "Shawny said you might come. I'm so glad too cuz there be too many fuckin' bitches! I just came out to get some air."

"I wasn't going to—"

But before Cyprian could come up with a lame excuse, Jam Jam put a giant arm around Cyprian's neck and led him inside. Even though Cyprian was a strong vampire, he was easily trapped.

Jam Jam rambled as they waded through the club. "Do you remember that game against Churchill and that fuckin quarterback that tried to do a fuckin' flea flicker, and I was all over that shit and fuckin' threw his ass down. I heard you is in the Army now cuz you were raped by Egyptians, did it hurt?"

Cyprian didn't even bother responding, since Jam Jam had that glossy drunk look in his eyes which meant he probably wouldn't remember anything the morning after anyway.

When they arrived to the table, Shanice had to tear Cyprian away from Jam Jam's arms. She gave him a big hug. "Took you long enough. You know Marco, and Flora, her boyfriend Jake, and that's Amy Lynn – we just met her. This is Cyprian. He's in the Army."

Cyprian exchanged hugs and handshakes with everyone. But none of them were Japanese. He thought for a moment that maybe Shanice's roommate had left already, and so, he felt a momentary sense of relief.

That lasted seven seconds.

"Oh, and that over there is my roommate from college." Shanice pointed to the dance floor. "Her name is Misake. She's soooo hot, *amirite?*"

Cyprian looked over to find Misake slowly dancing with her eyes closed. It really didn't go with the uppity jazz riff currently playing. It was like she was dancing to her own imaginary music inside of her head. She had a cute, inebriated smile.

"Is she okay?" asked Cyprian.

"Misake? Oh, yeah. She's just drunk," answered Shanice. "She's actually allergic to alcohol, so it affects her pretty hard."

Cyprian nodded and kept watching her. He was instantly riveted to Misake's carefree spirit, even though she was under the influence. She seemed to sense his gaze, since when she opened her eyes, Misake looked straight at him.

"Cyprian, no."

The couple met each other half way.

"You must be Cyprian," she said. "I've heard a lot about you."

They shook hands, even though Cyprian felt an instant connection and wanted to do more. "And you're Misake."

"Yep. Nice to meet you." She didn't even linger, moving past him and rejoining the others, giving Shanice a hug.

Cyprian stood back and observed, wondering if Shanice and Misake were a thing. But all of the women in the group seemed to be overly affectionate with each other, and Cyprian understood why Jam Jam complained about "too many bitches." They weren't really paying attention to the guys, whether they were straight, bi, tri, omni, pan, gay, or whatever. Cyprian grabbed the attention of a cocktail waitress and ordered another round of what everyone was having, and even made her switch the current tab to his responsibility. Of course, that won him kudos from everyone.

Jam Jam kept trying to talk about old high school memories with Cyprian, but the vampire was too enthralled with Misake. He was glued to her every move, and every so often, Misake would look back at him and smile. And all Cyprian ever had to say to Jam Jam was, "I remember that play, shit was fucked up," and Jam Jam would laugh and nod and give him more fist bumps.

When night turned to early morning, half of the club was empty. The band was playing music that was more mellow. Jam Jam, Marco, and Amy Lynn had left. Shanice, Flora, and Jake ruminated about pop culture. And Cyprian had invited Misake to join him in a corner booth.

"You're a long way from Japan," said Cyprian. "Do you miss it?"

"A lot. But I'll be back soon."

"Oh, yeah? When?"

Misake seemed to ponder. She curled a smile and repeated, "Soon."

Cyprian stared into her eyes. For some reason, he felt like he could carry on a conversation with Misake forever. It was more than a physical attraction. And he certainly didn't have a hunger to drink her blood. It also didn't hurt that his little sister's voice had disappeared. Whether Lucie had given up, or changed her mind, it didn't matter. Cyprian didn't feel one bit of guilt and found himself in an unfamiliar place. Misake had captured a part of his soul he never knew existed.

But there was still some kind of connection Cyprian couldn't decipher.

"Do you believe in vampires?" asked Misake, out of the blue.

And there it was. A possible connection. There was no way Misake could know Cyprian was a real life vampire, but her ironic question certainly seemed to come from *somewhere*.

"I do," said Cyprian.

"Really? Not many people think they're real."

"If you live in New Orleans, then you have to believe in them to a certain degree."

Misake looked over at her roommate, who was still engaged in what sounded like a conversation about Billie Eilish. "Shanice doesn't."

"She just doesn't want to. That's what you have here. People who believe, and people who don't want to."

"Why do *you* believe?" asked Misake.

Cyprian knew you weren't supposed to reveal yourself as a vampire to the living, but there wasn't a death penalty associated with it like other rules. And the fact that Cyprian felt a strong connection with Misake and the Oriental imagery he had encountered during his transformation gave him a certain comfort level. The alcohol helped, too.

"Because I am one."

There was a beat, and then the Japanese woman busted out a laughter that echoed through the club. Shanice looked over and rolled her eyes.

Misake rubbed a tear and simply said, "You're funny."

Cyprian was a bit offended at her disbelief. Even though she was letting him off the hook for his potential transgression, he wanted her to believe him. So he kept the topic going, curious as to why she asked the question in the first place. "Do you believe in them?"

"Oh, yes," Misake responded quickly. "In fact, what's why I'm actually here in New Orleans – don't tell Shanice. But I'm here to meet one."

The *Impundulu* vampire perked up. "You are? Who?"

"His name is Balzac St. Laurent."

Cyprian was surprised to hear Balzac's name. He never thought Balzac to be the type of vampire humans would seek and found it humorous. "Balzac? Really?"

"Yes. You know him?"

"Everyone knows Balzac. He's a trip. Why are you meeting him?"

"Just for information," said Misake. "I'm trying to get into the Castille of Charlemagne."

Cyprian straightened up and looked around the room for spies. Misake apparently knew a lot about vampires. Not just from folklore, but from real life. And now it might not have been a coincidence for them to meet. "And why do you need to get into the Castille?" he asked, still looking around, suspicious that someone might be testing him.

"To get some of the Nectar of… uh…"

"L'Auberge?"

Misake's face lit up. "Yes! That's it! You know about that?!"

The vampire sighed and looked grim, recalling Balzac's mention of the dubious concoction. "And pray tell why do you want some Nectar of L'Auberge?"

"I want to get close to a vampire in San Antonio and have him turn me into one."

That statement stung Cyprian more than he expected. He had hoped that he was the first vampire Misake had ever met, but apparently another one was on her radar. But that issue was actually beside the point. "Are you of French descent?" he asked.

"No."

"Latina?"

"No."

"And I know you're not Cajun or black."

Misake drunkenly looked down at her own skin. "No."

Cyprian stared into Misake's eyes. "Then no vampire will turn you, unless you find one willing to commit suicide."

Misake slightly recoiled and then seemed to reformulate something in her mind. For the first time, her normal confidence waned, and she looked vulnerable. She softened and slid closer to Cyprian, resigned to changing the subject. "So, anyway," she said. "Mardi Gras is fun."

The vampire warlock also softened, relieved he didn't have to reveal anything more about vampires. In fact, Cyprian didn't want to talk any more at all. The new and raw tenderness in Misake's eyes melted him.

"You want to get out of here and go to my place?"

chapter 22

Cyprian sensed Misake's emotional vulnerability, so the vampire made love to her with the sole purpose of allowing her an escape. Misake's eyes told an undeniable tale of tragedy, and there was a sense of fear buried deep in her psyche. Cyprian also noticed she had two scars – shaped like Japanese *kanji* figures – above each of her breasts that were undoubtedly related to her tumultuous past. He wanted her to forget all of that for at least one night.

And never once did Cyprian want to suck her blood.

That told the vampire that Misake was a woman on another level. Whether it be something cosmic or spiritual, mental or definitely physical, or a combination of all of the above, there was an unmistakable connection and attraction he instantly felt.

Misake's body felt like home.

Cyprian's brown frame encased Misake's fragile porcelain skin like a baby bird nestled into the palm of a hand. His muscles pulsated with her every heartbeat as her body disappeared underneath him in fluttering moans of ecstasy. The vampire didn't leave one inch of her body uncared for as it erupted in a euphoric, seismic wave over and over again until the seas calmed to tranquil bliss.

Misake climbed on top of the vampire for their final round. Cyprian didn't think she was a virgin, but she certainly seemed a bit timid and unsure of herself. He steadied her by placing his hands just underneath her soft behind and rocked her pelvic region forwards and backwards, until she mastered the rhythm on her own and rode him like a well-oiled churning machine.

The *Impundulu* vampire then placed his hands under Misake's legs and swiveled her completely around in a fluent motion. She didn't miss a beat, as her body continued to engulf him. Cyprian ran a finger down her spine and to the soft dip at the base of her back, where he relished the clear view of their sensual interconnection. The heat of their bodies and the fusion of their juices continued until they simultaneously released and Misake collapsed backwards.

Cyprian caught her and never let go.

After breakfast at Café du Monde the following morning, Cyprian had hoped that he deterred Misake's desire to get closer to a vampire in San Antonio. He had talked about the Vampire Extraction Squad and their practices of beheading any bloodsuckers who disobeyed the crossbreeding rules. He even mentioned his own brief experience, killing Emmanuelle Emond and her own, sired human. Since there were no Japanese vampires (or *Jampyres*, as Misake chose to call them) on record, then Misake would surely be put to death.

And even though Cyprian yearned to see Misake again and get to know her more, he knew that was not a good idea. He hadn't heard of many vampires in relationships with humans. Or at least healthy ones. And the vampires of real life didn't seem to have human "familiars," even though vampire mythology was riddled with them.

So Cyprian tried to let Misake go.

But later that day, he received a frantic text message from Shanice that Misake was missing, and she hadn't heard from her in a while. The last several messages she had received featured a photo of Misake posing in the Castille of Charlemagne.

Somehow – *some way* – Misake ended up literally entangled in a vampire orgy.

Cyprian immediately rushed to the Castille and found her slithering naked with a plethora of vampires in harlequin masks. Balzac was there. So was Tebeau. And a handful of other humans. They were all engaged in sexual intercourse. The *Impundulu* vampire stayed back, unsure of what to do. Part of him was turned on to see Misake enjoying herself with others, but naturally, Cyprian couldn't help but also feel jealous.

And when the vampires started tearing into the humans and blood rained all around, Misake was curiously left unharmed. Cyprian realized that she must've been tainted with a vampire's blood through a concoction called the *Revendique*. That meant she was claimed, and no other vampire could harm her without facing their own death. Of course, that didn't mean she still couldn't die – she could be the dessert for whomever had claimed her.

So Cyprian stripped and joined the orgy. Partly to protect Misake. Partly to get a fill of the human blood he could no longer resist. *The smell was decadent.* When it was over, Cyprian escorted Misake to the bathroom, where she cleaned up a little and then promptly passed out. Balzac explained to Cyprian that he gave her his *Revendique*, but someone must've slipped something else to her. He then wrote a note for Misake and gave Cyprian the concoction of Nectar of L'Auberge that Misake had sought after.

Back in his apartment, Cyprian took the time to clean Misake and dressed her in clean clothes. She slept until the next morning. When she woke up, the vampire thought about hiding the Nectar, hoping she wouldn't remember it. But his guilty conscience got the best of him.

"Just be careful with that. I don't want you getting hurt," said Cyprian.

"By you?"

"Anyone," said Cyprian grimly, knowing all too well the violence vampires seemed to revel in.

When Misake left him again, Cyprian was faced with a sad realization: nothing he had said to Misake deterred her from getting close to a vampire in San Antonio. She had her Nectar, and she was on a mission she was determined to accomplish. For the second day in a row, the *Impundulu* vampire tried to get Misake out of his mind. She seemed to be on a completely different path, regardless of the "signs" Cyprian thought were related to her. If she was to be turned into a vampire and subsequently punished by death, so be it.

And once again, Lucie seemed to be right.

"Cyprian, no."

chapter 23

But forgetting about Misake was easier said than done. It was like those movies where everything reminded the forlorn main character about their lost love. That's how it was for Cyprian. A song on the radio would have the slightest lyric about a tiger or love or even just plain sex (so, basically, *every* song). The vampire drove by sushi restaurants he never even knew existed prior to meeting Misake. Every Asian person Cyprian encountered – whether they were Japanese or Chinese or Korean or Filipino – put Misake on the forefront of his thoughts (even though he knew that was blatant stereotyping). And every so often, he continued to have that same dream with the tiger cub in the rice paddy, his defiant sister Lucie, and the beautiful Japanese goddess.

Cyprian casually texted Shanice once a few weeks later, to see how they were doing and if Misake "had found her friend yet." Shanice responded with a bitmoji that shrugged her shoulders. So either Misake had found him and didn't tell her roommate and everything was fine, or she hadn't succeeded yet. Regardless, Cyprian once again tried to move past the conundrum that was Misake.

It helped that the Castille finally gave him another real assignment.

Vampires had to kill humans in moderation, so the general public wouldn't grow suspicious of any odd, mysterious forces. There was an unwritten rule that celebrities were off-limits due to the media scrutiny that often followed. The Castille quite frequently discussed the possibility of a new ban, but the degree of celebrity status always came in question. Someone like George Clooney was obviously off limits, but what about the star of a reality home improvement show? Tearing into Taylor Swift's jugular was a no-no, but what about the local singer who had a modest tens of thousands Instagram followers? Though a "celebrity ban" was often placed on the Castille's agenda, an official one never came to fruition.

So, every so often, a vampire would kill a celebrity. But truth be told, it often occurred in dark rooms when the vampire rarely recognized their victims. Such was the case with the likes of River Phoenix, Kurt Cobain, Selena, Michael Jackson, and Brittany Murphy. When a vampire knew of a victim's celebrity status, they often killed in a moving vehicle to reduce any potential mystery and clean-up. James Dean, Lady Diana, JFK Jr., and Paul Walker were some of the more high-profiled deaths. In every case, the military intervened to provide plausible cover-up. Also in every case, the Castille gave the guilty vampire a "slap on the hand" and were told "to be more careful next time" and so on and so forth.

But then came the curious story of French vampire Toussaint St. Toussaint.

Toussaint had an obsession with cinema and all things Hollywood. He moved to Los Angeles in 1976 and worked as a theater usher in the New Beverly Cinema, where he fed most of his appetite on all of the classics. His daily routine usually consisted of watching a matinee and then going to work. Toussaint mostly stayed off the Castille's radar, until the year his obsession became quite unhealthy.

The French vampire began suffering from a bout of depression since Hollywood was no longer producing an abundance of future classics. What made it worse was that Toussaint's favorite actors of yesteryear were getting old and dying into oblivion. The past was fading, and Toussaint was outliving the love of his life. So, in order to cling on to the past, the vampire decided to get ahead of the inevitable. He began enjoying his cinema in a *different* way.

It was eight o'clock in the evening at his home in Beetsterzwaag, Netherlands when actor Rutger Hauer settled into his recliner and found vampire Toussaint St. Toussaint sitting across from him like the devil who had come to retrieve his gifted soul.

"Before you die, I want you to tell me stories," said Toussaint. "The more stories you tell me, the longer you live. And please… begin each with 'once upon a time.'"

For the next five hours, Rutger Hauer detailed his acting escapades from his early years as a Dutch performer and being discovered by director Paul Verhoeven to his first American film role in Sylvester Stallone's "Nighthawks" and the acclaimed popularity of playing Roy Batty in "Blade Runner." He chronicled his personal life and the antics of his thespian colleagues like Harrison Ford and Michelle Pfeiffer. When Toussaint asked him how he felt playing the role of a vampire on multiple occasions, Rutger Hauer simply said, "It felt like a natural transition."

Had the raw and intimate conversation been recorded and shown to audiences, it would've undoubtedly been nominated for a "Best Talk Show" Emmy. But alas, that was not the purpose.

Toussaint killed Rutger Hauer and enjoyed the taste of his blood for the next several hours. At times, he thought he could envision movie stills from many of his films as the warm blood trickled down his throat. The French vampire had found a new way to enjoy Hollywood. First hand retellings of the medium he loved so much by actors who had lived it and were on the verge of extinction. Toussaint almost felt honored that his heroes would die by his hands, immediately after they shared and expounded on their life's work.

In the span of two years, Toussaint had killed several celebrities who were already on the way out. Tim Conway, R. Lee Ermey, Burt Reynolds, Doris Day, Albert Finney, and director Franco Zeffirelli were among them. They were all in the same fashion and always began with Toussaint's directive, "Before you die, I want you to tell me stories."

After the death of Rutger Hauer, Chancellor Valiquette decided that he had had enough. Toussaint St. Toussaint had been given a fair amount of warnings to refrain from killing celebrities, whether they were already on their death bed or not.

So the Castille dispatched *Impundulu* vampire warlock VES agent Cyprian Dugas to Los Angeles, California. His task was to kill Toussaint St. Toussaint on the spot.

But the French vampire wasn't home.

He was already at the home of actor Morgan Freeman.

chapter 24

The blood of Toussaint led Cyprian to Morgan Freeman's rental home in the Hollywood Hills. Though the actor usually resided in Charleston, Mississippi and New York City, he kept a modest 7,350-square-feet house for when he was shooting in town.

It was just after three in the morning – eight hours after Morgan Freeman had begun to spin his yarn about his own Hollywood adventures – when Toussaint finally bit into the Oscar-winner's neck. For the first time, the French vampire felt slightly guilty, since he was putting an end to one of Hollywood's most iconic voices. But eight hours of the actor's regal rhetoric about the early days of being a dancer to his stints on "The Electric Company" and the soap opera "Another World" to his varied work with Clint Eastwood was enough to appease Toussaint for the rest of his own days. And if anyone had kept track, they would've counted Morgan Freeman starting his stories with "once upon a time" exactly sixty-four times.

Toussaint carefully laid the actor's body down and closed his eyes to death. He then spied a record player and turned it on; he was curious to hear what Morgan Freeman liked to listen to. It was the soundtrack to the movie "A Clockwork Orange," which featured mostly classical music by Beethoven and original compositions by Wendy Carlos. The first track was oddly appropriate for the moment, soothing yet simultaneously terrifying.

And that was when Toussaint sensed Cyprian enter the house.

Cyprian found Morgan Freeman's body in the living room. The second piece from the soundtrack – "The Thieving Magpie" by Gioachino Rossini – seemed to blare from unseen speakers throughout the house. Naturally, the *Impundulu* vampire was stunned to find the famous actor dead, with blood trickling from his neck and staining the cashmere carpet. Toussaint was missing, but Cyprian could sense that the French vampire was still present.

Somewhere.

He turned toward the long hallway that extended from the living room and drew his sword. Cyprian could still smell the French vampire's fading muskiness as it filtered away from him. He slowly began creeping down the hall.

The first door on the right was slightly ajar, leading into a dark void. Cyprian pushed it open to reveal a coat closet – too many for the Los Angeles climate, and none of them seemed to have been worn. He slowly split the two center jackets apart, half expecting to find two glowing eyes staring back at him. But no vampire was hiding there on that night.

Yet, he was still somewhere.

The next two doors on the left opened into an office and then a game room, respectively. After a close inspection behind long curtains and inside closets, Cyprian did not find Toussaint.

A set of stairs led up to the second floor. By the time Cyprian ascended, Beethoven's "Ninth Symphony, Fourth Movement" seemed to match his every step. The second floor hallway was dark, except for the moonlight spraying from a window at the end. Cyprian flipped up the light switch, but it clicked uselessly. He opened his cell phone and used the flashlight function.

The moonlight and Cyprian's bright beam competed to cast eerie shadows dancing down and across the hall. Several strategically placed vases and candelabras stretched like claws and shuddered with every move. There were five doors down the hall, and every one of them were wide open to complete blackness.

The music from below faded with every step and gave way to Cyprian's heartbeat.

Bump-da-da. Bump-da-da. Bump-da-da.

The *Impundulu* vampire stayed on guard, peering into the rooms with his flashlight. They were all bedrooms, some full of furniture and others sparsely decorated. Every so often, a shadow would fidget, causing Cyprian to pause in his tracks. His heartbeat raced faster each time.

Bump-da-da, bump-da-da, bump-da-da.

Reaching the end of the hall, Cyprian looked out of the window.

The moon was full, though tinted by the city's infamous smog.

Behind Cyprian, a large shadow with two glistening eyes moved. He turned, only to find his own shadow sprawled out before him.

But he could smell Toussaint's blood.

Bump-da-da, bump-da-da, bump-da-da, bump-da-da.

Down on the first floor, the record continued to spin with more of a muffle. It had reached "Timesteps" by Wendy Carlos.

Cyprian tried to zero in on Toussaint's fragrance, hoping it would lead him to the right bedroom. But it didn't need to. Something else alerted Cyprian to his mysterious whereabouts.

The record from downstairs scratched to a halt.

It was suddenly dead silent. Except for—

Bump-da-da, bump-da-da, bump-da-da, bump-da-da.

But then the needle was replaced and advanced to a new song. It was Gene Kelly's "Singin' in the Rain."

Morgan Freeman was dead. So it had to be—

Cyprian sprinted down the hall and leapt down the stairs back to the bottom floor. He paused momentarily, since the lights were now all turned off except for the glowing console of the record player. He squinted, able to see down the hall and the outline of Morgan Freeman's body still lying motionless. But no one was manning the phonograph.

Bump-da-da, bump-da-da, bump-da-da, bump-da-da.

Again, Cyprian sprinted with his sword, ready to cut down anyone or anything he found. When he reached the living room, he didn't find anyone.

But the front door was wide open.

The *Impundulu* vampire approached and stepped out to the porch, convinced his prey must've run off. He tried to sense Toussaint's blood.

The smell was still there.

And it was stronger than ever.

Bump-da-da, bump-da-da, bump-da-da, bump-da-da.

Through the window, the light from the record player barely produced a silhouette of a man standing in between the curtain and the window.

Toussaint's eyes glowed with vehemence. And before Cyprian could turn around, he pounced!

The French vampire smashed through the window and instantly wrapped Cyprian's neck with a wire and began strangling him.

Cyprian dropped his sword and tried to pry the wire away with both hands, but Toussaint was too strong as he straddled the warlock's back with his legs and pulled with all of his might.

The wire began to cut through Cyprian's neck, blood oozing down his chest.

The *Impundulu* vampire couldn't gain a good grip or any traction. His eyes began to bulge and emanate green steam. His breathing turned into exacerbated gasps.

In a nearby tree, Cyprian's lightning bird Lucie began to wobble, seemingly feeling the same effects.

Toussaint wasn't going to let go; the weight of his own body took Cyprian to the ground.

And it was only a matter of time before his head would be completely severed.

chapter 25

If Cyprian had enough oxygen being supplied to his brain, then he might have been able to conjure up a spell to help himself. But the French vampire was too strong, gaining the upper hand quickly.

But then something curious happened.

Toussaint abruptly released his hold and tumbled backwards. He clutched his back in pain and writhed on the floor.

Cyprian rubbed his neck and slid away. He turned to see Toussaint desperately trying to extract what looked like *wooden bullets* from his body. But before he could even get a hold of one, his head was completely severed by Cyprian's sword.

Except the black vampire wasn't wielding it.

"You alright, brother?" said a man's voice with a Southern twang.

Cyprian rubbed his eyes and found himself looking up at The Cowboy. He wore a denim jacket with jeans, with a black Stetson hat and boots. The vampire rubbed his eyes again to make sure he wasn't hallucinating.

The Cowboy placed his .44 Magnum – that apparently silently shot wooden bullets – back into its holster. He then put a hand down to help Cyprian up to his feet.

"I'm Benjamin Flynt. The Castille sent me to be your back-up. Sorry I was late."

Cyprian stood and continued to gather his bearings, still rubbing his neck.

The Cowboy said, "I thought you were supposed to have some amazin' powers or sumptin'?"

The *Impundulu* vampire ignored the question and finally realized who Benjamin was. He coughed and was barely able to say, "You're The Cowboy."

"Yeppers – that's what the Fangers like to call me." The human bounty hunter looked down at Toussaint's head and rolled it to the side with a boot. He then peered inside of the house. "Holy shit. Is that who I think it is?"

"Yeah."

The Cowboy rushed inside to get a better look. "That's the guy from 'Unforgiven.'"

"Yeah," nodded Cyprian. "Among other things."

"I think he was Darth Vader's voice too."

Cyprian almost corrected him, but left it alone. "I was a few minutes too late."

"That's alright," said The Cowboy, trying to console him. "He looks really old anyways. Probably only had a few more years left. Hey, brother – you got some of that goo so I can get rid of that Fanger's body?" He pointed to Toussaint.

"Yeah," said Cyprian, who was still staring sullenly at Morgan Freeman's body. He pulled out a small tube of liquid and tossed it to The Cowboy, who then walked back out and began humming a Country Western melody.

The vampire warlock kept staring at the dead actor, and then furled his brows in afterthought. He bent down and started rubbing his palms together. His eyes glowed green as he chanted, "*Oxlo mandu, Kwanili fino, Zenkwe intok.*"

Neon green vapors rose from his hands. He then placed them on Morgan Freeman's jugular.

It took a moment, but the two fang marks actually disappeared.

And then the Oscar-winner began to cough.

Cyprian threw himself back in surprise. *He never thought that would work.*

"Holy shit, shit, shit!" yelled The Cowboy, who returned to investigate the noise with a newly sparked up blunt in his mouth. Toussaint's body was already disintegrating within the flames behind him. "You brought Darth fuckin' Vader back to life?!"

"Yeah," said Cyprian, still shocked. "I guess so."

"The Castille was right, brother. You do have amazin' powers! I ain't ever seen a Witch Fanger do that before!"

"Warlock."

"Huh?"

"I'm not a witch. I'm a warlock."

Before Morgan Freeman could fully recover, Cyprian and The Cowboy moved his body to the porch and then slipped away. They hoped that the actor would just think he had a wickedly life-like dream and sleepwalked through the window. And he did just that, telling his girlfriend back in Mississippi that he had a "wickedly life-like dream and sleepwalked through the window."

The Cowboy invited Cyprian to an all-night diner called the Original Pantry Café. In any other city, a cowboy in full regalia sitting in a booth across from a rugged black man would be an odd sight. But not in Los Angeles.

Lucie – Cyprian's spirit bird – was fully recovered and perched on a parking meter outside of the window.

Cyprian was still in shock about the resurrection he had just performed, silently not touching his cup of coffee.

"So, you didn't know you could do that?" asked The Cowboy, cutting into his stack of pancakes.

"No. I'm still learning what I can and can't do."

"That's some God-like shit right there. In fact —"

The Cowboy pulled out his cell phone and pushed a finger on his IMDB app. After a moment, "I knew it! I thought I remembered that he played God once. So you kinda saved God's life, brother. Oh, wait... I was wrong. He wasn't Darth Vader's voice."

"Yeah, that was James Earl Jones."

The Cowboy looked up at Cyprian and immediately entered "James Earl Jones." "Oh, yeah – you're right. He *did* do his voice. Mufasa too. Oh shit, he was the blind dude in 'The Sandlot!'"

Cyprian smirked at the notion of a human vampire bounty hunter using IMDB. "How'd you get into this business anyway?"

"You mean killin' Fangers?"

"Yeah."

"You ever see that movie 'Kill Bill?'"

"Yeah."

"It was kinda like that."

Cyprian was confused, trying to replay the movie in his mind. It wasn't until The Cowboy had finished his story that he finally understood the reference.

birth of the cowboy

"It was damn near twenty years ago when I was livin' in Abilene, Texas. My daddy had moved out of the house cuz he was beatin' my mama, and so she kicked him out. Then she met this Mexican guy named Rodolfo at some Mexican bar, and they started datin'. Rodolfo was cool and all, but there was sumptin' bout him I couldn't quite figure out, cuz he really didn't seem like my mama's type. He had these shifty eyes and a really strong Mexican accent, but if I was a girl or a homo I could see why they'd find him attractive and all. You know what I mean, brother? If I knew the things back then that I know now I woulda figured Rodolfo was getting with my mama to get a Green Card or sumptin' or 'nuther. But it turns out he was a Fanger, and he just naturally had this look like he was always up to sumptin'.

"Anyways, I didn't know he was a Fanger until later when I was in my mama's closet lookin' through my daddy's porno magazines, and I heard my mama and Rodolfo come home – I reckon I didn't know they were comin' home on account-a I woulda high-tailed it outta there long before that, but I was too late, and I still had to rehide the magazines so I did that and tried to get out, but I ended up hiding under my mama's bed. She and Rodolfo came in, along with another Mexican guy, and they were drinkin' beer I'm guessing or tequila or whatever and took off all their clothes and had fuckin' sex with each other.

"Now, I was little shit pervert when I was that age, and I had seen my mama and daddy fuck before, but this was some new shit with my mama and two new guys, and she was really into it. I could see them through a mirror that was kinda tilted down, and Rodolfo and his friend like tag-teamed on my mama, and she was usin' her hands and all of her holy holes, and it was crazy like nuthin' I'd seen in my daddy's magazines – or maybe in that "Hustler" of his, but you know, I don't think they actually showed penetration – or did they? – well, I don't remember.

"So, it must've been an hour or such when my daddy came home and found Rodolfo and his friend both with their cocks in my mama's mouth, and I couldn't see his face cuz the mirror wasn't pointed that way, but it musta been a shock of a lifetime to see that, I tell you, brother. He ran to the closet and pulled out his .45 and shot both of them Mexicans right off the bed with three bullets each, and he probably woulda shot my mama if he had any more bullets. And then the strangest thing happened.

"My daddy started to cry and said he missed my mama so bad and wanted to come home and take care of her and me again. And then you know what happened? They fucked. There were two dead bodies on the floor, and my mama and my daddy had sex like nuthin'! But the weirdest thing really wasn't that, brother. I mean that *was* weird and all, and knowin' what I know now 'bout sloppy seconds and shit, but the weirdest thing was the fact that the two dead Mexican bodies weren't really dead since they were both Fangers and they just decided to lay there fer a bit until my mama and daddy were deep into it, and then they both stood up at the same time, watched them fer a bit, and then joined in! One of the Fangers held my daddy's body down and had sex with him while the other was with my mama. Now, I don't know how my mama really felt about all of that cuz her face was turned away from the mirror so I couldn't see her expression at that point, but my daddy I could tell was in pain. He prolly never been with a dude before in that way, you know what I mean. I tried to think 'bout ways I could help him, but by the time I did, I was too late.

"Course, that's when I actually found out the two Mexicans were not really Mexicans, but Fangers. I mean – *Mexican Fangers* – you know what I mean.

"Those Fangers bit into my mama and daddy's necks and started drinking their blood. And then they tore out all of their insides, including their long intestines. And I saw all of it.

"I saw all of it, brother.

"All of it.

"Through the fuckin mirror.

"I saw all of it.

"The blood dripped down the side of the bed and made puddles that ran towards me. I didn't move at all. My face, my shirt, my pants all got wet with my mama and daddy's blood. There was a couple times when I thought the Fangers saw me through the mirror, but they didn't. I just kept still and thought maybe it was a dream and I'd wake up soon.

"But it wasn't a dream.

"No, brother.

"It wasn't a dream.

"My mama and daddy both had their eyes open through the whole thing. I don't know when they died. I don't know how much they actually saw before they died. There was one point when my mama's eyes looked like they were pointed at me through the mirror. I always hoped that maybe I was her last vision before she stopped breathin'."

chapter 27

A server brought another stack of pancakes to The Cowboy.

"Oh, right. The animation part with O-Ren's backstory," Cyprian said to him, finally understanding the correlation with the "Kill Bill" movie. "Being under the bed and stuff..."

"Yep."

"So the vampires let you go?"

"They never saw me, just like the movie. Like I said, I was hidin' under the bed. Since my blood was a mixture of my parents, they just thought they were still smellin' theirs. Or at least, that's what I think happened. I laid there fer two days, until the Police finally came, and I went to live with my Aunt."

"And so now you're just out getting revenge?"

"Well, I already killed the two Fangers who murdered my parents. That was the first thing I did once I left the Seals." The Cowboy pushed over his empty plate and replaced it with his new stack.

"Seriously? I heard the Latino vampires are pretty tough."

"They are, brother. Tougher than most. I tracked them down in Corpus Christi and, usin' some Phantom Salt and a little bit of my own blood to lure them, eventually chopped off their heads."

"And then what?"

"President *Valley-kwet* was gonna kill me, but he said he was impressed. So, now it's not fer revenge, but fer my life... and fer the money."

"Still gotta be some satisfaction," said Cyprian. "I mean, vampires killed your parents, and now you get to kill them for a living."

"I guess so. Specially the Mexican ones."

Cyprian smirked. He watched The Cowboy as he drowned his new pancakes with more maple syrup. Of course, the vampire hitman was still hung up on one detail. He shook his head and, with a mouth full of food, said, "Still can't believe you resurrected Morgan fuckin' Freeman, brother."

After breakfast, Cyprian shared a joint with The Cowboy, thanked him for his help, and then they parted ways. The vampire immediately visited Imamu upon his return to New Orleans to get some clarification on his newfound power.

Imamu was vaguely impressed. "It is because of the soul that you carry. It guides you to an unmistakable power."

"Have you seen anything like it before?"

"Only in the High Priestess."

Cyprian nodded, unsure of how to feel. "So can I... *can we...* resurrect anyone from the dead?"

"No, no, of course not. Humans of your own race only, before the blood runs cold."

Cyprian thought what a stroke of luck it was for Morgan fucking Freeman to be African-American and to find him when he had just died. If Toussaint had chosen someone like Clint Eastwood or Betty White, then Hollywood would've mourned that morning after. When asked if he could resurrect *Impundulu* vampires as well, Imamu simply said, "With no head, you remain dead." That made sense, considering that was the most common way for a vampire to die.

Of course, word got back to Chancellor Valiquette about Cyprian's powers. The Cowboy spared no expense with the details. Viktor was impressed again but had a premonition that Cyprian's powers might come back to haunt him.

chapter 28

Misake. Misake. Misake.

That name drifted into Cyprian's head at least three times a day and during most showers when he'd masturbate to the vision of her slender back and pulsating ass bobbing up and down over his pelvis. No matter how hard he tried, he just couldn't forget her. The reoccurring dream with the tiger cub, Lucie, and the Goddess Amaterasu didn't help either.

So, when Christmas rolled around again and the Castille assigned him a job in San Antonio, Texas, Cyprian jumped at the chance to reunite with Misake. He also knew that he couldn't show up without a proper Christmas gift, so he had a lightning bird pendant molded out of pure silver.

He met Misake in the lobby of her dorms. They hugged, but it wasn't the memorable embrace Cyprian had hoped for. It was a bit cold and distant.

"What are you doing here?" Misake asked, who seemed genuinely surprised.

"I was just in the neighborhood."

"Ha, ha. Very funny. All the way from New Orleans?"

"I have business here."

Cyprian watched as Misake's face turned grim. It was obvious she was still embroiled in all things related to vampires. And maybe even the Latino one she favored. "So, I see you're not a vampire."

Misake sighed. "I'm sure you would've known if that happened."

Though Misake seemed disappointed, Cyprian was relieved that she was still human. But the fact that she was still pursuing another vampire made his body numb with more jealousy. He knew he had to try and change her mind again.

So, he invited her on his assignment.

Cyprian figured that was probably a no-no. But it was the only way he could think of to possibly discourage Misake from becoming a vampire.

Misake watched first-hand as Cyprian tracked down a Latino vampire named Julian at the Spaghetti Warehouse. When the criminal vampire ran, she was tasked to drive Cyprian's 1972 Pontiac GTO to catch up to them (and subsequently banged up due to her inept driving skills). And then when Cyprian finally beheaded Julian, Misake was accidentally (but not really) sprayed with an abnormal amount of blood.

Julian's decapitated head rolled to Misake's feet and blinked at her.

It couldn't have been a more perfectly staged scenario. And Cyprian hoped that it was enough to deter her.

But it didn't work.

Though Misake remained silent on the return trip back to her dorm room, things turned ugly later. As she washed her face in the sink, Cyprian laid on Shanice's bed and called out to her. "So... do you want to get something to eat?"

"You don't eat," replied Misake bluntly.

"You do."

"Not hungry."

"What about a drink?"

"No, thanks."

Misake entered the room with her bloody shirt in hand and tossed it into the trash. She stood at her closet and searched for another shirt.

Cyprian stood and approached. He wanted to rub his hand down her spine again, just like he had done several months earlier. He wanted to take her in his arms and cradle her – protect her – but the opportunity escaped, as Misake quickly covered herself with another shirt. She then blew past him to the other side of the room.

The *Impundulu* vampire sensed a bit of tension. But he also knew that he wanted to put an exclamation mark on the day's events. "So, anyway," he said. "Now you know what happens when vampires break the rules of the Castille."

Big mistake.

Misake whirled around, visibly angered. "I get it now. You're trying to convince me to change my mind. That I should quit trying to become a vampire."

"Of course," answered Cyprian, unsure of what else to say.

"Why?"

Cyprian was caught off-guard. He wanted to say the true reason – perhaps that it was because of love – but he wasn't convinced yet. So he tempered it, nestling one of her hands into his own. "Because I… I care for you."

Misake seemed to soften, for a moment, but then gritted her teeth with resolve. "You care for me? Enough to turn me?"

The vampire pulled away. "You know I can't do that."

"Then what? You think we can be some kind of interspecies couple?"

Deep down, Cyprian knew he'd take that label if it meant keeping her forever. But that also wasn't fair to Misake. "No… I just… I don't know."

Misake looked crestfallen and turned back toward her window. After a moment, she finally said, "I need for you to leave now."

Cyprian placed his colorfully-wrapped Christmas gift on her bed and reluctantly left. The drive back to New Orleans was excruciatingly lonely. He hoped for a phone call from Misake imploring for his return – or at least a thank you for the gift – but it never happened. He had even stopped at a Buc-ee's gas station on the outskirts of town and lingered around the aisles of Beaver Nuggets and freshly made bar-b-que brisket sandwiches, so as to not get too far away. Cyprian replayed the events and the conversation with Misake over and over again, and each time, he wished he could change one thing: he wished he could've said that he loved her instead.

It was abundantly clear to Cyprian that his heart was broken.

Cyprian was spared from his reoccurring dream about the tiger cub in the rice paddy for the next five months. He hoped that it meant he was starting down the road to letting his feelings for Misake go. But then the dream occurred one more time.

Except it had a slightly different ending.

Cyprian walked through a flooded rice paddy field and grazed his hands over stalk that was calmly swaying from a light wind. He happened upon a baby tiger, swaddled in a blanket that was stitched with the symbols of the Japanese goddess of the Sun and Universe. The vampire picked up the cub and held it against his chest, looking out over the rice paddy for its mother. But there were no other tigers in the area.

Suddenly, there was a voice.

"Cyprian, no."

The *Impundulu* vampire whirled around to find his sister Lucie standing at the edge of the rice field. She was shaking her head, holding Cyprian's lightning bird on her arm. She leaned over and whispered something to the bird. It then took off and landed on the belly of the tiger cub, still cradled in Cyprian's arms. It began to chirp excitedly – but also angrily – at the vampire, who had no idea what it was saying.

"I don't understand. Speak English!"

But then the bird pecked at one of the tiger cub's eyes and pulled it out.

Cyprian screamed. "What are you doing?!"

The bird couldn't respond, since it had an eyeball skewered on its beak that prevented it from opening. Cyprian plucked the eyeball from its beak and placed it back into the cub's eye socket, where it oddly resumed its functionality.

"Now speak," said Cyprian.

The bird chirped in indecipherable sounds again. And again. And again.

Cyprian looked over at his sister, but it was no longer Lucie. She was replaced by a line of cobras entering the water and hissing in unison. They swam across the flooded parcel of arable land and beelined toward Cyprian. He tried to run, but his feet were stuck.

The snakes swarmed him and the tiger cub and pulled the vampire into the water. Cyprian struggled for a moment, but his efforts were futile. He disappeared completely underneath, and soon the waters calmed to a macabre silence.

Cyprian woke up in a cold sweat, trying to catch his breath. And three seconds later, he received the phone call from the Castille that would change his life forever.

Latino vampire Uriel Santana had sired a Japanese woman, and Cyprian was being assigned to track and kill them.

There was no doubt in the vampire's mind that woman was Misake. So, he respectfully declined the assignment with a bogus excuse.

There was no way Cyprian could kill the woman he loved.

Instead, the *Impundulu* warlock vampire's inherent need to protect her kicked in.

"Cyprian, no."

chapter 29

Cyprian didn't have a plan to protect Misake. He just knew that he needed to. For whatever reason, he felt like it was his new destiny. Every sign seemed to point to it. From the Oriental motif during his vampire transformation, to the heaviness his heart felt with every thought of Misake, to the now foreboding premonition of a dream. Every sign, that is, except for his sister Lucie's continued advice against it.

"Cyprian, no."

But when the heart of a man starts to drive his urges, as opposed to his normal, carnal influences, then it would take a herculean effort to stop him.

And he knew the Castille would send their best – Tebeau.

So Cyprian made the trek back to Texas and first picked up Misake's scent in a cabin by a lake. She wasn't there but had left blood-stained clothing from her transformation. He immediately stashed the clothes into a delivery truck heading to north Texas, hoping that would distract Tebeau and buy Cyprian some more time to find Misake first.

It worked. Tebeau was sent on a wild goose-chase and found the bloody clothes in Fort Worth, Texas.

That bought enough time for Cyprian to scour San Antonio for Misake's whereabouts without any interference. Of course, he was ultimately unsuccessful.

Another familiar scent took Cyprian to a landing strip on Lackland
A.F.B., where he just missed a private jet that might or might not have had
Misake onboard. She also wasn't at her dorms, nor was she at Uriel's
house. The latter revelation was highlighted by a one-on-one melee with
Uriel's insatiable sister Gabriella Santana. After a one-sided ass-whoopin'
given by the Latina vixen, the *Impundulu* vampire managed to finally best
Gabriella with an assist from his healing magic.

"You should probably get your sword out," said Gabriella, as she bled
on the ground. "If you plan on killing me."

"I'm not here to kill you. I'm not even here to kill your brother."

"What do you mean? The Castille didn't send you?"

"No. The Castille sent someone else. I came here only to find the girl.
To protect her."

Gabriella stood and furrowed her brows. "Why?"

"Because I'm in love with her."

The words flowed easily from Cyprian's mouth. It was a confession
with a pronounced meaning. It was a revelation that spoke volumes within
the vampire warlock's psyche. Speaking it so freely and out loud to
Gabriella, Cyprian seemed to be relieved that his emotions were no longer
in a state of turmoil. They were clear and concise. And because of that,
what Cyprian did next made much more sense.

He left it up to Uriel Santana to track Misake down.

Since Uriel sired Misake, Cyprian knew that it might have been easier
for the Latino vampire to find her. Even though his jealousy for their
relationship ran rampant, he figured Uriel finding her first was better than
Tebeau. Another motivation for letting Uriel take the lead was that
Cyprian had no idea what Misake's true intentions were. It was obvious
she had a plan to become a vampire all along, but why? Uriel discovering
her first might be a safer way to find out, and perhaps the Jampyre didn't
even want to be found.

Jampyre.

Cyprian admired Misake for completing her mission of becoming
history's first Jampyre. The extreme and detailed actions she took over the
course of two years was a feat to be recognized. But now, she was a
fugitive on the run. The Castille was not going to let her or Uriel get away
with any indiscretions. And they had already killed his sister Gabriella for
helping him escape. In fact, they were also concerned with Cyprian's part

in the whole vampire ruckus (courtesy of Balzac's confession and Cyprian's own flippant effort in capturing Uriel). His refusal of the assignment suddenly became more heightened and confounding. So, they called for the *Impundulu* vampire's presence.

And he ignored them.

That was the point of no return.

Cyprian fled from New Orleans and to the West Coast. Several weeks later, he would find himself on a military cargo plane with Tebeau and the paralyzed bodies of Misake and Uriel.

But first, he had to deal with Ajax the Façade.

chapter 30

Cyprian escaped to Los Angeles because he liked what he saw back when he resurrected Morgan fucking Freeman. He also wanted to be on the West Coast for his impending trip to Japan, where he hoped Uriel would find Misake. Tebeau had been derailed trying to find them, first by Cyprian and then the sheer fact that Misake's blood was oddly no longer trackable. And Tebeau thought Uriel was still imprisoned in the Castille, so he didn't know to use the Latino vampire's blood.

After finding a cheap hotel in San Fernando Valley, Cyprian attempted to stay incognito until he was alerted of Misake's discovery. It wasn't too difficult, since there weren't too many vampires who lived in California. But he had forgotten about the one vampire who was more like brethren in those parts.

Ajax the Façade.

Though they'd never personally met, Cyprian and Ajax were connected in more ways than one. Both were from the same *Impundulu* clan. The seven-foot vampire was present when Cyprian transformed, even having the task of carrying Lucie's corpse from the boat to the village of the High Priestess. Ajax was also the instigator of the mysterious "whisper unheard around the world." And of course, both vampires had had sex with Atalia.

So when Ajax the Façade got word from his High Priestess that Cyprian was in his area and needed a consultation, he found his vampire blood brother in no time. He was in his black and yellow GTO, driving down West Manchester Avenue, and heading back to the Valley. The GTO was still a bit banged up from Misake's failed attempt at driving.

Ajax followed him in his own vehicle, which was an inconspicuous Toyota Celica. But after several miles of Los Angeles bumper-to-bumper traffic, Cyprian noticed his tracker suspiciously switching lanes every time he did.

And that was when the car chase began.

"Cyprian, no."

"Cyprian – no what?!" he shouted. "I'm not getting caught!"

Cyprian shot down East Vernon Avenue and headed north through Redondo Junction. Ajax kept pace, which confirmed to Cyprian he was a target. Assuming it was another VES agent on his tail, Cyprian had no intentions of slowing down. Even though he wasn't guilty of breaking any known vampire rules, he had a feeling the Castille would perceive his evasion as such. And of course, deliberately interfering with Tebeau's investigation would be frowned upon. Death would certainly be a possible consequence.

Ajax the Façade stayed on Cyprian as they zoomed through East Los Angeles and through Monterey Park. When they reached Fremont Avenue by way of Huntington Drive, Cyprian detoured to a sidewalk to try to shake his predator. He barely missed several innocent bystanders and clipped the side of a bus stop, spilling onto Lyndon Street and then up through Fair Oaks Avenue. They stayed on for several miles until they finally hit the 210, where they fast and furiously switched lanes back and forth with reckless abandon.

It wasn't until Cyprian reached La Tuna Canyon Park when his car ran out of gas. He immediately grabbed his sword and rushed up an uneven dirt trail. It was dusk, so hikers and their dogs were sparse. About a mile up, he reached a man-made stone labyrinth and a spectacular view of the Pacific Ocean. And that was when Cyprian turned to meet his foe.

His lightning bird Lucie soared up above him and circled.

Cyprian knew that he might have an advantage against the VES agent since he was an *Impundulu* vampire with special magic. But all of that went out the window when another lightning bird flew through the sky, and Ajax the Façade's tall frame finally came into view.

"Fuck," muttered Cyprian under his breath. Another *Impundulu*. Much larger and possibly wiser to his magic. Wasting no time, he instantly charged, hoping to catch Ajax off-guard.

The seven-footer easily sidestepped Cyprian's swinging sword and knocked him down.

Cyprian immediately sprang back up and twirled his sword around towards Ajax's torso, as they both moved across the stone artwork. Ajax kept his eyes on the blade, watching it whirl around, ensuring his safe distance. And then, just at the right moment, he kicked the hilt with his long legs, sending the weapon several yards away.

But that didn't deter Cyprian, as he began to combat with his fists. He landed several body blows to Ajax, who barely budged. He used his arms to block several of Cyprian's strikes, curiously never once going on the offensive. It was as if he was just content with protecting himself from any damage.

Cyprian began to tire and grabbed Ajax's large frame and tackled him to the ground. It was only then that his fists began to glow green, as if his inner magic (and perhaps Lucie?) sensed that he needed help.

But then Ajax the Façade made his one and only move. He quickly countered with his own magic and conjured up a large green ball of light and pushed it at Cyprian, soaring him through the air and sliding with a thud across the dirt.

Cyprian watched as a green, electrical current radiated throughout his body and fizzled away moments later. He looked up at Ajax with an astonished look. "How'd you do that? That was some 'Street Fighter' shit!"

Ajax the Façade stood and brushed himself off with a grin.

"You didn't even say 'Hadouken!'" added Cyprian.

"And you didn't utter a word when your fists lit up," said Ajax. "When your body and your soul are in sync, words and spells are no longer needed. One day you'll see."

Cyprian looked at his own fists, realizing Ajax was right. The glow didn't start from any type of spoken spell.

"I didn't know you were part of the VES," said Cyprian, finally standing.

"I'm not. Do you see a sword?"

And again, Cyprian was surprised he didn't realize that from the start. Ajax the Façade had actually tracked him unarmed.

"So then, you were just going to kill me with your magic?" asked Cyprian.

The super-tall *Impundulu* vampire laughed. "Who said anything about killing you? I only need to speak to you, and unfortunately, your cell phone said 'this number is no longer in service.'"

Cyprian grinned, understanding why he heard Lucie's voice telling him to stop. "Why didn't you just wave me down?"

"Would you have stopped?"

"Probably not. How do you even fit into that Celica anyway?"

"It's modified."

Ajax retrieved Cyprian's sword – admired some of the details – and then handed it back to him. "How many vampires have you killed?"

"Three. Well, unless you count that guy from my transformation. Then four."

"Ha, ha! That was an interesting night. I've never seen such a thing. And I don't think the High Priestess nor the Chancellor had either. You crushed that guy's head like a watermelon!"

"Well... I didn't really have a choice." Cyprian looked over at his lightning bird, who was curiously perched right next to Ajax's. They were excitedly chirping away at each other as if exchanging tales of high adventure.

"If he hadn't still been in transition, then your foot wouldn't have made a dent," added Ajax, as he knocked his knuckles hard on his own head.

Cyprian nodded and finally asked, "So, what do we need to talk about?"

Ajax the Façade walked over to the view of the Pacific Ocean. "The High Priestess is concerned with your recent actions."

"I would imagine she's not alone."

"What is going on with your heart?"

"My heart?"

"She knows that is what has taken over your mind."

Cyprian joined Ajax on the mountain side as the ocean breeze whipped around them. He watched the waves break and listened to their serene sounds as he contemplated the question. "Ever since my transformation, I've been... *pulled*... to something that's a mystery to me."

"The girl?"

"The girl. Yes. But more."

Ajax nodded. "The High Priestess sensed it as well. She saw the same images within your journey to the undead and wondered where they would lead."

"I'm still wondering," said Cyprian.

"Sometimes they are a memory. But most times, they are your future. This journey of yours will be ripe with danger."

Cyprian turned to Ajax. "So… she's letting me be? Not interfering?"

"The High Priestess has concern for you much like a mother to her child. But knowing your special abilities and your potential has put her in a quandary. As much as she respects the ways of the vampire regime, she has a keen interest in seeing where your path leads. But she wants you to tread with care."

"Will she help me?"

"A bridge she wishes not to cross."

Cyprian nodded. His eyes then shot up with a realization, "Hey – what was it you whispered to her… on that night… when I was transformed?"

Ajax looked a bit perplexed. "Whispered?"

"Yeah, yeah. The High Priestess looked like she was going to kick my ass, until you said something to her."

"Oh, right, right. I just told her that – with your potential abilities – you can be the answer to an *Impundulu* prophecy."

"Prophecy?"

"It is an old one that deals with the foretelling of an uprising and a restoration of power. But the specifics are unclear."

Cyprian turned back to the ocean with a roll of the eyes. He had hoped that it was something more profound, rather than some folktale gibberish. But he was glad he didn't know the answer when Balzac and Chancellor Valiquette had asked him, preventing laughter and ridicule.

"Good luck to you," said Ajax.

"Thanks… *Ajax the Façade*," responded Cyprian coyly.

The tall vampire smirked. "You are welcome, *Cyprian the Dominion*."

Cyprian furled his brows. "I have a nickname, too?"

"Oh, yes. For a long time now."

"The Dominion." It had a certain flare, yet subtly powerful. Cyprian wondered who came up with the name and under what circumstance. Was it after he duped and killed Emmanuelle Emond? Or perhaps because he resurrected Morgan fucking Freeman? He imagined a boardroom full of

Impundulu vampires throwing out suggestions like "Cyprian the Strong" or "Cyprian the Ripped" or "Cyprian the Brawn" or "Cyprian the Resurrector" and a majority vote of the winner. He would later discover that most *Impundulu* vampires had a nickname. Atalia was labeled as "the Versifier" due to her way with words.

Ajax and his lightning bird left La Tuna Canyon Park.

Cyprian remained overlooking the Pacific Ocean until the moon sprayed its luminescent reflection across the glistening water. He was appreciative having the support of his High Priestess, but he knew that would do nothing to prevent Chancellor Valiquette and the Castille from seeking him out.

Several days later, the *Impundulu* vampire found himself above the same ocean on a cargo plane carrying the paralyzed bodies of Misake Sakumoto and Uriel Santana. He was fighting Tebeau – one of the Castille's favorite sons.

chapter 31

It was a clunky sword fight on unstable ground that ended in victory. But Cyprian the Dominion didn't have time to admire Tebeau's body getting spliced by the propeller. A vicious lightning bolt from brewing thunder clouds had torn through the hull and caused the cargo plane to careen towards the Pacific Ocean, so he needed to try and save Misake. He threw himself onto the wooden crate that encased her and Uriel and began chanting, *"Usowe, Koki. Usowe, Koki. Usowe, Koki!"*

It was a protective spell that surrounded Cyprian and the crate and kept both intact as the plane splintered violently into the water. When the vampire finally emerged back to the surface, he laid on top of the crate as it floated. The wreckage surrounded him in thousands of pieces. A tuft of Tebeau's bloody, blond hair drifted by.

A strong gust of wind pushed the crate to the west. Cyprian turned on his back and stared up at the sun, knowing that west back towards Japan was certainly a better direction than east. It was then he noticed that there was no longer a single cloud in the sky.

Where did that lightning bolt come from?

"Was that you, Lucie?" he asked his soul.

Of course, no one answered. Cyprian wondered if the lightning was a product of what Ajax the Façade had mentioned. *"When your body and your soul are in sync, words and spells are no longer needed,"* he had said.

But the bolt hadn't originated from his body. Or at least, he didn't think it had.

Cyprian and the crate continued to sway in the ocean. It was a welcome moment of serenity in what had been complete chaos. He marveled at the silence and vastness of the sea and was glad that real vampires weren't effected by the sun like they were in literature and movies. Cyprian was also glad that he was dark-skinned, because he thought white people with sunburns looked ridiculous.

"Can you hear me, Misake?" he asked into the crate.

Misake and Uriel had been captured by Tebeau with one wooden stake plunged into their bodies as they made love. Or at least, that's what Tebeau had told the *Impundulu* vampire. Cyprian wondered what he might find in the crate and hoped that by the time they reached the shore, it wasn't too late for them. He knew that he'd have to put his magic to work.

"Well… hopefully we'll make it soon."

Cyprian ruminated about what a difference a year made in his life. A year before, he had just resurrected Morgan fucking Freeman and met The Cowboy. And now he was floating in the Pacific Ocean, protecting the bodies of two renegade vampires from two entirely different clans. He was also a renegade himself, now an outcast VES operative. At that moment, his lightning bird Lucie soared passed him.

"Oh. Thanks for finally showing up."

The lightning bird chirped and did another cross over, defecating into the water nearby.

"Oh, you're funny," said Cyprian. "You better watch out or I'll use some kind of spell on you. Maybe turn you into a hermit crab!"

His spirit bird squawked, almost in laughter.

Cyprian sighed and turned to his side. The steady motion of the waves was calming, so he closed his eyes and fell asleep.

He had woken up to the sensation of ocean water crawling up his leg and receding back across the Kikaijima shore. The wooden crate was still intact and beached several feet away from him. Cyprian immediately pried the lid open and worked his healing magic on both of the paralyzed – and almost dead – vampires.

That was when he found Misake's body to be adorned with new tattoos. Her left arm, shoulders, and back were completely covered with her own *irezumi* design composed of various elements in her life, including a small lightning bird buried within the ferocious tiger center piece on her back.

And her left arm?

It was exactly the same as the image Cyprian had seen during his Impundulu transformation!

Cyprian knew it was all tied together now. But now he just needed to find the meaning.

Several hours later, Misake finally emerged from the crate. She was plastered in coagulated blood, seaweed, and several organisms from the ocean. Cyprian escorted her into the ocean and helped her get cleaned.

"I know you're disappointed for what I did," said Misake, as they faced each other against the setting sun.

Cyprian continued to dab her wounds delicately. "Does it matter?"

"Of course it matters. You're a friend."

That label stung Cyprian the Dominion more than he anticipated. He knew his strong feelings for Misake weren't exactly being reciprocated, and especially since Uriel was still in the picture. Regardless, all three of them were in a dangerous predicament and needed each other. "Once the Castille gets wind of what I did to Tebeau, they'll be after me, too."

"Why *did* you interfere?" asked Misake.

Cyprian smirked and lied. "Cuz you're a friend."

For the first time, Misake smiled. The glow was finally returning to her skin, and the sunset gave her an ethereal, golden aura.

"So, how's the life of a Jampyre?" asked the warlock.

'Honestly? I love it, Cyprian."

"I have to admit – you make it look good."

Uriel finally emerged from his makeshift tomb and interrupted the moment. Cyprian left Misake and let the Latino vampire take his place.

Back on the shore, Cyprian continued to ponder life's meaning and had no idea what was in store for him. He knew Misake was somehow involved in the answers, so he stayed close to her as the trio settled back into Tokyo. He was relegated to being the third wheel in her relationship with Uriel, so he mostly tried to give them space.

To bide his time, Cyprian got caught up in the night life of the Kabukicho district. He satisfied his hunger – both literal and sexual – with the local Japanese women, who were always intrigued with the lone *kokujin* in the vicinity. He would also practice his spells every moment he could, including ones that involved hypnosis, the power of persuasion, and just general mind-altering magic. And sometimes, his voodoo would occur without any intention at all.

On one such occasion, he *accidentally* turned a woman named Suki into an *Impundulu* vampire.

Vampire?

Jampyre.

Impundulu Jampyre.

chapter 32

Suki was on the heavier side of things and loved her poke bowls. She had an exuberance for life and didn't have a care in the world about her weight or what anyone thought of her. She often frequented a karaoke bar called Shinjuku Loft and tried to serenade men into taking her home with them. That usually didn't work and was often met with laughter and ridicule and a lonely return home.

Except for the night when Cyprian the Dominion was already three sheets to the wind on red wine and sitting at a table right in front of the stage.

Suki went all in on the lone African-American man in the bar as she chose sultry R&B love songs to sing. First up was "If I Ain't Got You." Suki didn't have a voice like Alicia Keys, but the passion and fearlessness in her eyes gave the song what it needed to be powerful (albeit still sung in *Engrish*). She only left Cyprian's eyes twice for the monitor to make sure she got the lyrics right.

On her next turn (which was only two songs away), Suki chose "All My Life" by K-Ci & Jojo. Cyprian was oblivious at first that Suki was singing directly to him, until the rest of the crowd joined in. Knowing Suki's M.O., the patrons partly did it in jest, but also partly because they didn't mind Suki succeeding with a foreigner who had no idea what he was getting into. So when the night ended with Suki and the entire bar singing Boyz II

Men's "I'll Make Love to You" at Cyprian, the vampire finally took the hint and escorted Suki to his hotel room.

What Suki lacked in general appearance, she made up for in between the sheets. She was a voracious animal and ravaged Cyprian from the get-go by taking control, first with half an hour of biting-intense fellatio and another half hour of aggressively rolling his testicles like they were Chinese baoding meditating balls.

When Suki finally straddled Cyprian's hips, it didn't take long for the vampire to explode inside of her. Once the sensation and subsequent relief subsided, Cyprian's head pounded from alcohol poisoning, and he knew he needed food to help ease the pain.

So he bit into Suki's neck.

Her blood was surprisingly delicious, with the faint taste of orange peel. Or at least that's what Cyprian thought it tasted like. He kept sucking – more than he had ever done in the past – and while he did, began thinking about Misake. He wondered what she tasted like and wished that it was he who had turned her and not Uriel. Cyprian should've granted her wish way back when he first met her in New Orleans. After all, wasn't he now in the same predicament regardless?

Suddenly, the vampire's incisors began to radiate a green hue as he continued to suck on Suki's neck.

And then Cyprian passed out.

When he woke up the next morning, Suki was standing in front of the mirror and admiring her brand new fangs. Her slanted eyes were now in anime-proportion, and she had a giddy look on her face. She began to ramble in Japanese:

"Are you a vampire? Am I a vampire? I didn't know they were real! Can I go out in the sun? I'm really hungry! What do I eat? *How* do I eat?"

Of course, Cyprian didn't understand one word. He just stared at her, trying to recollect exactly what happened the night before. He remembered biting Suki. And then thinking about Misake. And then thinking about turning Misake.

Fuck.

His black magic must've translated his thoughts into turning Suki into the world's first *Impundulu* Jampyre.

Fuck, fuck, fuck.

Cyprian watched Suki take out her cell phone and start taking selfies, flashing her fangs and the obligatory "peace sign" with her fingers. He immediately sprang from the bed and snatched her phone. "Vampires don't do that," he said and promptly smashed the device to pieces.

Of course, Suki was taken aback. She blinked rapidly at him, waiting for answers. And preferably in her native language.

Cyprian scrutinized her transformation. He was curious as to why Suki's fangs were casually protruded. Usually, they would only extend prior to eating, or when angry, or faced with fear. Suki's fingernails and toenails had grown into razor sharp claws – something he had never seen before, even when he was himself transformed. There were subtle, unrefined differences that caused Cyprian concern.

His mind raced for a solution.

"Stay. Here. Wait. Here." Cyprian said, slowly speaking so that Suki would hopefully understand.

She slowly nodded.

"Good. I. Will. Be. Back. Do. Not. Open. The. Door. For. Anyone." He pointed to the door and shook his head.

Suki nodded again.

After Cyprian got dressed, he left and visited Misake at her father's estate. "I think I may have made a boo-boo," he told her.

"A *boo-boo*? Really?" said Misake wryly at his choice of words.

"I accidentally turned a panda bear into a vampire."

"What? How do you *accidentally* do that?!"

"I don't know. I was drunk. I mean… I have an inclination of what happened, but that's not really the point."

"That's some boo-boo."

"Yeah, I know."

"That's against vampire rules. Haven't you ever heard of the Crossbreeding Ban of 1972?" said Misake with a straight face.

Cyprian was completely oblivious to her ironic sarcasm. "Of course, I do! But I don't know what to do now."

"What do you mean? What are your options?"

"I don't know. All I know is that there's a new hybrid vampire in my hotel room."

Misake's eyes suddenly lit up at the blunt perspective. She now seemed genuinely excited. "Oh my God – I wanna meet her." She immediately grabbed her samurai sword and pulled Cyprian with her.

Naturally, Misake called Uriel to meet them at Cyprian's hotel room. When the three vampires entered, they found a gruesome sight. The entire room was covered in blood. There were four bodies dead on the floor – a housekeeper, a front desk clerk, a concierge, and perhaps the hotel manager? Their bodies were all torn into shreds.

Suki sat like a feral cat on the bed, licking the back of her hands; her nude body caked in crimson. And she also had newly developed horns on the top of her head.

"That's no vampire like I've ever seen," muttered Uriel. And then he seemed to have an afterthought, but only mumbled, "So, it's true. They *can* make beasts."

Cyprian blinked hard. "She… she didn't have horns when I left."

Misake spoke to Suki in Japanese. "Hello. How are you? My name is Misake."

"I'm Suki," responded Suki. "Are you a vampire too?"

"Yes, I am."

"All of you?"

Misake turned back to Uriel, who was still aghast at the bloody scene. "Yes, we all are. And I guess you are too?"

Suki nodded. "I'm still hungry." And then she started to cry.

Misake looked at Cyprian, who shrugged. "She's definitely different. Look at her nails too. How she mutilated these bodies. Almost… *animal-like*."

"And she has a fucking tail," added Uriel, as-a-matter-of-factly.

All three tilted their heads slightly, getting a better view of a scaly tail slithering behind the newborn vampire.

"What are they saying?" asked Suki.

Misake lied in Japanese. "They're just saying they've never seen such a beautiful vampire before."

Suki smiled, appreciative. Of course, now Cyprian was confused.

"What did you tell her?" he asked Misake.

"Nothing," she answered and quickly addressed Suki again. "Did you have sex with Cyprian last night?"

"Yes."

"It was good, right? I've done it, too."

Even though she was covered in blood, everyone could see Suki blush.

Cyprian started getting aggravated. "Okay, c'mon. What are you talking about?"

"Nothing," answered Misake again. "So what are we going to do?"

Uriel finally chimed in again. "We just need to kill her."

"What? Why?" asked Misake.

"Look around," said Uriel. "She's a savage. And we have no idea what's she capable of. She has a mixture of blood we've never seen before."

Misake furled her eyebrows. "Would I... would I have become that if you had turned me, Cyprian? And not Uriel?"

"I have no idea," said Cyprian, who now looked ashamed. He hadn't turned anyone into a vampire before – let alone his own species – so he was unsure of what could or would happen.

"I guess that's why they have the crossbreeding ban," said Uriel with a sting in his voice. "Some breeds aren't meant to mix."

Cyprian gritted his teeth, but didn't look at the Latino vampire. "So what do we do?"

"If we don't kill her, then what?" said Uriel. "We just let her roam free? Cover her horns with a black hat?"

"Why does it have to be a *black* hat?" asked Cyprian. "Cuz I'm black?"

"What? Are... are... you serious?" stammered Uriel, with an incredulous look.

"Freudian slip?"

"Bro. Whatever. She can wear a red one. I don't care," said Uriel, but then he threw another jab. "Unless you have one of those fake afros."

Cyprian made a step towards Uriel, but Misake blocked him with a hand. "You two are so stupid. It's like you're still in high school."

"To be honest, it's only been a couple of years for you and I," quipped Cyprian to Misake. "How long's it been for you, *Urinal*? Like... *forty years*?"

That time Uriel took a step, meeting Misake's other hand. She shook her head. "Are both of you done yet?"

Neither male vampire nodded, but kept silent.

Misake turned her attention back to Suki, who was wide-eyed to the indecipherable male-ego-laced banter. "I actually think the horns are kinda cool."

Both Cyprian and Uriel gave her a half-shrug.

"Cyprian can take care of her. Groom her even," offered Misake.

"More like *tame* her," said Uriel.

Cyprian shook his head adamantly. "No, no, no. I don't want to do that."

"It was your *boo-boo*."

"I know, but I don't have time to babysit."

"You have all the time in the world to babysit," said Misake. "All you do is go out and get drunk and get laid."

"And that's a full-time job."

Uriel muttered under his breath, "That's a cool full-time job."

Misake smacked Uriel in the shoulder and sighed. "Well, I'm not going to take care of her. I actually do have a full-time job, helping my father with his business."

Suddenly, the body of the concierge coughed. All three of the seasoned vampires jumped back in fear.

"Shit, he's still alive," said Cyprian, patting his heart. "Okay, okay. So what else can we do? I'm not killing her. You're not killing her—"

"I'll do it," said Uriel. And before anyone could react, the Latino vampire grabbed Misake's samurai sword and swiftly beheaded Suki.

Both Cyprian and Misake stood silent, as the first and last *Impundulu* Jampyre's horny head rolled to a stop in front of them.

"Okay. Now you two can clean all of this up," said Uriel, as he gave Misake her *katana* back and promptly left the room.

There was a long moment of silence until the concierge gurgled again. Both Cyprian and Misake recoiled slightly.

"I'll go find a mop," said Misake abruptly. "You put an end to that guy."

Misake left Cyprian alone in the room. He walked over to the concierge and crushed his neck with a foot. He then surveyed the mass carnage of five bodies in his hotel room and shook his head shamefully.

Cyprian then opened a drawer and pulled out a concoction of rat's blood and venom. He had made a fresh batch only days before, thinking it might be wise to have some handy, but also out of boredom. Little did he know, however, he would be needing it again only days later.

And it would be for an old friend.

chapter 33

The day would be a monumental turn in the lives of the outcast vampires hiding in Japan. Misake's father – Yakuza *oyabun* Shintoku Sakumoto – was killed by Uriel's sister Gabriella, who had been thought to be dead. And then in an epic battle inside of Tokyo's Senso-ji temple, Misake bested Gabriella and beheaded her. Uriel had to make a painful choice by helping Misake instead of his sister, losing a hand in the process.

When Cyprian received a phone call in the aftermath of what the Japanese headlines would later describe as "Yakuza Crime Lord Assassinated," he was sleeping in bed with a massive hangover.

Misake had said with a sullen voice, "Cyprian? Do you have any more of that rat's blood stuff? We need some. Enough for five vampires."

Five vampires?!

Cyprian thought he heard wrong. Maybe she said "fine." There was no way five vampires were dead and needed to be disposed of. Was one of them Uriel? There was a bit of sadness in Misake's voice, so it might have been possible. Were they all VES agents? If so, the department was quickly getting a reputation for being inept. First Cyprian's own rejection, Tebeau's death, and now four or five others? Regardless of the situation, the *Impundulu* vampire got dressed and left his hotel.

When he arrived to the temple, the first thing he saw outside of the five-story pagoda was his own lightning bird. It was crouched over another lightning bird.

A dead one.

That meant only one thing. There was a dead B.M. *Impundulu* vampire somewhere in the vicinity. Imamu had told Cyprian once that when one dies, so does their spirit animal.

Cyprian's bird poked its beak at the dead body, trying to wake it up. When it didn't move, the bird looked up at his vampire with glossy black eyes.

Cyprian actually recognized the bird. It had distinct features he had seen before. But he didn't want to believe it, reluctantly entering the building.

But there she was.

Atalia Venable. Atalia the Versifier. The *Impundulu* vampire whom Cyprian had begun and shared his intimate journey to the undead with.

And she was beheaded.

Misake was still kneeling by her own father's dead body, when she noticed Cyprian's moment of recognition. "Did you know her?"

"Yeah. I did," choked Cyprian.

"Very well?"

Cyprian wasn't in the mood for explaining, so he lied to Misake instead. "No. Not that well. Just in passing."

"She knew Japanese," said Misake, almost in admiration. She then turned back to her father.

The *Impundulu* vampire crouched down and noticed that Atalia's hand still adorned the heart-shaped garnet ring she had taken off of murdered French vampire Emmanuelle Emond. There was other jewelry as well; Cyprian assumed they were all souvenirs from her subsequent jobs as a highly-regarded member of the Vampire Extraction Squad. He covertly took the garnet ring and slipped it into his own pocket —

His own souvenir. A memory of a lost friend.

And because he had lost his own claymore sword during the plane crash in the Pacific Ocean, Cyprian took Atalia's – the one with the dangling set of golden dice.

Misake looked back up and saw Cyprian still lingering. "Just so you know, I didn't kill her. It was Gabriella. In fact... *she killed all of them.*"

Cyprian nodded, slightly appeased.

The other four bodies ended up being three other unrecognized VES agents and Gabriella Santana herself. Uriel was safe, even though he had lost a hand. Cyprian actually felt a moment of relief when he found Uriel alive. Even though he was jealous of the Latino vampire, Cyprian knew that would've crushed Misake even more. And ultimately, he cared for her happiness more than his own feelings for her.

"I'm sorry about your father," said Cyprian, when he had a moment hours later.

"Thank you."

"I know that… I mean… I know now that he was a motivation in you becoming a vampire."

"It was my only motivation," said Misake harshly, a fact it seemed she wanted Cyprian and anyone else within earshot to know. "He was my way of life, and it was taken from me. So I took it back."

Cyprian nodded, admiring Misake's determination and will. "So now that he's gone, what happens next?"

"Nothing changes," said Misake, with a stoic expression. "As far as I'm concerned, he still lives in my memories, and I will make sure he lives in the minds of his enemies."

The hair on Cyprian's arms tingled with fear as Misake's words resonated through him. They were laced with venom, and he was momentarily glad to be on her side.

Misake had won another battle in a war that was just beginning. In the days and weeks following her father's funeral, her enemies would regroup and realign with more strength. The world's only Jampyre would need to build her own army of allies if she was to succeed in her quest of maintaining her father's legacy and shaping her own.

It was going to be a long era of discord with plenty of bloodshed.

And Cyprian the Dominion would be in the middle of it.

Part Four

Power is venom.
It roars when it prowls unchecked.
Heavy wings falter.

chapter 34

A foreboding cloud lingered over the three fugitive vampires as they continued to hide in Tokyo, Japan. They knew it was only a matter of time before the Castille regrouped and sent more VES agents after them.

Uriel was especially vigilant, since he had betrayed the Goddess Mictecacihuatl – the Queen of the Underworld – and his clan *Los Vampiros Oscuros*. He knew that she might seek revenge as well, utilizing her spiritual powers and influence. Uriel had already buried the Queen's golden Aztec sword deep in the Pacific Ocean, to minimize any link that might have remained.

Cyprian was almost in the same boat, unsure of what his High Priestess Kwan'de'melu'da had heard about his antics in Japan. He knew she had an awareness of the highest power about his activities. Did she know he *accidentally* turned someone of a different breed into a vampire? Was she aware that the whole tempestuous affair with Misake led to the murder of *Impundulu* vampire Atalia the Versifier? But most importantly, was she still going to allow him the freedom to continue his mysterious journey? There was a vague prophecy he might or might not be associated with, but was it worth finding out?

Misake herself was dreadfully aware that her mother – the Goddess Amaterasu – was saddened by the death of her former husband and held Misake completely responsible. Though she didn't think her mother would harm her own daughter, Misake also had a feeling she might not be getting any more divine assistance anytime soon.

But regardless of the spiritual conundrum being experienced by the three vampires, it was business as usual in gangland Tokyo.

In the days following her father's funeral, Misake met with the family's *saiko komon* and *so-honbucho* to reassure them that nothing would change. The Sakumoto-*kai* organization would continue without a hitch and keep its reign as Tokyo's premier Yakuza family.

Uriel took an official position as a *wakagashira* and accompanied the Jampyre on most of her business. Though many of the *kobun* didn't care for a foreigner being so entrenched in their ways, they were just glad to be under the protection of Misake, who many had already witnessed as a skilled and powerful warrior.

The same first lieutenant position was offered to Cyprian as well, but he declined. The *Impundulu* vampire didn't want to appear to be "settling," even though he had no idea what the future had in store. He also perceived the position as an insult and consolation prize for not winning Misake's affection. So instead, Cyprian promoted himself to the unofficial position of being Misake's personal bodyguard and guardian angel, though he wasn't around her nearly as much as a guardian angel should've been.

One day, after the zen rock garden was renovated and the pond was refilled with brand new koi fish, Misake invited Uriel and Cyprian to join her. As they approached her from behind, Misake sat on the stone bench and stared into the pond and began to speak.

"I've ruined both of your lives," she said.

"What do you mean?" asked Uriel.

"If it wasn't for me, you'd still be living in San Antonio with your sister. And Cyprian – you'd still be in New Orleans being a dutiful soldier for the Castille."

Cyprian exchanged glances with Uriel. "We're big boys. You didn't twist our arms to do any of this."

"Well… she did mine," said Uriel, shrugging. "Sort of."

The *Impundulu* vampire turned his head in thought, and then nodded in agreement.

Misake continued her train of thought, following the path of a silver and gold fish whom she had named Katsu Hiro, "I've been preoccupied running the business, so I feel like I've neglected both of you lately. But I just want you to know how much I appreciate the sacrifices you've made so far."

Both of them nodded behind her back.

"I had something made for both of you," said Misake, as she reached under the bench and pulled out two, long cylindrical boxes. "It's not much, but it's the least I can do."

Cyprian opened up his box to reveal a custom-made samurai sword. The *saya* was black and yellow with embossed artwork depicting lightning birds outlined in a green sheen. The *tsuka* was intertwined with a bright, marigold *ito* and the *tsuba* was adorned by a lone bird.

Uriel's *katana* did not lack his own personal flavor. It was mostly black and purple with a bejeweled King Cobra that wrapped around the scabbard from top to bottom. His handle wrap was laced with dark violet, and the hand guard was a serpent's mouth with sharp fangs.

"Reminds me of my car," said both Cyprian and Uriel at the same time, each having to ditch their similar-colored sports cars when they fled their country.

"I know," said the Jampyre demigoddess with a smirk. "And look at your *kashira*."

Both vampires looked at each other with confusion.

"Your end caps," said Misake, translating herself.

Cyprian looked at his to find the name "Lucie" carved in metal. And Uriel found the name "Gabriella."

"Both of you have lost a sister," explained Misake. "In case you didn't know that about each other."

Cyprian nodded, hugging Misake in appreciation. Uriel waited his turn, and then did the same. Afterwards, both vampires drew their *katanas* and took another moment to admire the perfectly balanced blades. They each tested the sharpness on a nearby bonsai tree, slicing two neatly trimmed branches off.

Misake held a finger up. "Um. You guys know how long it takes to manicure a full size bonsai tree?"

Both vampires stared at her in silence.

"Never mind," she said.

And from across the way – on a rooftop – two beady eyes observed.

chapter 35

Her father. Honor. Redemption.
Her father. Honor. Redemption.
Her father. Honor. Redemption.

The mantra Misake had repeated to herself over and over again ever since she left Japan to become a vampire had faded away since her father's funeral. Those words sparked her and validated every move she made back in the United States, including those that involved the lives of others. Some deaths. Betrayals. Deception. But now she had a new mantra.

Her father. His legacy.
Her father. His legacy.
Her father. His legacy.

Those words were born from the conversation she had with Boss Oh at the end of the grand funeral just weeks earlier.

"Forgive me, Misake, if this is disrespectful. But it is imperative that we talk," Tokyo's lone female mob boss had said.

"What about?"

"The future," said Boss Oh, flashing her complete and ominous set of gold teeth. "I believe it is in our best interest to join our families and fortify control over Tokyo."

"I'm very honored that you would want to join my family," said Misake snidely.

Boss Oh frowned. "No, Misake. With your father gone, your family is no longer. I'm asking you to join mine."

For what seemed like an eternity, Misake stared at who was now apparently going to be her newest rival. She then curled a grin. "I have always respected you the most, Boss Oh. As the sole female Yakuza boss, you've shown the utmost strength to lead your family. You are wise and a cunning strategist. And because of that, I do have to agree with you... *this is absolutely disrespectful.*"

"My sincere apologies," said the older Yakuza boss in perfect English, as her face twisted. "We will have a discussion later, once the death of your father has cooled, and you've matured. See you soon... *Jampyre.*"

Boss Oh left, leaving Misake with a bad taste in her mouth. Not only did Boss Oh insinuate the Jampyre no longer had a valid family and wouldn't be recognized as the new *oyabun*, but she also knew of Misake's vampire transformation – something that had only been rumors and speculation by others in Japan. To top it off, Boss Oh knew perfect English. That was a sign of practice and education.

Regardless, the proposed future conversation with Boss Oh never happened.

Since Misake spurned Boss Oh's suggestion that they join families, the elder female Yakuza *oyabun* corralled Boss Watanabe's family instead, along with what was left of the dismantled Tamaki-*gumi* organization. When the dust settled, the newly established Okamakiri mushi-*kai* (Praying Mantis) crime syndicate had three times the members of what was left in Misake's. It was an unprecedented move in Japan's gangland history.

"Maybe you should reconsider her offer," said Uriel, on the day they found out about the reorganization and expansion.

"No. She disrespected me. Just because I'm so young, it doesn't mean I'm not capable of running my own family."

"Maybe she can teach you some things."

"My father taught me everything I need to know. And I helped him get back to where we belong – on top. I'm not about to let anyone change that just because he's gone."

"She's going to come after you," said Uriel. "It's only a matter of time."

"Let her," responded Misake confidently. "I'll take her out, just like I took out the Tamaki's."

Uriel remained concerned. He didn't know much about the Japanese criminal underworld and how it operated, but he did know about greed and power from his knowledge of some Latino gangsters back in San Antonio and Mexico. One such organization – the *Murciélagos* Cartel in Mexico City – was fronted by two vampires named Camazotz and El Galán. They were ruthless in their methods and built an unrelenting reputation. The internal forces of greed and power were strong influences in any culture. And scorned egos never rested for long periods of time.

It didn't take long for Boss Oh to make some aggressive moves.

Two bathhouses in Yokohama owned by the Sakumoto-*kai* family were ransacked and vandalized. A dry-cleaning facility in Nagoya was set on fire and burned to ashes. In both instances, several members of Misake's *kobun* went to survey the damages and to possibly recoup losses, but it was far too late, and the Okamakiri mushi-*kai* group had swarmed the area with too much manpower.

Misake had concentrated on keeping her father's foothold in Tokyo, neglecting everything else outside of Japan's capital city. It was a bold and strategic move by Boss Oh; a successful campaign that either halted or yielded several of Sakumoto-*kai's* primary sources of income. But before Misake could react and possibly counter-attack, Boss Watanabe made another move down south.

A cargo ship owned by Sakumoto-*kai* was on a return trip to Kagoshima from Seoul, South Korea. It had dropped off two hundred milligrams of uncut cocaine to a major buyer and now had approximately five million dollars in exchange on board.

Five trimarans carrying thirty outsourced sea pirates attacked the ship about midway and hijacked it, killing the entire crew, but not before a distress signal was sent out.

Misake quickly dispatched her nearest men to intercept the ship when it docked. But they themselves were ambushed. Once they jumped on board to fight the pirates, Boss Watanabe had his own men trap them from behind.

They were all brutally slaughtered, especially by the pirates, who were known to be violently savage with no regard for finesse. They tied some of the corpses to the ship and dragged them across the sea until they docked. The cargo ship was then set on fire and slowly burned and disintegrated into its watery tomb.

When Misake took Uriel and Cyprian with her to Kagoshima to survey the aftermath, they naturally found no remains, even though the blood of her men had a scent that lingered in the breezy coastal air. They questioned several dozen people around the docks and finally happened upon a witness from a local fish market who mentioned the arrival of vagabond sea pirates on that day, curiously spending money in the local bars and bath houses.

Misake called her senior advisor and discovered there was one prominent outfit of sea pirates who were capable of such a deed and were often hired by the Yakuza. They were based in Fukuoka and called themselves The Genkai Wokou.

Her father. His legacy.

Her father. His legacy.

The three vampires went alone.

Cyprian and Uriel could not wait to test out their new samurai swords.

And from within the shadows of their journey, two beady eyes followed.

chapter 36

It was just before nightfall when the trio arrived in Fukuoka and Hakata Bay. The sky was almost fuchsia and speckled with gray clouds. Water from the Genkai Sea broke heavily against the docks as bells, wind chimes, and seagulls blended into a chorus of oceansong.

The Genkai Wokou were anchored a hundred yards away in a superyacht called The Ronin. It was apparently a brand new extravagance paid for by the commission they earned on the stolen five million dollars. Since making money wasn't the primary motive for Okamakiri mushi-*kai*, they were very generous in giving the pirates over fifty percent.

Music and clinking glasses and debaucherous activities drifted faintly through the air from The Ronin, which was completely lit up on every level. Latticed strings of fluorescent lightbulbs illuminated guests of the pirates as they mingled on the top deck.

"The ones on top don't look like pirates," said Cyprian.

"No, but that's their ship," said Misake. "Must be having a party."

"So we wait?" asked Uriel. "Wait until the party's over?"

Misake mulled it over and then shook her head. "No. We show no mercy. I want to send a message to Boss Oh. If you party with the pirates, you die with the pirates."

"So what do we do? Swim to the boat?" asked Uriel.

Misake was already tying her hair up into a bun.

Cyprian reluctantly sighed, apparently not a big fan of the aquatic activity. He slung his samurai sword over his shoulder.

All three vampires slipped into the water and swam towards the yacht. The water was already cold from the disappearing sun. When they arrived, the night sky and twinkling stars had completely consumed the day.

They used the anchor to traverse the side of the boat.

When the three undead figures plopped onto the deck, there was total silence. All of the guests – mostly prostitutes and shady pimps – stared at the odd trio.

Cyprian whispered to the others. "They still don't look like pirates."

"Who owns this boat?!" shouted Misake in Japanese.

A timid woman spoke up. "The Genkai Wokou."

"Where are they?"

The guests all exchanged glances. A scraggily man stepped up. "They left for a while. They told us to have fun and would return soon and —"

Before the man could finish his sentence, all of the electricity turned off on the boat. Lights disappeared with an alarming spark. The music cut off to the whispering winds and breaking waves of Hakata Bay.

Within the darkness, the eyes of the vampires glowed. The lone set of green ones blinked and spoke, "We were set up."

From the coastline came an ominous sight. One by one, flames ignited from the tips of arrows. The dancing lights revealed they were being held by members of the Okamakiri mushi-*kai*. The thirty or so Genkai Wokou pirates stood in the back with long scraggily hair and grinned dirty and toothless faces. And even further back were two gloating figures – Bosses Oh and Watanabe.

There was a moment of tense silence, until the arrows were pulled back and launched.

The night sky illuminated with fire, and a perfectly bowed light apricot haze preceded the arrows. The boat guests screamed and started frantically running around for cover, some jumping ship into the frigid waters.

But Misake, Uriel, and Cyprian remained in their place. Even as the arrows punctured the deck all around them and flames billowed, neither of them wavered. They were more pissed than frightened. Pissed that they had been duped.

Some of the arrows hit guests in the back, igniting their bodies into cylindrical fireballs. Cyprian's lightning bird barely dodged a wayward one.

The *Impundulu* vampire yelled at it, "Get out of here, Lucie!"

The bird careened to the left and then soared away.

One arrow nicked Uriel in the shoulder. He looked over at Cyprian as he swiped away a flame. "You got a spell to save us, witch?"

"Fire won't hurt us," said Cyprian.

"Yeah, I know. But it'll burn off our clothes and I don't feel like fighting naked tonight."

"You ashamed of what God gave you?"

"No."

"You should be. I've seen you."

"You're so funny," said Uriel with a bored tone. "It's just easier to protect myself when I don't have dangling appendages."

Both Uriel and Cyprian looked at Misake, expecting her to shush them like she was always prone to do. But she had a stone cold gaze that locked with the other bad bitch across the bay —

Boss Oh picked one of her gold teeth with a long fingernail, even though she didn't need to.

The Ronin began to tilt and sink.

"Well, for once *Urinal*, you actually make sense," said Cyprian. "And by the way, I'm not a witch. I'm a Goddamn warlock!" He clasped his hands together and chanted, "*Usowe, Koki. Usowe, Koki. Usowe, Koki!*"

The familiar green orb shaped like a lightning bird surrounded the three vampires, just as flames engulfed their area. It encased them until the boat finally sank completely under the water and came to a rest on the ocean floor.

The trio bobbed back up soon after.

Some charred bodies floated nearby. The flames on the superyacht debris started to dissipate all around them. And once they did, the vampires were met with another harrowing sight —

All of the vagabond pirates had jumped onto their five trimarans and were barreling toward them at full speed.

And they all carried harpoon guns.

chapter 37

The first four harpoons sailed past the vampires and darted into the water. Without any time to figure out a defense strategy, each of them then plunged deep under to the wreckage of the superyacht and let the five speedboats pass overhead with a flutter of waves. When they returned back up to the surface, the pirates had already circled back.

Uriel had pulled up two corpses that were caught in the boat's sunken cabin. When two more harpoons shot toward them, he threw the bodies up and caught them in their paths. He then yanked each rope and brought pirates into the water, where the Latino vampire quickly disposed of them with hard twists of their necks.

Both Misake and Cyprian looked impressed with the one-handed Latino vampire.

But not to be outdone, Cyprian caught a harpoon in midair and instead of tugging, flipped it around and launched it like a spear back to its origin, impaling two pirates through the groin.

Misake ducked under another harpoon into the water and then shot back up with her *katana*, slicing an outer hull of the yacht right in half. The boat dipped enough to throw its riders into the water, where Misake sprang on them like a Great White and severed flailing limbs. The disabled trimaran veered off into the darkness.

Another set of pirates raced toward Uriel's head. At the last possible moment, he shot up into the air and caught himself on the mast. He then slid down and met the pirates, who had pulled out their own swords and braced themselves by grabbing onto a sail or a life line. Uriel held his own stance with great balance as the boat continued to speed out of the bay.

There were three boats full of pirates still left in the area.

Cyprian took a cue from Misake and managed to latch onto the bow of one and twisted with all of his might. Pirates plunged into the cold sea where Cyprian ripped out jugulars. His lightning bird helped by returning and pecking out eyeballs. When the damage was done, the water glowed a luminescent green around the new corpses.

Misake prepared herself for the trimaran coming towards her. But she didn't notice the one at her back controlled by the lone group of female pirates—

"Misake! Behind you!" yelled Cyprian.

But it was too late.

A harpoon penetrated her back, just under the right shoulder, knocking her sword away. When Misake turned, the other boat launched another aquatic dart, impaling her symmetrically on the other side. One boat then joined the other and dragged her out of the bay like she was a jerking tarpon.

And as she was being pulled away, Misake managed to take one last glimpse of the docks. Boss Oh curled a satisfied golden grin and walked away. Boss Watanabe and the rest of the Okamakiri mushi-*kai* followed.

"Misake!" screamed Cyprian. The *Impundulu* vampire darted to the recently emptied boat and climbed on. He then started it back up and took off after Misake.

The superyacht chase carried on under Aratsu Bridge and darted several miles until it reached Shikanoshima Island. The pirates plowed across the beach to a stop and pulled Misake's skewered body out of the water, pulling it several yards until they braced themselves against the bottom of a hillside.

When Cyprian finally arrived, he found himself confronted with eleven sword-wielding pirates and Misake right in the middle. She struggled to get loose of their hold, but the harpoons were lodged perfectly between bones and cartilage, hindering any great effort.

"Are you okay, Misake?" asked Cyprian.

Misake looked up from the protruding metal and the blood that continued to run from each wound. "Yeah, sure. Don't I look okay?"

"Does it hurt?"

"Not really. More annoyed than anything."

A couple of the Genkai Wokou female pirates approached Misake. They scrutinized the Jampyre's wounds and marveled in Japanese at how she wasn't dead yet. They also squeezed her perfectly shaped breasts in admiration.

"It's cuz I'm a vampire," said Misake in their native language, with a school girl grin.

All of the pirates burst into laughter. Some of them put up two fingers to their toothless mouths to pantomime fangs.

"I'm guessing you told them you were a vampire?" said Cyprian.

"Yeah."

When the laughter subsided, Misake spoke to the pirates again. "I'm also the daughter of Amaterasu-O-Mi-Kami, Goddess of the Sun and the Universe."

Several pirates looked up into the starry night as if they expected to see an image or constellation of the renowned goddess. And then they exploded in laughter again. Some of them having to rub their dirty bellies in pain.

"Is he a vampire too?" asked one of the pirates, feigning fear.

"He sure is," said Misake, locking eyes with the *Impundulu*.

"Is his father Kevin Hart?" asked another pirate, who apparently didn't know any famous African-American gods, let alone many others at all. Of course, that took his comrades over the edge with knee-slapping hilarity.

Cyprian raised an eyebrow. "Did he just say I look like Kevin Hart?"

"He asked if he was your father," clarified Misake.

The *Impundulu* vampire seemed insulted. And too tired to continue a meaningless banter. So he closed his eyes and concentrated. After a moment, his body started to radiate a green aura. And when he reopened his eyes, they glowed a toxic waste green that looked ready to spit Hellfire. His mouth hissed, showcasing the glistening, razor sharp fangs.

All of the pirates hushed in awe.

"You ever see Kevin Hart do that?" asked Misake in Japanese jest.

Just then, Cyprian's lightning bird landed next to him. It looked up at his spirit master and then seemingly tried to flex its own muscles.

"That's his bird," said Misake. "It can probably kick your ass too."

The Genkai Wokou pirates all whispered to each other in a conference. One of them then spoke to Misake. She translated, "He said go away, or they'll kill me right now. There's eleven of them so you stand no chance."

Cyprian's eyes continued to glow as he spoke. "What do you think?"

"I've seen your sword play and you need some work."

"I agree. But I'm pretty fast."

"Yeah, but they'll get some licks in."

"True. So what do you suggest?"

"You have anything in your bag of voodoo tricks?"

Behind the warlock's glowing aura, he pondered. He remembered Ajax the Façade's nonverbal fireball trick, so he tried to concentrate on that. After a moment of psycho-building and soul-connecting, he threw his hands out – one pointed at the six pirates on Misake's right side, and one pointed to the remaining five on the other.

But nothing happened.

He dropped his arms and threw them back up. The veins on his forehead pulsated.

Still, nothing continued to happen.

In fact, the green super juice all around Cyprian's body dried out, and if he was animated, everyone would've heard an engine sputter and die.

Some of the pirates giggled.

"What happened?" asked Misake.

"It didn't work, obviously."

"Obviously."

"Obviously."

A beat and then Misake said under her breath, "Obviously."

Cyprian looked down at his lightning bird, who looked up at him like he was a buffoon and chirped something that could've been construed as the word "obviously."

The pirate closest to Misake was getting impatient, so he raised his sword to Misake's belly and began puncturing her skin. Blood began trickling out. He barked at Cyprian with a verbal lashing.

Misake – hardly reacting to the pain, but now almost fearful – translated, "He said leave or I die now."

Cyprian zoned in on the blood oozing down Misake's stomach. He then looked up and caught the soft vulnerability in her eyes; a look that had already melted his heart on many previous occasions.

And then *something* grew inside of him.

It was a different rage.

A natural one.

The greenness returned, but this time only in Cyprian the Dominion's hands.

The lightning bird stepped away to a safer distance.

The *Impundulu* vampire warlock gritted his teeth and shouted, "*Hadouken!*"

And with that, two perfectly round spheres of electricity shot from his palms and blasted the two groups of pirates backwards until they slammed into the ground. They all twitched and convulsed to their deaths. Green fumes escaped with their souls and floated up into the night air.

Misake collapsed to her knees, finally feeling the effects of losing so much blood from her shoulders.

"Misake," said Cyprian, as he quickly went to catch her body from falling.

Misake was woozy, trying to keep her eyes open. "Did you really just yell '*Hadouken?*'"

"Yeah. Yeah, I did."

"Super cool."

Cyprian nodded but turned his focus to the harpoons. "I'm going to pull these out now. It's gonna hurt like a mother fucker."

"I know. Do them both at once."

Cyprian sighed and gripped both ends and paused.

The lightning bird covered its beady eyes with a wing.

And then the vampire yanked on both simultaneously.

Misake's scream echoed throughout Shikanoshima Island. Anything that was asleep was now wide awake in terror. And had it been any louder, the pirate corpses might have risen from the dead.

Cyprian carried Misake's body to one of the trimarans and placed her down gingerly. The last words she spoke before she passed out were, "Who's Kevin Hart?"

chapter 38

The sun began to rise on a new day.

Misake opened her eyes to find Cyprian sitting on the bed beside her. A green mist plumed from the puncture wounds underneath her shoulders. She smiled at him. "Hey, Ryu."

The vampire smirked at the "Street Fighter" reference.

"What would I ever do without you?"

"Die, probably," said Cyprian in jest.

Misake nodded and repeated, "Probably. Why are you so good to me?"

The *Impundulu* vampire seemed to ponder his words carefully. He stood and walked to the window and looked out at the sun peeking over the horizon. "I have… a sort of… *bond*… with you."

"A bond?"

"Yeah… a bond that wasn't born from a vampire concoction."

Misake grinned, knowing Cyprian was facetiously referring to the Nectar of L'Auberge she had used to attract Uriel. "Tell me," she said.

"When an *Impundulu* is transformed, they often see a premonition of the future. You remember Atalia – the *Impundulu* killed by Gabriella at the temple?"

Misake nodded her head.

"We were transformed on the same night," said Cyprian. "She told me she saw herself get strangled to death by a snake."

The Jampyre's eyes widened. The symbolism in Atalia's premonition was pretty clear cut. The King Cobra was the spirit animal of *Los Vampiros Oscuros*. "So... what did *you* see?' asked Misake cautiously.

Cyprian turned back from the window. "I saw you."

"Me? But you hadn't even met me yet."

"Well... I didn't see your face," said Cyprian as he sat back down beside her. "But I saw your arms. They grabbed me from behind and held me... pulling me..." He pointed to her arm with the very distinct tattoos.

Misake followed his finger and remained silent for a moment. "I killed you?" she finally asked.

"No."

"So then what?"

"I saw my High Priestess, and then I woke up as a new vampire," answered Cyprian with a shrug. "I haven't been able to figure out what it all means."

"So, you've been staying close to me just so you can figure it out?" asked Misake with a sting, almost offended.

"No, no, of course not. I..." Cyprian paused, seemingly conflicted with what he was about to reveal. "I'm in love with you, Misake."

Misake let out a small gasp. Even though she had heard Uriel speak those same words to her before, she always had doubts in the back of her mind. But this time, the words seemed truly genuine. "I... I... don't know what to say, Cyprian."

"You don't have to say anything. I know that deep down you've always known that I loved you. But you're in love with Uriel, and that's okay."

Misake frowned with struggling thoughts.

Cyprian noticed. "What's wrong?"

"I know he cares for me, but I know he resents me too for everything that happened with his sister. And I forced him into a life no vampire would've ever chosen for himself."

"You don't think he loves you?"

"We have a connection that will last forever. He transformed me into a vampire. But sometimes I wonder if what we're feeling is because of that, and it's not really love at all."

Cyprian stared into Misake's eyes, as if he could see the mental turmoil in them. It was obviously a thought she'd been fighting for a while.

She continued, "And why was it you who came after me and not him?"

"Well… he was tied up."

"Exactly. You stayed close to me."

"Yeah, but I don't think he meant to—"

"—And where is he now?"

Cyprian shrugged. The last time either of them saw Uriel was when he jumped on the trimaran full of pirates and it sped off into the night. "I don't know," he answered. "If he's not back in a couple of hours, I'll go look for him. But I'm sure he's okay."

Misake remained silent, unsure of her thoughts.

Cyprian looked like he was trying to read them. "Well, if you want my opinion," he said. "I think he really does love you."

"And now you're protecting him, too." The demigoddess smirked and grabbed Cyprian's hand and cupped it on her chest. There was no doubt that she felt a comfort and safeness with him in her life and no more words needed to be spoken that night. But when Cyprian stood and approached the door to leave, she asked him, "What do *you* think your premonition meant?"

Cyprian drew in a breath and pondered. "Either you're holding me forever… or escorting me to Hell."

Misake nodded and smiled. "But we're together in both scenarios, right? In life… *or death.*"

The *Impundulu* warlock returned a nod, reluctantly agreeing.

"And I don't plan on dying," added the Jampyre, whose smile evaporated to one of steel resolve.

Outside of the room, Uriel listened to their conversation with concern. Jealousy. And completely covered in blood. He heard Cyprian approach, so he walked away and then swiveled back around and feigned as if he was just arriving.

"Oh good," he said. "Is Misake here too?"

"Yeah. What happened to you?" whispered Cyprian.

"I fought off four pirates with one hand. Ended up close to the Korea Strait? I think. You?"

"They managed to snag her with two harpoons and pulled her away. I chased them down to some island and got her back."

Uriel nodded and spoke through his teeth with heavy sarcasm. "Thank God you were there for her."

Cyprian seemed to ignore the masked insult and pointed towards Misake. "Go to her. She's worried about you."

The Latino vampire slightly harrumphed. He moved past Cyprian and peered inside of the bedroom. But Misake was fast asleep. Without saying another word, Uriel entered and shut the door on Cyprian.

Outside of the compound, two beady eyes shifted with interest.

chapter 39

It didn't take very long for Misake to recover since she was a vampire demigoddess. And when she did, she immediately went back to Hakata Bay to retrieve her fallen samurai sword. Misake's plan was then to travel straight to Boss Oh's Tokyo residence – which was a four-story lair masked as a bathhouse – and burn the whole place down with the hopes that the Yakuza bitch was still inside.

But when she found several dead pirates still floating in the bay, she came up with another idea. The Jampyre wanted the female *oyabun* warlord to know she could play her game just as well. So she corralled as many Genkai Wokou corpses she could and had their heads severed and delivered in boxes to various Okamakiri mushi-*kai*-owned businesses. She then had two full bodies delivered in caskets to Boss Oh and Boss Watanabe's doorsteps with a note that read "You wanted to play. Let's play."

Naturally, both Uriel and Cyprian disagreed with Misake's tactics.

"She's already proven to be fairly conniving," said Cyprian. "We should just take her out once and for all."

"Unless she's already on our doorstep," added Uriel.

"I want her to fear me," said Misake. "I want her to fear so much that she eventually surrenders."

"And then you'll be satisfied?" asked Uriel.

"The shame she would have to endure for the rest of her life will most definitely satisfy me."

"She won't surrender," said Cyprian. "The Japanese have always been known to face death before shame."

"Like *kamikazes*, right?" said Uriel, who looked proud to throw in a Japanese reference.

Misake shrugged. "Then she will die. But I want her to be last. I want Boss Watanabe and his family first, to suffer a regret for joining her. And then all of her own. Boss Oh's last vision will be of her solitude in life and the knowledge that her greed was responsible for spilling every last drop of blood within her family."

Just then, Misake's *saiko komon* approached her. "Boss Sakumoto – pardon me – but we have just received some disturbing news."

"What is it?"

"The rest of the families in Tokyo have pledged their allegiance to Boss Oh, and together are asking for the immediate dissolution of your family."

There was a long silence as everyone took in the profound union.

"How many families is that?" asked Cyprian.

"Three other families, making it six total," said Uriel. "But since Watanabe and Tamaki had absorbed into Boss Oh's organization, that's really only four."

"*Only?* With how many men?"

Misake's advisor chimed in. "Close to a thousand."

Both of the male vampires looked at Misake with concern. But oddly, she didn't look concerned at all. The Jampyre smiled.

"So be it," she said. "Tokyo's too crowded, anyway."

Cyprian approached Misake with a straight face. "Our heads are already wanted halfway across the world. And now all of Tokyo wants them too? We need to make peace, Misake, before it's too much for us to handle."

"You're exactly right, Cyprian," said Misake. "We *will* make peace before it's too much for us to handle." And then she winked and smiled even wider. "The train's about to leave boys. Either grab a seat or jump off."

And with that, Misake left the room with her advisor.

Cyprian shook his head disparagingly at Uriel. "She's your girlfriend. Talk some sense into her."

"Do you really think I can do that, let alone anyone else?" said Uriel. "Both of us have tried to talk sense to her even before she was a vampire."

"And she never listened."

"And she never listened," repeated Uriel. "We can both leave right now. She just gave us the green light."

Cyprian frowned, almost disappointed those words came out of Uriel's mouth. "And go where?"

"You can go hide in Africa. I'm sure your High Priestess will protect you."

"And you? You think your Queen will have your back now? After you betrayed her?"

Uriel bit his lip, mulling it over. "Maybe."

Cyprian shook his head again, not even giving the proposition another thought. "Go get your sword. Buckle up. We're going to war."

The *Impundulu* vampire left Uriel alone in the room. The Latino vampire looked at the stump that replaced one of his hands.

And then he sighed.

chapter 40

Uriel indeed jumped back on the Jampyre *Shinkansen* with Cyprian. He was in too deep and wasn't about to abandon her.

Misake was still going to make Boss Oh suffer. But now she had a few more steps before that could be accomplished. The first thing she did was fortify her compound with more men and ammunition and put all of her businesses on high alert.

She then wasted no time in going after the first family.

The Teruya-*gumi* organization was the smaller of the four families and closest to being a completely legitimate operation. They ran a string of pachinko parlors all across Japan, with a couple serving as a front for money laundering. Boss Teruya resided on the entire top floor of the luxurious Park Hotel Tokyo, which was located on top of the Shiodome Media Tower. The 34th floor had a spectacular view of the city.

The three vampires rode the elevator up nonchalantly. But there was nothing nonchalant about their appearance. Misake and Uriel both made it a habit to wear something that showed off their tattooed arm sleeves. Of course, anywhere Cyprian went in Japan he was sure to garner looks being a muscular, bald black man taller than most of the native population. And they all wielded splendidly ornate samurai swords.

"So what's the plan?" asked Cyprian, under the lethargic jazz instrumental piping through the elevator speakers.

"No one survives except for Boss Teruya," answered Misake, as she stared up at the floor markers lighting up.

The elevator stopped on the 26th floor. A housekeeper joined the vampires with a stack of clean towels. She gave a side eye to the strangers and pressed the button for the 28th.

"What about the hotel staff?" asked Uriel, pointing a chin to the lone housekeeper.

"If they get in the way," said Misake. "They die."

The housekeeper turned slightly, as if she might have understood English. When the elevator doors opened to her floor, she quickly bolted out in fear.

Misake grinned, finding it amusing.

The elevator continued up to its destination. When the doors opened, the vampires were immediately faced with ten Teruya-*gumi kobun*, all sitting in chairs on either side of the hall, guarding the entrance to the floor. They all immediately stood and drew their guns.

And then the elevator door promptly shut.

Both Uriel and Cyprian looked at Misake, who blinked hard and sighed. She then repeated her mantra to herself.

Her father. His legacy.

Her father. His legacy.

"Sorry, for some reason I wasn't ready," she said. "But I'm ready now." Misake drew her sword and pressed the DOOR OPEN button with the tip.

Uriel and Cyprian drew their weapons as well.

And when the door opened, the *kobun* were in the same exact position.

"Is this where we can get a hot, steaming blood bath?" said Misake seductively in Japanese.

The gangsters all exchanged confused glances. And that was enough time for Misake to quickly cut down the first couple of men with slashes to the chest.

The others began shooting at the three vampires. Many of the bullets harmlessly entered their immortal bodies and some were actually batted away by the clanking steel of the swords. But it didn't take long to cut down the ten guards.

Of course, the hallway ruckus alerted the rest of the floor.

Doors were thrown open and more Yakuza soldiers spilled out. Some of them were still half-dressed, some were entertaining female partners, some were housekeepers, and some female partners were housekeepers who were half-dressed.

The hallway exploded in a melee of hyperactivity and screams and bloodshed. The vampires continued to progress, even as armed men surrounded them from behind. But the quickness and skilled prowess of the bloodsuckers were no match for what Teruya-*gumi* threw at them.

When the vampires finally arrived at the end of the hall, and the dust settled with dead bodies, not one inch of the hotel carpet could be seen. Blood dripped down the walls in a cool, splattered motif resembling something from "The Shining."

Misake pushed open the final door to find Boss Teruya standing against the window, wearing urine-soaked pants. His own personal bodyguard shot a bullet towards Misake's head, but her quickness split the bullet in half; each half of the steel case tapped the two vampire counterparts in the foreheads behind her.

Both Cyprian and Uriel dropped their jaws in awe.

"You just cut that bullet in half, Misake," said Cyprian. "Did you try to do that?"

"Of course I did. It was coming for my forehead."

"No, no – we get that you were defending yourself. That was natural. But did you literally try to cut the bullet in half, and not just knock it away?"

Misake thought about it and shrugged. "Yeah, I guess so. I saw it, I aimed, and then cut it. Why? You guys can do that, can't you?"

The two male vampires looked at each other. And then instantly nodded and lied.

"Of course we can," said Cyprian.

"I do it all the time," said Uriel.

"We just didn't know that you could."

Misake rolled her eyes and turned back to the bodyguard, who promptly shot a bullet through the window to shatter it and jumped out to his death thirty-four stories down.

Boss Teruya was left alone, the wind from the outside now whipping through his thinning gray hair. He looked out the window, envious of his employee's hasty decision.

"Hello, Boss Teruya," said Misake. "Do you remember me?"

The Yakuza leader slowly nodded his head.

"The last time we saw each other was when my father had called a meeting with all of the bosses," continued Misake. "You remember that, don't you?"

He nodded again. "Yes. How could I forget? It was when he showed us the head of Boss Tamaki, and you beheaded his distant half-breed relative."

"That's right," said Misake. "And you went home with blood stained in your hair and on your face. I would imagine it took a while for you to wash that off, no?"

"It did."

Misake approached the boss and circled him. "And even after all that, you still decided to betray my father by joining others against him."

Boss Teruya gulped. "Forgive me, but he is no longer with us."

"Isn't he? Can you not see him in my eyes?" Misake gazed into the boss's eyes, only an inch apart from the mobster. "He may not physically be with us, but his legend will endure through me, his one and only daughter. His blood is my blood. His life is now my life. So – let me ask you again – can you not see him in my eyes?"

He nodded and quivered.

And then there was the sound of a puncture and anguished grunt.

Misake's eyes widened. She looked down to see that Boss Teruya had penetrated his own stomach with a *tanto*.

The Jampyre shook her head and sighed deeply. "Why, why, why do you guys always do that? It's so annoying. I wasn't even done with my speech." She turned back to Uriel and Cyprian. "You guys didn't see him pull that out or anything?"

They both shrugged.

"I was kind of into your speech," said Cyprian.

"Yeah, seriously," agreed Uriel.

Misake blushed. "Really? It was that good?" Behind her, the Yakuza boss dropped with a thud and died. But she didn't even pay attention. "You didn't think it was too over-the-top and dramatic?"

"Nah, it was on point," said Cyprian.

"It was wicked," said Uriel.

Misake's face dropped and realized, "Wait – you idiots don't even know Japanese."

Both of them shrugged. "Still sounded good, though," said Cyprian.

Misake smirked and shook her head.

Cyprian motioned to all of the corpses lying in the hallway. "I'm sure the police are on their way by now. Can we get a quick lunch?"

"Chow down," said Misake.

And chow down they did.

From a hotel supply closet, two beady eyes peered out.

chapter 41

Kokusai Street in Naha, Okinawa was their next destination. Even though Boss Ito had an influence in Tokyo, he was the sole Yakuza *oyabun* on Japan's southernmost island. And he ran the infamous mile-long stretch of stores, restaurants, and hotels like an old-school Brooklyn gangster; every commercial tenant paid him a small percentage in exchange for his protection.

The three vampires exited the monorail at the Makishi station and found themselves in the middle of robust activity highlighted by food booths and street performers. It was an overcast Sunday evening during an event called "Transit Mall," so most of Kokusai Street was blocked off to vehicular traffic and only open to pedestrians.

A magician slid next to Cyprian and pulled a 100-yen piece from behind the vampire's ear. He then made it disappear into thin air and waited for a reaction.

"Wanna see some real magic?" asked Cyprian.

"No," said Misake bluntly, waving a finger at the warlock.

The magician recoiled away to another potentially gullible tourist.

Thunder cracked from up above, and the clouds ominously swirled. Many of the food booths started to shut down to avoid the impending rainfall. Shoppers scattered to shelter down various side streets.

But the vampires remained calm.

"So, where do we find him?" asked Uriel.

"He'll find us," said Misake as she scoped out rooftops. "All of the bosses are already expecting our visit."

Cyprian looked concerned. "So, now they'll all be prepared?"

"They'll think they are. But how do they really prepare for something they've never had to face before?"

The black clouds completely covered the sun, prompting storefront neon lights to spark up and down the street. The rain started to fall, washing out the rest of the street occupants down the various side outlets.

And then something odd happened.

All of the businesses down Kokusai Street shut down simultaneously by locking their doors and rattling down obnoxious metal barriers. When the sprinkling rain finally graduated to a torrential downpour, the three vampires were alone on the street lit up by reflecting neon signs across the glistening rain pitter-pattered road.

"Closing time already?" asked Uriel.

"No," said Cyprian. "They were told to close."

Instinctively, the three immortals formed a triangle with their backs to each other and slowly circled with their swords drawn. They were in the middle of an intersection, and from their standpoint, couldn't see another soul in the area. Except for Lucie the Lightning Bird, perched under an awning with a crazy-eyed pigeon.

Suddenly, motorcycle engines roared to life from somewhere. A headlight turned on and beamed from down each of the four streets, about a block away. The riders were all in black leather with matching *katanas*. They continued to rev up their rides.

"Sure has a way with theatrics," said Cyprian.

"Like a movie," added Uriel.

Misake panned her head around the area to each of the four motorcycles. "They're going to wish this was a movie."

"Swords this time," noticed Uriel. "I guess they found out bullets don't stop us."

The motorcycles spun out on the wet asphalt and began rocketing toward the vampires with cocked swords.

"Yeah, but one thing I forgot to tell you guys," said Misake. "Boss Ito only employs ninjas. So they wouldn't use guns anyway."

"Oh, fuck! Real ninjas?! Who's taking out the extra one? You, Uriel?" said Cyprian.

"I only have one hand, asshole!"

Cyprian laughed just as the four ninjas converged on them. All three vampires simultaneously leapt up into the air and swiped their swords, clanking against their bladed counterparts.

Misake took the task of handling the fourth ninja, throwing her scabbard through the motorcycle's front rim, launching its rider high up into the air and smashing against a storefront. Once the Jampyre landed, she immediately pounced on the fallen enemy and stabbed him through the back.

The three other motorcycles circled back around and returned. But once they were a half block away, the ninjas stood up on their seats and jumped towards the vampires, who had to contend with the wayward machines by dodging them before righting themselves and facing the airborne assassins.

Each vampire took on their own enemy.

And it wasn't pretty for the two American citizens. Neither of them knew a lick of martial arts.

Each time Cyprian and Uriel lifted their swords, they were met with roundhouse kicks and jabs to the face, the chest, the groin, and kept spilling across the rain-soaked road.

On the other hand, Misake matched her opponent with every move. It was a righteous battle of alternating and slick offensive and defensive moves and the clanking metal of their sharp swords. The continuous heavy rain didn't seem to deter either warrior one bit.

Cyprian and Uriel continued to get their asses kicked. At one point, they smacked into each other's foreheads and crashed against a light post. They remained on the ground as they watched their opponents square up for another round.

"It really annoys me that you're not using your magic," said the Latino vampire, wiping the blood off his mouth with the back of his hand.

"I haven't mastered it," said Cyprian, popping his shoulder back into place. "I still have to really concentrate, and right now, I don't have that much time—"

One of the ninjas brought down his sword toward Cyprian's forehead, but he managed to parry it just in time. Both vampires sprang back up to their feet, only to have their noses smashed by ninja boots. They fell on top of each other.

Uriel asked, "What about your bird? Can't it distract them or something?"

Underneath the awning, Lucie seemed to be frolicking with the crazy-eyed pigeon.

"Lucie! No!" yelled Cyprian. "You don't know where that bird's been!"

The spirit bird ignored him.

The vampires both wearily stood back up to face the ninjas, each holding up their swords without any confidence at all.

"You know what?" said Cyprian. "These things are distracting me." He dropped his *katana* and held up his fists.

"Are you kidding me? It's your funeral," said Uriel, keeping his sword up.

Both of the ninjas exchanged glances through their helmets and then simultaneously dropped their swords.

"Oh yeah. It's on now," said Cyprian, as he charged both of them.

The two ninjas threw punches and kicks, but each time Cyprian managed to block with his fists and forearms. It wasn't pretty, but it was pretty effective. The *Impundulu* vampire continued to push them across the slippery street until he managed to catch a ninja fist in each of his large palms, returning them into their helmets and shattering their Plexiglas visors.

And before they could regroup, he smashed their heads together in a crunching explosion of skull and fiberglass.

Uriel seemed impressed, giving Cyprian a silent clap.

They both then whirled around to go help Misake, but her ninja was newly decapitated.

All three vampires gathered back in the intersection.

"I'm guessing that was the appetizer?" said Uriel.

"And here comes the main course," said Misake, motioning in the air.

From every rooftop, down the block and behind them, more ninjas scaled down roped grappling hooks to the ground. There must've been at least a hundred men and women all dressed in black, at one point completely covering all of the neon signs to darkness. It was an ominous spectacle.

"Just a thought," said Uriel. "Why don't *we* just use guns?"

"Where's the fun in that?" asked Misake.

"Oh, this is fun for you?"

"Guns are so loud and obnoxiously violent. Swords are an elegant way to die."

Uriel rolled his eyes, as if he wasn't appeased with the answer.

All around, the ninjas landed. And then they charged with war cries.

The male vampires held their own for a while, but mostly on defense. Their sword skills were enough to at least keep them alive.

Misake naturally dispatched her opponents. Most of them with ease. And when she had an opening, she took the opportunity to help out Cyprian and Uriel. They were grateful for the help, but annoyed that their personal opponents were being replaced by fresher ones.

The rain-soaked battle raged on for what seemed like an eternity. Neither side gave up and even when the ninja body count rose, reinforcements replaced them. The vampires endured a fair share of cuts, but didn't waver.

Cyprian wished he could do hand-to-hand combat instead, or better yet, use his magic in one fatal swoop, but the conditions weren't working in his favor. That was, until he took a deep gash to his shoulder.

The shoulder with his lightning bird tattoo.

The tattoo that was a portal to his soul.

Cyprian the Dominion belted out a loud, anguished cry that seemed to create a charge of electricity that surged from his shoulder and down to his feet and then shot a neon green, circular wave across the asphalt about a block's diameter in length.

Every single body touching the ground was knocked from their feet, and once their bodies hit the electric canvas, they sizzled to their untimely deaths.

And then in a flash, the surge was gone.

Cyprian dropped to his knees, clutching his shoulder.

Lucie flew down to check on its master, consoling him with a head nudge.

And when the *Impundulu* warlock realized that the rain drops were the only sounds left surrounding him, he looked around.

Kokusai Street was a sea of death.

No one was left standing.

Not even Misake and Uriel.

chapter 42

Cyprian crawled over to Misake and instantly began rubbing his palms. But before he could recite his healing chant, she coughed to consciousness. Her immortal body withstood what no human (or ninja) could apparently endure.

"What… what happened?" she said, sitting up.

"I don't know. My magic… *did something*," said Cyprian.

Misake looked around at all of the dead ninjas. "Did something alright. You really should get some kind of voodoo instruction manual."

"I left it back in New Orleans," said Cyprian nonchalantly.

Misake wasn't sure if he was joking or not. She looked over at Uriel, who was just then getting up to his elbows.

"What happened?!" he grunted.

"Cyprian saved our lives once again," said Misake. "What is that like… three or four times?"

"Three," answered Cyprian bluntly.

Misake smirked and stretched up to her feet.

"Well, a little warning next time," said Uriel. "Maybe you should get some kind of voodoo instruction manual."

"He left it in New Orleans," said Misake, tapping a dead ninja body with her foot. She then looked down the now deserted street. "Do you think you killed everyone? Like… even the ones inside the buildings?"

"I don't know," said Cyprian, as he took his hand off of his shoulder to reveal a gash that radiated a green beam like a lighthouse beacon. He quickly covered it before the other two vampires noticed. "I mean... does it matter to you? You didn't spare any of the housekeepers back at that hotel."

Misake raised an eyebrow – Cyprian was right. "Well, it's time to find Boss Ito."

"There's no need," said a distinct and formidable man's voice.

The three vampires whirled around in surprise to find Boss Ito standing in the middle of the mass carnage. And behind him stood another two hundred ninjas.

Uriel spoke under his breath, "When you say *ninja-like* you're not kidding."

Lucie squawked in fear and flew back up to its perch.

Misake, Cyprian, and Uriel all raised their swords again.

"No," said Boss Ito in Japanese. "I'm not here to fight. I'm here to pledge our allegiance to you, Boss Sakumoto."

Both Cyprian and Uriel looked over at Misake and waited for a translation.

"He just surrendered," she said.

The two male vampires sighed and looked like they were going to collapse in overwhelming relief.

Misake approached Boss Ito and calmly stood face-to-face with him, even though the rain continued to spill down their faces.

"You had already done so with Boss Oh," said Misake.

"I know. But I was mistaken. Your father was always the most respected Yakuza *oyabun,* and I idolized him for his shrewdness. I have no doubt you will follow in his footsteps, as I've already witnessed. I do apologize."

"I appreciate the words, but you know I cannot accept your apology."

"I know that as well," said Boss Ito. "If I were in your shoes, I wouldn't trust myself. I *couldn't* trust myself. So I'm offering you the allegiance of my *kobun.*" He motioned back to all of the ninjas, who simultaneously dropped to a knee and bowed to the Jampyre. "They will be loyal to you for the rest of their lives."

Misake looked past Boss Ito to his warriors. "Prove it."

Without hesitation, Boss Ito raised both of his arms to the side. Two lead ninjas approached and swiftly chopped them off. They then returned back to their original bowing positions.

Boss Ito buckled to a knee, blood spewing out of the stumps where his arms used to be. He tried to keep a dignified face, but he couldn't stop his salty tears from merging with the rain drops already on his cheeks. "Please… show me mercy."

"I appreciate the gift of your *kobun*," said Misake. "But for your betrayal, tonight you die until you are dead."

And with that, Misake turned and trudged through the blanket of ninja corpses. Her new ninja army rose, passed by their bleeding and now former boss, and followed her down the street. She motioned Uriel and Cyprian to join her.

Uriel whispered to Cyprian, "What just happened?"

"If I'm not mistaken, Misake just took over an entire island."

They joined her upfront of the marching ninjas. And behind them, Boss Ito wavered for a bit before collapsing to his death.

Down a side street and behind a dumpster, a shadowy figure shifted on the ground. El Enano stood and opened his beady eyes.

chapter 43

On their return back to Tokyo, Misake sent her new ninja *kobun* to Kujukuri Beach to fortify her family's presence there. The Sakumoto-*kai* organization had a few lucrative businesses that remained untouched by Boss Oh and Okamakiri mushi-*kai*.

And since Boss Ito was gone, only three bosses were left.

Uehara.

Watanabe.

Oh.

Her father. His legacy.

Her father. His legacy.

But Boss Uehara didn't wait for a surprise visit like the one that finished off Boss Teruya in his top luxury floor of Park Hotel Tokyo. He also didn't prepare a well-conceived surprise ambush like Boss Ito had attempted on Okinawa's Kokusai Street. Instead, Boss Uehara sent an invitation to Misake for her to join him in a banquet that was to be held in her honor. Naturally, the Jampyre read between the lines.

"It's obvious he's just trying to switch sides," she told Uriel and Cyprian.

"And I suppose you're going to attend?" said Cyprian with a weary sigh.

"Of course I am. He invited both of you as well, along with fifty of my own *kobun*."

The two male vampires exchanged bemused glances.

"And he said no guns or swords allowed," added Misake, noticing their expressions and pointing to the fancy parchment-like invitation written in equally fancy *kanji*. "So really… what can possibly go wrong?"

"I think those were General Custer's last words," said Cyprian.

Uriel nodded. "Santa Anna too."

"Were Custard and Santana bad ass immortal Jampyre demigoddesses?" asked Misake coyly.

"No."

"I didn't think so. You guys have a couple of days to get new suits. I'm going to Kujukuri Beach to check on some things and then find me a nice dress." And with that, Misake ended the conversation and promptly left. It was as if she was too anxious to accomplish another task.

"Check on some things?" repeated Uriel to Cyprian.

Cyprian only threw his arms up and shrugged. "I don't know any more. She seems to be operating on auto pilot."

Uriel frowned, an overwhelming sense of dread displayed on his face. "You ever sense that the Castille is watching us?"

"They are."

"They are?!"

"Watching us. Taking notes. Formulating a plan."

Uriel looked out the nearest window, but there was nothing to be seen. Cyprian chuckled. "You won't see him. He's pretty sly."

"Him? You've seen *him?"*

"Oh yeah. A few times. He's been tracking us for several weeks now."

"Why haven't you told us? Or better yet, killed him?"

"There's no point," said Cyprian. "He's not here to do harm. He's only gathering info and communicating it back to the Castille. There's nothing we can do. And whatever the Chancellor is planning is already inevitable."

Uriel seemed to shudder in fear. "And so, we just wait to see what happens?"

"As we've been doing," said Cyprian. "And hopefully… we still come out on top."

"As we've been doing," nodded Uriel.

"Exactly. But right now – in case I die – I'm gonna go buy me the most fucking expensive suit I've ever owned. I think I deserve it."

A smile finally curled on Uriel's face. He seemed to wholeheartedly agree with that plan. The two vampires walked out of the room.

"Tell me something," asked Uriel. *"Who* is watching us?"
"El Enano."

Across the street – behind a bush – El Enano's beady eyes narrowed.

chapter 44

As they strolled through the men's formal clothing section of Tokyo's Isetan Shinjuku department store, Uriel was still laughing.

"I had always heard stories about El Enano," he said. "But then you start wondering if they're made up or not."

"I saw him in passing at the Castille once."

"Is he really that small?"

"Yeah, he really is."

Cyprian paused at a rack of Brioni suits. "Oh, Hell yeah." He began sifting through the selections.

Uriel was still hung up on El Enano. "It amazes me how no one ever notices him."

"Only those who aren't supposed to notice him, don't notice him. Everyone else, I suppose, do," clarified Cyprian. "And now that I've seen him, I can't unsee him. I'm going with all black, with maybe a yellow tie. You?"

Uriel nodded, "I'm not surprised. Maybe something with purple." And then, "Is he here now?"

"Who?"

"El Enano."

"Oh. Yep."

"Where?"

Cyprian scrutinized the stitching of the jacket he was holding as he slowly spoke. "Very slowly look over at your nine o'clock and at the bottom of the rack."

Uriel cracked his neck and covertly looked over to his left.

Inside of a circular rack filled with Desmond Merrion of London jackets, two little work boots poked out.

The Latino vampire nonchalantly turned his head back and then squeaked out laughter. "No, way. You're fucking with me."

"That is the infamous El Enano, I'm telling you," said Cyprian with a straight face, now looking at another jacket.

Uriel's grin quickly faded with one of star-struck hope. He then started whispering. "I want to meet him."

"No."

"Why not?"

"You'll embarrass him."

"But he's a Latino *hermano*," said Uriel excitedly, but subdued. "A very famous one. In fact, he might be the most famous of our breed. Even more than El Galán."

"Who's he?"

"Gangster in Mexico City who also sings. He's actually put out a couple of albums."

"Huh. Well – your sister Gabriella was famous too."

"True, but not for the right reasons."

The *Impundulu* vampire smiled, coming around to the notion of engaging with El Enano. "Watch this." He slowly moved to another suit rack, closer to where the little spy was hiding. The little boots instantly disappeared, and then reappeared within a rack farther away.

"Oh my God," said Uriel. "He's so good. I didn't even see the jackets move."

"I know. And the only reason I caught onto him was I saw his reflection ducking away in my sword when Misake gave them to us."

"He's been following us ever since then?!" marveled Uriel.

"At least. And I thought I might've accidentally killed the little guy in Okinawa when all of those ninjas went down."

"Well… I mean… he *is* a vampire," said Uriel.

"A really tiny one," said Cyprian as he slipped on a Dormeuil jacket to try on.

Both vampires suddenly busted out in laughter. In fact, tears began rolling down their faces as they held onto the nearest racks to stop themselves from falling.

"Okay, okay," said Cyprian, wiping a tear. "Let's meet him."

"How?"

"You act like you're going to the bathroom and circle behind him. And then at the same time, we try to catch him."

Uriel was giddy. But he quickly put on a straight face and his acting shoes. "Nah, I think that jacket makes you look fat. Hey – I'm gonna go take a piss." He left Cyprian and disappeared into the men's shoe department. He then circled back and crept up to El Enano's rack.

Both vampires met each other's gaze and nodded. They silently counted to three.

From each side of the rack, Cyprian and Uriel shot their arms through the jackets to corral El Enano, but they only grabbed each other.

"Where'd he go?" shouted Uriel.

Cyprian looked to his left and just managed to catch El Enano's little feet disappear around the corner. The *Impundulu* warlock instantly took off after him.

Uriel followed as they crossed several sections of the department store in hot pursuit. El Enano was elusive, as he never brushed merchandise or hit a dangling hanger or knocked over any customers.

The two taller vampires – on the other hand – brushed a lot of merchandise, hit many dangling hangers, and knocked a couple of customers to the floor. They kept catching just a glimpse of the vampire spy, enough to stay on his tail.

After a couple of revolutions around the floor, El Enano finally descended the escalator. Cyprian and Uriel reached it, only to have several customers block their path. Down on the floor below, El Enano had already gotten off, and it was the first time the vampires caught a glimpse of his entire body.

Miguel "El Enano" Soler wasn't actually a dwarf as his nickname would suggest. He was just a Latino man who was small in stature – just slightly over four feet tall. His crooked and patchy goatee tried to mask a baby face, but it only made him look ridiculously cuter. And oddly, he was missing two fingers and an ear; large scabs currently taking their places.

The little spy turned and looked back up at Cyprian and Uriel. He threw them a stubby, but defiant, middle finger. And then he nonchalantly descended another escalator. He pulled out a cell phone that looked too large for him and began texting.

"C'mon, let's get him!" urged Uriel, who looked ready to jump from floor to floor.

"We'll get him. Have patience," said Cyprian, who casually slid onto the escalator behind an older Japanese couple staring back at the rare black man. "*Kone-eechie-wah,*" he said to them in his embarrassing attempt at Japanese.

Uriel joined him, but fidgeted from side to side, trying to see El Enano on the other escalator. "We're going to lose him."

Cyprian continued to walk at a normal pace to each set of escalators. They must've started on the sixth floor, since it took them that many sets to reach the bottom. Of course, Uriel was highly perturbed the whole time that his counterpart didn't have a sense of urgency.

"Seriously?" he said, every time they got stuck behind customers and came to a dead stop. "Let's just go around them."

But they didn't.

When they finally reached the first floor – and El Enano was nowhere to be found – Cyprian paused and perked his ear into the air. The overhead speaker constantly chimed in with the store jingle or a spontaneous sale announcement on cream pan.

Uriel continued his impatience. "What are you listening for—"

"—Shh."

Suddenly, the alarm at the east entrance blared loudly.

Cyprian immediately bolted for the sound and found the department store's security team surrounding a confused and highly annoyed El Enano.

"*Gomenasai, gomenasai,*" said Cyprian, who had apparently learned how to say "sorry" in Japanese with better pronunciation. He reached down into El Enano's jacket pocket and pulled out a lone security sensor, unattached to any store merchandise. "*Gomenasai.* Just a ha-ha joke."

The security guards took it and mumbled to each for a moment. They then nodded and walked away, insulting the foreigners in their native language.

El Enano narrowed his eyes up at Cyprian. He then spoke with a lisp that made him even more adorable. "Thmart. But not funny, you fucker."

"We just wanted to meet you," said the *Impundulu* vampire. "Uriel is a big fan."

Uriel walked up to El Enano and held out his hand. The little Latino looked like he was going to spit into it, suspicious of the renegade vampires. But he finally relented and obliged.

"You wanna get some coffee or something?" asked Cyprian.

"Fuck coffee. I want thum blood," said El Enano.

chapter 45

Back at the Sakumoto compound, Uriel laid a nude Japanese woman on a table. She was already dead, with several vampire fang puncture wounds in her body. "This one's only aged two days."

El Enano settled into a chair and grabbed a wrist. He dug his teeth in and began drinking.

Cyprian and Uriel sat on the other side and joined in. Cyprian bit into the back of a knee, and Uriel took the other wrist, first shaking some salt and squeezing lime onto the skin.

The little vampire spy noticed Uriel's garnishments and perked his chin. Uriel obliged by sharing, sliding the items across the dead woman's belly.

The three vampires drank until their bellies were full. After a couple of belches and sips of red wine, they settled back into conversation.

Cyprian started with a question. "Are you here alone?"

"You thee anyone elth, fucker?"

Uriel smirked at the small vampire's smartass lisp-laden vulgarity. That was one of the few things he had heard about the infamous El Enano, including his diminutive stature, amazing surveillance skills, the fact that he used to be a Siamese twin, his penis was supposedly thirteen inches long, and he was a necrophiliac. "I heard you had a Siamese twin," he said.

"I did," said El Enano, motioning to the side of his body. "Johnny and I were attathed righth here. But when I was thurned inthoo a vampire, that fuckhead vampire forgoth he had thoo bithe thoo neckth, so I was lefth with a human attathed to my thide. Of course, after I fully tranthformed, I immediately thmelled Johnny's blood and bith out his fucking jugular before I realithed who he wuth. So, then I had a dead body attathed to me until I ripped ith off."

Both Uriel and Cyprian fell silent.

And then El Enano busted into laughter. "Oh my fucking God. You thood see the lookth on your faytheth! They look fucking thtupid! Yeth, I had a Thiamese twin but he died three dayth after we were born."

Cyprian looked over at Uriel and gave him a stern "don't ask him any more stupid questions" look. "So, what are you telling the Castille?"

"Just giving them updateth about whath you're doing. Who you're killing. Who you're eathing. Who you're fucking." El Enano winked at Uriel.

"That's it?"

The small vampire sighed. "How ofthen you've yuthed your black magic. How it almotht fucking killed me, you *cabron*! How you've thaved your pretty litthle vampire'th life theveral timeth while thith guy over here givth her the nightly burritho injecthion. Ha, ha, ha! I thaw all three of you on that boath while hiding underneath the pier. That demon vampire with the fucking hornth—"

"—You saw that?" exclaimed Cyprian.

"Fuck yeah I did. What the fuck happened? Thee had hornth and clawth and whithkerth and thit."

"I don't think she had whiskers," said Uriel, who was bored with the conversation.

El Enano shrugged. "Maybe thee did, maybe thee didn't. We'll never fucking know. Hey – what happened thoo your thithter... er... um... Gregoria?"

"Gabriella. She was killed."

"Oh, whath a fucking thame. Thee was a good lay."

Uriel clenched his teeth. Even though it was a backhanded compliment, he didn't want her to be the subject of any conversation, let alone those sexual in nature.

Cyprian caught his counterpart's disagreeable nature and redirected the topic. "So what's the Chancellor going to do now?"

"I have no idea whath his planth are, if he hath any ath all," said El Enano. "And even if I did know, I wouldn't fucking thell you."

Uriel continued to grit his teeth. "Then we'll just kill you right now. Won't be a big deal. We've already killed five VES agents, and you're just a messenger – no, wait – you're half a messenger."

El Enano curled a wry and tired grin, as if he'd heard every "small" joke a thousand times each in his life. He downed the rest of his wine. "Ith that all? Can I fucking go now?"

"No," said Cyprian. "I want your cell phone."

The pint-sized vampire stared at the warlock's eyes for a long time; he could see a green storm brewing. He slowly extracted his phone and placed it on the corpse's belly. "There. Any more fucking questionth?"

"What happened to your ear?" asked Cyprian, who didn't really seem to care but was a tad curious.

El Enano reached up and lightly caressed the hardened scab. "The devil bith ith off. Thook thoo of my fingerth thoo." He held up both of his hands and wiggled his remaining fingers. "And that thame devil ith going thoo do worth thoo you."

There was a long moment of tense silence between the spy and Cyprian.

Uriel noticed but couldn't care less. "Is it true your dick is thirteen inches long?" he asked, his mind apparently reverting back to the legend of El Enano.

"I'll thell you whath," the spy said. "Leth me have this corpthe, and I'll thow you."

Cyprian abruptly stood and kicked back his chair. "You can have this corpse, but we're not watching." He motioned to Uriel to follow him out of the room.

The Latino vampire lingered for a moment – morbidly fascinated – but then caught up to Cyprian. Behind him, El Enano climbed onto the table and unzipped his pants.

Outside, Cyprian stood over the koi pond and stared at El Enano's cell phone. He had it turned to the "placed calls" page and the number labeled "Chancellor V."

Lucie – his lightning bird – was dozing off on the branch of a nearby bonsai tree.

"I can't believe you gave him that corpse," said Uriel as he approached.

"Fair trade."

"For what?"

The *Impundulu* vampire flashed the Chancellor's contact number to Uriel.

"So... you're going to call him? Maybe try to negotiate peace?"

"Maybe. Worth a shot," said Cyprian.

Uriel shrugged.

Cyprian took another moment to weigh his options. He then pushed the button and waited. It rang.

And rang.

And rang.

And then, a groggy voice answered. "El Enano? Is there something wrong?"

Cyprian opened his mouth to speak, but the words escaped him.

Chancellor Valiquette repeated himself. "El Enano? Are you there? Is something wrong?"

"This isn't El Enano," said Cyprian finally, trying to put a little more testosterone in his timid voice. He put the Chancellor on speaker.

There was a long silence on the other end of the line. And then the Chancellor cleared his throat, "Cyprian the Dominion?"

"That's right."

"How are you, my boy?" said Viktor in his usual overly exuberant self.

"I'm fine."

"That's good to hear. Are you ready to come home?"

Cyprian looked over at Uriel, who slowly nodded. "Yeah, I think so. In fact, I think we're all ready to put this behind us and start leading normal lives again."

"Oh, Cyprian Dugas," started Viktor, who then gave a thirty second pause. "I'm sorry, but that can't happen. All of you must still face the consequences for your actions."

Cyprian looked like he wanted to crush the phone. "We've easily disposed of everyone you've sent to kill us, including your beloved Tebeau, Uriel's own sister Gabriella, my own sire-mate Atalia, and now your fucking midget messenger. We're willing to forget it all. All you need to do is forget as well."

Another long moment of silence. That time it was excruciating as Cyprian and Uriel had no idea what was going on within the Chancellor's mind in New Orleans. But then, they heard a mysterious voice in the background.

It was an older woman. And knowing the Chancellor's lascivious reputation, she was probably a new lover.

The mystery woman seemed to be having a hushed argument with the Chancellor. The tone in her voice was stern but had a regal air about it. And when the argument ended, it appeared that she had won.

Viktor Valiquette returned to the phone and began with a sigh. He then whispered only three more words.

"Prepare to die."

chapter 46

Cyprian used one hand to crush the cell phone into a thousand pieces of glass, palladium, lithium, and magnesium and sprinkled them into the pond. He then looked towards the house, pointed at it, and barked, "Go cut off that mother fucker's dick and then place him on the nearest boat back to New Orleans!"

Uriel calmly returned to the house.

Lucie rustled to Cyprian's voice from the bonsai tree.

From the outside, Cyprian heard El Enano say, "Fucking perverth. I knew you wanthed thoo watth!" And then a frantic, "Waith! Whath are you doing?! Fuck – *ahhh!!!!*" And then the miniature vampire's voice faded with a whimper and repeated, "*Why? Why? Why?*"

Cyprian sat on the stone bench, pondering the past and accepting his future.

Lucie flew over and sat next to him, following the koi fish with its beak.

It was almost two hours later when the water from the koi pond splashed up, revived Cyprian from deep reflection, and scared Lucie away.

Uriel walked up and sat next to him.

"Sorry," said Uriel.

The warlock wiped his face. "What did you throw in there?"

"His dick."

Cyprian grimaced and witnessed the koi fish pecking at the severed appendage as it sank to the bottom. And yes, the legend seemed to have been true. "Jesus. Looks like it belonged to a horse."

"So, I found a boat headed to Hawaii."

"Close enough. I'm sure he'll find the rest of the way."

"He wouldn't stop crying the whole way. And you know what? He never cursed once."

"Karma, man," offered up Cyprian. "God shortchanges you at birth, then evens it out with an advantage that most men would trade their souls for, and then loses said advantage when you keep polluting the air with indecency."

"And having sex with dead people."

"Yeah, that too."

The two vampires sat in silence for a moment as they watched the fish return to the surface with full bellies. A penis carcass followed.

"What do we tell Misake?" asked Uriel.

"We tell her nothing for now," answered Cyprian. "She needs to concentrate on the task at hand."

"Retaking Tokyo?"

"Exactly. If the Chancellor makes a move before then, then we'll handle it. But for now, we need to focus on helping her, too."

Uriel sighed deeply. Almost too deeply. It was obvious he still wasn't satisfied with their current situation and what the immediate future was holding.

"We really just have three more families to conquer, and that'll be it," said Cyprian, trying to read Uriel's mind. "And the next one is pretty much giving himself to us on a platter."

"And that worries me. It's all been too easy."

"Like Misake said, we're a master race in these parts," reasoned Cyprian. "They have no idea who they're dealing with and how to counter against vampires."

"And warlocks," said Uriel, slightly grinning.

Cyprian returned a smile and nodded. Apparently a day of suit shopping and chasing down tiny vampires was a recipe for vampire brotherhood bonding.

Uriel stared into the koi pond with a worried expression. "I haven't heard from her," he said. "Have you? She's not answering her phone."

Cyprian pondered, concern also brewing on his face. "I still haven't been able to sense her. Not since that lake house of yours in Texas."

"It's like her blood mutated or something when she came over."

"She recovers quicker than us, too."

"I've noticed," agreed Uriel.

Cyprian walked over to Lucie – perched back on the bonsai tree – and stroked its head in deep thought.

Uriel gave him a moment, but then impatiently interrupted. "So what do we do?"

"Where was it she said she was going?"

"Some place called Kujukuri Beach."

"If we don't hear from her by morning, we'll go find her."

Uriel nodded and stood. "I'll go clean up that mess on the table. Unless you still want some of it?"

"Gross, dude."

Misake returned from her business on the coast with a renewed sense of vigor. She felt closer to her ultimate goal with every Yakuza boss she took down.

Her father. His legacy.

Her father. His legacy.

And now she was ready for the next step.

The Jampyre visited fifteen department stores in Tokyo and tried on thirty-one dresses. When she finally found the right one, she treated herself to a mani/pedi and went to a hair salon. When the primping and preparation was done, Misake was almost unrecognizable.

If it had been an 80s teen movie, Misake would've walked down a set of stairs in slow motion to reveal herself. But since her bedroom was on the first floor, an exit from the house to the zen garden where Cyprian and Uriel were waiting would have to suffice.

And both of them were mesmerized.

For whatever reason, the Jampyre had decided to wear a completely pink ensemble, and she was a sight to behold. Her dress was simple, yet elegantly hugged her perfect figure. It showcased her shoulders and shimmered in strapless wonder. It was accented with pink, high-heeled Jimmy Choo's, bright fuschia lipstick, matte neon pink eye shadow, rose quartz and pink tourmaline costume jewelry – and to top it off – Misake had her hair completely dyed in bubble gum pink and styled in Audrey Hepburn's iconic updo.

From the roof, Lucie catcalled and flapped its wings.

"What do you think?" asked Misake, giving the guys a bit of a twirl.

Cyprian approached her in his dashing all-black suit with yellow accents. "You look absolutely gorgeous. And like something from a comic book."

Misake looked at Uriel – wearing a purple version of Cyprian's style – who was still marveling at her. She raised her brows, anxious for his opinion.

"Yeah! Gorgeous! I mean... wow," he said. "How... how are you going to fight if we need to?"

The Jampyre shifted and revealed a slit that spilled out a curvaceous hip and the long, toned leg that followed. "Are we ready?"

Under different circumstances, the vampires might have fully enjoyed dressing to the nines and enjoying a night in downtown Tokyo. They were about to paint the town red – but unfortunately – it wouldn't be the "type of red" they hoped for.

chapter 47

The three beautiful vampires showed up to the Grand Nikko banquet hall with fifty handpicked *kobun*. Misake had chosen the members who had been loyal to her father the longest; many of them almost reaching retirement age. That included her inherited and trusted *saiko komon* and *so-honbucho*.

And of course, all of them were unarmed.

They entered the hall named Palais Royal. It was decorated with exquisite chandeliers and walls painted with a garden motif. Boss Uehara sat at a table in the middle of the large room by himself. All of his own fifty men and women were split up at the other tables.

They all stood in unison and bowed. Naturally, the vampires took note that they did appear to be unarmed as well.

"Boss Sakumoto, you look absolutely radiant," said Boss Uehara. "Thank you for accepting my invitation. Please join me at my table and have your team sit wherever else they'd prefer."

Misake sat directly across from Boss Uehara. The other two vampires took strategic positions behind her right and left shoulders. All of her *kobun* filled in the other empty seats, reluctant and hesitant in sitting with the enemy. And when everyone settled, Misake stood out like a beacon of pink splatter amidst all of the black suits.

Boss Uehara clapped and banquet servers flocked in masses with bottles of wine, filling the already laid out glassware.

"No swords and no guns," said Misake to Boss Uehara. "But perhaps you're using poison as a weapon?"

The senior boss laughed. He switched glasses with Misake and eagerly took a sip. "I assure you there is no poison."

The Jampyre looked around the room to find her entire family looking back at her. She nodded, and they all began enjoying their wine.

Boss Uehara added, "My *kobun* are completely unarmed. No hidden steal within the secrets of their suits. Tonight they are only equipped with charm for their new guests."

But the boss and his *kobun* had a dark secret—

Underneath every single table in the banquet hall, a bomb started to count down.

Tempura appetizers made their way from the kitchen and began populating the center of the tables. The room suddenly roared with the sounds of chopsticks being snapped in two and a collective sigh of relaxation.

Of course, Misake didn't snap any chopsticks.

"Please eat," said Boss Uehara, soaking a battered shrimp into his *ponzu* sauce/wasabi concoction and placing its entirety in his mouth.

"I will soon," said Misake.

"Your *gaijin* friends aren't eating either," observed Boss Uehara. "I can have the kitchen make whatever it is they'd prefer. Perhaps an American cheeseburger? Or wings of the buffalo?"

Misake grinned, recalling her first experiences in San Antonio and her college roommate Shanice having her try every famous fast food staple. "They'll be fine. They are just concerned with my well-being."

Boss Uehara slowly placed his chopsticks across his appetizer plate and smiled. "I've heard of your talented bodyguards and no doubt, my men wouldn't stand a chance against them."

"No, they wouldn't."

"And against you as well, Boss Sakumoto. My *kobun* still speak of that day in Sapporo when you faced all of Boss Tamaki's trained samurai by yourself."

Misake grinned wryly. "Much of it an exaggeration, I'm sure. But without it, how entertaining would stories be?"

"Yes, I agree! I'm fascinated most by the one that says your mother is a goddess."

"That one is true."

A moment of silence. And then Boss Uehara belted out a hearty laugh.

The entire room took notice and relaxed even more. The conversation between the two bosses appeared to be going well.

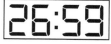

Cyprian took a sip of wine and observed the others at his table. Members of each family were in casual conversation with each other. Even though it was all in Japanese, he could tell that some of it was about baseball or sumo wrestling or new local hangouts.

At Uriel's table, much of the same was going on. Conversations about meaningless things with mouths full of *Tempura*-battered sweet potato and asparagus. The Latino vampire's eyes shifted every so often to each entrance and exit to ensure their safety. He even scrutinized the banquet hall employees, making sure they didn't have any hidden weapons.

"I remember your father when he was only Boss Tamaki's driver," said Boss Uehara. "In fact, I was there on the night he took a bullet for him."

"Really?" said Misake, suddenly interested in hearing stories about her father.

"Yes. We had a mutual deal with some Russians that turned sour. All Hell broke loose. But your father was willing to sacrifice his life for his boss and soon after was promoted to first lieutenant. Many were concerned – and perhaps even jealous – since he was so young."

"How young?"

"Barely twenty, twenty-one perhaps."

"And then what happened?"

"I don't know the details of why your father left the Tamaki-*gumi* organization. I only remember the sudden appearance of his new family and how he took something from each of us. He was like a tropical storm sweeping over the island, and none of us were prepared for his strength. When the clouds cleared, we all bowed to a new force in Tokyo."

"Except for Boss Tamaki?" asked Misake.

"Yes. Except for Boss Tamaki. He felt betrayed that his own first lieutenant – a man he saved from a petty criminal life and groomed from an early age – would do such things."

Misake clenched her teeth. "And later on, his son would rape me."

Boss Uehara frowned and fell silent.

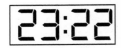

The banquet dinner was moving along at a rapid and super-efficient clip. The soiled appetizer plates were being picked up and simultaneously replaced with teriyaki steak dinners and bowls of white rice.

Cyprian motioned to one of the servers, "You have any cooked rare?"

The server nodded and smiled and gave him a fork.

"No, I didn't ask for a fork," said Cyprian. "I wanted my meat bloody."

Of course, the server had no idea what the *Impundulu* vampire was saying.

"Never mind," sighed Cyprian, who began thinking how amazing it would be to drink the blood of Boss Uehara's soldiers. Some of the females had a sweet lychee-like smell.

Cyprian looked over at Uriel, who continued to look suspicious. The warlock smirked and glanced back at Misake.

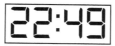

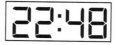

"We were all shocked Boss Tamaki made that move," said Boss Uehara. "But for a while, it seemed to have worked. Your father was weakened."

Misake sipped her wine, reflecting on those moments and how it changed the course of their lives. That path directly led her to the current seat at Boss Uehara's table.

Her father. His legacy.

Her father. His legacy.

Boss Uehara took a bite of his steak and savored the flavor.

The Jampyre had a sense that the Yakuza *oyabun* knew it was going to be his last meal on Earth, and he was going to enjoy every bite of it.

"This place is better than any restaurant in Tokyo," he said. "In fact, I've used the chef for many of my private events."

That certainly sounded like something someone having a last meal would say, thought Misake. Boss Uehara was having his favorite meal, made by his favorite chef.

"You really need to try this," he said.

Misake didn't want to offend Boss Uehara, noticing that Cyprian and Uriel had also left their plates untouched. She motioned to a server. "I'm sorry, but my stomach can only handle meat cooked rare. Would you mind making three new plates, one for myself and each of my American friends?"

The server nodded and took off.

Boss Uehara nodded at Misake, savoring another bite.

It didn't take long for the new slabs of meat to arrive, since they were barely cooked.

Cyprian was surprised to receive his. "Oh. She *did* understand me." He utilized the only fork in the room with a steak knife to cut into it. He then placed it into his mouth and chewed for what seemed like a minute.

The others at his table appeared to wait for his opinion.

He shrugged. "It's not a two-hundred-pound white boy from Mississippi, but I guess it'll have to do."

Naturally, no one understood what he said and resumed eating their own meals.

Misake ended up eating half of her steak. She downed it with a lot of wine to mask the bitterness of the cooked meat.

Her table mate was already done with his. "Absolutely delicious. I hope the afterlife will be filled with such delicacies."

"The afterlife?" said Misake, who didn't want Boss Uehara to know that she was already assuming the inevitable.

"Yes. I mean… I'm assuming you are here to kill me and take my men as your own?"

The Jampyre dabbed her mouth with a napkin and placed it neatly across her plate. "Yes, I suppose so. But I guess I had hoped to hear an attempt at a negotiation."

"If I were to successfully negotiate my life with you, then I fear I would ultimately lose respect for you, Boss Sakumoto."

"Very well put, Boss Uehara."

She reached over and offered her glass for a toast. He obliged. *Clink!*

Uriel attempted to take a visual lesson to use his chopsticks. But he failed miserably – stabbing more than grabbing – and dropped one, watching it roll underneath the table. He stooped down to retrieve it, but was immediately stiff-armed by one of Boss Uehara's men.

"No, no, no," he said with a wave of the finger. The Yakuza henchman then snapped the same finger at a server, who immediately gave Uriel a new set of wooden chopsticks.

Uriel was slightly taken aback by the sudden and aggressive block. But he nodded and said, "Thanks."

"*Domo*," said the *kobun*, offering an impromptu language lesson.

"Right – *domo*," repeated Uriel, who definitely knew of the translation.

The *kobun* didn't stop there. "*Domo arigato*."

"*Domo, aree-gat-too*," said the Latino vampire.

"*Ari-gah-toh*."

"*Ari-gay-tah*."

"*Ari. Gah. Toh*."

"*Ari. Gah. Toh*," said Uriel, finally getting the pronunciation down.

The *kobun* clapped and said in his best English, "*Belleee guud!*"

The plates were getting cleared and made way for bowls of mochi ice cream.

Misake looked over to see the reaction of her vampire cohorts.

Uriel looked curiously at the bowl of round ping-pong ball-sized goodness. He picked up a green *matcha*-flavored one and rolled it in between two fingers. He then squeezed a bit too hard, shooting his new *kobun*-translator friend in the forehead with gooey ice cream.

Misake squirted out a giggle.

Cyprian rolled his eyes and pushed his bowl away.

Boss Uehara wasn't devouring his ice cream like he had the tempura and teriyaki steak. It was almost as if he made a conscious decision to slow down, stalling his upcoming execution.

And Misake suddenly felt sorry for him. "I want to thank you for your hospitality. My *kobun* will not soon forget this meal."

"Is it enough to warrant me a quick death?"

"I'd say your chances are good. When?"

"After coffee?"

"There's coffee, too?"

"Espresso is what I think I chose off the menu."

"Very well then," said Misake. "You die after espresso."

A female *kobun* from another table traded seats with the one sitting next to Cyprian. She began speaking English slowly, as if she just finished three weeks of night classes and wanted to practice.

"Hello," she said. "I finishing three weeks of night class learn English. May I practice for you?"

"Sure." Cyprian leaned back, slightly amused, slightly attracted.

"Do you like to eats pizza?"

"Pizza? Um, sure. I guess."

"Are you of interest in basketball?"

"Am I interested in basketball? Yeah."

"Are you... *vampire*?"

Cyprian paused, leaning forward. "Say that again?"

"I hear... we hear... that you are... vampire," said the pretty *kobun*. "Is not true?"

It seemed like the entire room waited for Cyprian to answer. *Kobun* from other tables leaned in. The vampire mulled over his options and decided to lie, unlike the last time a pretty Japanese girl approached him with the topic.

"No, of course not," he said finally. "Vampires aren't real."

The curious *kobun* narrowed her eyes and looked suspiciously at Cyprian's uneaten mochi ice cream.

The *Impundulu* vampire took the hint and popped one of the balls into his mouth. It was obviously gross, but he tried to put on a straight face. "Mmm mm mm. That's sooo good." And then he suffered from a serious bout of brain freeze.

Uriel sighed in aggravation when he saw the banquet servers start their rounds of serving espressos. He moved his head from side to side, trying to get Misake's attention to urge her to kill the Yakuza *oyabun* already.

But she never looked over.

His gaze then wandered to other members of the Uehara organization. For some odd reason, more than a few were looking at the clock on the wall. Some of them glanced at their watches. And even others the digital clocks on their cell phones.

Apparently, they were ready to go home, too.

At that moment, Uriel's coffee mug was flipped over. But the vampire placed his hand over the rim and politely refused the espresso.

Boss Uehara spun the spoon in his espresso. Sweat beads began to form on his forehead.

"Why Boss Oh?" asked Misake.

The Yakuza boss nodded as if he expected the question. "She convinced all of us that joining forces was the best plan for our livelihood and survival."

"And what do you think now?"

Boss Uehara paused, choosing his words carefully.

"I think it is still the best plan. Unfortunately, it must take many sacrifices."

The Jampyre mentally analyzed his words. "So, you believe Boss Oh will still triumph in this war? Over me?"

The boss gulped. "I do."

"Even after I've already defeated three other families?"

He nodded.

Misake's face dropped in surprise. "And yet Boss Oh has disappeared, allowing all of you to fall."

"Disappeared? No, we know exactly where she is."

"Where?"

"In America."

"America? Where?"

Boss Uehara pondered. "New Orleans."

From the other table, Cyprian turned slightly in recognition of his hometown and the only English words to come from Misake's conversation.

Misake clenched the table cloth in her fist. Her face boiled in anger. She asked a question she already knew the answer to. "Why is she in New Orleans?"

"To learn about you and your friends, of course." He motioned to Cyprian and Uriel.

The Jampyre released the table cloth and straightened it out, trying to calm herself. "She won't find out anything," she said defiantly.

Boss Uehara loosened his tie. "She's apparently discovered so much already. Much of it before she even departed. In fact, it was the trail that led her to America."

"What do you mean?"

"She captured a little man who was spying on the three of you. A man with a foul mouth."

Misake turned around and motioned to Cyprian. "Have you heard of someone from the Castille spying on us? Supposedly a small man who curses a lot?"

Cyprian paused. Conflict on his face.

"El Enano," said Uriel, who didn't seem to care about any conflict. "We found him a couple of days ago."

Misake scrutinized Cyprian's shameful face. "And you didn't think to tell me?"

"You were out of town," said Uriel again. "And then here we are."

"We'll talk about this later," said Misake sternly, as she turned her attention back to Boss Uehara. "So, what things has Boss Oh learned?"

"You broke a law over there, and now you're a wanted woman."

"Haven't we all broken laws, Boss Uehara?"

"Your friends – the ones with you tonight – are also wanted."

Misake grinned. "Friends often have things in common, otherwise how can you even define them as friends?"

"Your dark friend has special powers," continued Boss Uehara. "He is a witch."

"That's definitely not true," said Misake with a straight face. "He's a warlock."

The Yakuza boss paused and looked annoyed with her flippant attitude. "Your father wasn't murdered by any of the other families. He died by your own hands."

Misake raised her voice in anger, "No, he didn't—"

"—You were directly responsible for his death," shouted Boss Uehara. "You may not have pulled the trigger, but it was your selfishness that killed him!"

All of the other tables watched the two sparring bosses in morbid silence.

Cyprian and Uriel moved to the edges of their seats in case they needed to intervene.

Misake closed her eyes in rage. Her mind exploded into turmoil. When she reopened her eyes, they were bloodshot. "I've changed my mind, Boss Uehara. Your death will be slow."

Oddly, the Yakuza *oyabun* smiled. "Good. I would've lost respect for you otherwise."

At that moment, Misake looked over at Uriel. She finally read the impatience on his face and nodded. It was almost time.

"Finish your espresso, Boss Uehara," she said. "I'm anxious to see your blood."

He nodded and sipped, loosening his tie again.

Cyprian still looked shameful that he hadn't told Misake about El Enano, especially since he knew about the little spy tracking them for weeks. He hoped that it wouldn't bite him in the ass. The vampire glanced down to his porcelain mug of espresso – which he had accepted but not taken a drink – and saw something odd.

There was a steady tremor in the brown liquid.

He looked up to find the pretty *kobun* shaking her leg like she had a jittery tick. It banged against the leg of the table. "Are you nervous?"

She feigned a smile and said in English, "Sorry. Too many... ahhh... *caffeine.*"

The *Impundulu* vampire glanced inside of her mug to find it empty. Seemed logical enough. But then he looked across the room and all around. He finally noticed the same odd behavior occurring everywhere. Including the constant clock-watching Uriel had observed.

The two male vampires looked at each other with perplexed looks and shrugged.

And then they noticed a single tear run down the pretty *kobun's* cheek.

All three vampires suddenly heard a cacophony of heightened heartbeats. It was deafening. And the owners of those heartbeats began to sweat profusely.

Uriel noticed that all of the banquet servers were gone. Dirty dishes still remained to be picked up but had suddenly been abandoned.

Boss Uehara downed the rest of his espresso and seemed to relish that last drop just a moment longer, swishing it around his mouth. He placed it back down and closed his eyes.

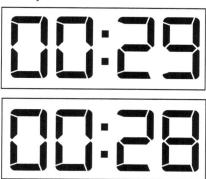

"Finished with your coffee? Good." Misake moved her napkin over to reveal a steak knife that she had hidden. "Any final words, Boss Uehara?"

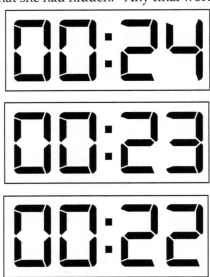

"Had your father betrayed me many moons ago instead of Boss Tamaki," he said. "I would've ensured that you suffered a greater pain."

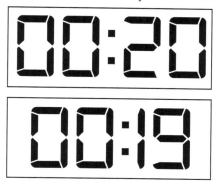

The Jampyre abruptly sprang from her chair and sliced through the *oyabun's* neck. A crimson waterfall began pouring down his white collar and black tie.

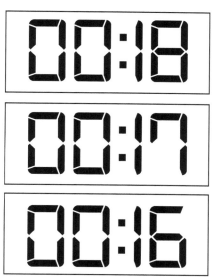

Misake braced herself to see if any of his men would retaliate.

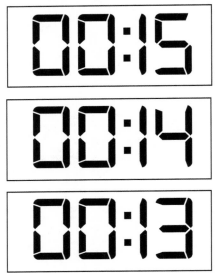

But they didn't.

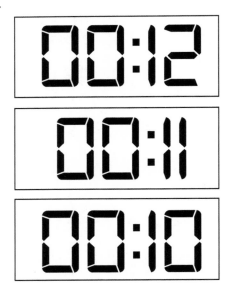

Instead, all of Boss Uehara's men closed their eyes and clasped their palms together in prayer. Their table partners from the Sakumoto-*kai* organization all watched in confusion.

Misake exchanged glances with Cyprian and Uriel. She suddenly had the horrific sense that it would be the last time she'd ever see them again.

Cyprian noticed the tears that suddenly engulfed Misake's eyes. He searched his soul for an answer; a resolution; a clue; *something*. He clasped his hands together and began rubbing them. They started to glow green. "*Usowe, Koki—*"

But before he could finish the protection chant, he cried out in pain and clutched his heart. Something was happening inside of him. The *Impundulu* vampire warlock dropped to his knees, unable to move a muscle.

Misake rushed over and caught Cyprian in her arms and then guided him down, until his head rested in her lap. Tears streamed from his eyes. "Cyprian! What's wrong?!"

Cyprian was catatonic. Gasping for air. Gasping for salvation.

Sensing the worst, Misake implored, "Don't go, Cyprian. I love you!"

Uriel watched Misake and Cyprian, feeling isolated. Feeling alone. And when Misake uttered her true feelings to Cyprian, the Latino vampire felt betrayed. Scorned.

Still on the ground and stroking Cyprian's head to comfort him, Misake looked over and caught a glimpse of one of the time bombs. It read—

Misake shot a glance at Boss Uehara. Blood continued to gurgle from his neck. And just before he closed his eyes to eternal sleep, he managed to turn a devil's grin at her.

The Jampyre looked down at Cyprian. His eyes bulged out in shock. His mouth was agape. He looked like a man enduring the last moments of his life. She then looked at Uriel with a hopeless expression. But his own wasn't comforting. In fact, the Latino vampire had his teeth clenched at her in vehemence.

All of Boss Uehara's *kobun* screamed in terror—

When the explosion occurred and roared, there was the unmistakable sound of three cosmic goddesses screaming in anguish within the depths of the celestial plains. It was a shrilling sound, ending with the dissipating sound of macabre sadness.

Outside, the Tokyo night sky lit up like the Fourth of July until dust billowed up from the crumpled building and blanketed the stars with an ominous, ashy-gray quilt. Half a city's block suddenly evaporated into oblivion.

And a stone's throw away, a lightning bird plummeted fifty feet to the hard, unforgiving asphalt and shattered every bone in its body.

Part Five

Home of the misplaced,
seek the guise not apparent.
Present your presence.

chapter 48

Noriko Suzuki killed her first man at the age of seven.

She had just woken up from a bad dream when Noriko noticed a stranger creeping past her room, heading to her sleeping parents. She tiptoed to her father's dojo, grabbed a *tanto*, and without hesitation stabbed the man up the anus as he contemplated his next moves at the end of her parents' bed. The home invader bled out and died before Father and Mother Suzuki knew what was happening.

And Noriko returned to a peaceful sleep.

At ten years old, the little girl had saved some money to purchase a couple boxes of Botan rice candy with toy surprises (way before they were replaced with lame stickers), but when she witnessed a homeless man kick his homeless puppy, she instead bought Japanese pan with a custard filling. She squeezed out the creamy goodness and replaced it with a mixture of bleach and rat poison.

The homeless man died of food poisoning, and Noriko got a new dog. She named it Daitetsu, after her all-time favorite sumo wrestler.

When Noriko was sixteen, a classmate she was smitten with walked her home from school. When they reached the middle of a bridge spanning across a canal, the boy found an opportune time to kiss Noriko on the lips. She was elated, but when the boy took it a step further and slid his hand up her shirt, she immediately pushed him over the bridge railing.

The canal below – at that point – was only three-feet-deep.

The boy broke his neck upon impact and drowned.

During her junior year attending the Gakushuin Women's College, Noriko asked an English professor for a meeting to discuss the lower-than-usual grade he had given her on an essay entitled, "A World Without Men." After thirty minutes of heartfelt arguing and defending her stance, the professor simply unzipped his pants and pulled out his penis, explaining the only way she could raise her points was to "raise *his* point."

Noriko promptly obliged by biting his manhood completely off, chewing it into a perfect ball of bolus, and spitting it back into the Professor's face. Of course, he'd already fainted from shock.

When Noriko Suzuki graduated college, she was still a virgin. Because of her short life's history with men, she made a vow to never give herself to a man, unless he truly earned it by winning her love, trust, and respect.

Only one man came close. But that man broke Noriko's heart into a million pieces when she found him with another woman on the eve of their wedding. She killed the woman first, and then made the man eat the corpse until his stomach ruptured. After that, other men died trying – or at the very least – became severely handicapped.

Noriko's resolve to keep the sanctity of her body unblemished steered the other facets of her life. She was an astute businesswoman and hard negotiator. She became a consultant for Fortune 500 companies and was even recruited by several Yakuza *oyabun* to help drive some of their illegal operations.

One of them – a man by the name of Boss Kenji Oh – offered to recruit Noriko into his organization as a full-time advisor. He promised her the highest salary she'd ever received and even the most luxurious living quarters.

Noriko accepted and quickly helped the Oh-*gumi* organization become one of the most successful in Tokyo, joining the ranks of the families led by Boss Tamaki and Boss Watanabe. Her business savvy, penchant for hard research, and general confidence became highly touted traits, and her reputation grew into one of respect throughout the criminal underworld of Japan.

It would be eight years later when Noriko Suzuki would take the next step in her life and secure herself as Japan's most formidable woman. It was during a Christmas party hosted by Boss Tamaki at his luxurious snow-covered estate outside of Sapporo, Japan. All of the bosses and their senior advisors and headquarter chiefs and first lieutenants and high ranking *kobun* were invited.

Towards the end of the night – when everyone had filled their bellies with top shelf liquor – Boss Kenji Oh found Noriko outside, admiring the sprawling view of snow-capped *sakura* trees against the twinkling stars of the night's sky. The moonlight gave her a radiant glow.

"What are you doing, Noriko?" asked her Boss, as he stumbled over the crackling snow underneath him.

"Just admiring Mother Nature and her breathtaking gifts."

The Boss slightly slurred. "Yes. But they are not alone with you out here."

"Thank you." Noriko turned slightly – recognizing a compliment – but hoping it wouldn't go further than that. In fact, she quickly tried to change the subject. "The party is going well. All of the bosses seem satisfied."

"All of the bosses *are* satisfied," said the Boss. "But it's because they will have a warm body to help thaw their icy souls when they retire for the night."

"I'm sure they can let you borrow one of their handmaidens, Boss Oh."

The Boss barked into the night. "I'm tired of handmaidens! They no longer do anything for me! I wake up with an emptiness I want to dispose of."

Noriko gave him a side-eyed glance. "And how do you propose to do that?"

"Marry me, Noriko. Be by my side. Together we can become Tokyo's most powerful Yakuza syndicate. More powerful than Japan's ever known!" The Boss's words echoed loud enough that it seemed to draw the attention of the party inside.

Noriko remained calm and said, "I appreciate the offer, Boss Oh. It is most generous and gracious, and most women would be honored to be your wife. But the day I marry will be the day I'm truly in love."

Boss Oh frowned and stumbled to the side, catching himself against a tree. He began mumbling to himself. "I've loved you since the day I met you eight years ago. And for all those years, I didn't take a wife. I waited for you. I waited for you to fall in love with me."

"I'm sorry, Boss Oh."

He continued, ignoring her. "And all those years you never took a lover. I thought for sure you were waiting for me as well."

"True love has eluded me thus far," said Noriko. "And though true love is not the one prerequisite for the gift of my purity, it will only be given to a man who is able to return something I cannot achieve for myself. I will not and cannot be your wife. You haven't earned that. Again – Boss Oh – I am truly sorry."

The Yakuza *oyabun* grunted in anger and attacked Noriko. He threw her into the snow and started clawing at her custom-made Angel Takuya kimono, layer by layer until her skin was exposed.

But Noriko's annoyed expression never changed. It never wavered. She remained calm, even as Boss Oh's actions were a flurry of hyper-aggressiveness and his hands and arms flailed with intoxicated yearning. It wasn't until the Boss attempted to unleash his own flesh when Noriko pulled out a hidden blade and slit him across the throat.

Blood sprayed across her porcelain face and breasts and the crisp, white snow surrounding her. Not to mention her now-ruined one-of-a-kind kimono. And when her Boss finally collapsed to the side in death, Noriko still had the same expression. She was annoyed, like the many times before when a man she admired and respected failed her.

Noriko Suzuki fully expected to die that night for murdering a Yakuza kingpin. The commotion had attracted an audience from the house.

But instead, her life was spared, and the party continued without another hitch.

On her return trip to Tokyo, Noriko Suzuki fully expected to arrive and die for murdering a Yakuza kingpin.

But instead, the Oh-*gumi* organization left her alone.

As she settled back into her home, Noriko Suzuki fully expected to be fired and begin her search for another job.

But instead, the Oh-*gumi* family – including a couple of rightful blood heirs – bestowed her the "keys to the car."

Noriko gladly accepted and resumed business as usual. She didn't bother to change the name of her new crime syndicate as a sign of respect to the family. And she just assumed the name and title of her predecessor. It was soon after the transition that Noriko also suffered from an aggressive periodontal disease, prompting her to lose all of her teeth and replacing them with a set of solid gold ones, which would set the stage for her future, formidable reputation and later nickname of *Madamu Gorudo* (Madame Gold).

Such was the creation of the current Boss Oh.
One of the two baddest bitches in Tokyo.
And still a virgin.

chapter 49

Several years later, Boss Noriko Oh found herself back at the Tamaki compound where she had killed her former employer. She spent only a few seconds reminiscing at the spot of the murder; a hand tight across her chest on her chic tightly-patterned Komon kimono as if she was protecting herself from his spirit. And then Boss Oh turned her attention to the one hundred and six samurai corpses organized into the Jampyre symbol Misake had created on her epic and bloody revenge spree in Sapporo.

It was the aftermath and downfall of the Tamaki-*gumi* organization.

Boss Oh walked around the bodies with her *saiko komon* and scrutinized their fatal injuries. Most had died by *katana*, but a few had some of their innards ripped out. Snow had continued to fall and filled open wounds like cups of shaved ice. She took special notice of those victims, bending down and examining the jagged lacerations made by bare hands.

"Someone very strong," offered her senior advisor.

The female *oyabun* nodded and continued to walk around and accidentally kicked something metal, buried within several layers of fresh snow.

It was some remnants of the rocket that blasted Misake in the chest.

Boss Oh looked up at the entrance of the Tamaki compound, to the snow underneath her own feet, and then back to the rocket. It was almost as if she could sense and track its path by deciphering the evidence presented in front of her. "Where did this hit?"

"Probably one of Boss Tamaki's samurai—"

"—I checked all of them," said Boss Oh, raising her voice. "None of them were hit by a bazooka rocket."

The senior advisor gulped, leaving it at that.

Inside of the warehouse-converted mansion and Boss Tamaki's bedroom, the *maneki neko* was still moving, its right paw swinging. Boss Oh used a finger to stop it and paused as if she was channeling the thoughts of the porcelain cat. She then turned away, bent down, and procured a floored *wakizashi*, snapped in two.

"That never left Boss Tamaki's side," said the senior advisor.

Boss Oh nodded. "And yet, here it is. Not by his side and disrespected, snapped in half like a stick of pickled *daikon*."

They moved back downstairs and examined each room until they came across Boss Tamaki's torture chamber. It was the one he had specifically designed to cast revenge upon Misake for killing his youngest son Sanju-Hachi. And it was also the one where his decapitated body was currently decomposing.

"Where's his head?" The *saiko komon* looked around the room.

"Taken as a symbol, no doubt." Boss Oh ran a finger across every torture device in the room, admiring the mechanics and ingenuity and macabre history of the older ones. When she reached the back of the room, she turned to see the large portrait of Sanju-Hachi covering an entire wall. It was defaced with the word "#rapist," written in *kanji* and blood.

Boss Oh curled a smile.

"What is that symbol?" asked her advisor, pointing at the hashtag.

"It's what all the young kids use these days," answered Boss Oh. Her smile remained as the possible suspects in her mind suddenly dwindled in size.

"So this was done by kids?"

"One kid in particular."

The advisor was skeptical. He seemed to carefully choose his next words since he undoubtedly didn't make it a habit to disagree with his boss. "How could – one kid – do all of this? Kill all of those samurai?"

"That's what I plan to find out."

Boss Oh left the Tamaki compound and retraced Misake's steps in Sapporo like she was a modern day Japanese Miss Marple. Her first stop led her to the third floor of club King Xmhu where she observed the crimson stained carpet, currently cordoned off by police tape. All of the massacred bodies were gone, but some entrails remained in dried and shriveled up pieces. The blood-splattered birthday cake also remained.

The senior advisor walked up. "The owner showed me the recording. It looks like a woman walks up and throws a smoke bomb, but it's hard to see anything after that. It might be that same woman from the email."

He was referring to the hazy picture of Misake that had been circulating around the families after she was caught on camera in a hotel room, when she killed Rokuju-Ichi and eluded some of Boss Tamaki's men and their Gatling gun. But no one had recognized the daughter of Boss Sakumoto. In fact, the thought never crossed anyone's mind. Until now.

Boss Oh stood in that now infamous hotel room suite. The corpses had also been long removed. The windows were all still shattered out, and the furniture was riddled with bullets. She looked over the window frame edge as the wind from the outside swirled. Behind her, the senior advisor watched the captured video of the entire fight and gasped once Misake jumped out.

"There's no way she could survive that!" he exclaimed.

"And yet, she did," said Boss Oh, looking at the rooftop directly across. She looked back and mentally calculated how much power and force it would've taken Misake to have leapt and reached it. "I've seen enough," she said, abruptly swiveling around and leaving the room. "We must get back to Tokyo."

"But what if she's still here? In Sapporo?"

"She's not."

"How do you know?"

"Because her job is done here," said Boss Oh. "And her father awaits her."

chapter 50

Boss Oh played it cool when Boss Sakumoto arranged a meeting with all of the Tokyo Yakuza leaders at his home. She played it even cooler when he reintroduced Misake as his new *wakagashira*. And her venomous veins ran with ice water from a frozen tundra when Boss Sakumoto proudly displayed his archenemy Boss Tamaki's head and then subsequently beheaded a distant mixed-race relative and permanently stained her brand new white Kyo-bingata kimono with blood.

The female *oyabun* vowed to wait patiently until she was ready to make her first move in the retaking of Tokyo. Of course, she had no idea that outside forces would intervene and present her the favor of killing Boss Sakumoto only weeks later. And then when Misake spurned her offer to combine families, the pieces were set for Boss Oh to make some power moves. Of course, she would've lost all respect for the Jampyre had she accepted anyway.

"Your prey has taken the bait," said a Genkai Wokou pirate.

Boss Oh and Boss Watanabe approached the coastline with their bow and arrow-wielding *kobun* to find the superyacht anchored in the middle of Hakata Bay.

"All three of them?"

"Yes."

"Cut the lights."

A pirate flipped a switch on a remote. The party lights on the boat immediately sparked and fizzled out. There was a collective surprise and grumble from the ship guests.

Boss Watanabe then motioned to the *kobun*, who lit the gas-soaked cloths on their arrow tips. They then launched them, watching a perfect crescent of light attack the starry night and ignite the superyacht into a floating island of flames.

"Get your crew ready," said Boss Oh to the lead pirate.

The pirate paused, confused at the directive. He watched the ship burn as passengers were engulfed in a fiery tomb. "They will not survive."

"Get your crew ready!" repeated Boss Oh with a stinging echo. "This fire will not stop her."

All of the pirates obediently boarded their trimarans and revved them up. They then prepped their harpoon guns. The next time they looked up at the doomed luxury yacht, it had sunk into the depths of the bay. Steam rose off the turbulent waves like escaping spirits into the celestial plains. And there were only three lone survivors bobbing out of the water.

Boss Watanabe was floored. "How is that possible?"

"Did you see that green orb?" asked Boss Oh, referring to the green light produced by Cyprian's protection spell.

"Yes. What was that?"

Boss Oh squinted in thought and stroked the inside lining of the original Maiwai-style kimono she chose to wear on that night. "The stories about Misake may have some merit," she said. "Her mother being a goddess, giving her immortal blood."

It took a moment for Boss Watanabe to process the information. "And the other two? The *gaijin*. Do they have divine blood as well?"

Boss Oh stared hard at Uriel and Cyprian, as the pirates took off and harpoon guns at the ready. "I don't know. Perhaps they are just being protected by her." She watched the ensuing melee and listened to some of the reactions of those around her. They were mostly gasps of surprise at how skilled Misake and her foreign friends were.

And then she took note of a wayward lightning bird in the distance, flapping its wings in midair as if it was keenly observing the action below.

Once Misake was snagged by two harpoons and dragged away, Boss Oh began to leave. She had a feeling the Jampyre would still prevail. In fact, she hoped she would. The chess match had only just begun, and it was much too fun. And that was about the time Boss Oh would make a discovery that would change the course of the game forever.

From the corner of her eye, she saw a movement under the docks.

It was a small figure with beady eyes.

chapter 51

El Enano was chained to a chair by the ankles. His wrists were in the same predicament behind him. Two fingers laid severed on the ground. His face was battered and bruised, blood streaming from every orifice. And the hilt of a *tanto* was protruding from his belly button.

Yet he continued to smile.

Boss Oh watched him smile. She had changed into a jumpsuit and now stood in front of the diminutive vampire alone, in the middle of an empty warehouse much too large for the barbaric event. Her knuckles were skinned to the bone. Perfectly coifed hair no longer perfect. El Enano's blood speckled across her body. There was a rolling tray next to her, with already-used surgical instruments.

She was waiting for a death that wasn't coming.

"I already told you," said El Enano, who oddly didn't have his famous lisp. "You have to fucking cut off my fucking head if you want me to fucking die!" He spat at her.

"So if I want to kill Misake, that's the only way I can?"

El Enano sighed. "Who is Misake?"

"The one you were spying on."

"I told you. I wasn't spying. I was just—"

"—Fucking fishing. Yes, I know. Yet you had no fishing rods. No fishing nets."

"I had a spear, but I dropped it into the water. When you found me, I was just about to fucking leave."

Boss Oh twisted her lips in annoyance. She looked down at the instruments currently unused and picked up a scalpel. She approached El Enano, gripped his throat and squeezed, and promptly sliced off the tip of his tongue when it made an appearance.

"Fuck! You fucker thlut!" screamed the Latino vampire. With his new lisp.

"Are you going to start speaking the truth?!"

"Fuck you!"

The female *oyabun* stabbed El Enano in the thigh with the scalpel. He shrieked a pain that echoed throughout the warehouse.

"Now?"

"Fuck you!"

Boss Oh bent down to El Enano's ear and whispered. "I can do this all night, until you are only a piece of your former self. Now tell me what I want to hear."

The little vampire sputtered blood and whispered, "Go fuck yourthelf with a thorny rothe and thpin."

The boss grinned her solid gold teeth and bit off El Enano's ear.

That scream was even louder, rattling the rafters.

Boss Oh chewed and chewed and chewed and then spit the unrecognizable ball of skin and cartilage onto the floor.

El Enano finally had tears running down his face. He whimpered. "Who. The fuck. Are. You?"

She didn't answer. Instead, Boss Oh removed the blade from El Enano's abdomen and wiped it on her sleeve. She then pointed the blade at his crotch.

"That's the next thing to come off."

"As long as you yuthe your pretthy mouth again," said El Enano. "And hope you don'th choke thoo death firtht."

Boss Oh promptly reached for his zipper with a stone cold countenance. She had finally run out of patience. And that's all it took for El Enano to throw up his proverbial white flag.

"Okay, okay! You win! I'll thell you everything you wanth thoo know!"

"Good."

"Will you leth me live?"

"Depends on what you tell me."

"What do you wanth thoo know?"

"Everything."

El Enano pondered his predicament for a moment. And then nodded. "If I thell you everything, can you promith me one thing?"

"No," said Boss Oh bluntly.

He asked anyway. "I just can'th have my bawth know I thold you."

"And who is your boss?"

Again, El Enano paused. Severed appendages aside, he knew that what he was about to do could warrant a worse fate by breaking vampire codes of ethics. "Thanthellor Vikthor Valiquethe of the Casthille of Tharlemagne."

"I've never heard of him."

"Of courth noth."

"And why is that?"

El Enano sighed. His next words would be the point of no return.

"Heeth a fucking vampire."

chapter 52

"Heeth a fucking vampire. I'm a fucking vampire. Mithawkey ith a fucking vampire. Her boyfriend Uriel ith a fucking vampire. Thiprian – the black one – ith a fucking vampire."

"Misake calls herself a 'Jampyre,'" said Boss Oh.

"A 'Jampyre?'" said El Enano. "Thath fucking thoopid. Theyrth know thuth thing ath a Jampyre. Thee made thath up when thee wath thurned illegally."

And thus began the riveting eight-hour conversation Boss Oh would have with El Enano about everything having to do with vampires. She was enraptured and gave him her full attention. El Enano expounded on their history and culture up to present day. The rules, the bans, the crimes, the secrets, the cover-ups. He detailed the strengths and weaknesses of the real life bloodsuckers. And of course, he spoke of what he knew about renegade vampire Misake Sakumoto and the Castille's recent failures to capture her.

"And I thought she was some kind of demigoddess," said Boss Oh.

El Enano scoffed. "Imagine thath. A vampire and a goddeth? Thee would be unthoppable."

Boss Oh smiled. Even as a "simple vampire," Misake was thus far unstoppable. But now she had secrets and more importantly – weaknesses – suddenly revealed.

El Enano was released. Boss Oh made the promise to him that she wouldn't tell Chancellor Valiquette about what had occurred if she ever had to cross that bridge. The little vampire immediately resumed his surveillance duties on the three vampires, recuperating his wounds on-the-go.

Boss Oh went home after the long night of inflicting torture that morphed into an early morning impromptu lesson about vampires. She soaked in a steaming hot bath and absorbed all of her newfound knowledge. She then went to sleep with new plans and strategies swirling and formulating in her mind and then deep into her dreams.

She slept peacefully for sixteen hours.

When Boss Oh woke up, she was advised of a large package that had been delivered. It was the casket with the dead body of a Genkai Wokou pirate, with a note from Misake that read, "You wanted to play. Let's play." Of course, Boss Oh was already entrenched in the game and made her next move by calling an emergency meeting with the other Yakuza bosses.

"I received the same thing," said Boss Watanabe. "What do we do?"

"The Sakumoto-*kai* have not interfered with any of my businesses," said Boss Teruya. "So why are we here?"

Boss Uehara spoke up. "I ask the same question. This is a problem for only Boss Oh and Boss Watanabe."

"I did not agree with the union of your families," added Boss Ito. "But as long as my own businesses were not interfered with, then I had no problem. Apparently, Boss Sakumoto has taken exception to it."

"Boss Sakumoto?!" yelled Boss Oh. "Boss Sakumoto is dead! Do not recognize this petulant child as a boss! She is too young and irrationally fit to lead her organization."

"She's done nothing thus far for us to think otherwise," said Boss Uehara. "And it was you who instigated the attacks on her businesses. It was you who hired the pirates to raid her vessel."

Boss Oh began turning red with rage and frustration from the accusations. But she closed her eyes and calmed herself and spoke softly. "Indeed, I did. But it was only because she disrespected me at her father's funeral. She said she would ensure that her family would remain the most powerful. And if you think you won't be affected, then take a look at this." She threw down Misake's handwritten message on the table before them.

But it was altered to read, "You wanted to play. Let's play. When the game is over, I will be the only boss left in Tokyo."

The three men turned to the fourth – Boss Watanabe. He said with a stammer, "Yes. My message... said the same thing." He then glanced concern to Boss Oh, who rolled her eyes at his ineptitude in lying.

"A child's game is what she's playing," Boss Oh quickly countered. "She's in way over her head, and we have no time for this." She read everyone's silent and skeptical faces and added an exclamation mark. "And truth be told, wasn't the Sakumoto organization started with the betrayal of an already established family? The Tamaki family goes back in history to the origins of the Yakuza. Sakumoto-*kai* should not even exist, and now they want to be the sole and premiere organization in Tokyo."

There was a long moment of silence until Boss Ito finally asked, "So then what is it you propose, Boss Oh?"

"Simple. I want to send a message back to her. One that says the rest of the families will stand together against her, unless she dissolves her organization."

Boss Watanabe added, "With a united front, hopefully that will be enough for her to back down."

"And if she doesn't?" asked Boss Teruya.

"Then we take her down."

"She's just one family. Surely that won't take much."

Boss Oh grinned. "Misake Sakumoto is not who she appears to be. Though she's young and impetuous, she has a unique strength that none of us have ever seen before. I was fortunate enough to meet a man who gave me much information about her and what transpired during the time she was apparently abroad in the United States. I'm still not entirely convinced that what he told me was all true, so I will be taking a trip to validate this information."

The female *oyabun* proceeded to give the men a general overview of what she discovered. However, the other four Yakuza warlords were highly skeptical and in fact, laughed at some of the outrageous details.

Boss Oh knew that was natural. As she retold some of the vampire findings out loud, she even thought to herself that some of it was absurd. Too absurd. Too incredulous. And sometimes downright comical.

And that's why she was on the next plane to New Orleans, U.S.A.

chapter 53

Boss Oh stood inside of the New Orleans Museum of Art. She wasn't wearing her customary high-end designer kimono, but instead business casual attire in pastel colors with a Coindivi sun hat.

She perused through a section of paintings by a British artist named Hush, who – coincidentally – had a collection of "Street Geishas" depicting Japanese women in a mix of graffiti and anime styles. Boss Oh tilted her head, unsure if she was impressed or offended, especially since it was the third straight day of scrutinizing it.

El Enano had briefly mentioned the Castille of Charlemagne being disguised as the museum, but Boss Oh didn't imagine she'd have such a difficult time figuring out how. Thus far – after three days – she hadn't noticed anything to give her a clue. The patrons all seemed normal enough, especially since many were students on field trips. By the end of the day, Boss Oh was ready to return to Japan, recapture El Enano, and perhaps bite off his other ear to obtain the secrets of the Castille.

But then she got lucky.

As Boss Oh was about to exit, a dapper male holding a harlequin mask in his hand brushed past her and beelined for a door with an access code pad. He punched in some digits and entered. Just before the door closed behind him, Boss Oh noticed him putting on his mask.

And descending?

She had seen others enter the door before, but she always chalked it up to employees reporting for work and never from that angle. Her current vantage point allowed her to peer slightly inside to what must've been an immediate stairway down. *Very odd.* And why would that handsome man be putting on a fancy mask?

Boss Oh backtracked and nonchalantly leaned against the wall. She watched a slightly risqué-dressed woman enter the museum, pull out what looked like a fancy invitation from her purse, and silently read off the code to gain access through the now mysterious door.

That was when Boss Oh became thoroughly skeptical and unimpressed. Surely access to a vampire fortress took more than a simple code? Thus far the two visitors shielded their fingers when entering the numbers, but it all still seemed too basic.

Nevertheless, several more beautiful people with masks in their possession entered and disappeared. Boss Oh looked at her watch.

It was 4:50pm. *Did something begin at 5?*

If so, the Yakuza warlord was now pressed for time. If something was about to begin, it was likely that visitors would stop. So, she approached the coded door and acted like she was about to punch in numbers, waiting for the next visitor.

It was a statuesque red-headed vampire named Joelle.

Boss Oh feigned a gasp. "Oh no. I forgot my mask!" She turned and acted like she didn't notice the woman, and then exclaimed, "Oh! Do you think they'll mind?"

Joelle curled a grin. "The mask is just for shits and giggles. If it makes you feel any better, you can just wear mine."

"Oh, that's so nice of you – if you don't mind?"

"Of course not," said the French vampire, who gave a cruel pucker of the lips. "I'm sure I'll get it back when it's over."

Boss Oh nodded as she watched Joelle punch in the code and open the door. She followed her down the abnormally long stairs into the depths of the Castille.

"So who invited you?" asked Joelle.

"Invited? Oh… um… I'm so embarrassed. *I forgot his name.*" Boss Oh gave Joelle a cheesed schoolgirl grin.

"Oh, that's funny," said the vampire.

"Who invited you?"

"Oh – no honey. I did the inviting."

Though Boss Oh wasn't sure if Joelle was a real vampire, she certainly carried herself like one. Or at least, that was how the Yakuza *oyabun* imagined a French vampire from the old world would act.

When they finally reached the bottom and walked into the Great Hall of Bastien, Boss Oh was floored. Much like Misake's reaction when she first entered a couple of years earlier, the Gothic architecture was a site to behold by any "foreigner." Or just plain human for that matter.

Joelle turned and handed Boss Oh a glittery, orange and yellow mask shaped like two connecting autumn leaves. "Here you go."

"Thank you," she said, slipping it on.

The vampire paused a moment, looking into Boss Oh's eyes. "Why are you here?" she asked with eyes that seemed to lock into her subconscious mind.

"What... what do you mean?" said Boss Oh, suddenly concerned that her ruse was uncovered.

"You just don't seem like the usual type to come around here."

Boss Oh tensed as the vampire lingered on her breath. All she could do was shrug and ask, "What type is that?"

"Dumb." Joelle smiled and whirled away. "By the way, I love your teeth. They are to die for."

Boss Oh sighed and concealed a grin. She liked Joelle and her persona. She looked up to find the portrait of Chancellor Viktor Valiquette. "Will he be joining us?"

Without even looking up at the portrait, the French vampire knew who she was referring to. "He may. If he's hungry."

If he's hungry?

Joelle continued to the door on the far end, past the parlor with lounge chairs.

Boss Oh paused, suddenly wondering if she should've tried a different tactic. She didn't feel prepared entering something that required a vampire to be hungry. "You know what?" she said. "I'm sorry, but I'm not sure if I'm feeling too well. Here's your mask back."

Joelle stopped at the door. It took a while for her to turn around. And when she did, her face twisted with evil. "It's too late to change your mind."

"Why?"

"Your invitation is very exclusive. Surely, your *unnamed* friend made that clear to you. And you – *honey* – have seen far too much already."

Boss Oh smiled, thinking momentarily that she would've lost respect for the vampire had she let her go. "You are right – must be nerves." She joined Joelle at the door and slipped on her mask.

It was 5:00 p.m.

Right about time for a vampire orgy.

chapter 54

Even though she was still a virgin, Boss Oh had seen her fair share of naked people. She made her home on the top floor of a brothel masked as a bathhouse, so nude employees and customers were the norm. But the vampires slithering on the floor before her in bare flesh was a decadent mosaic of living art. The unknowing soon-to-be-dinner humans weren't that bad either, seemingly handpicked from the crème de la crème.

Joelle was already nude when she tugged on Boss Oh's sleeve. "C'mon. Don't be shy." She began unbuttoning the Yakuza leader's Anthropologie button-down top for her.

"Wait," said Boss Oh, placing a hand on top of the vampire's. "Is he here? The one from the portrait?"

Joelle looked into the mass of perfect skin and erect reproductive organs. "No. I don't think so. That's okay, though. You'll still have fun."

"But I need to see him."

"No, you don't. Is whomever invited you in there?"

Boss Oh peered around her and lied. "Yes."

"Then that's all that matters."

"No, I really need to see him."

The French vampire frowned. She closed the door to the orgy and backed Boss Oh into the wall, her erect nipples grazing against her chest. "Listen. If you don't go in there right now, you will embarrass your friend. No one declines an invitation to *this* kind of party."

The Yakuza warlord buckled down. She wasn't about to lose her lifelong virginity in a meaningless vampire orgy, and meeting the Chancellor was thus far her primary priority. "I completely understand that, and I don't mean to offend anyone. But I just need to speak to him first," she said calmly. And then she glared into the gorgeous vampire's green eyes. "And you will not convince me otherwise."

Joelle clenched her teeth in anger and promptly clutched Boss Oh around the throat with a slender hand. She then lifted her two feet into the air and barked with sharpened incisors. "I couldn't wait to fuck your brains out. But now no one gets that chance!"

Boss Oh kicked her feet and tried to gasp for air. Her harlequin mask and summer hat fell to the ground. "Please! I just need to speak to him!"

"No one gets to speak to him!"

"Only... *two... words...* that's it!"

"Only two words? Tell *me* these two words that he must know!"

The Yakuza boss continued to flail and started losing her strength. But she managed to squeeze them out. "*Misake... Saku-moto!*"

Joelle's eyes blinked twice and then she dropped Boss Oh, who collapsed hard to her knees, gasping for air.

"What about Misake Sakumoto?" asked the vampire.

"I can get her... for him. I know she's wanted by... *your kind.*"

The redhead perked her brows, impressed at a human's knowledge. "Really? So you know about *our kind*? And you know she's our enemy number one?"

"Yes. She's actually why I'm here. I... I wasn't invited."

Any anger left quickly dissipated from the vampire's face. "Wasn't invited? And yet you got inside." She smiled wryly. "Because of my negligence."

Boss Oh finally stood up with her fallen hat and mask. She handed the mask back to Joelle. "Because of my supreme acting skills."

Joelle laughed. "You see? I knew something was off about you."

"Because I'm not dumb?"

"Definitely not."

Joelle took in a breath and looked down the hall. "I will take you straight to the Chancellor, on one condition."

"Name it."

"No one finds out I let you in."

Boss Oh pondered, remembering El Enano's plea deal with her. "Vampires are really afraid of other vampires finding out they broke a code."

"You've got that right."

"Deal," nodded the Yakuza *oyabun*.

Joelle reopened the door to the orgy to retrieve her clothes. And when she did, Boss Oh caught a glimpse of the first human getting his neck bitten. For the first time, she thought about how similar she was to a vampire, having bitten off her own fair share of body parts.

"How did you get in?"

Chancellor Valiquette stood in a robe in his parlor, visibly annoyed.

Joelle was next to him with her arms folded, acting equally perturbed. "Go ahead, tell him what you told me."

Boss Oh calmly spoke. "I waited until someone – I don't know who, I didn't pay attention – entered the coded door and threw a shoe to prevent it from closing all the way."

"A shoe?!" Viktor laughed. "Imagine that! Infiltrated by a shoe! And then?"

"I walked down the stairs, through the hall, and managed to catch – I'm sorry I never got your name." She pointed at the red head.

"Joelle."

"Yes, Joelle. She was entering a... *room*."

The Chancellor walked up to Boss Oh and circled her. "Let me get this straight. You walked – unescorted – through a vampire fortress with no interference..." He sniffed her neck. "... and no one smelled your blood?"

Boss Oh looked at Joelle, who quickly covered for her.

"I smelled her, but I honestly thought it was one of the other invited humans."

Viktor read Joelle's face for a moment. He then approached her and grabbed her hand, which was still holding her harlequin mask. "You missed out on the feeding."

"And the fucking," said Joelle.

"Indeed, indeed," he responded. The Chancellor walked across his parlor and slid an ornamental sword off the wall. He returned to Boss Oh. "And you risked your life so that you can speak to me?"

"I did. We have a common interest. Or shall I say... *enemy*."

Chancellor Valiquette turned grim. Even without saying her name, the mere mention of an "enemy" seemed to conjure up mental images of the Asian headache that had consumed him the better part of the last year. "Misake," he muttered.

Boss Oh slowly nodded.

Viktor then suddenly swiveled and promptly sliced off Joelle's head. He turned the blade and placed it under Boss Oh's chin.

"Why'd you do that?!" she yelled.

"You still have orange and yellow glitter around your eyes."

The Yakuza *oyabun* turned her eyes down to the harlequin mask, still being held by Joelle's decapitated corpse. The Chancellor was astute. But she had no time to admire him or feel bad for the beautiful, fallen vampire.

"And now, you're next," said Viktor.

chapter 55

"I've come all the way from Japan for your help," said Boss Oh, as the tip of the Chancellor's bloody sword remained precariously on her neck.

"I'm in no business to help a human."

"Not even if it's to take down Misake Sakumoto?"

"We'll get her in due time," said Viktor. "She's been a nuisance, but I've had to deal with worse in my century and a half of being undead. Tell me... how did you even come to the knowledge of the Castille and the vampires?"

Boss Oh remembered her promise to El Enano. And though she couldn't help Joelle, she still wanted to honor it. Besides, she had a better fib to tell. "Misake is flaunting it all around Japan. She speaks regularly of vampire culture and about the Castille and about you."

"About me?"

"Especially about you. And how you have an insatiable appetite for sex... but the inability to lead a people." Boss Oh braced herself for the Chancellor's reaction.

But he only curled an amused grin. "Well... stories can only go so far."

"She calls herself a 'Jampyre.'"

"Jam-py-er," repeated the Chancellor, pronouncing it slowly. He shrugged. "Has a certain ring to it."

"So, will you help me stop her?"

"We had planned on stopping her, regardless of your visit today."

"But I can offer you any of our resources."

"You asking me for help proves your own resources have been futile."

Boss Oh slumped her shoulders. It didn't appear that there was anything she could say to convince the Chancellor otherwise.

"What is your name?" asked Viktor.

"Noriko. Why?"

The vampire leader dropped his sword to his side. "Because I like to know the names of anyone I drink." He instantly flashed his fangs.

"Wait!" implored Boss Oh. "I can give you something in return."

"There is nothing you can offer that I need."

"It's not a need," said the Yakuza *oyabun* quietly. "It's a… *prize*." A sorrowful tear sparkled from her eye.

"A prize? I'm intrigued. What is it?"

"My body. It has been untouched by any man."

The Chancellor's brows raised. "You're a virgin?"

"My entire life," said Boss Oh, with a touch of sadness. "I've been waiting for the perfect moment. But it has eluded me… *until now*."

Viktor seemed touched, silenced by her sincerity.

"And if I am to still die by your hands," added Boss Oh. "Then why not do it after your hands have be stilled me?" Without waiting for a response, she began to slowly undress. Layer after layer, the Japanese criminal warlord stripped in tantalizing fashion. For a middle-aged woman, she had a body to die for.

The Chancellor's fangs slowly receded. He grabbed Boss Oh's hand and escorted her to his bedroom that oozed sensuality. His satin-covered bed was the size of two kings with a plethora of plush pillows. It was an amusement park for the sexually deviant.

They fucked for the next several hours. And then again the following day. Chancellor Valiquette even cancelled a general session with his government board members to spend more time with his new lover.

Boss Noriko Oh was enraptured by the enigmatic vampire. Though she had always imagined a spectacular wedding night with a handsome and strong-willed Japanese man when she'd lose her innocence, she couldn't think of a more satisfying alternative. And the fact that she never once thought about Misake Sakumoto or Yakuza business in general while she was being tended to by the uber-talented and experienced Viktor

Valiquette allowed her to truly experience a mental getaway. A welcomed release. A vacation to an erotic resort.

The former Noriko Suzuki, now known as the Yakuza *oyabun* Boss Oh, and revered as Madame Gorudo, was no longer a virgin.

It wasn't until the finale of the umpteenth time, after she shuddered in an orgasmic crescendo and collapsed onto Viktor's chest, that the topic of the Jampyre was finally brought up again.

"So, Noriko," started the Chancellor. "How is it you'd like my help?"

Boss Oh slipped to his side in sweat. "I want to know everything and more about her. Her weaknesses, her strengths. I want to know about everything she did while she was here stateside. Where she went. Who she met. What she touched. And then I want to know the same for her two male counterparts."

The Chancellor nodded. "Ah, yes. Quite the fugitive trio. A renowned member of *Vampiros Oscuros*, a highly once-promising Black Magic *Impundulu*, and an – what we'll call temporarily – an ambitious and impetuous Jampyre, who I've heard may be part demigoddess?"

"How did you hear that?"

"A Queen Cobra told me. Is it true?"

Boss Oh continued her skepticism of the rumor. "No."

The Chancellor chuckled. "Well, anyway, I'll put you in touch with our historian. He has done an excellent job documenting the pieces of Misake's misadventures here and especially in Texas."

"Thank you. And we are continuing our efforts to stop her back home."

Suddenly, Viktor's cell phone rang. He picked it up to read the display. "Ahh. My informant in Japan." He watched Boss Oh's expression as he answered. "El Enano? Is there something wrong?"

There was silence on the other end.

"El Enano? Are you there? Is something wrong?"

"This isn't El Enano," said Cyprian's voice finally.

Viktor gave a concerned side-eye to Boss Oh. "Cyprian the Dominion?"

"That's right."

"How are you, my boy?" said Viktor, turning on the speaker and his charm.

"I'm fine."

"That's good to hear. Are you ready to come home?"

"Yeah, I think so," said Cyprian. "In fact, I think we're all ready to put this behind us and start leading normal lives again."

"Oh, Cyprian Dugas," started Viktor, who then looked at Boss Oh and shook his head with a mocking grin. "I'm sorry, but that can't happen. All of you must still face the consequences for your actions."

Cyprian's voice turned to stone. "We've easily disposed of everyone you've sent to kill us, including your beloved Tebeau, Uriel's own sister Gabriella, my own sire-mate Atalia, and now your fucking midget messenger. We're willing to forget it all. All you need to do is forget as well."

The Chancellor placed his hand over the phone and turned to Boss Oh. "These efforts of yours. Will they work?"

"Ultimately."

"The *Impundulu* actually has a point," said Viktor, who seemed to be playing devil's advocate. "We can cut our losses and just allow whatever has transpired to stay isolated in Japan."

"Never!" Boss Oh pulled away from the vampire, offended at the notion. "I want her destroyed to the point that even her memory will be erased from all history! That includes anyone she's ever been associated with!"

The Chancellor smiled proudly. He uncovered the phone and sighed, "Prepare to die." He then promptly clicked off and waited for his lover's appeasement.

"If it's the last thing I ever do in my life, so shall be it," she said.

"You needn't worry," offered Viktor.

Boss Oh nodded and returned to his side. "I'm sorry about your informant. He was – without a doubt – the toughest I've ever faced in extracting information." El Enano was apparently dead, so there was no more need to keep his end of the deal. And it was a good opportunity to prove her worth to the Chancellor. Boss Oh held her breath for his reaction to the confession.

The Chancellor pondered for a moment, smiled, and then stroked her hair. "My, my, my. You continue to surprise me. Such a ruthless bitch. If you were of French descent, I'd turn you in a heartbeat. In fact, I might not even be upset if you told me you lied and weren't a virgin."

"That was not a lie."

"I know. I could tell."

Boss Oh smiled and thought back to the phone conversation. "Cyprian – he's the black one, right?"

"Yes."

"He knows magic?"

"He does."

"Does that pose a problem?"

"Most definitely.

"How do we combat that?"

Viktor went into deep thought for a moment. "There's someone else you should meet."

chapter 56

"Chancellor Valiquette! What a surprise!" said Imamu, almost choking on his hookah.

Viktor escorted Boss Oh into the curio shop. They both perused it as if genuinely interested to see its inventory.

"Is there anything I can help you find, Mr. Chancellor? I wish I had known of your arrival, and I would have tidied up the place a little."

"No need," said the Chancellor dryly. "A store of this nature has more charm the more in disarray it is."

Imamu nodded, though he was beginning to look nervous. He waited patiently for the two customers to finish. Boss Oh picked up an oriental vase with tiger artwork; the same one Cyprian had picked up many moons ago. She brushed off the dust.

"You can have that if you'd like," said Imamu. "Special price for friends of the Chancellor."

Boss Oh placed it back down. "No, thanks. It's made in China."

The Chancellor approached Imamu. "Imamu. If my memory serves me, those sired by your high priestess all must visit you at some point, correct? To... erm... *activate*... their powers?"

"Mm hm. 'Activate' is an interesting word, but yes... I guess so."

"What is that process?"

Imamu turned grim. He furled his brows. "Mr. Chancellor?"

"No need to worry, Imamu," said Viktor. "My friend Noriko is fascinated by our customs and would like to know."

"But she is of… *human blood*… Mr. Chancellor."

Viktor leaned into Imamu and whispered, "Just humor tonight's dinner, won't you?" And then he smirked.

It took a moment, but the wise old *Impundulu* vampire finally figured out his meaning. He sniffed and got a whiff of the *Revendique* made with the Chancellor's blood in Boss Oh's system. Imamu wholeheartedly laughed. "Come follow me inside." Imamu escorted them through the beads and into the back room. "After our High Priestess Kwan'de'melu'da—"

"—Kwan'de what?" asked Boss Oh.

"Kwan'de'melu'da. After her yearly ritual of turning one male and one female into a vampire, they each visit me in this room where their souls I guess you can say – *are activated* – within their bodies to become the spiritual guides of their powers."

The Yakuza warlord looked around the unkempt room at all of the voodoo staples. She looked highly skeptical that anything would help her in the war against Misake. Until a large, wooden chest caught her attention. "What is in there?"

"Ah," said Imamu. "That is the most important step of the entire process." He opened the chest to reveal all of the voodoo dolls. A couple of new ones sat on top. "These are the physical conduits of their spirits."

"They look like voodoo dolls."

"Many call them that. Mm hm."

Boss Oh eyed several of the dolls, taking note of one that was completely bare. The fake hair and clothes had all fallen off. The stitching looked frail and ready to unravel. "What's wrong with that one?"

"Oh! I forgot to take that one out." Imamu reached for the naked doll and its discarded components. "She passed on, unfortunately."

"Atalia the Versifier?" said Viktor.

"Yes. May she rest in peace. I will give it a proper burial."

Boss Oh squinted and recalled Atalia's name from the conversation Viktor had with Cyprian the night before. That prompted the abrupt question, "Where's Cyprian the Dominion's?"

Imamu blinked hard and looked at the Chancellor.

"You heard her," he said. "Where is his?"

The *Impundulu* vampire reluctantly pointed to a red Nike Air Jordan shoebox sitting on a shelf. "He wanted his to have a special home."

Without seeking permission, Boss Oh grabbed the box and opened the lid. Inside, Cyprian had lined the interior with pictures of his sister Lucie throughout her life. Many of them were of each other together in happier times. And the voodoo doll that resembled her laid embedded within her favorite dress, scrunched up to make a cushiony bed. "Why is it dressed like a girl?"

"His soul is driven by a female," said Imamu.

"The one in the pictures?"

"Mm hm."

"Interesting. Do they work like real voodoo dolls?"

"How do you mean?"

"If I stick a pin into it, will he feel it?"

Again, Imamu looked at the Chancellor with concern, who only implored him to answer with stern eyes. "Yes."

"I need to borrow it," said Boss Oh, promptly taking the doll out of the box.

"No, no, no. They must stay here," decreed Imamu, reaching for it.

The Yakuza *oyabun* pulled it away.

Imamu turned to Viktor. "Mr. Chancellor, please. The High Priestess would not allow it."

"She's just borrowing it, Imamu. She will return it. You have my word."

The *Impundulu* thought long and hard about his next word. "No."

Viktor barked. "Imamu the Pundit. Do not disobey your Chancellor."

"I'm sorry, Mr. Chancellor. But the conduits all stay with me. They are to be under my protection at all times."

"Then there will be consequences."

Imamu stared into the vampire leader's eyes. His mind was obviously in mental turmoil. After a moment, he said, "So be it." And then his eyes radiated green. But before he could unleash his magic, Boss Oh promptly extracted a wooden chopstick from her hair bun and stabbed him in the gut with it.

The color in his eyes quickly dissipated, and he dropped to a knee.

Imamu looked up at Boss Oh, completely stricken. He then looked over at his leader and implored, "Chancellor... *please... do something.*"

But before Viktor could react, Boss Oh seized a claymore sword leaning against the corner of the room and promptly sliced off Imamu's head.

The *Impundulu* vampire's head rolled to the Chancellor's feet. His eyes were still wide open like two full moons. A single tear rolled down the face as he gasped his last breath.

Viktor was shocked. "What have you done?!"

"You told him there would be consequences."

"Imprisonment! That is what I was referring to!"

"Oops," said Boss Oh, not really caring. She zeroed in on her new prized voodoo doll, as the Chancellor still wallowed with concern.

"The High Priestess will be upset," he said.

"So? Are you not her leader as well?"

"I am," said Viktor. "But she can be an unreasonable bitch."

Boss Oh grinned and approached him. She seductively put a hand on his shoulder and kissed him lightly on the lips. "Get used to it."

The Chancellor inhaled her essence, and his concern seemed to quickly turn into one of sexual compulsion. Boss Oh's impetuous nature and wild abandon seemed to be an erotic drug he couldn't get enough of. He escorted her down to the rickety cot, where they made unbridled love.

And Cyprian's voodoo doll never left Boss Oh's hand.

chapter 57

When they finally left Imamu's curio shop, Boss Oh nearly stepped on a dead lightning bird. She paused momentarily at the corpse, staring at its bent neck. She recalled the moment when she noticed a similar bird hovering over Cyprian in the pirate battle on Hakata Bay. Coincidence? Probably not. For good measure, she went ahead and stepped on it anyway, crushing its skull into the pavement.

Back at the Castille, Boss Oh gave Boss Watanabe a call. "What is the status?"

"Boss Teruya is dead. As all of his *kobun*."

"He never stood a chance," said Boss Oh. "Was he backed into a corner of the hotel?"

"Yes. But he managed to die with honor."

"I'm sure the Gods will be so proud," remarked Boss Oh dryly.

"There's more," said Boss Watanabe. "Boss Ito lost half of his ninja, and then surrendered the other half to her."

"Stupid fool."

"Yes. He did *not* die honorably. Regardless, your plan is still proceeding accordingly," said Boss Watanabe. "Two of the families have been wiped out, leaving only Boss Uehara and ours. Misake is doing exactly as we hoped. Soon it will be our family as the sole power in Tokyo."

Boss Oh pondered. "So then Boss Uehara will most definitely be next. Is he prepared?"

"He sent Misake an invitation to accompany him in a ceremony in her honor."

"Ceremony?"

Boss Watanabe proceeded to explain Boss Uehara's plan to trap the vampires inside of the Grand Nikko banquet hall with hidden explosives. Naturally, Boss Oh was skeptical it would work, but came up with her own idea to assist.

"Let me know when it begins," she told Boss Watanabe. "To the exact second."

On the night of the banquet, Boss Oh ensured she was not in the middle of fucking the Chancellor when the thirty-minute countdown began. In fact, she had to abruptly cut a session short when she got the text message.

The Chancellor wasn't very pleased. "What are you doing?"

"I'm sorry, but I have something important to tend to." Boss Oh set a timer on her phone and stood naked by an armoire.

"More important than my unsatisfied loins?" Viktor laid on his back, his manhood reaching for the ceiling.

"This could be the end of Misake Sakumoto."

"My, my, my," said the Chancellor. "That statement just gave me the tingles."

Boss Oh smirked and returned to the bed. She sat on the edge and placed her cell phone before her so she could monitor the countdown. And then with one hand, she continued to appease the Chancellor.

After switching hands several times, Boss Oh wasn't able to bring the Chancellor to a climax. So she went ahead and climbed on top and shrouded him, placing the cell phone on his chest. She barely moved, instead practicing Kegel exercises.

Viktor was amused at the Yakuza *oyabun's* concentration on the duty at hand and her willingness to please him by multi-tasking. But he let her be, glued to her highly anticipatory face as she, in turn, kept her gaze on the timer.

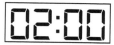

The Chancellor had his eyes closed, relaxing to the slow and rhythmic pulses occurring in his nether regions. But when the timer reached two minutes, he felt Boss Oh shift and reach over to the bed stand. She opened the drawer and pulled out Cyprian's voodoo doll and placed it next to the phone, hardly missing a beat.

Boss Oh plunged an ice pick through the heart of the voodoo doll. She lifted it, sending the sharp point all the way through. She then began riding the Chancellor like he was a horse nearing the finish line of the Kentucky Derby.

When the alarm on her cell phone jingled the end of the countdown, it was intertwined with the faint sound of three cosmic goddesses screaming in terror and the orgasmic frenzy simultaneously climaxing from Boss Oh and the Chancellor. The Yakuza warlord collapsed onto the French vampire's chest. She didn't bother to turn off the cell phone alarm, letting it chime what was hopefully a symbolic victory.

Twenty minutes later, Boss Watanabe called Boss Oh. It was difficult to hear him, since chaos reigned in the background with sirens blaring. "The entire building is gone, so is half a city block!"

"Any survivors?"

"All I see is rubble and dust right now!"

"You have men all around?"

"Of course!"

"It doesn't matter what it takes," said Boss Oh. "Pay off whomever, however much you need to. I want all three of those bodies in our possession. If limbs have been separated, I want every limb. If organs have been crushed into a million tiny pieces, then I want a million tiny pieces."

"As you wish."

Boss Oh was about to click off when she had an afterthought. "Do you see any dead birds anywhere?"

"Excuse me?"

"Birds! The animals with wings that fly in the sky! Do you see any?!"

"No, I don't think so."

"Have all your men look for dead birds. I don't care what kind, or how many. If they see any, I want it. Do you understand?!"

There was a long silence on the other end of the phone. "I understand," he said finally. "Three bodies. All of the pieces. Any dead bird as well."

Boss Oh clicked off the phone as more sounds of chaos and shouting authorities filtered through. She didn't look very satisfied.

"I love hearing you speak Japanese." The Chancellor rolled to his side and faced her. "So?"

"It's time for me to return to Japan."

"What for?"

"To confirm Misake's death, or finish her off once and for all."

Viktor nodded. "Tomorrow you speak to our historian. And then I have a gift for you."

"A gift?"

"A going-away present."

chapter 58

Early the next morning, Boss Oh found herself in the Arts District of New Orleans and sitting in a loft on a couch with three cats. Balzac St. Laurent sat across from her, wearing a purple wig and matching robe.

"Oh, I remember Misake, *dahling*," he started. "She got me into a whole lot of trouble."

"How?"

"She had a marvelous story about a fortune teller in San Antonio who was an Almost and threw out a Vee name to make me think her intentions were on the up and up." Balzac paused and appeared to read Boss Oh's confused face. "They weren't, obviously."

"So what did you do?"

"I got her some Nectar so she could get close to a Latino hunk. I thought it was for true love, but Misake just ended up using him to turn herself into a Vee."

"They're still together in Japan."

"So I've heard. He *does* love her. I could tell it in his eyes when his sister Gabriella – who I believe *also* fell for her – helped break him out of the Castille. And they're there with Cyprian Dugas, who as far as I'm concerned, was manipulated just as much. What a complete shame for the two bad boys."

Boss Oh nodded, stroking Pekkle the Cat, who had crawled onto her lap. "Do you think she's still using them?"

"I think they must've grown close, being branded outlaws together."

There was a moment of silence as Balzac curled a grin. "Still... I did admire Misake. She was headstrong and knew what she wanted. She was also gracious enough to include me in my first Vee orgy."

"You hadn't been in any before?"

Balzac's face turned sincere, recalling. "I avoided the ones at the Castille, not wanting to feel the pain of possible rejection... *for obvious reasons, dahling*." He waved a hand down his body and uncrossed his legs, exposing his missing genitals. "But she pulled me in, and I had the time of my life."

Boss Oh remained silent, partly shocked at the impromptu visual, partly to let Balzac continue his happy reflection, and partly because she didn't care to hear anything positive about the Jampyre bitch.

"But I know she is an illegal Vee and must be stopped," said Balzac with a sigh. "The Chancellor said you plan on doing that?"

"She has caused chaos in my homeland and a war to erupt on the streets of Tokyo."

Balzac perked his brows.

"The Chancellor mentioned there might be other parties that want her dead?" said Boss Oh.

"If you believe in legend, then the Goddess of the Underworld, *La Madre of Los Vampiros Oscuros*, most assuredly would like to have her head as well."

"How's that?"

"It was believed that Uriel and Gabriella Santana were the caretakers of her spirit. So when Misake was responsible for Uriel's betrayal and Gabriella's death, it left the Goddess in dire straits."

Boss Oh still didn't want to believe in the existence of celestial beings, but they were being mentioned more and more. And now that she believed in real life vampires, perhaps it was time to change her stance.

"And supposedly it was their Goddess who alerted them of the divine blood running in Misake's own veins," added Balzac, helping Boss Oh's cause.

"So... is that Goddess still in dire straits?" asked the Yakuza *oyabun*.

"I've heard she found new caretakers from Mexico City. Two delicious Vees named Camazotz and El Galán," answered Balzac, who didn't say any more than that. "It's almost time to take you back to the Chancellor."

"He said you were taking me some place new?"

Balzac stood. "That I am. But first… makeover!"

chapter 59

Boss Oh was dolled up and given curls. Balzac was more conservative than usual with a brunette wig and matching dress, but he still looked gorgeous.

The French almost-transgendered-vampire took Boss Oh to a sprawling piece of private land outside of New Orleans. Chancellor Valiquette owned a restored plantation house with curled staircases leading up to it. He was already waiting for them on the ground, admiring Boss Oh's new look. "You just couldn't help yourself, could you, Balzac?"

"Gorgeous skin like hers? No, sir," he said. "It's true what they say – Asian don't raisin."

Viktor led them behind the house to a set of locked storm doors. He used a key to open them and then descended down the stairs into a musty room with lit lamps. "This used to be slave quarters back before the Civil War."

"What is it now?" asked Boss Oh.

"*Slave quarters*," said Balzac with a dry grin.

As the room opened up, Boss Oh saw a large flat screen television on the wall illuminating the rest of it. There was a pool table, foosball table, a miniature bar, and four cots arranged in the corner. And at a poker table in another corner, there were four Latino vampires playing cards.

But they weren't your average, everyday vampires.

They had horns. Long tails. Sharp claws. They looked very much like Suki, the Japanese woman Cyprian had accidentally sired several months earlier. Except they were all stocky, dark-skinned, and almost seven-feet tall.

Boss Oh's jaw dropped at the sight.

Viktor offered an explanation. "Our spy in Japan witnessed Cyprian sire a Japanese woman and turned her into something similar to these hybrids. We had heard that that's what B.M. *Impundulu* vampires were capable of, if allowed to sire anyone from another race. When El Enano described the details, needless to say, I was intrigued. So I had Placide the Laconic indulge me with a science experiment."

Unseen until now, Placide the Laconic waved from another corner, "Wassup." He was an *Impundulu* vampire, currently reading the latest Frances Trilone novel.

"Where do they come from?" whispered Boss Oh.

"Illegal immigrants from Mexico," said the Chancellor. "We offered them jobs on my land, food, and eternal life."

"The American dream, *dahling*," added Balzac.

"So they're just different-looking vampires?" asked Boss Oh.

"They're also bigger and stronger. Something in their genetic composition increased their muscle mass and length of their limbs. Thus far we haven't seen any signs of magic capability. Right, Placide?"

"Nah."

"And you said you discovered something new yesterday?"

"Skin."

"Oh, right! Their skin is impenetrable by metal."

Boss Oh perked a brow. She spied Placide's sword leaning next to him – and in an almost identical scenario to Imamu's death – promptly sliced off the head of one of the hybrids.

Blood spewed and sprayed all over the room. The other three Latinos quickly backed away from the table in fear.

"Why do you keep doing that?!" cried the Chancellor.

"You said their skin was impenetrable by metal," said Boss Oh. "I was testing it."

Viktor looked over at Placide, who didn't flinch, but was vaguely amused at the violent act. "Not that one." He pointed to the Latino hybrid in the corner.

The Chancellor shook his head. "So only *one* of them cannot be harmed by metal?"

Placide nodded.

"That would've been nice to know, Placide."

"You didn't ask," said the *Impundulu* vampire.

Boss Oh was unfazed, even though she was dripping in blood. She stepped closer to the "impenetrable" Latino and noticed his skin was scalier, resembling a reptile's. She touched it and marveled. "Amazing. I wonder why this one is different?"

The Chancellor was still perturbed, wiping his face, eyeing Placide like a disappointed father.

Balzac offered his opinion, "Probably not a pure Mexican."

"Half Puerto Rican," chimed in Placide.

"See?"

Boss Oh continued to admire the Latino hybrid. "So you're just going to use them to work on your land?"

"Oh, no, no," said Viktor, finally coming back around. "I am grooming them to be a new division of my Vampire Extraction Squad. An elite division."

"A secret division," said Balzac.

"Yes. Placide has trained them in some fighting techniques." The Chancellor motioned to Placide. "What have you taught them?"

"Punching," he said, without looking up from his book.

"That's it?"

"Kicking."

Viktor rolled his eyes. "And Balzac came up with a name for them. What was it?"

"*The Beastly Boys.*"

The Chancellor blinked at Balzac for a moment, and then turned back to Boss Oh. "The name is a work in progress."

The Yakuza *oyabun* encircled the trio, now deeply fascinated.

"Pick one," said Viktor.

Boss Oh raised her brows, almost giddy. "Really?"

"To be your own personal bodyguard until you take complete control over Japan."

Still glued to his book, Placide the Laconic chimed in. "Tail. Hat."

The Chancellor looked at Boss Oh and confirmed with a nod. "Yes. You obviously can't flaunt them in public unless the tail is tucked in and claws and horns are hidden. Beanies work the best."

Balzac started clapping in excitement. "Yay! Hat shopping!"

chapter 60

Boss Oh ended up choosing the reptile-skinned half-Mexican, half-Puerto Rican, vampire hybrid Beastly Boy named Severo, who coincidentally was the most attractive. He had flowing black hair, massive biceps, dimples, and a passing understanding of English.

After hat shopping with Balzac and returning back to the Castille, Boss Oh began packing her things.

The Chancellor was just finishing up a phone call. "Good. Stand by and wait for further instructions." He hung up and smiled at Boss Oh. "You will be getting one more gift soon."

"Oh? Another handsome vampire, perhaps?"

"Let's just say it's the ace up your sleeve you asked for. If you need it. Procured by our one and only mortal bounty hunter."

"Mortal?"

"He's human, but quite the character. We call him 'The Cowboy.'"

"I'll see him in Japan?"

"Yes. And he may be of more use to you."

Boss Oh approached the Chancellor and sighed. "You've been too good to me."

"Your success will be my success."

"Is that all?" She put her arms around his neck. "Will you miss me?"

"Of course I will."

"I'll miss you. I can't imagine fucking anyone else."

"Ah, but you will," said Viktor. "Now that you've been soiled, you will undoubtedly sample more flowers with wild abandon!"

Boss Oh broke away. "And you won't be jealous? That another man will *soil* my body after you were the only member of the exclusive club?"

"It would be selfish of me to cast any feeling upon you that may be detrimental to you enjoying your waning days to the fullest," said the Chancellor. "Since you are a mortal, live your days as if they were your last."

The Yakuza warlord frowned with jealousy. "What if I want to become immortal? Have we not shared enough to warrant that?"

Viktor sighed. "I cannot break our laws."

"But did you not just create those mixed-breed monsters in secrecy?"

"I didn't personally sire them. It was Placide."

"But you sanctioned it."

"For the good of our people."

"Says every politician."

The Chancellor shrugged and grinned smugly, ending the topic of conversation.

Boss Oh nodded in defeat. She wasn't sure if she actually wanted to be a vampire, but she wanted to test the Chancellor. She wanted to see what kind of influence she had won over him in the previous days. Apparently not a lot; it was obvious she wasn't any more to him than a pawn in his own game against Misake.

The Chancellor's phone rang. "Yes," he said after he answered, and then listened intently for a few seconds. He frowned. "Of course. Anything you can." He then hung up and remained silent.

"What is it?"

"It appears that El Enano was not killed after all. He just showed up to our infirmary and remains unconscious in a bed."

Boss Oh winced. "She sent you a message."

Viktor slowly nodded and gritted his teeth in anger. "Message received, Misake." He turned to the Boss. "Take care of that bitch. And when you do – and if you so desire – we will continue the conversation of your prospects in becoming immortal."

She nodded in agreement (and smug victory) and then approached the drawer in the bed side table. Boss Oh opened it and pulled out Cyprian's voodoo doll – which still had an ice pick through the heart – but found many of the attachments – including the hair and clothes – had fallen off. The texture of the body looked weathered and stale. She recalled the doll she had found in Imamu's chest with similar traits, revealed to belong to a dead vampire name Atalia. She curled a sneaky, golden grin.

And then a moment later, Madame Gorudo received a text message from Boss Watanabe. All it said was:

WE HAVE HER. 😁 👍

Part Six

Obtain the low plain,
vain and pain one in the same.
Abstain to regain.

chapter 61

It was still the wee early hours of morning when the Japanese *shobo-shi* (fire fighters) continued to work furiously to subdue the blazes that roared from the rubble of what used to be the Grand Nikko banquet hall. Crowds gathered in throngs down every extended block to get a better view, as they received push back from what must've been Tokyo's entire *Keisatsu-cho* work force.

Boss Watanabe's men patiently waited. They were tasked to get first dibs on the bodies of three vampires. And certain police authorities already knew that; paid off with a ridiculous amount of bribe money.

They were also on the lookout for any dead birds. Thus far, they had found only eight. A few sparrows. A couple of house swallows. One thrush.

But there were no lightning birds.

When Lucie had dropped from the sky, its body crumpled into the street and against the curb. Every bone in the bird's body was broken, including its beak. And then shortly after the fire fighters arrived to extinguish the flames from the explosion, the overflow of water cascaded against the curb and picked up the lightning bird's light and frail body, carrying it into a nearby drainage system and dropping it down to the sewer system below.

Lucie the Lightning Bird – Cyprian the Dominion's spirit animal – was gone.

It wasn't until late the following day when Misake's newly-dyed pink hair finally glowed from within the debris. Her body was almost unrecognizable; crushed in too many places. Impaled by several objects. Charred everywhere else.

But there was still movement in her heart. One beat per minute.

The Jampyre was still alive.

Boss Watanabe's men intercepted Misake's gurney and took it to a military hospital on Yokota Air Base, which was in western Tokyo. The Yakuza had a long-standing partnership with the local American influence and was allowed to access their medical facilities with discretion.

Misake was placed into a room surrounded by Boss Watanabe's twenty best men. For good measure – and suggested by Boss Oh – they hammered wooden stakes through her wrists and ankles to prevent her from escaping.

Physicians attempted to piece the Japanese vampire back together, but a few hours into several simultaneous surgeries, they realized that Misake was healing all on her own. They backed off, incredulous. It would take nearly half a day for her wounds to fully heal and seal back together.

When Misake finally opened her eyes, Boss Watanabe stood at the foot of her bed. His eyes were wide open, as if he'd been frozen in shock for hours. "Never in all my years would I ever have believed such a story."

"Which one?" asked Misake groggily.

"Both. The goddess one. And now the vampire one."

The Jampyre attempted to move her arms, but then realized she was paralyzed from the wooden stakes puncturing her skin. She curled a touché-type of grin. "Where am I?"

"In a hospital on Yokota Air Base."

"Yokota Air Base?"

"Surely you've heard of it. In Fussa?"

Misake didn't respond, instead looking around the room. She craned her neck to look out the window, but only saw blue skies. "Where's Cyprian? And Uriel? Are they here too?"

Boss Watanabe smiled. "Your *gaijin* friends? No. Unfortunately, they didn't survive."

Misake frowned. She attempted to "sense" them, but knew that Uriel would be the only one she might have success with. But no trace was coming to her. Living or dead. So she surmised only one conclusion. "No. You're lying."

The Yakuza boss shrugged. "The rest of the bodies were beyond recognition." He looked at her bare arm, which was previously decorated by a full *irezumi*.

She followed his gaze and noticed the same thing. "What happened?"

"Your body must've lost at least two layers of skin," said Boss Watanabe. "The healing process was not kind to the art." He pulled out his phone and showed Misake a picture. It was one of her body, freshly extracted from the rubble. Completely and utterly gruesome. "You were the only survivor. But don't worry – your friends looked far worse."

Misake turned her head to the side and finally shed a tear. "So, what happens now?"

"We wait for Boss Oh. She should be flying over Hawaii right about now."

"From New Orleans?"

"Oh yes," said Boss Watanabe, with child-like enthusiasm. "She can't wait to see you."

"I'm sure. And then how long until she eliminates you?"

The Yakuza warlord quickly lost his smile.

Misake continued. "It's obvious she wanted me to do the dirty work and get rid of the other families. Otherwise, she would've helped. I mean – do you really think that she went to New Orleans only for *research*?" She attempted to raise her arms, but they collapsed. "Sorry, I attempted to do finger quotes there. But you know what I mean. No – she was out of the country so she could avoid having to protect everyone after she told all of you that joining forces would be in your best interest."

Boss Watanabe pondered. "But we joined our families prior to all of that."

"And you relinquished your title?"

"No."

"When I'm gone, Boss Oh will not be satisfied sharing a title with you. I guarantee it. She's only using you until then."

The Boss pondered and sighed, as if a part of him found the notion to be logical. "So then what? You want me to help you escape and then we can join forces against *her* now?"

"Hashtag hell no," said Misake. "I wouldn't join you. Besides, you're going to be dead soon."

Boss Watanabe snorted through his nose. When he saw that Misake was dead serious, he frowned and promptly stomped out of the room.

Later that night, Misake stared out the window at the crescent moon that seemed to be chastising her for the predicament she was experiencing. Her arms and legs were still staked to the bed. The intense healing process made her crave more blood than usual. And the Jampyre's loneliness swelled to higher levels.

But then the moon suddenly evaporated from the sky.

It was like someone flipped a switch to simulate a lunar eclipse.

chapter 62

After the massacre on Kokusai Street in Okinawa, Misake had sent her newly recruited two-hundred ninja *kobun* that were gifted by Boss Ito to Kujukuri Beach. She not only wanted to increase her influence there, but also thought it would be a low-key risk if they turned out to be traitors and remained loyal to their former leader.

But then Misake had an epiphany.

She left Uriel and Cyprian in Tokyo so that they could buy new suits for the upcoming ceremony hosted by Boss Uehara. That was strategic on her part, knowing that her two male vampire counterparts probably would not agree with her next move to solidify her stronghold as the premiere Yakuza boss. In fact, the Jampyre had a feeling they might have tried to stop her.

Misake gathered her new ninjas in an abandoned warehouse. They stood in formation, ten rows of twenty. "As you all know," she said, "The remaining families in Tokyo had formed an alliance with the sole intention of taking the Sakumoto-*kai* organization down. And as all of you should know, they have thus far failed in their attempts. Your former leader Boss Ito was the latest."

All of her newly recruited men and women continued to listen, as the Jampyre weaved in and out of their lines.

She continued. "Defeating you was not an easy task. In fact, I would rank you as the most challenging foe I've faced thus far. More challenging than Boss Tamaki's samurai, even though they only *dressed* like samurai."

Chuckles from the crowd.

"More challenging than Hanta was in our battle in the *pachinko* parlor."

Knowing nods, especially from the female ninjas of the group.

"The Genkai Wokou pirates were very tough, but the stench was their greatest strength."

That time there was uproarious laughter.

"Boss Teruya's *kobun*? I'm right-handed, but I only needed my left on that day."

The ninjas continued to laugh, many of them holding their stomachs in pain.

Misake waited for some of the laughter to die down before she continued. "But then, when I faced your team, I had finally met my match!"

The ninjas started to hoot and holler, clapping at themselves.

"But!" screamed Misake, beckoning for silence. She waited until she could hear a pin drop. "You have only been the most challenging *Japanese* enemy I have ever faced."

All of the *kobun* exchanged curious glances with each other.

Misake changed the tone in her voice, almost sounding like she was telling a campfire horror story. "The most challenging foe I've ever faced... was the same one I see in the mirror every day." She took a few more steps to drawn in breaths. "The vampire."

A hushed gasp filtered through the warehouse.

"It was a vampire who captured me in my most vulnerable state and nearly killed me. If it wasn't for an ally of mine, I'd surely be dead. It was a vampire who killed my father right before my very own eyes while I stood helpless." The Jampyre read their horrified faces as she continued her walk. "I know all of you have heard the rumors. That my mother was the Goddess Amaterasu-O-Mi-Kami, making me a demigoddess. And more recently, you may have heard that I – myself – am a vampire, making me an undead immortal. Well... I'm here to tell you... that all of it is true!"

The warehouse echoed with rumbled skepticism through the crowd. Misake waited for it to subside before she spoke again.

"I know that it's hard to believe," she said in a whisper. "The connection with my mother has been undeniable. But the transformation into a vampire has been my crown achievement. It has been my awakening. It is the source of my dominance. It will carry me to the end of time. And today… I offer the same to all of you."

The warehouse exploded with hyperactive activity. Some of the *kobun* were still skeptical and found the notion to be farcical. Some were very excited. And there were even others who looked mortified.

"I need one volunteer!" shouted Misake over the noise, which screeched to an abrupt halt. From the front of the group, she surveyed their faces until one female ninja slowly and bravely rose her hand.

"Good! What is your name?" asked Misake.

"Aiko."

"How would you like to become the world's second Jampyre, Aiko?"

Aiko bowed. "It would be an honor, Boss Sakumoto."

Since Misake was sired by Uriel – a Latino vampire – she wanted to be cautious at first. After all, Cyprian had recently turned a Japanese woman into a vampire with less-than-desirable results in the form of horns and claws, a tail, and an insatiable hunger. So Misake wanted to start with one. And that would be Aiko.

The Jampyre bit into her neck in front of the enraptured audience. In fact, the rest of the ninjas all broke formation and gathered into a circle around the ritual.

It took about forty-five minutes for Aiko to open her newly opaque eyes and see the world through an undead lens. When her sharp teeth protracted, everyone took a step back and gasped incredulously.

The results appeared to be successful – at least – in Misake's eyes.

There were no horns or claws or tails or an insatiable feral-like hunger. At least, not yet. Nothing irregular compared to what had happened to her. At least, not yet. There was no interference from Misake's mother. At least, not yet. In fact, being a demigoddess didn't seem to have an effect positively or negatively on the vampire transformation. At least, not yet.

Or did it?

It wasn't until Misake had converted three other ninjas into Jampyres that she heard Aiko's voice approaching her.

"I feel so alive," she said, even though Aiko hadn't opened her mouth.

The OG Jampyre stared at her new spawn number one. She answered back only through her mind, "And it's only the beginning."

Aiko smiled, nodding. "Yes. I can't wait."

And there it was. The anomaly in the breeding of the Japanese race.

The French had strength, power, and centuries-old influence to pave their trail. *Los Vampiros Oscuros* had even more strength and abnormal self-healing powers and were sexy AF (if you want to call that a distinct trait), and had the Queen of the Underworld to guide them. The *Impundulu* had magnificent physiques, and some harnessed the spiritual power of other souls (as initiated by their High Priestess) to use voodoo and black magic.

And now the Jampyres? Apparently had the power of telepathy. Whether it be a byproduct of Misake's divine bloodline, or just because of the differing Japanese genetic make-up was of unimportance.

Misake looked over at the third Jampyre she had created. "How do you feel?" she said in silence, zeroing in on the ninja's brain waves.

He looked up and thought, "My vision is perfect now."

The demigoddess smiled proudly. Thus far she was tickled at the aberration. Not to mention that her new recruits were already skilled ninjas. So, when Misake finally converted the rest of her team – an act that took the next sixteen hours – she had two hundred new vampire ninjas.

Jampyre ninjas?

Ninja Jampyres?

Two hundred fucking Nin-Jampyres.

chapter 63

Misake spent the next day with her newly formed Nin-Jampyres, teaching them the ways of the bloodsucker, and giving them a more theatrical appearance. She gave them custom made designer suits with stretched lining to give them more mobility. The backs of their jackets were embroidered with her own original Jampyre symbol she had designed back in Sapporo. And then she bought them all red kabuki masks that only covered the top half of their faces.

This would be her new army. And she wanted everyone to recognize them.

The Jampyre had just equipped them with matching samurai swords when Uriel and Cyprian finally found her in the warehouse.

"Misake?" said Uriel, as she whirled around.

She grinned. "Hello, boys. Do you like my new army? Perhaps my enemies will now show me more respect."

Cyprian took a step forward, scrutinizing the ninjas. It seemed that he could already tell in their eyes that something was off. "Misake – what have you done?"

The Jampyre's grin flat-lined as she stomped her foot with a war cry.

All of the Nin-Jampyres copied her and followed suit. But when they shouted, their fangs were on full display.

Uriel and Cyprian were both stunned to silence.

"Why didn't you tell us?" asked Uriel, almost choking on his words.

"So that you could stop me?"

Another long moment of bated breath as the two vampires knew she was right.

"I wasn't positive that this would work," said Misake to break the silence. "So I just wanted to do it on my own and see for myself."

Cyprian walked through the lines of newborn vampires, examining every detail. "You sired all of them personally?"

"That's right."

"How long did it take you?"

"I don't know. Most of the day."

Uriel remained at Misake's side, still befuddled. "I've never heard of such a mass transformation."

"Neither have I," chimed in Cyprian from the back of the warehouse. "And especially not by any one vampire. Siring one human alone is enough to exhaust a vampire for hours."

Misake perked a brow. "Hm. Perhaps another advantage of being part demigoddess?"

Cyprian returned to the front. "The Chancellor's gonna shit a brick when he hears about this. How are you even going to feed all of them?"

"Local blood bank," said Misake nonchalantly.

"Oh? You've already got all of this figured out?"

"We did this morning. Where are you, Hirohito?" she called out to the Nin-Jampyres.

One of them raised his head.

"Hirohito has a connection with the blood bank," said Misake. "His sister works there and should be able to give us a hook-up, or at the very least, notice of a new supply for us to raid every so often."

Cyprian sighed. "So they're staying here? Not using them in Tokyo?"

"Not until I need them. I think we've done pretty well on our own so far. Which reminds me – did the two of you find new suits?"

Both of the vampires shot curious glances to each other. They had been distracted by their side adventure in capturing El Enano and never returned to the department store. They had also agreed to not tell Misake and give her any unnecessary worry.

"They are getting tailored at the moment," lied Cyprian, even though they both did get a sense of what they would've picked out.

The Jampyre looked skeptical, trying to read the *Impundulu's* face. "Tailored? Really?"

"Yep." That was all Cyprian could counter with.

But before Misake could question any more, Uriel turned the tables on her. "What about you? Didn't you say you'd go shopping for a dress?"

"I know, I know. But, obviously, I got distracted. I'll find something."

"You should go with pink," said Uriel.

"Pink? Why?"

"I think you'd look good in it."

Even though Misake was a demigoddess and a vampire, she was still a young woman who liked to play dress-up and get pretty. So her mind went into a fashion-frenzy overload at the possibilities that could make up a pink ensemble. "Yeah. Maybe."

And that was that.

Any more conversation about the Nin-Jampyres was futile, since the deed was already done. Both Uriel and Cyprian were relegated to accepting the statement that ended all useless discussions, "It is what it is." And they had a more pressing event coming up.

The trio returned to Tokyo, leaving all two hundred Nin-Jampyres behind to protect Sakumoto-kai's coastal businesses and to be on stand-by if they were needed.

And that need would come fairly quickly.

Several days later, Misake would fall for a trap and be a victim in a catastrophic bomb explosion and find herself paralyzed in a hospital on an American military air base near Tokyo.

Boss Watanabe stood in front of her.

"Where am I?" she asked.

"In a hospital on Yokota Air Base."

"Yokota Air Base?"

"Surely you've heard of it. In Fussa?"

And that was all that was needed for the Nin-Jampyre's to find their injured and hindered leader's location. They swarmed the hospital like the plague in a third world country.

chapter 64

The sweeping blackness outside of Misake's window was interrupted every few seconds by the vision of a red, horned kabuki mask. It was an utterly horrifying sight, signaling the arrival of blood and death.

The moonlight returned from the outside as the last Nin-Jampyre scaled the wall and passed Misake's room. She listened closely as chaos erupted on the ground level with shouting by both American and Japanese patrons. But they were all abruptly silenced by the succinct sounds of slicing samurai swords.

Bodies continued to fall down the hall when Misake's door finally opened. A lone Nin-Jampyre entered and flipped up her mask. It was Aiko. And she was escorting Boss Watanabe into the room, who had blood streaming down from his ears.

"Pull out these stakes," said Misake.

Aiko approached her leader and slowly and gingerly pulled out the wooden shards.

Misake shrieked in pain as her flesh was pulled by the splinters. When they were all extracted, she remained in bed for a moment, stretching her limbs and allowing the wounds to heal. She achingly swung her legs around and sat in her paper hospital gown. "Boss Watanabe – give Aiko your cell phone."

Boss Watanabe pulled a bloody hand away from his ear and gave it to the Nin-Jampyre.

"Where are my friends?" asked Misake, as she attempted to stand on her own two feet.

"I told you. They are dead. Along with Boss Uehara, all of his *kobun*, and all of the banquet hall staff. Only you survived the blast."

Misake approached the window and looked out. She squinted at something that drew her attention, but she soon shook it off. "I don't believe you. Where are they?"

Boss Watanabe shook his head.

"Punch him in the ear again."

Aiko curled a fist and punched Boss Watanabe square in the ear. His head twisted violently in pain.

"Did you hear that?" said Misake. "I heard it. It was the sound of your eardrum exploding. You only have one left. So I will ask you one more time. Where are they?"

Boss Watanabe collapsed to his knees. "Please, Boss Sakumoto. My only priority was you. As far as I know, both of your *gaijin* friends did not survive."

"Then where are the bodies?"

He shook his head and shrugged. "Boss Oh did not disclose that to me."

"And yet you still think she will not betray you?" The Jampyre finally approached him. She motioned to Aiko. "Use his phone to record this. And then send it to Boss Oh."

"What... what are you going to do?" pleaded Boss Watanabe.

"I'm going to drink all of your blood."

"I swear to you, I don't know what happened to the bodies!"

"It doesn't matter anymore," said Misake. "I'm just fucking hungry." And with that, the Jampyre dug into his neck and ravished him. The color in Boss Watanabe's face faded as he was drained of all life.

Aiko recorded the whole feeding, until Misake looked up at the camera with her lips crimson-stained. "Hashtag – and then there was one."

The video was immediately sent to Boss Oh.

The Jampyre dropped the ragged corpse and faced Aiko. "I want all of you to turn Tokyo upside down until you find Uriel and Cyprian. If they are indeed... *dead*... then I want their bodies. Do not report back to me until you do!"

Aiko nodded and left the room.

Misake stared at the limp body of Boss Watanabe and whispered, "I know they're alive. They have to be." Tears started streaming down her face, as doubt began to plague her. She then began stomping on the Yakuza *oyabun's* head in anger until the skull shattered. She slipped down to the ground and whimpered, "Please... *please*... let them be alive."

Instinctively, Misake reached up to her neck and realized she had lost her lightning bird pendant. Again. But this time, she had the sinking feeling it would not be found. And even worse, a dread washed over her that she would never see who had given her the gift again.

Cyprian.

The Jampyre recalled her last moments in the banquet hall. The *Impundulu* vampire attempted to protect her for the umpteenth time. But then he collapsed into her arms with horror painted in his eyes and a hand across his chest like an unseen spirit had suddenly taken over his body. Misake had felt hopeless, and even though they were all heading toward impending doom, for a moment, she only felt concern for Cyprian.

"Don't go, Cyprian. I love you!" Those were Misake's final words to him.

And now he was gone. And so was Uriel.

The hospital was hauntingly quiet until sirens began to ring several miles away.

Misake stood back up, used Boss Watanabe's body to shatter the window, and then jumped to freedom.

She ran all the way home, where she found more death.

chapter 65

Her home had been pillaged and vandalized, and any *kobun* left protecting it was massacred and placed in the rock garden, forming the *kanji* letter for "OH." Misake knew she was being mocked for her corpse display back at the Tamaki compound in Sapporo. To top it off, all of the koi fish were skewered with wooden stakes, including Katsu Hiro.

The walls inside the house were drenched in blood and every piece of furniture destroyed and unsalvageable. Her father's business office – the one she had kept as a shrine to her own mother – was turned into a sea of undecipherable junk. And when Misake entered her bedroom, she was met with an even more gruesome and unapologetic visual.

The corpse of her father Shintoku Sakumoto had been dug up and hung in the corner of her room. He had the name "OH" carved into his belly.

Misake immediately brought her father down and laid him on her mattress, which had been ripped to shreds. She began to cry, burying her head into his decayed chest. "I'm so sorry I have failed you again, Papa," she said to the dead body. She continued to weep until slumber fell upon her.

When morning arrived, Misake began the arduous task of putting things back together. She first reburied her father, but kept him on the property instead of the cemetery. She placed all of her dead *kobun* into the meat locker. Even though she felt bad for losing them, there was no sense in wasting the blood, even though it was nearing the "best by" date due to being exposed to the sun for so many hours. And then Misake attempted to scrub the house clean.

It wasn't until the end of the day when Misake was thoroughly exhausted that she finally realized her divine *katana* was missing. In fact, so were the handcrafted samurai swords she had gifted to Uriel and Cyprian. Since the invitation to Boss Uehara's banquet had asked for no weapons, the vampires had placed all three on a sword rack.

That sword rack was smashed into pieces and missing its riches. Only Cyprian's claymore sword (previously Atalia's) remained on the floor, unworthy of theft or destruction.

Misake picked up the sword and flicked at the dangling dice. She then furrowed her brows in anger. She thought that by now Boss Oh had surely returned from New Orleans. And she also thought it was time for the bitch to die. But without her own divine weapon, without Uriel and Cyprian, and now with her formidable Nin-Jampyre army on assignment seeking her vampire friends, she knew she needed to wait. She called out to Aiko telepathically. "Aiko – status?"

"We believe we have found them, Boss Sakumoto," said Aiko. "We are on the way now."

"Uriel and Cyprian?"

"Yes. We found a Police Chief who had accepted a bribe from Boss Watanabe. We beat his children until he revealed their whereabouts."

Misake lingered on the "beat his children" part and was momentarily mortified. Even though Boss Oh was pulling out all the stops in destroying Misake, the Jampyre thought she herself had at least an ounce of scruples.

"His children are in their thirties," said Aiko, as if she could sense her boss's moral dilemma.

"Ah. Okay," sighed Misake. "Where are they?"

"In a horse stable outside of Osaka."

"How far are you?"

"About ten miles out. Shall we wait for you?"

Misake knew that she was about two-hundred and fifty miles away from Osaka. Though she wanted desperately to rescue her friends herself, it would take her much too long to get there. "No. Get them. And leave no survivors. Not even Boss Oh."

"Understood, Boss Sakumoto."

Misake wrung her hands and waited ten minutes. And then she waited another ten. Five minutes later, she began to worry. How long should it take for two-hundred Nin-Jampyres to infiltrate a horse stable and rescue two vampires? Was it heavily guarded by Boss Oh's *kobun*? Surely her immortal ninjas wouldn't be a match. Misake couldn't wait any longer. "Aiko? What is happening?"

There was a long moment of silence.

And then Aiko finally answered with a shaky voice. "Boss Sakumoto – we stormed it from all sides. There doesn't seem to be anyone in here."

"No one?"

"No. Not even your friends."

"Horses?"

"No. It's completely empty. But the floor is covered in something sticky. I don't know what it is. It's, like, all over the walls too."

Misake's eyes widened.

"A lot of dead rats too… like they were gutted."

And that's when Misake screamed in her mind. "Get out of there!"

"Why?"

"It's snake venom and rat's blood! You've been set up!"

Aiko didn't say another word. In fact, Misake couldn't get a hold of any Nin-Jampyres. Her mind remained a quiet vacuum of despair. It wasn't until a pain ripped through her cerebral cortex and continued to radiate for several minutes that the Jampyre realized a horrific truth.

All of her spawn were dead.

chapter 66

Misake took a train from Tokyo to Osaka. It was a dreadful trip, trying not to think about what carnage might be laid before her and the house she left in shambles behind. Her life was in complete disarray, so it was difficult distracting her mind with any positive thoughts. Whether or not she'd find Uriel and Cyprian was a mystery, but she knew it wouldn't be good news. Either they were dead with her army, or still missing.

For brief moments, she managed to recall some happy thoughts about Uriel Santana. Their wickedly terrifying but erotic courtship in San Antonio and the passionate reunion in Tokyo were certainly the highlights. She felt a great deal of regret for swooping into his life and destroying everything he had. Including his life, if that was the case. She continuously sensed his blood – in fact, it was more so at that moment – but she also knew his blood was a part of hers.

But when Misake's visions turned to Cyprian Dugas, she realized she had many more positive memories to draw from. She met him in New Orleans with her roommate and bestie Shanice Roberson. He was the first man she ever made love with and to this day, the most satisfying. Cyprian joined her and a transgendered vampire named Jacinda (Balzac) in an intoxicating and surreal vampire orgy that still filtered into her dreams every so often.

Cyprian had also saved Misake's life from VES agent Tebeau when he was hauling her in an airplane across the Pacific Ocean on the way to Chancellor Valiquette and the Castille. And then again against the Genkai

Wokou pirates with his surprising "Street Fighter" move. And the *Impundulu* vampire also single-handedly put an end to the battle against Boss Ito's second wave of ninjas. He was always there for Misake, and she couldn't return the favor. Her last vision of him – the pain-stricken eyes as he was cradled in her arms – was something that would be emblazoned in her conscience forever.

Misake held her breath as the train pulled to a stop. It didn't take long to find the stable, since the stench of two-hundred dead vampires still wafted through the air like Hell's fragrance. The foundation of the stable remained; the rest of it was in ashes. The bodies were mostly gone, burned and dissolved to oblivion. All that remained were some samurai swords. Some of their motorcycles. Charred kabuki masks. And a couple Jampyre jackets.

Misake had promised the ninjas immortality. But in a matter of a week, all of her newborn baby vampires were dead. Uriel and Cyprian were gone. And what *kobun* she had remaining in other parts of Japan were undoubtedly ready to jump off the sinking ship. The Jampyre had never felt lonelier than she did at that moment.

She dropped to her knees and ran her fingers through the ashes. She picked up a burned kabuki mask – which was still amazingly intact – and ran a finger along the charred edge of a single horn. She placed it over her head and laid on the ground. And then Misake cried for six straight hours until she finally dozed off.

When the sun began to set, she was awakened by a tiger.

A real, honest-to-God, wild Siberian tiger.

It nudged Misake in the back and then sniffed the back of her neck.

The Jampyre opened her eyes through the mask but remained still.

The tiger gave her a healthy lick across the nape and then strolled off into a heavily wooded area about fifty yards away.

Misake turned and managed to catch a glimpse of the tiger as its backside and tail swayed and disappeared into the darkness. She was momentarily stunned, since tigers had never been indigenous to Japan, even though they had always been revered in the culture. Was that a beckoning from her vampire spirit animal? Did it want her to follow it into the trees? She stood and took a curious step.

But then she was interrupted.

By someone humming?

The humming blended with a cold wind that sifted through Misake's hair and brought the slightest aroma of marijuana. She shivered and sensed that someone was watching her. In the distance, she saw a figure standing on a high plain. The outline was distinct and quite the dichotomy against the pink and purple sunset of Japan.

It was The Cowboy.

chapter 67

The Cowboy silenced, snuffed out his joint, and then positioned himself into an old Western standoff formation. Both of his hands were cocked near the holsters cradling his two .44 Magnums at the hips. His two bandoliers were completely stocked with wooden bullets.

Of course, Misake didn't have any guns. In fact, she was completely defenseless, having had her own samurai sword stolen. About five feet away, she spied one of her fallen Nin-Jampyre's swords. But instead of diving for it, she turned and faced The Cowboy – with her kabuki mask still on – and formed the shapes of guns with her own fingers. She then "holstered" them.

The Cowboy sneered.

The Jampyre sniffed his blood and realized he was human and not part of the Vampire Extraction Squad she knew of. But she also knew she couldn't take him lightly. After all, he might have been responsible for killing two-hundred ninja vampires.

"Say when," he said dramatically, a la Val Kilmer's Doc Holliday, his voice drifting through the breeze.

Misake cracked her neck and inched up onto the balls of her feet. She then drew her hands and shot air with her fingers and shouted, "Pew, pew, pew!"

The Cowboy drew his guns at the exact same time. But he didn't shoot air. Wooden bullets soared toward Misake's body as he pulled the trigger twice in each hand.

The Jampyre contorted her body and dodged each one with ease. She then tumbled to the ground and rolled over to the samurai sword and sprung back up.

And now, she was armed.

The Cowboy quickly unloaded four more bullets from each Magnum.

Misake twisted and sliced her sword through the air, knocking all but two completely away. One of them grazed her shoulder. The other nicked her ankle. She blamed the injuries on the clumsy and clunky sword she was using, only then realizing how much her own sword, gifted by her mother, was truly a product of divinity. It was light and effortless and synced with her strategic mind, proving that the Jampyre's prowess and reputation as a warrior wasn't only a result of her demigoddess and vampire genetics.

Regardless, her current sword sucked.

Across the way, The Cowboy looked astounded. His revolvers were still poised at Misake, smoke pluming from their barrels.

The Jampyre demigoddess wiped the blood off her shoulder and quickly returned to her battle stance with her blade completely vertical. She wasn't sure how long she could last with her mediocre-suck ass-dime store *katana*. But then she realized a very simple fact.

Twelve bullets had been discharged.

So now, The Cowboy's guns were empty.

And that's why he was currently reloading.

Misake looked over to her left at the heavily wooded area the tiger had disappeared into. The innards morphed into darkness for what seemed to stretch for miles. And even though a deadly Siberian tiger – who might or might not have been friendly – was somewhere inside, she immediately bolted towards it.

The Cowboy ran with her, reloading as he moved. When his guns were ready, he pulled the trigger several times.

Bullets whizzed past Misake as she swerved and ducked. One grazed her heel, and another clipped her ear. She dove into the woods to the ground as two more splintered the tree directly in front of her.

All of her injuries radiated and throbbed in pain.

The Jampyre quickly rose to her feet and ran deeper into the foliage. It got darker and more ominous. Behind her, more bullets began chasing her, smacking against the trees and spraying pieces of bark into her eyes.

Leaves were clipped and rained to the ground. When Misake reached a clearing, she threw her samurai sword in one direction, her mask in another, and then darted a hard ninety-degrees to try and shake The Cowboy.

He was only thrown momentarily and remained hot on her trail.

"I can do this all night!" he shouted from behind her in his famous Southern twang. "There's nowhere you can hide!"

Misake felt herself get tired, but more because the injuries to her heel and ankle were taking way too long to recover and hobbling her progress. Had it been any other material besides wood, she would've undoubtedly healed by now. So, she beelined to the nearest and tallest tree and promptly scaled it like she was a monkey until she reached the highest branch that could support her weight. She then drew in her breath and waited.

Below her, the faint sound of crunching footsteps approached.

They passed her.

And then they returned.

And then they paused.

"Oh, come on now," said The Cowboy. "That's not really fair. I ain't the climbin sort. You ever try to climb with boots?" He shot two bullets in a couple of directions that ripped through leaves of other trees.

Misake closed her eyes and remained still, realizing he was just guessing and hoped he wasn't a successful gambler.

A couple more bullets soared nearby and cracked into branches.

"Aight then. I'll just wait for ya," said The Cowboy. He slid his back down against a tree and sparked up his joint again. He then continued to randomly speak.

For over an hour.

Misake waited patiently high up above as he rambled. And rambled. And rambled.

His ramblings were all over the place.

"I heard you was a shifty Fanger and pretty hot, but I couldn't tell with that stupid mask you had on. What was that? A homo devil or sumptin'?"

"Were you impressed at how I killed all of your baby Fangers? I was fuckin' shocked when they all went inside of that stable and didn't even leave five or six lookouts outside or nuthin'. Dumb as rocks inside of a creek bed if ya want my opinion."

"This is my first time in Japan. I reckon I gotta catch me some sights. What do you recommend? They got rodeos here?"

"You're one popular Fanger. You know, I just met two of em scopin' you out like sum Goddamn perverts."

"You know, your baby Fangers squealed like pigs when they were burnin'? Ain't ever heard that before comin' from any Fanger I ever killed. I'm guessin' you'll do the same."

"Japan. Japan. Japan. This is where sushi came from, right? In my opinion, they should just take it right back. Shit. Is. Nasty. Cook your food, fuckers!"

"I had to use Amazon Prime International to git all that snake poison here. You know how much that shit cost me? Like two thousand dollars. But I can write it all off as a business expense and such on my taxes."

"You know, I met your boy – Cyprian. He was a cool dude. Did he tell you how he resurrected Morgan fuckin' Freeman?"

"Did I just hear a lion?"

"Is weed legal here in Japan?"

"I took some of them motorcycles and swords and kept them. Imma try to git them back to the U.S. of A. and sell em on Ebay."

"I was kiddin' a while ago, I don't pay taxes."

The Cowboy sang, "Come on baby give just a little. Why can't we meet in the middle? I can't do nothing when you're gone. This place couldn't be any colder. I need your head on my shoulder. My hearts been breakin' way too long... way too long." He then laughed. "That was one talented Fanger. A fuckin' Cole Clark. You know those guitars are from Australia? You ever heard that song? 'Way Too Long' by Adam Hood?"

"You got lions or tigers in Japan? I swear I just heard one."

"You ever wonder how they figured that the venom from a Golden Lancehead viper, rat's blood, and fire would disintegrate Fangers? I mean – did they have scientist Fangers tryin' to figure that shit out? Like they had all these different venoms from different snakes and just did some mixin' and matchin' til one of dem scientists fuckin' melted?"

"You prolly don't even know what country music is over here."

"I heard you went all the way to San Antone just to be turned into a Fanger so you could come back and help your daddy be like Scarface or sumptin'? That's kinda funny. I heard a Fanger killed him, though. That's even more funny. What do they call that?"

"Do they have pancakes in Japan? I could sure go fer a short stack right about now."

"Fuck. I thought I brought an extra blunt."

"Ironic! That's what they call it!"

"San Antone has a pretty decent rodeo."

"I wonder what Adam Hood's been doin' these days?"

"Hey – if Cyprian did tell you about the Morgan fuckin' Freeman story, did he tell you how I thought he was Darth Vader's voice? I felt as stupid as your baby Fangers. It was some other black dude that played Darth Vader – I forgot his name already. You think they got a black dude to do his voice cuz he was black? I mean, like, his armor and shit?"

"I swear to God, this forest must have tigers."

"I need to give the Chancellor a call soon – what's the time difference?"

"Wait – you prolly don't even know who Darth Vader is. They have good movies here or just Kung fu movies and cartoons with the big eyes?"

"You know... come to think of it... I think I'd like some waffles. Not pancakes."

Suddenly, The Cowboy shot one bullet into the air. It missed every branch until it hit Misake right in the thigh.

She squealed in pain.

"Ha! I thought that was you!" shouted The Cowboy. He stood and aimed for where her head should be.

But then there was a tiger's roar.

The Cowboy squinted to see its monstrous shape creeping toward him in the darkness. Its eyes glowed a mixture of flaming reds and sunlight yellows. "Holy shit. I knew I heard one! Nice, kitty, kitty." He started to backtrack away from the area. And then he rubbed his eyes, wondering if he was just really high.

But the tiger was real, drawing closer, now more visible. It was the same one that had awoken Misake. It was salivating, razor sharp teeth glistening.

"Don't come any closer," said The Cowboy, raising his Magnum. "I got bullets for ya."

"They're only made of wood," said Misake, as she gingerly climbed down the tree and limped to another.

The Cowboy exchanged glances from Misake to the tiger. "Is this... is this... your tiger? He understands you?"

"Maybe he does. Maybe he doesn't. Let's find out." Misake addressed the tiger in Japanese and said, "Kill the white boy."

Even though The Cowboy had no clue what she said, it seemed he could tell that it was a violent directive. He turned and instantly bolted.

The Siberian tiger roared at him, but stood its ground until the trail of the foreigner was long gone. It then turned and strolled over to Misake, licking her wound until the bullet was extracted from her thigh.

"Thank you," she said, stroking it underneath its jaw. She continued to rest and welcomed the tiger's company.

Misake remained until she felt well enough to leave on her own two feet. She continued to pet the tiger, and then they walked together until they came upon another clearing, on the opposite side of where the stable was located. She said good-bye to the tiger, and they parted ways.

The Jampyre would later find out that the tiger wasn't actually a wild animal in its natural habitat, but rather one that escaped from Osaka's Tennoji Zoo a day earlier. And coincidentally, it was named "Shin" (a short, derivative form of her father's name Shintoku).

She had wished that she could keep her vampire spirit animal as a pet, but knew that would be a difficult task. Shin was subsequently recaptured and returned safely to the zoo.

Regardless, Misake felt a momentary reprieve, knowing she still had *something* on her side. The loneliness was still vast, but there was an ounce of hope.

On the train ride back to Tokyo, her thoughts were reformulated.

Misake's focus was on Boss Oh.

It was time for the bitch to die.

Part Seven

The bullet train speeds.
The same track leads another.
No hope for resolve.

chapter 68

Misake didn't have to waste any time looking for her. When she returned home, there was already an invitation from Boss Oh waiting for her. And a gift.

The invitation was written in human blood. It read "Come visit me, and no one else will die." Misake sniffed it. The blood was vaguely familiar and must've belonged to one of her remaining *kobun*. They were the only humans left in Japan that she remotely cared about, and Boss Oh must've known that.

When she opened the gift, she found a fresh, human kidney. From the same exact person. Misake instantly felt bad for whoever the victim was. It was an invitation that she couldn't refuse, even if it was another trap.

But it didn't matter.

The war needed to end.

Misake was going to kill Boss Oh once and for all, or die trying. The remaining sole, opposing Yakuza *oyabun* had already gone too far. She had hurt many of the Sakumoto-*kai* businesses that resulted in financial loss. She took away her vampire companions whom Misake adored. And last but not least, Boss Oh desecrated the body of her fallen father.

And that brought Misake back to her mantra.

Her father. His legacy.

Her father. His legacy.

The journey that began with the desire to win her father's respect back was now going to end with returning respect back to her father.

Misake knew it wasn't going to be a simple task, especially since it appeared Boss Oh had learned about a vampire's weaknesses and so much more. She also had help sent from the Castille, and it probably wouldn't end with just The Cowboy. The Jampyre held onto hope that her mother – the Japanese Goddess of the Sun and Universe – would assist her daughter in some way, but she'd been spurned thus far after she was responsible for having Amaterasu's one true love killed.

Somehow, some way, Misake was going to have to do it all by herself.

Instead of having a new, traditional samurai sword made, The Jampyre had a double-bladed *katana* forged instead. It was basically two swords connected at the end caps. Misake didn't know what Boss Oh would have waiting for her, but she knew that whoever or whatever it was wouldn't be as prepared to counter such a weapon.

And if Misake were to die, she wanted to look her best as a corpse. First, she had her arm and back re-tattooed, since it all had been lost with the injuries sustained in the bomb explosion. It was mostly the same designs and motifs she had previously, but she made the homages to Uriel and Cyprian larger with a more pronounced *culebra* and lightning bird fiercely facing each other. Her hair was still pink, but she re-dyed it with jet black. The outfit she chose for her would-be corpse was a black leather one-piece jumpsuit that hugged her body like another layer of skin.

The Jampyre was ready for battle. And for whatever came next.

It was almost midnight when Misake approached Boss Oh's residence and first scoped it out from a hiding spot. It was a four-story building in the heart of the Kabukicho red-light district in Tokyo called Nagomi no Thermae Yu. Masked as a legitimate bathhouse, it was notoriously known to be a full-scaled brothel.

Misake had only heard stories of the infamous spot. Government officials, police authorities, and *kobun* from all of the Yakuza families were regular visitors. Not to mention tourists from around the world. Boss Oh took up her residence somewhere in the building, which was ironic for someone having the reputation of being a devout virgin.

The Jampyre sniffed the seedy air that wafted from the open front entrance. There were certainly a lot of humans inside. There was also blood of an irregular sort, something Misake couldn't place. And then there was the blood from the invitation and the kidney. It was the strongest scent, signaling that whoever it was, they were still bleeding.

Several Japanese men in business suits exited the building. They didn't look very satisfied, arguing and pointing back at the establishment. And then, curiously, the door behind them closed, and the neon lights overhead shut off.

It was only midnight, and the brothel was closing?

And then it dawned on Misake. Boss Oh anticipated she would accept the invitation and closed shop for the Jampyre's arrival.

The "party" was scheduled for midnight.

And it was time to party.

chapter 69

Misake nonchalantly walked across the street with her double-edged sword slung over her shoulder. When she neared the building, a hostess in a kimono opened the door and bowed.

"Welcome, Boss Sakumoto," she said in hospitable delight. "Boss Oh is expecting you."

The Jampyre entered to find *tatami* floors in a wide corridor with rooms at regular intervals on each side. A couple of decorative rock fountains with koi fish inside of shallow coin-filled ponds splashed water to sounds of serenity.

And waiting for Misake on each side of the corridor were two lines of fifteen women dressed only in undergarments and wearing *Okame* masks. Though the masks depicted a large woman with smiling eyes, they were actually somewhat terrifying. Especially since all of the women were holding their own samurai swords.

They all simultaneously raised their weapons and pointed them at Misake.

The Jampyre had heard that the women Boss Oh employed in the brothel were not only beautiful (albeit currently in masks), but also lethal. It was a requirement since many of their customers were shady and dangerous individuals.

Behind her, the hostess ceremoniously locked the door.

Misake took a step. And then something curious happened.

To the right of her and sitting in the corner, a renowned Japanese-American musician named Kevin Masaya Kmetz began playing a *shamisen* (three-stringed instrument). The song was called "Dragon String Attack," and it was as if Boss Oh had hired him to specifically score the battle in the bathhouse.

Misake found the theatrics vaguely amusing but enjoyed having a beat to time her movements. The music and rhythm provided by the *shamisen* would be more than appropriate for her dance with death. She brought her sword down and leveled it horizontal to the floor.

The *Okame*-masked women slowly approached.

And when Kevin Masaya Kmetz kicked his strumming into high gear, they all attacked.

It was a frenzied melee highlighted with feminine war cries as the women brought power and finesse with their blades.

But Misake was equal to the task and then some. Her two blades took turns parrying and stabbing with a whirlwind of slanted movements. The prostitutes were getting sliced and diced and soiling the bamboo floor with blood splatter. Some of the *Okame* masks were split in half, revealing the porcelain cheeks of the victims.

The Jampyre felt bad having to kill so many gorgeous women. She hadn't been with one in a couple of years and wouldn't have minded sampling one. But her burning loins certainly would not be a priority on that night.

Half of the women had already been dispatched when the background *shamisen* song slowed down. As if on cue, Misake and the rest of the women paused, circling each other and catching their breaths. And then when Kevin Masaya Kmetz transitioned right into the "Second Wave" of the same song, the battle resumed.

Misake wasted no time in taking down the other half, utilizing some of her acrobatic skills. She scaled the walls and managed to even behead a couple of the prostitutes. When the second round was done, she was left with three more foes.

One was a Japanese man wearing women's lingerie. The other two were female bodybuilders. All three had on the same *Okame* masks and were visibly guarding a stairwell that led up to the next floor.

The Jampyre began to realize why Boss Oh ran such a successful brothel. She appeared to cater to many types of fetishes. She stepped up and crouched into her favorite *Hasso No Kamae* battle stance just as the second song ended.

There was only a brief moment of silence, as Kevin Masaya Kmetz already knew what he'd be playing next. It was the final part of his "Dragon String Attack" quartet – "Finishing Blow." From the other side of the room, he began to play with fevered intensity.

Misake attacked with equal fervor. The three fetishes held their ground much longer than expected, utilizing some brute strength and a couple of jabs to the Jampyre's face. Bodies got entangled in sweat and blood. But when the dust settled, the three remaining fighters were all toppled into a pool of blood.

The music instantly stopped as the virtuoso *shamisen* player eagerly took a break and wiped his brows of sweat.

Misake couldn't help but grin and surveyed the aftermath of the room. It was a gory display of corpses. The koi ponds overflowed with water and crimson. Oddly, the hostess continued to stand by the door. Her eyes were wide as saucers at the carnage, knees trembling in fear.

But the Jampyre ignored her, sniffing the air for the familiar blood Boss Oh used on the invitation. It was stronger. And definitely closer.

She took a step towards the stairwell leading up to the second floor.

"Wait!" cried out Kevin Masaya Kmetz. He gathered his things in a ruckus and picked up his stool, struggling to rush over to Misake. Without saying another word, he passed her and made his way up to the next floor. His items clamored against the railing and walls.

Again, the Jampyre smiled in amusement.

She then followed.

Whoever was waiting on the second floor had better be ready.

Misake was just warming up.

chapter 70

The second floor was not unlike the first. But instead of faux koi ponds, there were 100-gallon fish tanks in between every door. All of them were salt water, so the aquatic life inside was vibrant and colorful.

Misake's awaiting enemies were also different. Instead of women, she now faced the brothel's team of Japanese male escorts. They all wore tighty-whitey underwear and white robes and *Daikoku* masks depicting a jovial farmer. And of course, they were all armed. Each of their hands held a ninja *sai* (3-pronged dagger).

The Jampyre had heard that the men Boss Oh employed in the brothel were not only handsome (albeit currently in masks), but also lethal. It was a requirement since many of their customers had jealous husbands and boyfriends.

At that point, Misake wondered why Boss Oh hadn't equipped her army with automatic weapons. There was no way the Jampyre would've been able to withstand such an onslaught and would've had to retreat. And there was the answer. Boss Oh didn't want Misake going anywhere. She was making it a somewhat fair fight. Ultimately, she probably wanted the vampire to prevail so she could face her. And of course, there was also the whole theatric spectacle of it all.

Kevin Masaya Kmetz finished setting up in the corner. He sat on his stool and had his *shamisen* ready. He looked up at Misake, who was actually waiting on him.

"Ready?" she asked.

He seemed slightly surprised that the Jampyre was waiting on him. "Yes."

Misake nodded and moved into battle stance.

The musician started to strum "Metal-Jongara Attack." And that's all it took for the male escorts to scream and charge the Japanese vampire.

Misake's offensive techniques proved to be a bit more challenging, since the *sai* was useful in blocking and redirecting and unarming sword wielders. After two men were cut down, a third managed to lock his weapon through hers and tossed the double-edged *katana* across the room, shattering a fish tank. Water and flapping fish cascaded across the floor.

The Jampyre had to use her martial arts knowledge to punch throats and kick more than one set of testicles. As the escorts reeled in pain, Misake then bit and tore into jugulars with her fangs and bare hands. She felt bad having to kill so many handsome and sculptured men. She hadn't been with a non-undead male since the airman in Misawa and wouldn't have minded sampling one. But her burning loins certainly would not be a priority on that night.

A few more fish tanks exploded upon bodily impact. Misake picked up a flopping, exotic fish and stuffed it into an escort's mouth, right before she punctured his abdomen and tore out his intestines.

When all of the escorts were dead, she was left with one more foe.

It was a Japanese man the size of a Sumo wrestler. In fact, his hair was styled in traditional *oichomage* and he was wearing the *mawashi* (belt) they normally display. He did not have a mask but definitely guarded another stairwell leading up to the next floor. He also stood on Misake's wayward sword.

The Jampyre again ruminated about why Boss Oh ran such a successful brothel. She catered to many types of fetishes. But Misake wasn't actually positive that the Sumo wrestler was a male prostitute. Perhaps he was just a hired gun.

"Do you work here?" she asked, wiping her mouth of blood and repositioning into another stance.

"I do," obliged the big man, also shifting his feet.

"How much do you cost?"

"Depends on the services."

"Sex."

"The works?"

"Sure."

"A hundred thousand yen."

Misake perked a brow. "Business good?"

"My next available appointment is in three weeks," said the Sumo wrestler, keeping a hardened face.

"Cool," said Misake, unsure of what to say next. "I... um... was just asking for a friend."

"Tell your friend I'll give her a discount."

"That's mighty generous of you. How come?"

He positioned his hands like a boxer. "She'll be in mourning for losing a friend."

The Jampyre nodded. *Touché.* She turned back to Kevin Masaya Kmetz, who had stopped playing and was riveted to the impromptu conversation about brothel prices between a Sumo wrestler/prostitute and vampire demigoddess.

"Sorry," he said and began playing an arrangement called "Tar Bomb Attack."

Misake squared up and attacked the Sumo wrestler. But he batted her away with his bulky arms. When she tried to claw into his belly, he used that same belly to smash her chin, spilling her across the slippery, saltwater floor. When the Jampyre lunged for his jugular, he caught her hand into the palm of one of his gigantic ones and threw her against the wall.

The Sumo wrestler rumbled toward Misake before she could stand back up and placed a massive foot across her larynx. Her face instantly turned red, eyes bulging out from the weight of his nearly-half-a-ton body.

The Jampyre clamped onto his feet with both hands and pushed upwards with all of her might. She managed to create some separation and used the wet floor to propel her away, just as his foot hammered down next to her face. She then turned and bit a mouthful of his shin off.

The large man yelped in pain and staggered backwards. The weight of his body caused his injured leg to collapse into his foot, much like a tree does at the hands of a lumberjack. He timbered onto the hard floor with a loud thud. And before he could regroup, Misake stood over him, holding her retrieved sword.

"Don't kill me! What about your friend?!" implored the Sumo wrestler.

Misake rose one of her blades high into the air. "I lied," she said. "I don't have any friends." She then sliced off his head.

The background music stopped, and all that was left were some fish that continued to slap against the water.

The Jampyre rubbed her neck and regained her color. She looked over at Kevin Masaya Kmetz, who seemed flabbergasted at all of the bloodshed. "What's your name, anyway?" she asked.

"K-kevin," said the musician, stuttering his visible fear.

"Hi, K-kevin. I'm Misake. You play really well."

"Th-thank you."

"Are you ready to go up?"

Kevin Masaya Kmetz looked the Jampyre up and down. Most of her body was covered in someone else's blood, including her face. She had a few torn slits in her outfit. "Are you?"

Misake took a deep breath. "I guess so. Thanks for asking. Here, let me help you with that." She walked over and grabbed a couple of bags. They both proceeded to maneuver around fallen corpses and fish.

"Are you like... a vampire... or something?"

"Yeah."

"That's cool. Is that why they're trying to kill you?"

"Sort of. It's a long story, Kevin," said Misake.

They reached the stairwell. Misake took another healthy sniff. The familiar human blood was even more pungent now. It definitely belonged to someone she knew, but she still couldn't place it. She hoped that whoever it belonged to was coping with having only one kidney left. Judging by the structure of the building and her progress, the Jampyre figured she was about half way through before she discovered who that was.

chapter 71

The third floor of the building had been converted into a large waiting room with velvet upholstery and old world décor. One half of a wall was a bar, completely stocked with the finest of spirits.

Misake emerged onto the floor and slowly placed the *shamisen* musician's things down. What she saw standing before her gave her pause.

Thirty of Boss Oh's *kobun* stood before her. They all wore fancy suits. And all of them held Uzis, pointing right at her chest.

The Jampyre kicked herself for creating the auspicious manifestation. "You might not want to stay for this one, Kevin."

"I was paid to play on each floor."

"Then I hope you know how to play on your back."

Misake took a step forward and raised her sword.

Kevin Masaya Kmetz quickly took a corner and set up. He began playing the song "Last *Shamisen* Master Attack" before he even sat down and settled.

All of the *kobun* put a finger on a trigger. But then they did something curious. They split into two groups, so that the other end of the room was now visible to Misake. The other end and the stairwell. The stairwell and its new defender. The boss at the end of the level.

It was Severo, the Latino/*Impundulu* vampire-hybrid-temporarily-classified-as-a-Beastly-Boy. The one Chancellor Valiquette had graciously loaned to Boss Oh. He stood a good two feet taller than the nearest Yakuza soldier. His tail slithered behind him. Severo threw off a designer Banana Republic beanie, revealing his horns.

The music scratched to a halt, as all eyes were glued to the formidable figure.

"What the—," said Misake, astonished.

All of the *kobun* lowered their weapons and placed them at their sides. It was obvious they were letting Severo have the first crack at the Jampyre.

"Did Cyprian turn you?" asked Misake, recalling the *Impundulu* vampire's accidental and botched attempt in siring a Japanese woman.

"No," answered Severo in a hard Hispanic accent. "It was another."

The Jampyre approached him and circled his body, fascinated at the hybrid. She now knew where the scent of the irregular blood came from. "Are you considered a part of the *Vampiros Oscuros* family? Or the *Impundulu*?"

"I don't know. The Chancellor only recently created us."

Misake smirked at the hole that was created in his Docker jeans, so that his tail could wiggle freely. "Us? There are more of you?"

"A couple," said the Beastly Boy.

Misake found it interesting that the Chancellor would allow such crossbreeding after all that time. Since 1972. For a brief moment, she thought perhaps there was hope for a "Jampyre" race. But if there was, she knew the Castille would never allow Misake to be a part of it, for everything she'd put them through.

When she returned to Severo's front, she walked backwards a few feet and took up her battle stance again. And then with a tilt of her head, the *shamisen* resumed its play. Misake charged the hybrid vampire and aimed right for his neck.

But the Beastly Boy didn't even move.

Misake's katana clanked hard against his scaly neck and didn't even make a scratch. Pain shot up the Jampyre's arm as it caused a wicked vibration to resonate up her bones.

Severo immediately grabbed the sword away from Misake, snapped it in two over his knee, and then plunged each blade through her abdomen.

Blood squirted from Misake's mouth. She stumbled backwards until she hit the wall and slid down to the floor. The shock in her eyes was more profound than the pain she was feeling.

Again, the music halted to succinct silence. The musician looked over at the fallen Jampyre, a mixture of concern and confusion.

All of the *kobun* were also utterly astonished. They exchanged glances from the injured vampire to the indestructible beast that was Severo, who stood his ground and waited.

Misake slowly extracted the two blades and tossed them aside. She wiped her own blood from her mouth, tasting it for the first time on that night. "Interesting," she said, as she slowly stood back up.

"Are you okay?" asked Kevin Masaya Kmetz.

"I've been better, Kevin."

"You should run away. Maybe try again another time?"

Misake looked over at him and smiled appreciatively at his concern. "I'm ready for all of this to end. With either victory or death. I don't have much outside of this to live for anymore."

The *shamisen* musician nodded, understanding. "No matter what happens, I will write a song in your name."

The Jampyre returned a nod and took a few steps towards Severo. "Now I'm ready," she said and put up her dukes.

This time Severo charged, rumbling down the corridor. He lunged a fist at Misake and landed on her cheek, sprawling her against the wall again.

She stood back up and was immediately gifted with a kick to her chest and another cracked wall behind her.

Blood sprayed from her mouth as she put an arm across her bruised chest.

But Misake wasn't deterred.

She quickly regrouped and began sparring with the Beastly Boy. Her super-fast jabs and kicks weren't doing any damage, but they were steadily pushing Severo back.

When they reached one end, the Beastly Boy countered with his own offense of right and left hooks and kicks to the chest. His power and strength moved Misake several feet at a time, and even though she wasn't sustaining any damage either, the pain in her face said she was certainly feeling it.

On the next round, Misake began using her acrobatic prowess more. She jumped and gave Severo some roundhouses to the face. She crouched and swept his legs from beneath him. Each time, the hybrid vampire felt an impact, but he kept going.

At one point, Severo managed to pick up the Jampyre and lifted her high over his head. He then threw her over some of Boss Oh's men, smashing her against the wall and creating a large crater in the sheetrock.

Misake was equal to the task, however, and quickly rebounded and slipped behind Severo, sweeping his legs and then grabbing his tail. She then swung him around several times and let him fly over the bar and against the shelves of liquor. The Beastly Boy collapsed in a shower of shattered glass and alcohol.

But Misake didn't stop there.

She leapt over the bar and jumped on Severo's head several times, mashing it into broken glass. The hybrid finally began to bleed, until he managed to find a large broken shard and sliced a gash behind her knee.

The Jampyre buckled and fell backwards.

Severo sprung to his feet and pounced on top of her, using his entire body to keep her flat on her back. He continued to hold the glass shard and attempted to plunge it through her neck.

Misake managed to put two hands against his wrist and stopped the tip an inch away from her jugular. Blood poured from Severo's palm as he gripped the glass with all his might, now placing his free hand directly on top to give him more force.

It was a monumental battle of strength.

The glass was now grazing Misake's neck. Her own blood began to spill.

And then she made one last power move.

The Jampyre twisted her body, slightly rolling Severo's body. Unbalanced, the glass shard shifted and sliced the side of her neck and stabbed into the floor.

Even though blood began to spew, Misake released one hand from Severo's wrist and clawed into his eye socket, pulling out an eyeball.

The Beastly Boy instantly screamed and rolled completely off of Misake, writhing on his back and crunching against more glass. Both of his hands covered his hollow socket as he cried and whimpered in pain.

Misake pulled herself to her feet and put a hand against her own neck wound, still draining profusely. She beckoned with a finger to the nearest *kobun* to approach her. When he did, she handed him Severo's eyeball and grabbed his Uzi away from him.

The rest of the *kobun* quickly aimed their weapons at her. They rushed to the bar and had her dead to rights.

But Misake was unfazed.

She turned to Severo and said, "Let me see."

Unsure of the Jampyre's intentions, Severo slowly moved his hands away from the grotesque hole where his eye used to rest.

"I'll make the pain go away." Misake promptly shoved the tip of the Uzi inside and pulled the trigger.

Severo's head exploded in a shower of skull and brains.

The Jampyre then handed the Uzi back to its owner, who oddly returned the eyeball back to her. She crushed it with her hand and tossed it.

Misake then threw her arms up in surrender.

Every Uzi in the room pointed directly at her head.

Some were only inches away, positioned like news reporter microphones.

"Go ahead," she said. "Hit me with your best shot."

chapter 72

But no one pulled their triggers.

Misake sighed and turned around. She found a bottle of 1800 Patron tequila that miraculously survived the destruction of the bar. She unscrewed the lid and found several shot glasses. "Anyone want a shot?"

None of the *kobun* moved. In fact, they continued to keep their guns on her face.

"Kevin? You going to make me take a shot all by my lonesome self?"

The *shamisen* musician looked disparagingly at the scene. From his vantage point, he could see every Uzi in the room poised on her. "Um. Okay," he said and approached the bar.

Misake filled four glasses with tequila and slid two over to him. She held one up for a toast. "Here's to your music."

They clanked glasses and downed the first shot.

Kevin Masaya Kmetz grimaced as he swallowed. He regained his voice and said, "Are they going to kill you now?"

"No," said Misake. "They would've done it by now. Their job was just to make sure I get up to the fourth floor if it so happened I had an alternative plan." She grabbed the other shot glass. "Your turn to make a toast."

The musician held up his final shot reluctantly. "How about... to life?"

The Japanese vampire turned grim. She contemplated a moment, nodded, and then downed the tequila like a professional drunk.

Kevin Masaya Kmetz struggled again, clutching his throat at the burning sensation funneling down into his system. "Is it going to be bad up there? Do you think I should skip it?"

Misake shrugged. "If you're going to write a song about me, don't you want to know how it ends?"

"I was hoping you could just tell me tomorrow," he said with an uncomfortable grin.

"You're sweet," she said. "If tomorrow comes for me, I will owe you a conversation." She motioned to some of the nearby *kobun* and asked, "Anyone have any cash on them?"

Some of them exchanged confused glances.

"Come on, come on. Cough it up."

With their free hands, the *kobun* began rummaging through jacket and pant pockets, delivering a cluster of wadded up *yen*. It was an impressive haul.

Misake pushed it all over to the musician. "Here's your tip."

The *kobun* all dropped their jaws in dismay but were immediately distracted when Misake hopped out over the bar. They quickly regrouped and surrounded her.

"Take it easy. I'm heading upstairs now." Misake approached the third floor stairwell and took one final whiff. The mystery blood was only a level away. An overwhelming cloud of anxiety overcame her as she realized – or at least hoped – that Boss Oh would also be present.

Their war was coming to a head.

Misake remembered she was unarmed and looked back across the room to her discarded and bloody blades. And then she had an epiphany. A slow realization. "I'm not going to need any weapons, am I?" She looked at all of the *kobun* in general, but wasn't really looking for an answer. Instead, she got uneasy stares.

The Jampyre took a deep breath and climbed the stairs.

chapter 73

The entire fourth floor was converted into Boss Oh's business office and living quarters. A large mahogany desk sat at the opposite end. Priceless art lined the walls above love seats. There were several closed doors between them, leading to what was probably a bedroom, bathroom, and storage closets.

And, curiously, there was a wooden coffin on the side of the room. Its lid was wide open.

Misake had wondered why the plush waiting area and bar were on the third floor, and not the first where customers could possibly wait for their sexual escorts. But then she realized that the waiting room was probably more for the leader of the Okamakiri mushi-*kai* crime syndicate, doing most of her illegal business from one floor up above.

The Yakuza *oyabun* sat behind her desk, nonchalantly sliding left on her cell phone. She spoke without looking up. "Hello, Misake."

Misake ignored her and darted her eyes around the room for any traps. She then zeroed in on one of the closed doors, closest to Boss Oh. "Who's in there?"

"My bedroom? Ah – you smell the blood. Of course. I'll show you in time. But first, have a seat."

The Jampyre shook her head. "I'll stand, thank you."

Boss Oh grinned her gold teeth and stood. She approached Misake and stood a few feet away from her. "I haven't spoken to you in a minute."

"Since my father's funeral."

"Ah, yes. When you disrespected me."

"It was a mutual disrespect," said Misake.

"And that video you sent me of Boss Watanabe. What was that you said?"

"And then there was one."

Boss Oh curled her lips, recalling, "Ah, yes. *Hashtag...* and then there was one."

"Very cruel how you manipulated him. Was it always your plan to become the only Yakuza boss in Tokyo?"

"Always? No. But the opportunity arose, so I seized it."

"*Opportunity*. Meaning me?"

"Of course," smiled Boss Oh. "And then there was one," she repeated. "More apropos for tonight, wouldn't you say?"

Misake only nodded.

Boss Oh scrutinized the Japanese vampire's body. Her attire. Her wounds. All of the blood caked on her that mostly belonged to the warriors she had thrown at Misake. "Very well done." She circled around to her back. "Did you enjoy the show I put on for you?"

"The music was a nice touch."

"Oh! You liked it? He wasn't my first choice. I was trying to get Poppy – you know her?"

"I. Love. Poppy."

Boss Oh came back around to Misake's front. "So do I! But she's on tour in Europe." And then she began another revolution around the vampire's body.

"Too bad," said Misake. "The *shamisen* player was really good, though."

"Where did he go? Did he die in the crossfire?"

"I told him to leave. I said this floor would be the most dangerous."

Boss Oh giggled. "You're probably right. Too bad. I had a song picked out for him to play." She returned around to Misake's front, even closer to her body.

The Japanese vampire took a healthy whiff of her blood. "Boss Oh. *Madame Gorudo*. The legends told about you haven't been true."

Again, Boss Oh continued another circle around. "Oh? What legend is that?"

"The one that says you've remained a virgin for your entire life. I can smell in your blood you've been tainted."

The elder Yakuza *oyabun* giggled. "What an amazing talent that is. That legend was true only up to a couple of weeks ago."

Misake raised her brows in surprise. "Really? A man earned his stripes enough with you to warrant such a treat?"

Boss Oh paused directly behind Misake. She leaned into the nape of her neck and whispered. "Not a man. A vampire."

A shiver rippled through Misake's spine. She knew exactly which vampire the *oyabun* was referring to. *Chancellor Viktor Valiquette.* The vampire of all vampires. The leader of them all. If one were to lose their virginity and make it memorable, there certainly weren't many men or women who could top that.

"Our fucking was driven with the common desire to rip off your face," continued Boss Oh in a whisper. "It was worth every drop of sweat." She moved back around to Misake's front, both of their lips almost grazing each other.

"I can easily rip your throat out right now," said the Jampyre, clenching her fists.

"Oh, I know," said Boss Oh. "I know. But you're much too curious to see what's behind door number one, and you must know that my death causes another."

Misake sniffed the air. She still couldn't place the scent of the blood. It was too familiar just to belong to one of her *kobun,* but she couldn't imagine anyone else in Japan. "Eye for an eye. Small sacrifice, I'd say."

"You think so? Why don't you find out?" Boss Oh positioned her throat right in front of Misake's mouth.

Misake sniffed the intoxicating scent of her enemy's blood and shuddered at the proximity. Her fangs elongated and dripped saliva. And then she shivered with restraint.

"Come on, Misake. You know you want to. Just kill me right now. Get it over with! Be the only Yakuza boss left in Tokyo! Be the loyal daughter you still want to be!"

The Jampyre hissed and immediately placed her mouth on Boss Oh's throat – who held her breath and seemed to relish the moment – but Misake's amazing will power prevented her from biting. She backed off and walked away, leaving only a slight puncture wound in Boss Oh's throat.

One drop of blood spilled. The elder boss actually looked disappointed.

"Who's behind the door?" pleaded Misake.

Boss Oh sighed and smirked. "Your heart has always been your downfall. It was the reason you became a vampire. And it will be the reason you die as one."

Misake faced the opposite corner of the room. Her peripheral vision landed on the mysterious coffin. "So, what do you want from me?"

"I want you to renounce your title as a Yakuza boss and hand me sole control over Tokyo and all of your businesses."

"That's it? And then you leave me alone?" She turned back around.

"And everyone you know."

Misake paused, staring into Boss Oh's eyes with a look of contempt. Her statement triggered more unanswered questions. "Where's Cyprian?"

Boss Oh twisted the side of her lips. She walked back to her desk and opened a drawer, pulling out the *Impundulu* vampire's weathered voodoo doll. It still had the ice pick rammed through the heart.

"What's that?" asked Misake.

"You don't know? According to his breed, it's the physical conduit for a vampire's soul. This one belonged to your dark-skinned friend." Boss Oh poked at the tip of the ice pick with her finger.

Misake stared at the doll for a moment, confused. But then she gasped, once she realized the significance of the ice pick. She recalled the moment Cyprian felt a pain in his chest, right when he attempted to protect her in the banquet hall.

And Boss Oh seemed to notice her revelation as well. "Yes. Right before the bombs all exploded."

"You did that?"

"Of course I did."

Misake fumed through her nostrils. "So where is he now?"

"Who knows?" said Boss Oh. "Heaven. Hell. Where do dead vampires go?"

"You bitch." A single tear ran down Misake's face as she continued to stew. She regretted not ripping out Boss Oh's jugular a moment ago.

"He definitely won't be needing this anymore." Boss Oh opened another drawer and pulled out a *tanto* knife. She then abruptly sliced the head off the doll, withdrew the ice pick, and stabbed it into the desk, and threw both parts to the floor in front of Misake's feet. "For good measure."

Misake picked up both pieces and placed them together. She didn't want to believe Cyprian was gone, but something told her it was the truth. She held the doll close to her heart and closed her eyes. When she reopened them, her voice cracked with sadness. "And Uriel?"

"Ah. The boyfriend. We're sending his body to New Orleans. What the Chancellor plans on doing with it, I don't know. But I understand his Queen might want him back and is one pissed off woman." Boss Oh waited for a reaction, but the Jampyre remained silent, her face boiling with anger. "I heard the both of you had his sister killed? Tsk, tsk." She seemed to be having fun now.

For the first time, Misake noticed a samurai sword rack sitting behind Boss Oh's desk. It housed her mother's sword, along with the ones she gave Cyprian and Uriel. Her eyes narrowed in more vehemence, until she saw something else that drew her attention.

It was Uriel's Aztec sword. The one his Goddess had gifted to Gabriella. The one Gabriella used in their fight-to-the-death battle in the Tokyo temple. And the one Uriel had supposedly buried deep into the Pacific Ocean. *How the Hell did it get into Boss Oh's hands?*

Boss Oh continued. "Did you know they were lovers?"

"Who?"

"Your boyfriend and his Queen. But then you stole him away from her."

"That's not true."

Misake watched Boss Oh shrug with a smug smile. She didn't want to believe that fact, but it wasn't so farfetched. It certainly wasn't a detail she would've expected Uriel to openly confess. Regardless, she was still hit with a twinge of jealousy.

"She has a new lover now," added Boss Oh. "Someone by the name of... *Camazotz*... I think. From Mexico. You know him? I heard he's a pretty big deal."

Misake slowly shook her head. She could care less about any other vampires. Her mind was still trying to wrap itself around the fact that Cyprian and Uriel were gone.

The *oyabun* allowed her to wallow for a moment. And then she appeared to lose her patience. "So, what's it going to be, Misake? Will you hand all of Tokyo over to me?"

The Jampyre wiped a tear and gritted her teeth. "I'm not destroying my father's legacy for you, and I doubt you'd feel comfortable with me running around still alive."

Boss Oh smiled. Her golden teeth glistened Hellfire. "You're probably right. That's why I have another option." She walked over to the empty coffin. "Get inside and allow me to ship you off to the Chancellor."

"Then I'm as good as dead anyway."

The grin disappeared off of Boss Oh's face. It was as if she didn't want to play games anymore. "I'm afraid this is the only option you have left, little girl."

"Unless I kill you right now."

Boss Oh pointed at the mysterious door.

The Jampyre never looked over. Instead, she paraphrased a Poppy song. "Right now, there is no other life worth sparing if it means I can *'bury you six feet deep, cover you in concrete, and turn you into a fucking street.'*"

"Is that so?" Boss Oh seemed to mask her amusement of the recognizable lyrics and stared at Misake with bitterness for a moment. She then slowly knocked on the wall.

The door to her bedroom opened.

And then that all-too-familiar, foreboding hum.

The Cowboy walked out. "Howdy, again. Where's your kitty cat?"

Misake looked surprised. "That was *his* blood? I could care less about this asshole." She took a few steps towards Boss Oh. But then the Cowboy interrupted her.

"Wait, little miss cat lady," he said. And then he motioned into the bedroom. "C'mon, darlin'. Don't be shy."

Footsteps shuffled from within.

A shadow emerged.

It was Shanice.

chapter 74

Shanice looked completely haggard. She was only wearing a bra and panties and a large bandage across where her kidney was taken out. She had fresh cuts all over her body, so her blood ran continuously.

"Shanice?!" Misake took a step, but the Cowboy raised one of his Magnums and pointed it directly at her forehead. His other hand blocked Shanice from progressing.

"Misake?" said Shanice wearily, her eyes glazed over to despondence. "Is that really you?"

The Jampyre squirted out tears at the sight of her battered, old college roommate. "Yes! It's really me! Are you okay?"

"I feel pretty good. They said something about you being with Cyprian? Where is he?"

Misake gulped, looking down at the doll still clutched to her bosom. "He's... he's... not here right now."

"That's too bad. I miss him."

"Yeah," lamented Misake. "Me too." She spilled more tears.

"Oh, and they said you have one of my kidneys?"

Misake wiped her eyes and barked at Boss Oh. "How could you do that to her?! She has nothing to do with this!"

"I wish I could take the credit, but it wasn't my idea. Not the removing of kidneys part. Just the 'using her as a bargaining chip' part." She stared into Misake's eyes with a conniving grin.

But the Jampyre only had Shanice's well-being on her mind. She looked at the Cowboy, who still had his gun steady on her. "Let her go. You've got me now."

"I only take orders from one Fanger," he said. "And he ain't here."

Misake sullenly met Shanice's eyes and whispered, "I'm so sorry, Shanice. I'm so sorry I got you mixed up in this."

Her former dorm buddy managed to smile. "It wasn't your fault. You had no idea I'd be picked to be your roommate."

The Jampyre squeaked out a giggle, with more tears flowing. "How was volleyball going?"

"We made the playoffs last year. Lost in the second round."

"Well, that's pretty good."

Boss Oh sighed impatiently, the look of death incarnate painted across her face. She raised her *tanto* and placed the tip at Shanice's remaining kidney and ordered Misake. "Get in the box or we take out the other one."

"And then you let Shanice go?"

"Yes."

"How do I know you will?"

"You don't."

"Let me at least get her to a hospital."

"You are in no position to bargain," said Boss Oh dryly. She placed the tip of her knife further into Shanice's side, puncturing it slightly.

Shanice winced.

"Okay, okay!" cried Misake. She stepped over to the coffin as the Cowboy kept his weapon trained on her forehead. She slowly climbed in with Cyprian's voodoo doll and sat upright. "I'll see you later, Shanice."

"Promise?"

"I promise," said Misake. "We'll go to Whataburger."

"Can't wait."

Misake turned to Boss Oh. "And keep Tokyo warm for me. When I return, I'll be drinking your blood."

Boss Oh nodded. "I wouldn't have it any other way."

The Jampyre laid down and closed the lid over her.

The Cowboy immediately rushed over and secured the latches and sliding locks. He tested the lid and made sure it was fastened solidly. "Lookin' good." He returned to Boss Oh's side and motioned to Shanice. "What are you going to do with her?"

"I don't need her anymore." Boss Oh slowly and deliberately stabbed her knife all the way through Shanice. She cried out in pain and dropped to her knees.

From inside the coffin, Misake sensed Shanice's demise and screamed in anger. She began punching the interior of the lid with brute force. The wooden box rattled and shifted and pounded until the wood started to splinter and the Jampyre's bloodied fist shot through. Her hands then clasped to each side of the hole and she pried it open even further until the entire lid cracked in half, and she flew out of the coffin in a shower of debris and both parts of Cyprian's voodoo doll.

Misake landed on her feet and then leapt for Boss Oh.

But the Cowboy promptly put a wooden bullet into her forehead.

The Japanese vampire demigoddess dropped with a hard thud right next to Shanice.

"Misake!" she shrieked.

Boss Oh approached the vampire's still body and rolled it over to her back with a foot.

Misake's eyes were wide open, frantically looking around. But she remained helpless and paralyzed, the wooden bullet lodged into her brain, rendering her all but catatonic.

Boss Oh knelt down close to Misake's face, flashing her golden teeth. "Who's the bitch now?" She then spat onto the vampire's cheek and stood back up.

The Cowboy leaned into Misake's line of vision, his gun still smoking. "Gotcha. Meow."

The Jampyre's consciousness began to waver. Through her peripheral vision, she managed to see her bestie Shanice, with a dagger still lodged in her side. Blood and saliva dripped from her lips. Shanice's body then began to collapse, her head coming to a rest across Misake's belly.

Their eyes met and spoke to each other in pain. In friendship. In love.

And then everything went black.

Epilogue

Down and out behold;
for the strength will come tenfold.
Hold on to your butts.

chapter 75

Camazotz entered the lair of Queen Mictecacihuatl. He was a chiseled Jason Momoa-version of a Latino vampire with eyes hardened by his criminal history. From Mexico City, the notorious and seasoned cartel drug lord was recruited by the Queen to replace Uriel and Gabriella Santana as her new caretaker. He was also her new lover.

The golden casket that accentuated the room full of Aztec treasures began to rumble. Blood started to spill down the sides as the lid slowly opened. Cobras hissed and slithered out and disappeared into the confines and crevices of the sparkling wonders of the room.

The nude body of the Queen surfaced, and she slowly stepped out, approaching the beefy bloodsucker with a lick of her bloody lips.

"You have returned?" she said as her voluptuous body grazed his.

"I have, my Queen," said Camazotz. "And I bring you gifts."

Behind Camazotz stood his bearded comrade-in-arms; a crooning vampire who was known as El Galán. And he was supporting another Latino vampire, who could barely stand on his own two feet.

It was Uriel. His back was riddled with wooden bullets.

Queen Mictecacihuatl was visibly excited to see Uriel. Her eyes lit up with an undeniable yearning for the Latino vampire. She had missed him, and it was obvious.

"Uriel," she said with unbridled enthusiasm. "Is it really you?"

"Yes, my Queen," he said with fatigue in his voice.

"Have you returned to me?"

"I have."

"Forever?"

El Galán pushed Uriel towards the Queen, who embraced him with arms still dripping an abnormal amount of blood.

Uriel rested his chin on her shoulder. The conflict displayed on his face spoke magnitudes. His lot in life had taken a difficult turn in the past several months. And now he had returned to the deity he had betrayed, who could end his days with the snap of a finger.

"Yes," he said.

That was the only word Uriel knew his Queen wanted to hear.

Somewhere in the sewers of Tokyo, the corpse of a lightning bird rotted with rigor mortis in the corner, buried in a mixture of mold, maggots, and feces. A large rat squeaked and shuffled by the stale body, not even giving it a healthy whiff.

Suddenly, neon green smoke sizzled and plumed from the bird's beak.

And then Lucie opened its eyes.

acknowledgements

I'd like to thank all of my friends and family members for the incredible support in purchasing the first book. The pictures you sent me warmed my heart. Every book I signed shot adrenaline into my creative soul. I will forever be grateful for the outpouring of love. On this Earth, you are all family, and will always be.

To my wife Johanna who is the magic fairy dust in my life. Without you my journey would be meaningless. You're my one constant; a beacon of light when the roads can be dark and desolate.

To my strong sisters – Liz, Beverly, Debi, Sandy, Tina (yes, you are), Jenny (yes, you are) – who are always the loudest cheerleaders on my sidelines.

More hugs to my beta readers, including Frances Trilone, who continues to indulge my sometimes absurd sensibilities.

Thanks to Jorge "El Galán" Gallegos, who was the first non-Beta reader to finish the book and for the amazing exposure. GO BUY HIS MUSIC.

To my fellow Daily Grind Warriors: Corinna, Mayra, Theresa, Erika, Jorge, Gladys, Irene, Yeralda, Krystal, Alma, Andrew, Lorenzo. You gave up a portion of your hard-earned paychecks not on libations or nachos, but to support me. Fist bumps!!!

To Michele Hernandez and the staff at the Twig Book Shop for supporting local writers and taking a chance on Misake's unscrupulous and violent saga. I'm still pinching myself for being placed on the shelf right next to Dacre Stoker – a direct descendant of the father of vampires himself, Bram Stoker.

about the author

Arakaki Soto is half-Japanese and half-American, raised as a military brat on bases around the world. As an only child, Arakaki had to utilize the creative mind and imagination to feed the soul. Arakaki is also a professional screenwriter, with such mega hits like AVENGERS OF JUSTICE, starring Amy Smart, MY DOG THE CHAMPION starring Lance Henriksen, and MY B.F.F. starring C. Thomas Howell.

Learn more about Arakaki and keep in touch at:

www.arakakisoto.com
Twitter: @alamohapa
Instagram: @arakakisoto
Facebook: @AuthorArakakiSoto
Pinterest: @alamohapa

Don't forget to check out Book 3 of The Vampire Haiku Chronicles:

Made in the USA
Columbia, SC
29 October 2020